THE PROTECTOR

BOOK 1 OF THE TALES OF CALEDONIA

PETER WACHT

Kestrel
Media Group, LLC

The Protector
By Peter Wacht

Book 1 of The Tales of Caledonia

This book is a work of fiction. Names, characters, places, and incidents are the product of the author's imagination or are used fictitiously. Any resemblance to actual events, locales, or persons, living or dead, is coincidental.

Published in the United States by Kestrel Media Group LLC.

ISBN: 978-1-950236-19-0

eBook ISBN: 978-1-950236-18-3

Library of Congress Control Number: 2021914033

❀ Created with Vellum

ALSO BY PETER WACHT

THE REALMS OF THE TALENT AND THE CURSE

THE TALES OF CALEDONIA

Blood on the White Sand (short story)*

The Protector

The Protector's Quest (Forthcoming 2022)

The Protector's Vengeance (Forthcoming 2022)

The Protector's Sacrifice (Forthcoming 2022)

THE SYLVAN CHRONICLES

(Complete Series available at Amazon)

The Legend of the Kestrel

The Call of the Sylvana

The Raptor of the Highlands

The Makings of a Warrior

The Lord of the Highlands

The Lost Kestrel Found

The Claiming of the Highlands

The Fight Against the Dark

The Defender of the Light

THE RISE OF THE SYLVAN WARRIORS

Through the Knife's Edge (short story)*

* Free short stories can be downloaded from my author website at www.kestrelmg.com

YOUR FREE SHORT STORY IS WAITING

THROUGH THE KNIFE'S EDGE BY PETER WACHT

This short story is a prelude to the events in my series *The Sylvan Chronicles* and is free to readers who receive my newsletter.

Join Peter's newsletter and get your FREE short story at www.kestrelmg.com.

SETTING THE STAGE

The Protector is set more than one thousand years before the events that occur in *The Sylvan Chronicles* and takes place in a separate land of *The Realms of the Talent and the Curse*. Caledonia, though a monarchy, functions more like a loose confederation of Duchies, much to the displeasure of the Crown.

It is during this time that some of the more adventurous and grasping members of the Caledonian nobility accept King Corinthus Beleron's territorial grants and begin to colonize the Territories far to the west on the other side of the Burnt Ocean. These Territories will eventually become the Kingdoms.

In Caledonia, as in the other realms, the ability to use the Talent sets apart the person gifted with this unique skill. But being able to use the Talent is only part of the dynamic. For if a Magus chooses to follow a darker path, the Talent becomes the Curse.

PROLOGUE
WORRISOME DISCOVERY

For the thousandth time, the tall woman with the piercing violet eyes pushed the strands of curly hair that swirled around her face back behind her ears, knowing that in just a few seconds she'd be doing much the same again. The wind was strong today, gusting off the mountaintops, and in her haste to start her day she had forgotten to bring her favorite scarf.

Rafia Riverstone had left her rooms before first light, poling herself across the calm surface of the lake in the small boat crafted specifically for that purpose. She had then hiked resolutely into the mountains. After a difficult climb of several hours, she had finally reached her destination. Looking back the way that she had come, the sight always thrilled her. She was the Keeper of Haven, the fortress and library built on the small island encircled by a glacial lake that itself was surrounded by the towering heights of the Shattered Peaks. With the sun almost directly above her, the midday light shone brightly off the glassy surface of the water. She never tired of the sight, but she didn't have time to dwell on it as she continued to hike deeper among the pinnacles. She had started this trek with a clear purpose in mind, and she meant to complete her task before the sun set.

Usually when she hiked in the mountains, she allowed her mind to wander. It gave her a chance to think. To let go of her work if only for a time and permit new thoughts and ideas to pop into her head unbidden. But not today. Today she couldn't afford to be distracted. Not if what she suspected turned out to be true. So she continued on her northernly route, moving quickly but quietly, halting every few minutes to get a feel for her surroundings, to make sure that she was alone.

After another hour, she stopped abruptly. She had come to the edge of the forest, beyond which was a small glade filled with dappled sunlight. She had tracked a stream for the last several miles so that she now stood at the top of a small waterfall that crashed down on one side of the clearing. She had planned on filling her water bag here and keeping on to the north, but something held her back, some small prickle of warning that had served her so well in the past, so she stayed concealed within the trees instead. Waiting. Watching. Worried.

Not certain why she decided to remain where she was, but trusting in her instincts, she surveyed the small clearing more carefully. Then she saw what had stopped her. By the rocks below the waterfall. Scratches in the mud. At first, she thought that it could simply be the signs of forest animals drinking from the water pooling beneath the waterfall. But these marks were too big. Although they were obscured somewhat, farthest away from the pool she could make out one good print in the muck. A large, clawed foot with four talons. That could have only been made by one creature. A deadly creature that had not walked these mountains for quite some time. Or so she thought.

She had heard the rumors of their return closer to the Winter Pass through her network of friends and peers, but she had not seen evidence of it herself until today. She hated that her suspicions had proven correct, because that meant that some of her greatest fears could be borne out in the future. If these beasts were making an appearance once again in Caledonia, it made sense that they would be in the Shattered Peaks, and certainly near Haven since her home was only a few dozen leagues south of the Weir. But there was really only one reason why these beasts would brave the deadly risk of forcing their way through that weakening magical barrier.

She was about to step out onto the rocks of the waterfall and climb down to get a better look at the mark in the mud when she froze, sensing movement not too far to her rear. Taking hold of the Talent, she wove the natural magic of the world around her in such a way so that she faded into the forest, taking on the colors of the trees and bushes she hid among, concealing herself from any searching eyes.

Only seconds passed before a large green shape shot between the trees just to her left and leapt off the top of the waterfall, landing deftly in the mud below, followed by another blur to her right, and then another to her left, until half a dozen Ghoules stood beneath the pounding waterfall, having returned to where they had camped the night before.

For a moment, she didn't know what she should do. Wait for the Ghoules to move on? Or would they be using the small glade as their campsite again for the night? Did she need to slink away as quietly as she could? Was she strong enough to take on so many of the foul beasts at once if she had no choice but to fight?

That choice was made for her when she felt the air move behind her, a barely felt disturbance that sent a chill down her spine. Moving based solely on a feeling, she ducked down and rolled backward, pulling the long dagger from the sheath at her hip and whipping it through the air in a back-handed motion. She felt the blade strike home, slicing across the back of the Ghoule's leg. The creature stumbled as the wound broke his stride and then the beast grunted in a combination of pain and surprise, but the Ghoule still had the presence of mind to pull his sword from his scabbard across his back and swing it in the space where he thought his attacker would be. But Rafia had already moved to the Ghoule's other side, driving her dagger deep into his groin. Tearing the steel free, before the creature could screech in agony, she slashed the blade across the Ghoule's throat, the beast crumpling at her feet as his blood seeped out onto the rocks and mixed with the water of the stream.

For several minutes she kept absolutely still, maintaining her control over the Talent so that she remained hidden within the forest. How had the Ghoule found her even though she was cloaked with the Talent? And then she realized that the beast probably hadn't been looking for her. The creature probably hadn't even known that she was there. He had simply been following the same route as his compatriots. It was just bad luck that he had been about to run into her. That realization allowed her to breathe a sigh of relief. Even better, it seemed that her fight atop the water-fall had not caught the attention of the other Ghoules down below, the pounding of the water on the rocks masking what little noise there had been while she dispatched the unlucky Ghoule.

But what to do next? She could sneak away and hope that the other Ghoules would not discover their missing companion long enough for her to be well on her way back to Haven. Yet she knew that could be no more than a vain hope. Even if she got a good head start on the beasts, the Ghoules were faster than she was. They'd catch her before she regained the safety of her home. No, better not to take that risk. She had taken the initiative and it had worked out for her. Better to continue to make use of it. Better to bring the fight to the Ghoules rather than relinquish the advantage and gift it back to them.

Kneeling down to wipe the black blood from her dagger before sheathing it again, she rose with a smile creasing her face. The Ghoules were bigger, stronger, and faster than she was, but she had the advantage of surprise. More important, she was invisible. The quick fight with the unsuspecting Ghoule had sent a rush of adrenaline flowing through her veins. It had gotten her blood up in a way that hadn't happened in quite some time. Her senses were sharp, her movements fast and decisive.

Taking in more of the Talent than she had held in years, she stepped to the edge of the waterfall. The Ghoules were sprawled about the small glade, apparently unconcerned that one of their party was missing. Leaping out into the air, she released a small portion of the energy that she controlled. Twin lightning bolts shot down from the clear sky and burned through two of the Ghoules, the only warning for the shocked creatures that they were under attack.

1

IN THE PIT

Bryen jumped back just in time, the black dragon's claw raking his arm rather than his torso. The sight of his blood, the red drops sprinkling across the bright white sand, sent the crowd to an even higher level of savagery. That's why thousands of people gathered here, after all. For some, it was an opportunity to gamble on the outcome and perhaps walk away with more than they had wagered. For others, it was a distraction from the mundaneness or the misery of their everyday lives. While some simply enjoyed watching the weekly spectacle of man killing man, man killing beast, beast killing man, woman killing man.

It really didn't matter to those drawn to the gladiatorial games in the Colosseum, because no matter why they chose to attend the contests, they were bound by one single, simple principle. Someone or something would die, and it wouldn't be them. Because of that, all who attended had cause to celebrate.

Judging by the jubilant screams that echoed down into the Pit when his blood splattered the sand, Bryen guessed that most of those watching expected the black dragon to kill him. He didn't blame them. No one had ever faced a black dragon in the Pit on their own and survived.

Black dragons were uncommon creatures, rarely seen in Caledonia, and they were deadly beasts. They lived in the Trench, and for one to have been captured and brought more than a hundred leagues to the south hinted at not only a huge investment, but also that the King felt the need to raise the level of entertainment that he was providing to the people of Tintagel. For that's what the gladiatorial games had become, a tool for the monarchy to distract the common people from the challenges, irritations, and burdens placed on them, often by the Crown itself. The fact that the King had gone to the trouble and expense of acquiring such a unique creature implied that the rumblings of unrest that Declan had reported during his wanderings through the city had grown more worrisome to the good King Marden Beleron, who seemed more interested in maintaining a reality crafted of smoke and mirrors rather than addressing the needs of his people.

Bryen pulled his mind away from his political ponderings and back to the very large and hungry adversary that stood before him, the dragon having pushed itself up onto its hind legs and stretched out its leathery black wings. The creature was as tall as a two-story tower, its body and wings blotting out the sun and putting Bryen into a shadowy twilight. The gladiator struggled to keep his feet in the blood-soaked sand, barely escaping another swipe of the beast's sharp, curled talons when he rolled to the side, feeling the hardened claws slide past him by no more than a whisker. Sensing victory, the dragon raised its head to the sky and shrieked in triumph, the earsplitting noise rising above the din of the fifty thousand spectators crammed onto the wooden benches circling the Pit and extending all the way up into the farthest reaches of the Colosseum.

The tall gladiator, his long, prematurely white hair still flecked in a few places with light brown, retreated from the beast, taking a moment to study his opponent. He ignored the wound on his arm as best as he could, locking away in the back of his mind the waves of fiery pain that spread from the slash. He had never fought a black dragon before. In fact, he had never even seen one before, and that ignorance had almost cost him his life. Though the dragon wasn't as large as some of its cousins, growing only to about twenty to twenty-five feet in length, it was just as dangerous. Black scales as hard as rock covered most of the animal, and sharp spikes ran down the length of its spine, functioning as a natural armor which had proven impervious to Bryen's sword and short spear.

Initially, Bryen had concluded that his only chance for success was to go for an eye, but much to his dismay he had found that to be next to impossible. The creature was too fast. Unlike many of the bulky, brawny gladiators who fought in the Pit, Bryen had a surprising strength contained within his wiry frame, which often gave him an advantage during his combats. But not today. Today, he had met his match when it came to speed and agility. Several times Bryen had attempted to attack the beast from behind, yet with each assault it had proven to be a losing strategy. The black dragon tracked him with a frightening intensity as the monstrous beast moved with an almost unnatural celerity, keeping Bryen to its front at all times.

Even worse, the dragon's sharp claws weren't the only danger that he faced. If he got too close to the beast, the dragon also had the option of spitting out a venom that ate through steel and burned through flesh to the bone. Bryen had learned of that alarming ability the hard way, losing his shield in a futile effort to put out one of the dragon's eyes. If he hadn't gotten his buckler up in time, he'd either have been blinded or killed.

His options on what to do next were diminishing with each passing second. Declan and the other gladiators had taught him a great deal about how to fight in the Pit, but this combat was like none of the hundreds of others that he had survived.

The dragon charged forward, teeth the size of Bryen's forearm streaking toward his head. Bryen spun out of the way and slashed down with his sword. He struck a hard blow across the dragon's snout, but the steel had no effect, simply clattering off the beast's scales and leaving his sword arm numb. The dragon's head whipped around, the animal clearly irritated that it had missed its prey once again, and that's when Bryen saw his chance. He lunged forward with his spear having aligned the tip of the steel with the dragon's right eye.

But, once again, he was too slow. The dragon turned its head just enough so that the point of the spear skittered across the beast's scales. Bryen recognized the danger imme-diately with the dragon's head now lined up with his chest and no more than a few feet between them. He dove to the side just as a stream of acidic venom shot from the dragon's mouth. Though most of the blast missed him, a few tiny droplets splattered his left arm and leg. Pinpricks of agony shot through his body, and he feared that he would seize up from the pain.

Bryen could have abandoned his efforts. He had given more of himself in blood, sweat, and tears to the spectators crowding the stands during the last decade than they deserved. There was no known way to kill a black dragon.

So what was the point? He had nothing left to prove and no way to escape the Pit other than to be dragged across the sand. But one of Declan's many sayings ran through his mind as he continued his roll away from the black dragon, putting several more feet between himself and the beast that stalked him. He heard the words in his head in the Master of the Gladiators' gruff voice: "Everyone dies. Not everyone dies with honor." That brought a smile to his lips and the spark of an idea to his mind.

Rather than wait for the dragon's next attack, he decided to change his tactics. Bryen sprinted forward, faking a lunge for the dragon's eye, then jumping into the air and flipping over the beast's head. Before landing in the sand, he jabbed with his short spear toward the animal's other eye. Based on the experience that he had gained during the last hour, he knew before he even attempted the attack that it wouldn't work, but that was fine with him. Having seen the dragon already tilt its head to defend against the strike, he pulled back his spear and instead swung down into the beast's maw with his sword. Yet even this proved futile. Though his sword struck hard and true against the dragon's front fangs, it was like hitting one of its scales. His steel blade bounced backward off the unyielding tooth.

Despite his failure, he kept pushing himself forward, cutting, stabbing, and swinging with blade and spear, seeking any of the weak spots that he had used so many times before when fighting other animals. Still, nothing that he tried worked. His anger getting the better of him, he feinted once more to the left, the dragon's eyes tracking him, before he leapt into the air again and tried to drive the point of his sword through the dragon's snout. A gasp went up from the crowd when they saw the blade shatter into hundreds of pieces, the steel no match for the dragon's scales. For a moment, all Bryen could do was stare at the broken blade in shock. Then, sensing the dragon turning toward him, he threw the remnant of his sword at the beast and dodged out of the way, the dragon's claws slicing through the air where his chest had been just a moment before.

Bryen stepped back for a few seconds, breathing deeply to calm his nerves. His shield and sword now gone, he was left with only his short spear. There had to be a way to get by the dragon's defenses, Bryen told himself. There had to be! Otherwise his time in the Pit would be coming to a bloody end.

He resumed circling the dragon, keeping a good distance away as he searched for a solution. Any solution. Because time was running short. He had been fighting for almost an hour, and he was down to a single spear point. Even worse, he knew his several wounds would begin to slow him down. And when they did, it would all be over. The dragon finally would have its meal.

The cheers and screams from the crowd washed over him, shaking the Colosseum to its very foundation, but it had little effect on Bryen. He was tired of it, tired of every-thing -- the cheering, the fighting, the killing, the pain, the blood. The crowd wanted to see blood. That's all they ever wanted to see. Every time he stepped onto the white sand of the Pit. Whether it was his blood or the dragon's, it really didn't matter to them. No matter how appealing the thought of escaping from the Pit might be, he decided that it wouldn't be his blood that colored the white sand red on this day. If Death wanted to take him, he would fight for every last breath.

DECLAN STOOD at the gate leading into the Pit, his hands clasped tightly to the steel bars as if he were going to pull them free from the bolts connecting them to the stone wall and rush into the Pit to join the fight. The Master of the Gladiators was a hard man, which only made sense since he had lived a hard life. An orphan, he had broken free from the poverty of his youth by joining the army.

Once in the military, he had risen quickly, his tenacity and lack of fear serving him well, but even more so his ability to gain the trust of the soldiers he led. He treated the men and women he was responsible for as his family, because he didn't have a family of his own. They respected him for that, and when he asked them to risk their lives, they did so, because they knew that he would be risking his life right along with them. He never asked his soldiers to do anything that he wouldn't do himself.

The life that he had built for himself had all fallen apart because of an arrogant dolt. When a young lord seeking to make a name for himself had ordered Declan and his troop to capture a village, they had done so with an efficiency that had earned him a great deal of praise. But when that same arrogant dolt then had ordered Declan and his soldiers to slaughter all the village's inhabitants, he had balked.

The lord argued that the villagers supported the bandits that they had been charged with removing from the Dark Forest. Eliminating the people who aided the brigands would make their task that much easier. Declan had told the lord that they had no evidence that these villagers were assisting the bandits; in fact, it seemed more likely that they were victims of the raiders, who stole their livestock and their crops on a regular basis. Moreover, even if the people living at the edge of the wood had some sympathy for the bandits, and Declan had been quite clear that he didn't think that was the case, that was not cause to murder them.

Upon hearing Declan's refusal to execute his order, the lord had made the mistake that had cost him his life, drawing his dagger and placing it at Declan's throat, telling him that if he refused to obey, he'd kill him then and there. Declan didn't take too kindly to the threat. Before the lord knew what had happened, Declan had taken the fool's hand and used it to drive his very own dagger into his throat. The inquiry that followed found Declan guilty with cause to be removed from the army, but the lord's father wanted him dead. So the commander of the Royal Guard, demonstrating some mercy for a soldier whom he had respected, had instead sentenced Declan to the Pit.

He had become a slave, a gladiator forced to fight in the Colosseum, but he was alive. And after ten years of surviving both man and beast, he had been named Master of the Gladiators, relieving him of the need to fight on the white sand. Still a slave, but more likely to remain alive. Since then he had done as he had when he was a soldier in the army, looking out for the men and women compelled to share his fate. He was hard on them, because that was the only way he knew how to lead, but also he wanted to keep them alive. For that, they respected him.

Which was why he felt a wave of shame surge through him as he watched the dragon pursue Bryen around the Pit. Declan had trained the boy to be a gladiator, to fight anything that might stand across from him in the Colosseum. But he had not prepared Bryen for a beast like this. How could he have? Black dragons had never been put in the Pit before, at least not since he had been enslaved. No one had ever been foolish enough -- or so desperate -- to try to capture such a deadly beast. Until now.

"I'm going to gut that fat fool," growled Declan.

Not very tall, the Master of the Gladiators was stout with broad shoulders and arms the size of most men's legs. He was built as solid as an oak tree, his body strengthened by his years as a gladiator. His strength had served him well in the Pit, but now it offered him little advantage. He could only watch as the boy he had raised battled for his life.

"Beluchmel did this?" asked Lycia.

The tall gladiator stood next to him, her eyes never leaving Bryen as he glided across the sand. He had done better than she had expected. Although the black dragon was winning the combat, Bryen continued to move across the sand with that agility and grace of his that seemed almost freakish in a person as tall as he was. She was only a head shorter than Bryen, and though she was quicker than any other gladiator in the Colosseum, her movements never flowed so smoothly as his.

"Aye, lass," replied Declan. "He felt the need to bring that wretched beast from the Trench. How he did it, I don't know."

"But why?" asked Davin.

The rangy gladiator with spiky red hair stood behind the Master of the Gladiators. Normally, even when he fought in the Pit, he had a smile on his face that often appealed to the fairer sex, but not now. Not when his friend had been sentenced to death.

"The King is with us today," grumbled Declan.

Davin cursed and then spit behind them. "He wanted Bryen to die. I have no doubt that he still holds a grudge."

"No," corrected Lycia. "You may be right about the ill will, but that wasn't his goal today. The King wanted to put on a show."

"Right, lass. Doesn't matter to Beluchmel whether Bryen

lives or dies, only that the King of Caledonia and his people enjoy the spectacle that plays out before them."

"So Bryen is the sacrificial lamb," muttered Davin. "The blood needed to quell the mob and satisfy the urges of our blockhead of a monarch."

"That he is," said Declan.

They all knew the odds were stacked against the young gladiator, regardless of how fast or skilled he may be. They had watched for the past hour as their friend had used every bit of knowledge that he had learned while fighting in the Pit to keep himself alive, but nothing he had tried had affected the black dragon in the least. Bryen had only succeeded in angering the beast and delaying the inevitable.

"He's survived worse," offered Lycia, who pushed her braid of long, red hair back over her shoulder. Davin and Lycia were brother and sister, forced into the Pit for stealing food while homeless in Tintagel.

"He's never fought worse," said Davin quietly. "None of us have."

There were many reasons to stay out of the Trench, but the black dragons that had made that grim terrain their own topped the list. The beasts, almost mythical in nature because they were so rarely seen, were known to take those foolish enough to enter that primeval land in a single bite. And as the red-haired gladiator watched his friend struggle to stay alive, he saw that the dragon hadn't tired. It seemed that the beast was intelligent as well, allowing Bryen to wear himself out, waiting patiently until he made a mistake. Then the dragon would have its victory, and Beluchmel would have the end to the story that he was seeking.

"Let's not give up on him just yet," snapped Declan, his worry getting the better of him. "I didn't waste all my time teaching that scrawny lad to fight just to see him end up in a dragon's gullet."

DURING THE PAST decade Bryen had spilled gallons of blood, some of it his own, on the white sands of the Pit. All with the goal of entertaining the crowd, to allow them to forget their problems and worries for a few hours, to let them bet on who or what would survive, to give them the pleasure of seeing death firsthand without having to risk their own lives. At first, the cruelty of it all had horrified him. Now, he barely paid any attention to it. He had seen too much death, been the cause of too much death, for it to affect him. Now he viewed fighting in the Pit as a way to escape. But he didn't think that he had the courage for that release -- not yet.

He had first stepped onto the sand a day past his ninth birthday, weighed down by a short sword that he could barely hold with both hands and a foot-long dagger strapped to his thigh. He was to be that day's entertainment, matched against a veteran gladiator from a western Duchy who was built like a rock and wise to the ways of the Colosseum. The huge gladiator, muscles bulging, face contorted by a series of bloodcurdling screams, soaked in the cheers and adulation of the crowd and played upon the desires of the onlookers. When the combat began, the experienced gladiator toyed with Bryen to start, nicking him first in the arm, then the leg, then the other arm, letting the crowd see the blood, savor it, and thereby incite them into a frenzy.

Bryen had been terrified, never having fought another person before, and still not sure why this was happening to him. He had only received a few weeks of training from the Master of the Gladiators, and when Bryen had been told to walk down the dark passageway lit at the far end by the sun gleaming off the white sand, the irascible Declan seemed to have little hope that he would be walking back this way at the end of the combat. Bryen had no choice then, just as he had no choice now, and he realized that he would die as soon as the veteran gladiator grew tired of his sport.

That thought had enraged Bryen, filling him with an anger that he had never experienced before, an anger that burned away the fear of fighting for his life in front of tens of thousands of screaming people that had almost frozen him in place. It was as if a door had been opened for him, a door that allowed him to see the world as it truly was -- kill or be killed. Discarding his sword because he knew that it would only be a detriment to try to use it against his much larger opponent, he had attacked the gladiator with his dagger with a speed and ferocity that surprised his adversary and had drawn gasps of shock and disbelief from the crowd.

Nimbly dodging the larger man's sword thrust, Bryen had dove past the gladiator, dragging his dagger across the back of the man's legs and slicing cleanly through a hamstring. The gladiator had fallen to a knee, one leg useless. Rather than giving his opponent a chance to regain the initiative and perhaps decide to kill him quickly rather than tease the crowd, Bryen had made the decision for the veteran fighter by mercilessly cutting across the back of his other leg, disabling him completely. Unable to believe what had happened, the gladiator barely felt Bryen's dagger sink into his back in search of his heart.

When it was over, Bryen had risen to his feet, his eyes locked on the now lifeless body. The pool of blood grew larger as it seeped onto the white sand. He had studied the dying gladiator for several seconds, still not sure why it had all happened, nor where he had found the strength and courage to fight back. But then he realized that thinking about it too much served no purpose. He was simply happy to still be alive.

Much to his surprise when he looked up from the fallen gladiator, after scanning the stone rows that rose above him, he saw nothing but astonishment and shock on the faces of the people staring down at him. Silence reigned in the Colosseum as the crowd also tried to figure out how he had proven victorious.

Slowly, the clapping had begun, followed by the cheers, as the crowd acknowledged the little victor. When Bryen raised his bloody dagger to the sky, the cheers had erupted into a roar, a few screams of *Volkun*, or the *wolf*, raining down upon him. Bryen had walked from the Pit to thunderous applause, the Colosseum swaying back and forth. Reaching Declan, he retched, what little was left in his stomach splattering the white stone, and then he had almost passed out. The entire experience had sickened him. Yet it was only the beginning.

The Kingdom of Caledonia, located on a peninsula of the same name with a northern boundary of almost impassable mountains that connected to the Trench, had become addicted to the gladiatorial games during the last few centuries. The capital city of Tintagel was known the world over for it, with many people traveling hundreds of leagues simply to catch a glimpse of the ultimate human struggle.

In the beginning, criminals, slaves, and prisoners fought one another. Then volunteers began to fill the fighting ranks, trading their freedom and risking death in search of glory and riches by binding themselves to the owner of a gladiatorial troupe. Sometimes these gladiators achieved it. If they performed well, they were entitled to a share of their owner's winnings. And after earning a certain amount, they could buy back their freedom, their reputations' intact and their fortunes made. More often than not, however, they fought until they died, living at the owner's school until they fell in the white sand of the Pit. They realized too late that slavery was simply that -- slavery.

Eventually, the King of Caledonia, in search of a new revenue stream that would not require another tax on the people, confiscated the gladiator schools and the combats in the Colosseum became the royal sport. Since then, no one in their right mind considered selling their freedom to fight in the Pit, reserving that place for the dregs of society, the criminals who willingly chose a gruesome death rather than wasting away in a cell and the unfortunate who had no say in the fate that had befallen them. But the crowd cared little about who struggled on the white sand; although, of course, they did have their favorites -- it was a money sport, after all. Their main concern was blood. They wanted to see the white sand turn red.

Bryen understood that better than anyone, having spent the past decade surviving animal or man, fighting on the days of the four principal lunar phases -- the new moon, first quarter, full moon, and last quarter -- since he had first arrived at the School of Gladiators located behind the Colosseum. An orphan forced to survive on the hard streets of the capital city, he had been caught stealing food. Sentenced to death or slavery, Declan had plucked him from the gibbet or the pleasure houses -- the bidding when he was on the slavers' block had been leaning toward the latter -- giving him instead a life in the Pit.

At first, he had been terrified, not knowing what that really meant. But he had learned quickly, taking in everything that Declan sought to teach him. And of the many lessons that the Master of the Gladiators had imparted, Bryen had learned perhaps nothing more important than the fact that life revolved around a simple proposition -- kill or be killed. Declan had drilled that understanding into him relentlessly. So much so that it had become a part of him.

But now Bryen was thinking less about survival and more about death. What if he died? Did it really matter? The thought had filled him with an overwhelming fear for years. When he was younger, he would wake up screaming in the middle of the night because he remembered his first combats when his odds of survival had been slim at best. But as he grew older, his perspective had changed. Death was the easiest form of escape. He would no longer be forced to entertain the bloodthirsty crowd of nobles, merchants, tradespeople, and others who could afford the admission fee to the Colosseum. And after so long a time on the white sand, after so many deaths, the thought of his own bothered him little. What if he didn't fight to the best of his abilities? What if he allowed his opponent to slip past his defenses in a brief moment of weakness?

Though he thought about it frequently, he knew that it would not be a satisfying escape, and he could never bring himself to do it. Declan had influenced him greatly over the years, and whenever his thoughts wandered to this dark corner of his mind, the Master of the Gladiators' words burned through his soul as a reminder, a reminder that he seemed to hear far more than he would like: "Everyone dies. Not everyone dies with honor."

He regained his focus as the dragon slithered forward, its jaws searching for his head once again. Bryen dodged out of the way, rolling to the ground to avoid the lunge, his spear once again scratching harmlessly against the scales near the dragon's right eye. Gathering some sand in his hand, he threw it into the face of the beast, blinding the creature for a time and winning a moment's respite to search for some way to take down his adversary. Every creature -- man or beast -- had a weakness. He knew that. He had found it hundreds of times before. Bryen simply had to find the dragon's.

Yet, it was easier said than done. The beast was remarkably fast, and its sharp claws gave it excellent traction in the sand. Further, based on his lack of success during the past hour, there seemed to be no way to pierce the animal's armor. Bryen could spend an entire day hacking at any part of the dragon's scales without a tangible result, but he couldn't even do that now because he had already broken his blade, having been reduced to a single spearpoint. No, there had to be a better way.

With an angry growl, the dragon lashed out again, its vision clear once more, and again Bryen jumped out of the way. He had barely avoided the lunge, but the beast didn't give him a chance to recover. The massive head rose up before him, unleashing a stream of venom that sizzled as it discharged from its teeth-filled maw. Tired from the long struggle and his wounds beginning to affect him, Bryen moved slower than he normally would have. Though he escaped the full force of the venom, several large drops landed on his left leg, sending a fiery agony from his toes to his core as the acid burned into his skin.

His scream of pain, the first sound he had made since he had entered the Pit more than an hour before, energized the crowd, sending them to a new level of hysteria. Sensing the end, the inevitable conclusion brought the thousands upon thousands of spectators to a fever pitch, their voices a dull roar that mimicked rolling waves of thunder on a stormy night.

Bryen continued the roll that brought him safely out

from under the stream of venom, but the dragon maintained its attack, the beast charging across the sand with its jaws open in anticipation of victory. Bryen came to his feet quickly, separating the pain in his leg from his consciousness. He then dodged to the side, allowing the dragon's head to slip past him. That's when he saw it. It was an opportunity that he simply couldn't pass up.

Stabbing with his spear, the sharp tip plunged into the dragon's exposed ear. He couldn't thrust the steel as deeply as he would have liked, but it was enough at least for the moment. The strike disoriented the beast and stopped its charge, the dragon rearing up once again and shrieking in pain. For the first time since the dragon had been released in the Pit, Bryen had drawn blood. But he knew that what he had done wasn't enough. Time was quickly running out. Still, his chances had improved at least somewhat, as Bryen had finally found what he was so desperately looking for.

Much to the crowd's surprise, Bryen charged directly toward the rearing black dragon, a cry of anger and pain escaping his lips. Bryen's tactic startled the dragon, but the beast recovered quickly, attempting once more to catch its prey with a stream of venom. As soon as the dragon began to open its jaws, Bryen realized that his plan would work. Before the first drops of venom flew toward him, Bryen pulled his foot-long dagger from the sheath on his thigh and changed his grip on the blade so that he held the tip between the fingers of his left hand. Just as quickly, he released it, sending the sharp blade spinning end over end through the air.

The dragon never saw the dagger as it slid through the stream of venom, the steel plunging deep in the back of its throat. The dragon's terrible screech of pain drowned out the thunderous roar of the crowd, which shockingly became silent. They had never expected the fight to turn so quickly. The dragon fell on its side, trying to tear the blade from its mouth with its claws, Bryen momentarily forgotten. And that's when the gladiator struck.

Bryen dove forward, driving his spear into the soft belly and chest of the black dragon with all his might, and then again, and again, and again, until finally he found the beast's heart and the dragon's magnificent head flopped to the sand, its eyes glazed over by death, a pool of bright red blood stretching farther and farther away from its steaming body and staining the white sand the color of the setting sun.

Bryen had been right. The dragon's weakness lay in its underside. He stood over the beast, offering his own private apology and a nod of respect to a worthy competitor. He had not wanted to kill such a magnificent creature, but he had little choice in the matter. Kill or be killed. That was his life.

Weary of the combat, Bryen backed away from the dragon, an animal much like him -- forced to fight for the pleasure of others. A feeling of regret rose up within him, whether because the dragon had died or because he had survived, he could not say. Ignoring the thunderous applause of the spectators and the pain of his injuries, many of the people in the stands howling like a wolf to acknowledge his victory or screaming for the Volkun, Bryen walked slowly across the Pit toward the large steel gate that had just opened. A familiar figure stood before him.

"A good fight," said Declan as he followed his fighter from the Colosseum, his short, grey hair standing straight up and highlighting his dark skin.

"A useless fight," answered Bryen, as he walked across the gladiators' stockade and entered the dim light of the training rooms beneath the Colosseum. The roar of the crowd thankfully dissipated as the door closed behind him, but not before a man a hand taller than Bryen with flaming red hair saluted him, three long spears clutched tightly in his hands, as he strode out toward the stadium. It was Davin's turn to test his luck in the Pit.

Declan studied his charge for a time before replying. The grizzled veteran tried to keep a distance from his gladiators. Why get close to someone who was going to die? But he had found it impossible to follow that stricture with Bryen. The frightened, willowy boy with the unkempt hair, the youngest person to ever fight in the Pit -- much less survive for so long -- had grown up before him, becoming a tall, lean young man. Declan understood that Bryen's experience in the Pit had scarred him, both inside and out. Three long slashes that had healed with time but never had disappeared marred his left cheek and neck. His sharp grey eyes were hard, and his long brown hair and beard were almost overcome by a premature white.

Though Declan would never admit it to anyone, he saw Bryen as a son, so he had trained the boy harder than he had trained any other gladiator to ensure that he had every chance of surviving in the Pit. Seeing the emptiness in Bryen's eyes when he passed by him tore through Declan's heart. The thought that he could do nothing to help Bryen break free from this life nagged at him constantly. He understood that Bryen had tired of his weekly struggles, and he knew what happened as soon as the hope for freedom, for a better life, disappeared. He had seen it too often in other gladiators. But what could he do other than give him the best chance at surviving? To train him. To teach him. To give him the tools that he would need to live, even if the life he lived wasn't the life that he wanted.

"You need to be faster next time," Declan said gruffly,

unsure of what to say, so he fell back into his more comfortable role as Master of the Gladiators. "Otherwise, you may
not be as lucky. If your aim had been off by just a hair, you
would have died."

"Probably," said Bryen as he dropped heavily to a
wooden bench and closed his eyes.

Declan noticed the grimace that played across his face,
so he told one of the boys who worked at the Colosseum to
find the physick. The slash and burns and other assorted
injuries Bryen had suffered needed treatment.

The expression on Bryen's face told Declan that his
young charge simply didn't care anymore. Declan cursed
the boy's luck. Bryen didn't deserve to be here. None of the
gladiators did. But few could challenge fate and win. There
was nothing that he could do about it, nothing except teach
them everything he knew, all with the hope that something
he gave to them would allow them to live -- if only for one
more week.

"Well done, Bryen. For a moment I thought the sand
would turn red."

Bryen looked up and grinned, seeing Lycia standing in
the doorway. Just a few days after Bryen had arrived in the
Colosseum, Declan had explained what the saying used so
frequently by the gladiators meant, as it referenced a gladiator dying on the white sand of the Pit, his or her red blood
soaking into the feathery, soft, pure white crystals.

"So did I."

"But not yet."

"No, not yet," Bryen confirmed.

"Death doesn't choose us ..." began Lycia.

"We choose our death."

Bryen finished the saying that was a mantra among the
gladiators. They clasped arms and then Lycia walked off

with a grin, giving his shoulder an affectionate squeeze as she headed toward the steel gate to watch her brother fight. She understood that she had to give the white-haired gladiator the space that he needed to release the tension of the duel, from the fight that in all his time in the Pit had brought him closest to death.

DEMANDS

"Are you enjoying the combat, Duke Winborne?" The question was a simple one, yet it held several meanings in the slightly mocking tone with which it was offered. "I understand you have a unique perspective on the games."

"Quite the spectacle," replied the Duke of the Southern Marches, who hesitated just a moment before responding. He chose to ignore the attempted insult. "I'm quite impressed by this gladiator. A lesser fighter would not have survived for so long against such a beast."

In actuality, Kevan Winborne despised the gladiatorial combats. They showed a lack of respect for human life, for the people compelled to participate. The Caledonian Kingdom had abolished slavery hundreds of years before, yet a form of it still remained here in the Pit, something that was accepted and overlooked because of its utility and profitability, and it left Kevan somewhat sickened. The privileged classes viewed the Colosseum as a place of sport and an opportunity for their own amusement and distraction. They cared little for the wellbeing of those forced to perform on the white sand, ignoring the hypocrisy of such a practice, as they were only concerned about the quality of the show. They wanted drama, excitement, bravery, skill, and a heroic end, having no concern for the people or creatures placed on their sandy stage.

"Very true," replied the handsome young man. Long black hair ran to the nape of his neck, and more often than not it fell into his eyes. His regular attempts to move the unruly strands amused and excited the many young, eligible women who sought to attract his attention. He had an easy smile, though the ladies pursuing him tended to ignore the fact that frequently it tended to curl into a sneer when he failed to obtain what he wanted, or he believed that the person he was interacting with was below his station or wasn't worth his time. When you sought to catch a king, the little things could be disregarded. "Very true. Tell me, Tetric, has anyone ever survived an encounter with a black dragon? I believe that we haven't had a beast as dangerous as this one in the Colosseum for decades."

"Not to my knowledge, Your Majesty. And you're right. The last time we had a creature such as this was well before your father's reign. Six gladiators fought the animal together. All six died." Tetric's words came out as a scratchy whisper. His intense black eyes, which had an almost hypnotic quality, added to the man's formidable appearance. Wiping a few drops of sweat from his bald head, then stroking his short, pointed beard as was his habit, he turned the full force of his gaze on Duke Winborne. "Of course, no man can escape his fate, no matter how hard he might try."

"Yet this young man continues to do so."

Kevan understood Tetric's reference quite well. Having to pay his respects once a year to the young King Marden Beleron, ruler of Caledonia, was a chore that he dreaded but couldn't avoid. To also have to deal with the likes of Tetric, the King's Chief Advisor, made the experience that much more unbearable.

The Duke of the Southern Marches sighed in weariness. He was still a young man, or at least he liked to think so, but the last few days in Tintagel had aged him. As soon as he and his contingent of soldiers had ridden under the gates of the Corinthian Palace, named for Marden's late father, a battle had ensued. Not one of steel or magic, but rather of words. Insinuations, threats, and promises that could be just as deadly as a dagger in the ribs.

"No man can escape his fate, Tetric. I will agree with you on that. But no man has to accept it willingly. No man has to give in. Though a man may be placed on a certain path, that man can still fight it. In fact, some would say that allowing others to choose your path is worse than fate. You never know what will come of the choice until it's too late."

Tetric flinched as if he had been struck a physical blow, yet he quickly recovered with a menacing glare. Kevan was pleased to see that his jab had hit home. Rumors circled Tetric like buzzards around a dying animal. And everyone knew that in any rumor there always was some hint of the truth.

Marden's Advisor had appeared mysteriously in Caledonia a decade before, quickly inserting himself as a confidant to King Corinthus, Marden's father. At the time of Tetric's arrival, Caledonia prospered. The harvests flourished, the Kingdom was free of the pirates who often marauded along the coast, and the Dukes and Duchesses of the various provinces had learned to settle their differences through diplomacy rather than war -- all aided by the King's wise and just leadership. Yet soon after Tetric had wormed his way into the Tintagel court, cracks began to appear in the Kingdom's foundations.

The Crown began to ignore the requirements of long-standing treaties, impinging on the rights of the provinces. New taxes were forced on the Duchies, and thus on the common folk, making it harder for average workers or farmers to pay their debts. The argument was often the same. There was a need for more soldiers in the Royal Guard. The Corinthian Palace had to be expanded. The navy required more ships. More, always more. While at the same time the commoners suffered and Tintagel, the capital of Caledonia, began to fall into disrepair. No one could trace these problems or crises directly to the new Advisor, because it was King Corinthus who signed every order or approved every action, but Tetric's influence over the King was clear and increasing by the day, much like a large snake winding itself slowly but inexorably around its victim. Then Corinthus' health began to wane.

In consequence, as time passed, Tetric rather than Corinthus appeared to be ruling Caledonia, yet there was little that the Duchies could do, if only because now several of the provinces were frequently at odds with one another, and individually no Duchy had the strength to stand against the much larger Royal Guard. The King's health continued to fail and after several years of deterioration the old man died. With a young, ambitious, and impressionable Marden following his father to the throne, in just the last three years Tetric had strengthened his grip on the Kingdom -- surreptitiously, of course -- and solidified his influence over the mercurial and short-tempered king.

"I disagree," replied Marden. "A man can be forced onto a path he hasn't chosen for himself. It simply requires a certain incentive. For example, just the other day I had a man drawn and quartered because he refused to admit his crime, proclaiming his innocence to the very end. If he had retracted his statement of innocence, then perhaps I would have been more lenient. Maybe a beheading instead. But that was his choice. He chose to fight, to deny. To try for a different path. In this instance, the man's decision to resist led to a more painful death."

Marden settled back into his chair, his attention once again on the combat that continued to play out before him. The gladiator now circled the black dragon, searching for an opening. Ah, well. No matter how good a fight the slave put up, it was all for naught. If he fought in the Pit, he was a man condemned and his sentence eventually would be carried out. Even if he survived his struggle on this day, and that likelihood was slim at best, fate would catch up to him on another.

"And then just yesterday a merchant accused of smuggling was brought before me," continued Marden. "He had a cart full of finely woven rugs, jewels, even some spices, all from the Western Isle. He was given the choice of turning over his contraband to the Crown and leaving the Kingdom peacefully or having his head chopped off. Though he, too, proclaimed his innocence, stating that he had paid the required taxes on the imports, he wisely chose the former course, losing his contraband but escaping with his head. Of course, he will be spending a good bit of time in prison for his crime."

"May I ask, your Majesty, what these examples have to do with me?" The Duke of the Southern Marches knew exactly what they had to do with him, but he had to play along, if only to massage the ego of this young, impetuous ruler. "I know you asked me to attend you here for a specific purpose. I'm curious as to that reason."

"You are the most direct, straightforward of my vassals, Kevan," said Marden, leaning forward now, his black eyes focused on the most powerful of the Dukes and Duchesses in the Kingdom. "Whether that's good or bad, we shall see. I should have expected you of all people to cut to the chase." Marden nodded toward his Advisor. "I told you he would do such a thing, Tetric, did I not?"

"You did, your Majesty," confirmed Tetric, twirling the pointed end of his beard in his hand. "As you said, Duke Winborne is one who goes straight to the heart of a matter."

Tetric eyed Kevan with a malicious intent in his eyes. Kevan's pointed comment had obviously struck closer to home than he had thought possible. Moreover, it had stayed with the Advisor, who was known for holding grudges and meting out retribution when the time was right.

"You see, Kevan," began Marden, "I'm faced with a problem." He clenched his fist and sneered as he watched the gladiator's blade shatter on the black dragon's snout. It wouldn't be long now. The slave's heroics would soon be lost to history. "I've sat on the throne of Caledonia for three years now. And the Duchies are growing restless. I'm sure you're quite aware of that."

Kevan shrugged and nodded his head noncommittally. The provinces were always restless these days because of the Crown's usually self-serving decisions. Before Tetric had arrived, King Corinthus had usually put the interests of the Kingdom before his own. With the King's Advisor and the coronation of Marden Beleron, that dynamic had been reversed. As a result, there were rumblings that several of the Dukes and Duchesses were interested in removing Marden from the throne. But none were willing to take that risk on their own. Yet.

No Duchy on its own had the strength to defeat the King's Royal Guard, and the distrust sown by Tetric during the last decade had weakened the former bonds between the Duchies. As a result, none of the Duchies but for a few trusted any of the others enough to form temporary alliances to achieve their goals. Thus, the Dukes and Duchesses spent half their time looking at their peers, worrying about what they might be planning, while spending the rest of their time trying to hinder Marden's many schemes. For Marden, it was an effective way to rule, keeping his greatest threats off balance, and Kevan gave Tetric full credit for engineering the current situation.

"To help soothe the Duchies, Tetric advises me that it's time to select a bride. Isn't that right, Tetric?"

"Yes, your Majesty. Absolutely correct. By picking a bride you can cement your position on the throne and remove any questions with respect to an heir, once the lucky bride is with child. Then the Duchies can turn their attention to more important matters rather than questions of succession."

Kevan listened to Tetric with half an ear, his mind having outpaced the conversation. An icy chill ran down his spine. He knew immediately what was coming next.

"I've thought about this for some time, Kevan. Marriage is not something that you simply jump into." Marden sat back in his chair, a broad smile on his face. "Your daughter Aislinn is a beautiful young lady, don't you think? And with the Southern Marches the most powerful of all the Duchies, I believe it only fitting that Aislinn become the Queen of Caledonia. Don't you agree?"

Marden said the words with such unassuming nonchalance, as if the proposal was no more than a topic of idle conversation and carried little import. Yet for Kevan the words drove a stake through his heart.

"Your Majesty is very kind for suggesting Aislinn as a possible match, but I must admit that I'm somewhat surprised by the choice." Kevan cleared his throat, trying to buy some time to think. "Aislinn is still just a young girl, and not yet ready for marriage. I would even suggest that she's a bit rough around the edges. Would you not, your Majesty, do better by selecting a young woman of greater maturity? A young woman who would have a much better understanding of what an alliance with the House of Beleron would mean and require?"

"Kevan, please give me a moment ..."

"Keep in mind as well, Your Majesty, that though I may rule the strongest of the Duchies, my House is still relatively young compared to some of the others. Choosing Aislinn is a great honor for me, I certainly can't deny that, but her selection may cause you ill will with some of the other Duchies."

Marden opened his mouth to reply, his face scrunched up slightly in anger, as his temper, which was never very far from the surface, threatened to erupt. He was the King! When he made a decision, there was no discussion or debate. No questions or resistance. There was only action. With an effort, he forced down his irritation. If he had learned one thing in his three years on the throne, it was that patience and cleverness at times trumped the application of force and unnecessary confrontation. And this was one of those times. Having regained control of himself, Marden was about to take a different tack, but before he could say what was on the tip of his tongue, Tetric interrupted him.

"King Beleron is well aware of the political ramifications of his choice," said the King's Advisor, leaning forward so that Kevan could smell his acrid, musty breath. It reminded the Duke of the Southern Marches of a newly opened crypt and sent another shiver down his spine. "And though your daughter is young, she is still of an age to marry. She offers more to our good King than any of the other eligible young women in the Kingdom. So much more."

With the Advisor's last comment, Kevan realized immediately that Tetric was much more dangerous than Marden, a thought that worried him, yet wasn't a surprise.

"As King Marden has said, he has given much thought to his decision," continued Tetric, his voice an unsettling wheeze. "An alliance between Tintagel and the Southern Marches would strengthen the Kingdom, so he asks for your daughter in marriage. It is not just a gracious request, but one to be valued and appreciated. What say you, Kevan?"

Kevan shot Tetric a hard glare, well aware of the insult offered by the King's Chief Advisor. Or rather the warning. To address a Duke of Caledonia with such informality was almost unheard of, occurring only between equals. Yet Kevan got the impression that Tetric saw himself as more than equal to Kevan and Marden. Kevan looked down briefly at the combat still taking place in the Pit. The gladiator was holding his own, having survived for more than an hour. He seemed to be quite capable, and the young man's patience was impressive as he waited for his opening, waited for the right moment to strike. Though almost everyone in the crowd likely believed that the black dragon would eventually kill the young man, Kevan knew the truth of it. The gladiator had become the hunter in just the last few minutes. It was only a matter of time before he proved victorious.

Turning his gaze back to Marden and Tetric, an uncomfortable lump in the pit of his stomach suggested that unfortunately for Kevan, he was now the quarry, a position that he detested. As a military leader, he was used to taking the initiative. To moving forward. But now, all that he could do was attempt to build up his deteriorating defenses as quickly as possible. Perhaps if he exercised the same patience as that of the gladiator fighting for his life, he could extricate himself and his daughter from this trap, at least for a time.

"Your Majesty, I must apologize. Truly, your request is overwhelming. I had never expected it." Tetric smiled slightly at the statement. Kevan was now certain that this entire plot was the Advisor's idea. More important, it was clear that Tetric held more sway over the son than he ever did over the father, and that was a frightening realization.

"It is overwhelming," answered Tetric in his quiet rasp. "But the King still needs your answer. He needs his bride."

"Your Majesty, obviously you know my decision, for there is no choice but one to be made. However, as I noted, my daughter is young and naive. She will most likely not understand what is going on between us, between the Crown and the Southern Marches. With your permission, I would like to speak with her first and present your proposal to her. I will then send you my reply, which of course is simply a formality."

Kevan held his breath, waiting to see if his delaying tactic would work. He expected Tetric to see through his maneuver immediately, and, in fact, he sensed that the King's Advisor was about to quash his attempt at deflecting the request, but this time Marden surprisingly aided him.

"Of course you may, Kevan. I must have your official response by the Fall Council of the Kingdom, so you have a few months to educate your daughter on the role she is to play. And I expect no further delays. If I don't receive word of your daughter's acceptance by then, I will, of course, be sorely disappointed, and we will have a much more serious conversation."

Tetric's face turned bright red, his rage barely contained, but control it he did. The fool! They had maneuvered the Duke of the Southern Marches into a corner from which he could not escape, but Marden had just given him a small path he could use to slip away.

"Of course, Your Majesty. Thank you for your generosity. If I may, Your Majesty, it is a long ride back to the Southern Marches. The sooner I am off, the sooner this matter can be settled to both our satisfaction."

"Then off with you, Kevan. I will wait on your reply. And remember ... *Father* ... don't keep me waiting."

"Thank you, Your Majesty."

Bowing at the waist, Kevan exited the royal box just as the crowd burst into a thunderous roar. He glanced down toward the white sand and saw exactly what he had expected. He had been right. The gladiator had won. As had he, at least for a time, having escaped Tetric's trap for the moment. But only for the moment. Kevan cursed his luck under his breath. What was he to do?

KEVAN TOOK his time as he made his way to the stable at the bottom of the Colosseum, used for the horses and carriages of only the richest and most powerful men and women of Caledonia, as he wanted to think a bit more about what had just happened and how to evade the net Marden and Tetric were attempting to throw over him and his daughter. It was there that he found Tarin, his Captain of the Guard, already in the saddle, the reins of Kevan's horse held firmly in his hands. Tarin seemed to have the ability to read minds, knowing that Kevan wanted to leave quickly. But he hadn't foreseen the dilemma that now plagued the Duke of the Southern Marches.

"Not yet, Tarin," said Kevan. "There is something that I must do first."

Tarin shrugged. "I had expected as much." He had served Kevan for more than a decade. He was well aware of his lord's moods and habits, and he could tell that Kevan's mind was working on a problem at a furious pace.

"Is it as we feared?" asked Tarin, sliding off his saddle and tying the reins of both horses to a gate.

"Worse, I'm afraid," replied Kevan. "Much worse." Kevan stood there for a minute, until finally the path that he needed to take formed in front of him. It just might be the solution, or at least part of the solution, that he was looking for. Besides, there was little risk to what he had in mind. "Who is responsible for the gladiator who just defeated the black dragon?"

Tarin gave his lord a quizzical look, not expecting the question. "I believe his name is Beluchmel," replied Tarin.

"Did you watch the combat, Tarin?"

"I did." It had been an impressive display for someone with little or no military instruction. True, gladiators were taught to fight. But as a soldier, Tarin had his prejudices and favored those with a military upbringing, as he believed that there was a distinct difference between that and the training that a gladiator received.

"And your thoughts?"

The Captain of the Guard waited a moment before answering. Tarin rarely answered anything right away, for he was a man of caution, a trait that certainly benefited him as a soldier, yet could also prove a hindrance at times.

"He fought with intelligence, with a patience and skill rarely seen in gladiators. Usually they come charging across the Pit, looking to end the combat as soon as possible, often not caring if they live or die. This one let the fight come to him, and his decision making is beyond dispute. He picked the perfect moment to make his move."

"Let us go in search of this Beluchmel," decided Kevan, nodding his head in agreement. "We have business to conduct."

~

"WHAT DO YOU THINK, Tetric? Will my soon-to-be father-in-law try to back out?"

"It will be hard for him to do so," replied Tetric. "Though I doubt that he has any intention of allowing his daughter to go through with the marriage if he can avoid it. His responses were quite vague, you know. He didn't commit to anything other than speaking to the girl about the proposal."

He and Marden had watched Kevan walk quickly from the royal box. They both suspected the decision that Kevan wanted to make. Therefore, they needed to ensure that he had but one option to select from, a choice that favored their plan.

"I agree," said Marden. "Still, do you think he will break if we apply the right amount of pressure?"

"No. He will not."

"We need him or his daughter, not both."

Marden tore his gaze away from the opened doors and glanced back to the white sand of the Pit. The attendants had already removed the dragon's body and the next combat was about to begin, this one pitting a tall, red-haired gladiator against two starved lions. He already had guessed the outcome, so he turned his attention back to his Advisor.

"We need to find some other way, Tetric. Some other way to ensure that the Duke of the Southern Marches does our bidding."

"Yes, your Majesty, we will. I will make sure that everything is in place."

A DEAL

"This is most unusual, Duke Winborne," said Beluchmel, his massive frame shaking as he pounded a large fist on the oak door wrapped in steel bands. His size was deceptive, as the luxurious silk robes that he preferred to wear hid more fat than muscle. "Most unusual. In fact, I can't even remember when a request such as this has been made, and I've been Master of the Colosseum for the last three decades."

Kevan ignored the chatter coming from the huge man. The bright sun gleamed brightly off Beluchmel's bald pate, long stringy hair near his ears running down to his shoulders. Serving as the Master of the Colosseum had its obvious perks, so long as you didn't bring too much attention to yourself. The fact that Beluchmel had survived in his position for such a long time, and had obviously profited from it, testified to his abilities, no matter how nefarious they might be. Based on his large, red, bulbous nose, the veins thick and obvious, Kevan assumed that much of the fortune the man had acquired was used to keep the Master of the Colosseum in drink and other pleasures.

"What's the price?"

An eyehole opened before them, then closed just as quickly, the grunt heard from the other side of the immense gates acknowledging Beluchmel's authority, though clearly with some reluctance. Slowly, the gates began to open, winches on both sides pulling them apart. Beluchmel squeezed his bulk through, stomping into the training ground, followed by Kevan and the always cautious Tarin, who placed a wary hand on the hilt of his sword.

Practice yard it might be, but to Kevan's eyes, it looked more like a prison stockade. A ten-foot wall made of brick and mortar surrounded the entire complex, and ten feet beyond that wall rose a twenty-foot wall. Ten feet beyond that barrier, a wall thirty feet in height loomed above the complex, blocking much of the late afternoon sun. Along each wall at fifty-foot increments a bored guard stood looking down at the activities taking place below.

Tarin's soldierly eye took it all in, guessing that something unpleasant waited between the walls of varying heights for any gladiator foolish enough to try to escape. Even a full-scale revolt would fail, he concluded. The gladiators' compound lay against the back of the Colosseum. On the remaining three sides just outside the walls was the permanent headquarters for the King's Royal Guard. If the gladiators somehow succeeded in escaping from their small enclosure, and the likelihood of that appeared to be poor at best, they still had to fight their way through a large army. All in all, it was the most effective prison Tarin had ever seen constructed.

On each side of the field, a long, ramshackle barracks stood in disrepair, the paint peeling off as the stone baked in the noonday sun. In several places, holes were visible in the roofs. Obviously, Beluchmel had done his best to siphon off as much of the money directed toward the upkeep of the gladiators' compound as possible.

A field several hundred feet long stretched out before them, more dirt than grass. Markers divided the field into distinct areas. The gladiators assigned to each space trained with specific equipment, honing their skills in order to improve their chances of surviving in the Pit. Tarin immediately noted that none of the gladiators were very old with perhaps just a handful beyond their early twenties. Try as the gladiators might to sharpen their abilities, he wasn't surprised that their efforts could only take them so far.

He understood that once a man or woman set foot on the white sand their death was assured, for most in a matter of months. When you were required to fight at least four times a month, it was inevitable that eventually your luck would run out. No matter how skilled a gladiator may be, all it would take would be a momentary lapse in concentration, a single poorly timed lunge or a slip on the white sand, and the end would come. Nevertheless, he was impressed by their diligence. Some balanced on a thin pole while trying to stave off the jabs of their compatriots' spears. Others lifted stones that he guessed weighed several hundred pounds, and then those same gladiators tried to run through sand placed there to mimic the fighting floor of the Pit. And still more worked to master a dozen other tasks, all designed to extend the time until their unavoidable death.

"The price will depend on the gladiator you select," answered Beluchmel, leading them across the field in a lumbering walk toward the main building that squared off the compound. Though this structure was in a better state compared to the gladiators' quarters, its age was apparent. Mortar crumbled slowly between the stones, and the roof, this one made of wood shingles rather than thatch, sloped dangerously toward the ground on one end.

Kevan watched as Beluchmel pushed his bulk through the opening, his sides scraping against the stone. The door had long since been removed, or perhaps it simply had disintegrated over time, mused Kevan. He and Tarin followed the Master of the Colosseum into a small room in which a man sat quietly behind a desk made of two sawhorses and what Kevan guessed was the missing door. The solidly built man, his grey hair shorn close to his scalp, ignored them, continuing to work through a stack of papers. He didn't seem to be a man who enjoyed his job. He had the hardened appearance of a gladiator, a man who had survived many combats in the Pit, and he had the scars on his arms and legs, revealed by the shirt and training shorts he wore, to prove it. Though the man was older, Kevan suspected that he could return to the Pit right then and still emerge victorious, though he doubted that the man had fought on the white sand for quite some time.

Beluchmel, obviously uncomfortable in his surroundings, cleared his throat a few times, hoping to gain the quiet man's attention. But the serious-minded fellow continued to ignore them.

"Declan, I bring with me prestigious visitors. Rise and offer them the appropriate courtesies."

The man failed to lift his head as he continued to sift through the papers on his makeshift desk. "I am busy, Beluchmel, and I have no time for visitors. I barely have time for anything but trying to keep my men and women alive." Having completed what he had been working on, finally Declan looked up from his papers, his sharp eyes giving a glimpse of the quick temper that lay just beneath his outward calm. "Now where is the fresh hay you

promised me for the roofs? And the other building materi-
als, Beluchmel? Where are they? We've waited for months.
If the King feels the need to put on this bloody show, then
he needs to take better care of the men and women
consigned to play a role in it."

Declan rose from his chair and walked around his desk.
Though Beluchmel towered over the shorter man, that was
of little import. Beluchmel wouldn't last a second alone with
Declan.

"How am I supposed to train my gladiators to fight in the
Pit if I can't even give them habitable quarters and good,
healthy food? And tell me, Beluchmel, how will you fill your
pockets with gold if you have no gladiators fighting for the
King's pleasure? How will you keep that large head of yours
on your portly body if the good King Beleron doesn't have
his favorite entertainment to keep the people's minds off
their own troubles?"

Beluchmel gulped loudly, a sheen of sweat appearing on
his forehead. Kevan and Tarin now understood why their
guide had seemed so reluctant to enter the gladiators'
compound. Though Beluchmel managed the Colosseum,
this kept man ruled the gladiators.

"You will have everything I promised you, Declan, everything. The shipments have simply been delayed. A few more
weeks is what I have been told. Surely you can wait that ..."

"I'm tired of your excuses, Beluchmel," said Declan,
stepping closer to the Master of the Colosseum and causing
the larger man to step back in fear. "If I had half a mind, I'd
break you in two and leave you for ..."

"Although that would truly be an interesting sight,"
interrupted Kevan, moving between the two men before
Declan could make good on his promise, "I have a bit of
business to discuss with you first. And since we must leave

within the hour, we need to take care of it now. Once that's concluded, you can do whatever you want to this one." Kevan pointed to Beluchmel, who clearly welcomed the interruption and had begun to sweat profusely despite the chill of the late afternoon. "I'm assuming that you are the Master of the Gladiators?"

"I am," replied Declan, the anger leaving his face, if only for a moment.

"Excellent. I am Kevan Winborne, Duke of the Southern Marches. And this is Tarin Tentillin, Captain of my Guard."

Tarin and Declan eyed one another, judging strengths and weaknesses in an instant. It was a common habit when two soldiers met for the first time. Satisfied by what each one saw in the other, they nodded a wary greeting.

"Duke Winborne," said Declan, giving the lord a perfunctory nod of his head. "You mentioned business. We have few visitors to the training ground. What can I do for you?"

"I am in need of a gladiator, Declan."

Declan chuckled softly. He had heard that some of the wealthy and powerful had strange tastes, yet this seemed a bit out of the ordinary. Declan picked up on much of what was going on in the Kingdom during his wanderings through the Colosseum and the city, but he had never heard anything unique, unseemly, or untoward about the Duke of the Southern Marches, no strange or upsetting predilections or tastes. In fact, from what he could tell from the various pieces of information that he had gathered, this Duke was more austere than most of his colleagues. Of course, not every rumor made its way to the Colosseum, Declan admitted, and every man was entitled to his private fancies, within reason, of course.

"May I ask the reason why you require a gladiator?" asked Declan.

"It's none of your concern," answered Tarin, who stepped forward, his hand caressing the hilt of his sword. The insolence of this Master of the Gladiators, former soldier though he might be, irritated the Captain of the Battersea Guard.

"It is my concern," grated Declan, his face red with anger. "I've trained these men and women, some since they were children, to be fighters, survivors. Fate gave them a bad hand sending them here to die, but I've done everything I could to ensure that they die with honor, and more importantly, that they delay their deaths for as long as possible. I will not release a single gladiator until I know your purpose, Duke Winborne. It is that simple."

"You will not release ..." sputtered Tarin, his blade half out of his sheath.

Kevan quickly grabbed the Captain's hand, forcing the blade back into the scabbard. Tarin was a stickler for everything in life, whether protocol or his own appearance, as seen by his spotless uniform, perfectly parted hair, and waxed mustache with the tips curled just so. But Declan didn't appear to be flustered by Tarin's display. In fact, he seemed to be less than impressed, obviously believing that he'd have little trouble dispatching Tarin if there was cause to do so.

"Declan, don't be a fool," said Beluchmel, worried that his business deal was about to fall through. "If the Duke of the Southern Marches requires a gladiator, then he will have one, even if I must bring a company of the King's Royal Guard in here to ensure that he gets one."

"Then you'd finally be giving me the opportunity that my gladiators and I have been waiting for," said Declan softly, his eyes glowing with a keen anticipation. Beluchmel took another step away from the Master of the Gladiators, quivering with fear.

During the entire exchange, Kevan had studied Declan, sizing him up. He saw loyalty there, and honor, and perhaps his most noble trait, compassion. He cared about the men and women whom he trained. That alone earned Kevan's respect.

"Enough of this," said Kevan in a thunderous voice, quelling the three men into silence, even the feisty gladiator. "Declan, I admire loyalty. It is a trait rarely seen these days, in even the best of men. You ask a fair question, and you will have an answer. I have a daughter, a teenage daughter. As the Duke of the Southern Marches, there are certain risks that I have to worry about, and it seems that those dangers are becoming more real, not only for me, but also for my daughter."

Declan nodded his head knowingly. Slave he may be, but he was not a fool. Duke Winborne was the leading contender for the throne should anything happen to King Beleron. Based on what he knew of the Duke of the Southern Marches that could be a good thing for Caledonia, though he doubted that the man would live very long if he ever demonstrated any interest in ruling the Kingdom, not with Tetric lurking in the shadows.

"I require a gladiator to serve as her Protector."

Declan studied the Duke of the Southern Marches for almost a full minute, until he was satisfied that he had spoken truthfully. Serving as a Protector was an honorable task, though much like a gladiator, a Protector had no personal freedom. But Declan was surprised by the admission. It was an archaic practice. No one had served as a Protector for at least five decades.

"And I'm assuming that you've already selected a gladiator to serve as your daughter's Protector."

"I have," answered Kevan. "The gladiator who defeated the black dragon. The one called the Volkun."

Declan's heart rose in his throat, choking him for a brief moment. Of course, he shouldn't have been so shocked. Bryen was one of the best gladiators to ever fight in the Pit, despite his relative youth. Why wouldn't the Duke of the Southern Marches want the best to serve as a Protector for his daughter? He searched furiously for a way to prevent the deal, but nothing came to mind. There was no legitimate way that he could stop the sale of a gladiator. Then again, perhaps he was looking at this from the wrong perspective. Perhaps this would help Bryen in some way. If nothing else, it would release him from the Pit. Bryen clearly wasn't interested in glory, the only thing attainable by a gladiator now.

True, slave Bryen would remain, but his life wouldn't hang in the balance based on the changing moon. And serving as a Protector couldn't prove to be a worse fate than the one that awaited him on the white sand, regardless of the threats Duke Winborne may have been concerned about. If Bryen could survive the Pit for ten years, then he could certainly endure watching over the Duke's most likely spoiled daughter. After struggling a few seconds more with what he knew had already been decided, he nodded his head in acquiescence, then quietly left the room through a doorway at the back of the office.

"Well, Duke Winborne, despite the trouble put up by our honorable Master of the Gladiators, it looks like you will have the gladiator that you require." Beluchmel rubbed his hands in anticipation. Matters were finally getting interesting, in his opinion -- another contribution of golds to his pocket.

"Your price?" Kevan asked the question sharply, clearly not interested in the drawn-out haggling so much a part of the general marketplace in Tintagel. Though some enjoyed it, and Beluchmel appeared to relish it quite a bit judging by the brief turn of disappointment on his face, Kevan did not.

"Fifty golds," answered Beluchmel with a straight face, his eyes sharp. They had entered his arena now.

"Fifty!" objected Tarin. "For a gladiator? That's robbery."

"Done," answered Kevan, judging the price cheap after having seen the gladiator in action. The cost of protecting his daughter was nothing to him, and based on this gladiator's performance, Kevan knew that he was buying the best.

"But Duke Winborne!" protested Tarin.

"The golds, Tarin," commanded Kevan.

Knowing from experience that arguing with his lord once he had made up his mind was a bad idea, Tarin began pulling out the pieces of gold from a large purse hidden beneath his cloak.

"Oh, my apologies, Duke Winborne. But I forgot the transfer fee required by the Crown. That's an additional ten golds, for a total of sixty."

Beluchmel grinned mischievously, knowing that he had won. The cost of this gladiator was obviously not a concern to Duke Winborne, so why not try to extract as much as possible.

Tarin was about to protest once again, but Kevan cut him off. "So be it. Sixty."

Throwing up his arms in mock despair, Tarin placed the heavy, thick coins in a smaller leather bag. The Captain of the Guard shook his head in frustration. The boy they were buying may be a fighter, but he was not a soldier. Hopefully that fact wouldn't cause the Duke of the Southern Marches to rue his decision.

"Stop moving around. How am I supposed to take care of your wounds if you flop about like a small child with a splinter in his finger?"

Bryen couldn't help but smile at Lycia's command, though her touch was anything but light as she first checked the slice on his arm from the black dragon's claw and then rewrapped that wound once she was satisfied that the physick had done good work with the sutures. She then turned her attention to the burns on his left arm and leg caused by the animal's venom. For those there was little that she could do other than make sure that Bryen continued to apply the healing ointment that would help with the pain and prevent the burns from becoming infected that sat next to him on the wooden bench.

"You're babying him, Lycia," said Davin. "Leave him be. He's had worse injuries than these."

"I'm making sure that he's well, that's all," said Lycia, her voice turning hard. Her brother had a knack for getting a rise out of her, often for the most innocuous of comments.

"You never show so much concern for me," protested Davin. "Besides, I had the harder fight. Two starved lions are much more difficult than a black dragon."

"The only reason it was a harder fight," corrected Lycia, "was because of those skinny legs of yours. You spent more time tripping over yourself than actually fighting those poor beasts. Besides, you weren't even hurt. Not even a scratch."

Bryen closed his eyes for a moment and settled the back of his head against the brick wall. The bickering between brother and sister washed over him, and he allowed his focus to waver for just a few minutes. After all that he had been through that afternoon, this being the closest yet that he had come to his own death, he found the incessant wrangling between Davin and Lycia relaxing.

Brother and sister had arrived in the Colosseum three years before, and Bryen remembered the day clearly. They had entered through the gates arguing with one another and it hadn't stopped since. When he had first seen Lycia, he had thought that she was the most beautiful girl he had ever laid eyes on, and he and Davin had become fast friends, one of his few here in the training barracks. There was a great deal of respect between him and the other gladiators. He had survived the longest of any of the men or women forced to bleed on the white sand, other than Declan himself. But because the prospect of death was always near that mutual respect rarely turned into friendship. Not when you might be charged with killing a friend in the Pit.

Thankfully, Bryen had not yet had to fight Davin or Lycia. Next to him, his two friends were the best gladiators in Tintagel, and Beluchmel had no desire to interfere with the stream of money he earned whenever one of the three entered the Pit. The Master of the Colosseum was a greedy, self-serving, soulless man, but he was not stupid. He would not do anything that would limit his potential earnings.

Bryen was drawn from his peaceful reverie by the silence that settled suddenly within the gladiators' quarters. He opened his eyes and saw that both Lycia and Davin were staring at Declan, who stood in the doorway. Bryen took in Declan's serious expression. Though the older man was always serious, this time his eyes suggested something else. There was a touch of sorrow and anger at the edges of his flinty glare and perhaps even a hint of hope.

"What's the matter, Declan?"

The Master of the Gladiators was about to answer, but he couldn't find the words, his emotions threatening to erupt, and that wasn't something that he knew how to manage effectively. So as he'd done all his life, he simply pushed the feelings roiling through him to the back of his mind and locked them away.

"I'm sorry, lad, but there was nothing that I could do. Come along."

Declan walked out of the gladiators' changing room, shaking his head in what Bryen took to be disgust but was actually sorrow.

Bryen had no idea why the Master of the Gladiators was acting this way. He looked to Davin and Lycia for guidance, but his two friends were just as surprised and confused as he was, both shrugging their shoulders in response. Declan could be moody at times, but they had never seen anything like this from him before.

Shrugging his shoulders as well, Bryen exited the room and hobbled after Declan as pain flared in his leg with every step that he took, a sense of unease settling within his stomach. He hadn't felt this nervous even when he was fighting the black dragon.

ONLY A FEW MINUTES had passed before Declan reappeared, and behind him came the gladiator from the Pit. He was younger than Kevan had expected, perhaps only a year or two older than his daughter, but his struggles on the white sand had aged him. His hair and short beard were mostly white, a few strands of light brown peeking through, and his grey eyes that contained faint specks of green held the haunted expression of a man who had seen the worst that life had to offer and not much else. Yet, there was something else there too, something that had confirmed for Kevan that this gladiator would defeat the black dragon -- an intelligence, or perhaps cunning, tempered with a self-confidence that displayed true character, not arrogance. All in all, Kevan was quite pleased with his selection.

"Bryen," said Declan, "this is Duke Kevan Winborne of the Southern Marches. He has a need for a gladiator, and he has chosen you. You are in his charge now."

The words seemed to physically injure Declan, the vigorous, strong man shrinking in upon himself. The Master of the Gladiators couldn't bring himself to look at Bryen while saying them.

Bryen was clearly stunned by the statement, Declan not having prepared him for the announcement. The gladiator stared painfully at the Master of the Gladiators, then examined the other men in the room. His eyes passed over Beluchmel with barely a pause -- someone who was not a threat, at least not directly, surmised Kevan -- then rested on Tarin for a moment, sizing him up. Kevan thought that he could read the gladiator's mind. A soldier, skilled and experienced, but then just as quickly, another kill if need be. Finally his gaze fell on Kevan, and a cold shiver ran down the Duke's spine for the third time in less than an hour.

For an instant, Kevan thought that he saw a flash of hate within those hard eyes, but then just as quickly it was gone, replaced by a deceptive calm. This gladiator did indeed have the appearance of a *volkun*, a *wolf* in the Old Tongue, waiting calmly, confidently, for its prey, pretending a lack of interest. But when the time was right, the volkun would strike quickly and with an uncontrolled ferocity. The moniker that Kevan heard being hurled down upon this young man after his victory over the black dragon certainly fit him.

Beluchmel reached for the bag of gold that Tarin had

dropped on Declan's desk, but Kevan stepped in front of him -- no easy task considering the large man's bulk -- before he could grab it with his fat, greedy fingers.

"I'm sure you can make better use of this than Beluchmel can," Kevan said, speaking to the Master of the Gladiators.

"But ..." Beluchmel's attempted protest was cut short by a sharp glance from Tarin, whose hand was once again on the hilt of his sword.

"Yes, Duke Winborne, I can. Thank you. But it is a hard price to pay." Declan's eyes remained on the stone floor, still unwilling and unable to look at Bryen.

Kevan nodded his understanding, then motioned for Tarin to come forward. The Captain of the Guard pulled wrist restraints and a short chain from his belt. Having no good reason to resist, and still a bit astonished by what was happening, Bryen held out his hands, his eyes boring a hole through the far wall. Tarin was careful to avoid the bandage on Bryen's right forearm, a reminder of the black dragon's sharp claws. Satisfied that the shackles were secure, Tarin stepped away and nodded to Duke Winborne.

Kevan immediately walked out of the small room, Beluchmel following after, trying to figure out some way to get a fair share of the gold now resting in Declan's hands.

"Time to go," said Tarin, giving Bryen a shove to his shoulder. Much to his aggravation he had to do it again, this time harder, as his initial effort had no effect whatsoever, the gladiator simply looking down at him with those eyes that revealed nothing. "You may be leaving the Pit, but that doesn't change your place in the world. Remember that. You're still a convicted criminal. Still a slave."

"Free he may not be," said Declan harshly, his eyes finally lifting off the ground and burning with their customary fire. "But he is not a slave. He is a gladiator. A fighter. Treat him as such, Captain."

Though Tarin knew that he should be insulted by Declan's outburst, he was more impressed than anything else and somewhat taken aback.

Bryen smiled grimly, locking eyes with his former instructor. There was no need for words as the master and the student studied one another for the last time.

"Thank you for giving me the skills to survive, Declan," said Bryen quietly, his soft voice sounding more like that of a poet than a man accustomed to the blade. He then shuffled out the door, slowed by the burns on his left leg from the dragon's venom, now wrapped in a loose bandage that Lycia had fiddled with until she had gotten it exactly how she wanted it. Tarin followed him outside, seeking to intimidate Declan with a glare, but failing miserably.

Declan nodded to his young charge, struggling to restrain the tears that threatened to fall as he watched the boy who had in many ways become his son take his leave.

BLOODED

The monstrous creature stood at the very edge of the wood, hidden by the shadows created by the trees as he stared at the snow-capped mountains of the Northern Spine that rose up in front of him. Those peaks were the southern extension of the mountains that he knew so well, the jagged spires running to the north from the Eastern River to the Shattered Peaks and separating the Breakwater Plateau from the Waste.

Every few minutes the creature's gaze swung to the left and then to the right, searching for any movement along the river. He hoped that the barge that had been grounded on the southern shore of the swiftly moving waterway would capture the attention of other traders plying their wares between Battersea and North Cove, one of the primary ports on the Bay of the Dead. If so, that would be a stroke of good fortune for his packs, though not for the men and women on those vessels, just as the humans on that now abandoned barge had learned. His soldiers needed to eat, and they preferred the taste of human flesh to that of animal.

One of his soldiers approached, the beast's clawed feet

ripping up the soft earth of the forest. His skin was a mottled green color that blended in with the tones of the surrounding trees and plants. That and the brown leather armor he wore made the Ghoule all but invisible in the Raven Wood. The dense forest was almost impenetrable at its very center, but here on the edge the only real hindrance was the dense undergrowth. That played to the Elder Ghoule's advantage, as he wanted to keep his packs hidden while they sought to complete the task given to them.

It had taken the combined strength of twelve of his fellow Elder Ghoules skilled in Dark Magic to create a temporary opening in the Weir near the Winter Pass that allowed him and his Ghoules to pass through the magical barrier, but even that success had come with a steep price. Though the Weir was weakening, the Elder Ghoule still had lost almost a third of his fighters during the crossing, the magical ward incinerating those Ghoules unlucky enough to be caught by its still potent power. Four of the Elder Ghoules who had crafted the flickering, unstable portal had died as well. It was a high cost, but it had to be paid if the Ghoule Overlord's plan to destroy the Weir was to be put in motion. Still, it was a huge sacrifice in the Elder Ghoule's opinion. He had fewer Ghoules than he had wanted for this mission, and he could have used the lost soldiers.

The Ghoules resembled men but were a head or two taller with angular faces and sharp, sawtooth teeth perfectly designed for tearing flesh and grinding bone. Their clawed hands were just as deadly as the short swords and spears that they carried, and many of his soldiers already had earned the prized bone knives sheathed on their belts, but not all. A Ghoule became blooded when he killed a human. To honor the occasion, the Ghoule would then carve the knife from the victim's femur or shinbone, after the Ghoule had eaten. There had been a dozen people on the barge who had made the mistake of landing this close to the unseen Ghoule camp, and as a result just as many Ghoules were now carving their bone knives, pleased to have earned the mark of honor.

His fighters were faster, stronger, and more vicious than the human warriors. But because the Weir limited how many Ghoules could enter Caledonia at one time -- the Ghoule Overlord had only so many Elders that he was willing to risk to prepare the way for crossing -- they were still few in number compared to their adversaries. So they needed to be cautious as they went about their mission, because if they succeeded in their assignment, the Weir would finally fall, releasing the Ghoule Legions for the first time in centuries.

For several minutes the Elder spoke with the Ghoule in a guttural language that sounded more like grunts and hisses than words. The scout had been tasked with exploring farther down the Eastern River toward the west, and he had discovered a patrol of human soldiers moving toward them along the shore. There were too many for the Ghoules to engage and have any hope of slaughtering without taking the risk that some of the humans would escape and spread word of the attack. When the Elder Ghoule asked how far away they were and learned that the humans would not arrive here for several more hours, he nodded. Then he gestured with the long staff of black ash that he carried and issued a quick stream of orders. The Ghoule ran off to inform the pack that they would be heading south shortly.

His Ghoules would have time to finish making their knives, but then they would hide the remains of their meal and move deeper into the Raven Wood. He had already identified a position closer to one of the many stone promontories that towered above the forest and gave it its name, as each cliff housed a conspiracy of ravens. The large birds were difficult to reach, and he had learned that the human soldiers preferred not to get too close to them, so it would be a good spot to wait before he and his pack turned east toward Battersea and the coast in order to join with several other Elder Ghoules and their packs.

He would achieve the mission that the Overlord had given him, but for now he needed to be patient. One time before the Ghoules had invaded Caledonia, leaving the Lost Land and sweeping down from the Shattered Peaks, killing and pillaging across the Kingdom until the Legions met defeat at the Bay of the Dead. He understood that the humans called that invasion the First Ghoule War, but he and his soldiers knew it as the War of Remembrance.

Although that incursion had taken place centuries before, the Ghoules still remembered how close they had come to winning that last battle, how close they had come to conquering all of Caledonia. The Ghoules would invade again once the Weir fell, and when they did, they would not fail. Once they found what they were seeking, their victory would be assured.

5

BAD DREAMS

With the sun still a distant thought the Captain of the Guard was about to kick Bryen awake, aiming the blow for the boy's feet, when he realized that the gladiator's eyes were open. Having traveled with the boy for a week and having watched him closely, tracking how he moved, his eyes never staying fixed on anything for longer than a second, he assumed that even with the shackles still affixed to his wrists, the gladiator could have jumped up ready to fight in a flash. Tarin nodded a reluctant greeting instead, then begrudgingly handed him a bowl of food that the boy accepted without a word, his grey eyes sparkling with green in the gloom but revealing none of the emotions hidden behind them.

Perhaps that's what Tarin found so disconcerting about the boy. His eyes. His expression. Tarin was good at reading people, at guessing their intentions or their thoughts. He had to be in order to do his job as Captain of the Guard, protecting not only the Southern Marches, but also the Duke who ruled the eastern province. But each time he looked into those eyes, the face a perfectly crafted mask, he couldn't get a read on the gladiator. The boy appeared passive. Tarin knew that he was anything but, remembering his handiwork in the Pit and his penchant for violence. No, there was a deceptive calm about the boy that was frightening, and the Captain had no doubt that the same look that he saw now on the gladiator's face would still be there when the boy tried to slide a dagger into his ribs. For the hundredth time since they had left Tintagel, Tarin was glad that the irons remained securely around the boy's wrists.

Grumbling to himself, the Captain of the Guard spent a few minutes checking the boy's wounds to make sure that they weren't going bad. He didn't want the boy in Battersea, he didn't want him anywhere near Lady Aislinn, and he had continued to argue with Duke Winborne about his decision until he knew that there was no use in continuing to do so, but if the Duke had a purpose for the gladiator, it was his duty to make certain that the boy could fulfill that purpose, and that meant ensuring that he stayed healthy.

"You should be fine in a few days," said Tarin, as he rose to his feet. "Have you always healed so quickly?"

The slash on Bryen's right arm had already formed a scar, and the pain of the burns had receded on his left arm and left leg, leaving only the mark of the black dragon's venom as a reminder of the experience.

"Just lucky, I guess," replied Bryen quietly. "Probably just the ointment the physick gave me."

Tarin grunted. "We leave in a few minutes. Be ready." The Captain then walked off before Bryen could nod his thanks.

Though Tarin was surprised at the speed of his recovery, Bryen wasn't. He had always healed quickly, and that ability had served him well in the Pit as the scars that crisscrossed his body testified.

The troops from the Southern Marches made good time after breaking camp that morning, riding along the Eastern River toward Battersea, capital of the Duchy. Bryen was thankful that he had adjusted to riding a horse for most of the day fairly easily after ten years in the Pit. The first few days had proven almost as painful as the wounds he had received while fighting the black dragon. But as the days passed, his confidence and comfort in the saddle had increased as his natural skill had returned. He had ridden in the Pit when required and had done well, just not as regularly as he was now.

Although he rode at the back of the column and ate the dust and dirt kicked up by the several hundred horses that trotted in front of him, he didn't mind, enjoying the experience of traveling through Caledonia too much to allow such a minor irritation to bother him. Seeing anything other than the white sand of the Pit for the first time in a decade was a treat. The day before they had crossed the border of the Southern Marches, taking them from the flat grassland on the eastern side of Tintagel that connected to the Breakwater Plateau to a hilly terrain of green grass and moss-covered rocks brought to life by wide swathes of heather, the purple and pink flowers coloring the landscape for leagues to the east.

As he followed along at the end of the troop, taking in the scenery, his thoughts unavoidably kept drifting to the many dreams that had disturbed him during the night. He had always had vivid dreams. Sometimes he could understand them. But most of the time they remained a mystery. The first wasn't much of a surprise.

He was fighting in the Pit, the setting more familiar than he would like. But he faced off against a beast that he had never come across before. A scaly, green creature with clawed feet and hands, an angular face, and sharp, serrated teeth. It was a head taller than he was, and it was fast, gliding across the white sand like a leopard. Bryen attacked several times, lunging and cutting with his sword, seeking a hole in the creature's defenses, but the beast spun away effortlessly from every one of his attacks. Then the creature took the initiative, swinging not only with his sword, but also his free claw, which sliced through the air in search of his neck or chest every time their blades met. Once the beast even flipped backwards, its two larger talons scything through the air and barely missing their mark thanks to Bryen's timely dive backward, the creature completing his flip in the air and then charging forward, angry that he had failed to cut Bryen open from his groin to his chest with his clawed feet.

From that point forward in the duel it was all that Bryen could do to stay clear of the creature. The combat had settled into one in which Bryen maintained his position in the center of the Pit while the creature circled him, waiting for his chance to strike. The fact that the beast looked familiar, that he had seen such a creature before, nagged at Bryen, but he knew that he had never met its like in battle. Maybe his sense of familiarity came from one of the books that Declan had given him to read. If he remembered correctly, the creature was a Ghoule, but he couldn't be sure, and those monsters hadn't been seen in Caledonia for hundreds of years. How one could have been brought through the Weir to the Pit, he didn't know.

For some reason thinking of the Ghoule next brought to mind his dream of a wooded place that he knew he had visited when he was a young child. Although the image of his father was faint, Bryen's memory of him fading with time, he did recall a few characteristics of note, such as his frequent smile and the strong grip of his hand while they walked through the dense wood, the smell of saltwater tickling his nose. Near the center of the thicket, they had emerged into a space several acres wide that had been carved out of the forest and formed a perfect circle. A gleaming tower made of an almost translucent, white stone stood in the middle of the clearing, soaring well above the tallest tree in the forest. The sun glanced off the stone, discharging a blinding white light. Looking up with his hand protecting his eyes, Bryen saw that the spire narrowed as it rose into the sky until it formed a sharp point at the very top. He had to look again because instead of rising straight up, the tip appeared to bend toward the west.

Bryen had stepped up to the spire, running his hand across it and discovering much to his surprise that there were no mortar or chisel marks. The spire appeared to be a single piece of stone. In several places scorch marks marred the otherwise pristine, pale white surface. Perhaps not unexpectedly, he couldn't find the door, and his father had made a game of it, wanting to find out if he could solve the puzzle. Bryen had walked the circumference of the tower, trailing his fingers across the stone, but never discovering any hint of where the door might be. Growing frustrated, and not knowing what else to do, he closed his eyes and kept his hand on the stone. He wasn't sure where the entrance was, but in his mind, he sensed where it should be. Trying to force himself to see what he was searching for, a bright white light flashed in front of him. He opened his eyes and to his amazement a stone door with vines and other plants carved into its surface appeared before him.

"Well done, Bryen," his father had said, coming to stand behind him with a hand on Bryen's shoulder, his pride obvious. "I knew you had it in you. Only those with the Talent can find the door. Come. You can wander around while I take care of a few things, but stay out of trouble."

His father pushed on the stone door, and though it was thick and heavy, it swung open easily on silent, hidden hinges. While his father did whatever he had to do, Bryen had explored every nook and cranny of the spire, until he had found himself in a room near the very top. What he found most odd was that this chamber appeared to be empty. Every other space in the tower was crammed with strange and interesting things. Tables covered by glass canisters, flasks and beakers, strange liquids running through tubes. Old weapons, ranging from swords to halberds to battle axes, all arranged around flags that he had never seen before. And most frequently, room upon room of books and scrolls, more often than not the texts crammed onto shelves that reached to the ceiling and ran off into the distance. Strangely, this room was empty. That, in itself, ignited his curiosity. But what was really peculiar was the spark of recognition that shot through him, almost as if he was meant to be here.

He stepped into the room, his interest piqued, and looked around. Not even a window. Just a large, circular room. He took a few steps farther in, then stopped. His foot had hit some kind of barrier, but there was nothing there but the image of the empty chamber. He put his hand out in front of him and felt the barrier again. He couldn't go any further. There was an invisible wall right in front of him, which only spurred his curiosity. He walked up and down the length of the unseen wall, pushing against it in several places. But nothing happened. It felt just as hard as a stone wall, though nothing appeared to be there. Then he decided to take the same approach as he had with the tower's door.

Placing his hand against the invisible barrier, he closed

his eyes, seeking a way past. After several seconds of probing, he opened his eyes once more. With just a little pressure, his fingers disappeared into the imperceptible wall. He
smiled, pleased with his success. Then he pushed his arm
farther into the invisible barrier, the image in front of him
shifting much like the surface of a pool of water that rippled
when you dropped a stone in it. He pulled his arm out from
the image, just to make sure that his suspicion was correct.

Satisfied, he extended his hand once more, then pushed
his entire body into the unseen barrier. It felt as if he was
walking through water, though nothing flowed around him.
The invisible obstacle had simply assumed a more viscous
form, much like jelly, that allowed him to slide through it
slowly. When he finally stepped across the barrier, he was
disappointed. All that work and there was nothing on the
other side except for an empty room that looked exactly like
the one on the other side of the unseen wall. That couldn't
be right. Why go to all that trouble in the first place? Now
even more curious, he took a few minutes to walk around
the large chamber. Although there were no windows,
sunlight still streamed into the room through the white
stone. How that worked, he didn't know, thinking that he'd
ask his father.

He stopped for a moment. There had to be a reason for
the disguised barrier. But what? Then he sensed something
unexpected. There was a power in the chamber, something
old and exceedingly strong. Yet it was muted somehow. He
wandered about the room once again, though this time with
purpose. In what he judged to be the center of the chamber,
taking into account the space segmented by the invisible
wall, he could feel the ancient energy pulsing just beneath
his feet. Basing his next action solely on instinct, he reached
down and touched one of the tiles in the floor, then had to

jump back to avoid getting hit in the head by the thin, stone pedestal that shot up from the floor. The stone was the same as that of the spire, very pale, almost translucent, but what caught his eye was the object that sat on top of it and was held in place by three barely visible gold threads.

The diamond was the size of his fist. He stared at it for several minutes, dazzled by the play of the light across the gem. He looked for imperfections, but found none. Unable to resist, he touched it with his fingers, and then everything around him disappeared in a blast of white light. He remembered waking up on the floor cradled in his father's arms, the diamond and its pedestal having settled back into the floor. He recalled that his father had been terrified at first, and then relieved when Bryen had regained consciousness. Then he had been angry, but with himself, not Bryen, castigating himself for letting his son wander the tower knowing what he could do.

What his father had meant by that, he didn't understand. But Bryen was having a hard time focusing on what his father had been saying as his mind remained fixed on the stone that he had touched. He had sensed the power that the diamond contained, both good and evil balanced on a razor's edge that could be tipped to one side or the other with barely a touch. It had been a frightening experience, but also an exhilarating one, as just a single jolt of the power contained within the gem had thrilled him. He felt a strange familiarity with that stone, but he couldn't explain why or what that really signified.

That dream had been followed by another, this one just as real. He was walking down an empty street in Tintagel, a light rain failing, his mother and father no more than shadows next to him. A strange fog had settled over the darkened thoroughfare, the moon blocked by the thick

covering of low-hanging clouds. He could tell that his
parents were worried, their gazes scanning around them
every few seconds, and then he felt their fear when several
large shapes wrapped in grey cloaks emerged in front of
them. The figures had simply stood there, not approaching,
but he sensed the violence that radiated from them. His
parents had stopped upon seeing the shapes, then they
decided to go back the way that they had come, but it was
too late. Several other cowled shapes had stepped out of the
gloom behind them. They were trapped on a dark street
with barely a candle flame trickling down from any of the
closed or boarded up windows of the shops and homes
lining the avenue.

One of the figures standing in front of them had
gestured, and for a moment Bryen thought that he had
glimpsed a scaly green forearm, but what really caught his
eye was the streak of black darker than the night that shot
toward them from the staff that the towering creature held.
A flash of white light blinded Bryen momentarily, and he
tumbled to the road, his father having pulled him to the
ground and fallen on top of him. More streaks of black
ripped through the air, but his mother stood before him
with what appeared to be a spinning shield of white mist
deflecting each attack. Bryen tried to get up, but he couldn't,
his father still covering him. He knew with a sick feeling in
his stomach that something was wrong. Finally, he was able
to wriggle out from beneath his father, and when Bryen did
he saw that he was not moving, his eyes open and glazed
and his upper chest scorched and smelling of charred flesh.

Then Bryen heard his mother scream. She had focused
so much on defending against the figure standing before
them that she hadn't seen the cowled shadows rush them
from behind. She slumped to the ground, the shield of

white mist disintegrating as she clutched at her side. Pushing himself out of the mud, Bryen ran toward his mother. Pulling free the dagger that his father had given him for his birthday, he leapt into the air and drove the steel into the back of the figure who had attacked his mother and now stood above her. The creature reared up and snarled, reaching for the blade now stuck in his back, his other arm swinging around and knocking Bryen back into the mud.

Dazed by the force of the blow, his eyes focused for a brief moment on the tracks in the mud. What looked to be a claw with four talons dug deeply into the muck, the imprint larger than the footprint of even the largest man. Bryen turned his head toward his mother, who kneeled in the street, hand to her side in a futile attempt to stanch the bright red blood gushing from the wound. The figure he had stabbed had moved out of the way, still struggling to remove the dagger, but he saw another shadow step behind his mother, a steel sword raised above her.

"Run," she had mouthed, and then he had watched in horror as the sharp tip of the blade had slid into her back. Not knowing what else to do, he had listened to his mother's last wish, dodging the sharp claws covered in green scales that reached for him and then scampering into an alley and losing himself in the maze of streets. He had been visited by that dream countless times during the past decade, and he still felt guilty, as if he should have done more to help his mother and father, that he had failed his parents and his running away made it all the worse. He had spoken to Declan about it once, and the Master of the Gladiators had been as gruff as he always was.

"Your parents couldn't protect themselves," said Declan. "If that was the case, how were you supposed to protect them? You need to let it go, lad. Focus on the present, not the past."

A new dream had then replaced that recurring nightmare. He stood in a training circle, eyes tight on a girl who stalked him. She held her sword loosely, balanced on her toes and prepared to attack as soon as an opportunity presented itself. Clearly, she knew what she was about with a blade. The girl was tall and slim, and as she lunged at him and then retreated when he flicked his wrist and his own blade deflected hers, he confirmed that she was quick as well. Only Lycia moved as fast as she did. Her long, auburn hair was braided down her back so that it wouldn't get in the way during the duel, and her eyes were intent, focused. She was not one to be distracted from her goal, and at the moment it appeared that her goal was defeating him.

Bryen knew that he had never seen the girl before. So why did she seem so familiar to him? And what about the girl troubled him so much? For some unexplained reason she confused him. He liked her but hated her at the same time. How was that even possible? As the beautiful young woman continued to circle him, his eyes never leaving hers, his free hand went to the silver collar secured around his neck. Why he wore it and how the torque had gotten there he didn't know. He just knew that it felt heavier than it should, its weight based on more than just the silver the collar was crafted from.

Bryen shook his head to clear it. Dreams such as these had plagued him ever since he had been a child. Rarely was he able to decipher them, though a few had proven useful after the fact. But for now, other than the one regarding his parents' murder that visited him almost every night, he had no idea what the others might mean, if anything other than the fact that he had a vivid imagination. So he turned his attention back to the terrain he rode through. Having spent the last ten years in Tintagel, and most of that time staring at stone and sand, he was excited to be going somewhere new, he admitted, even though the thought of continuing his servitude angered him. When he was in the Pit all he had wanted was to be somewhere else, anywhere else. And now he was, though perhaps not on the terms that he had desired. Not with irons fixed around his wrists.

Realizing that the column of soldiers had come to a halt, Bryen pulled back on the reins gently, his horse happy to comply. It was too early for the midday break, so he wasn't sure why they had stopped until he looked to his left and saw the large river barge grounded on the shore. Several soldiers jumped aboard. After a few minutes passed, they emerged from below decks, somewhat befuddled. They reported to the Duke and Captain that the large vessel was abandoned even though its holds were filled with goods. That discovery sent a murmur through the column of soldiers. No merchant left his or her wares unprotected. They would never risk their livelihood. As a few additional soldiers walked on board to conduct a more thorough search, Bryen felt a prickle running up his neck, almost as if he were being watched. He shifted his attention to the right, to the tightly packed tall trees that were no more than a hundred yards away from the riverbank.

Several ravens sat on the branches extending out from the wood, cawing loudly. To his ears it seemed like the large birds were calling to him, telling him that the prickle he felt was caused by something lurking within the pall, so he nudged his horse toward the Raven Wood until he was no more than a few yards from the edge of the forest. A sense of danger filled him, as if a threat lurked not too far away. Anything could be in the wood, he realized, and no one would know it. He couldn't see more than a few feet into the impenetrable shadows that the towering sentinels created. He stared into the gloom a bit longer, thinking that he might have caught a flash of movement heading deeper into the underbrush, but he couldn't say for sure. It could have just been the touch of the wind against a branch, but he didn't think so. Something had been there. Something fast ... and big. Then he looked down and saw a mark that he hadn't expected. In the dirt he picked out the tracks of a creature that brought to mind the dream that he had suffered through the night before and so many other nights. Several claws could be seen pressed into the ground, each imprint revealing four talons, each impression larger than a man's footprint.

Just then, Tarin rode up, his face red with fury. "I told you once to stay with the column, boy. I shouldn't have to tell you again. I expect my orders to be obeyed, or I'll tie you to your horse like a sack of rocks."

He continued to berate Bryen, but the gladiator simply ignored him, still looking down at the tracks in the dirt. Could it have been made by the same type of creature? Not having the patience to deal with the angry Captain of the Guard, he nodded toward the ground. Tarin was about to let loose another expletive-filled stream of consciousness when he finally looked down and the words caught in his throat. He saw the marks now as well, and by the silence that had settled abruptly over the soldier, Bryen was certain that the Captain recognized them.

"What kind of animal makes a track like that?" Bryen asked, seeking to confirm what he suspected.

Tarin didn't respond immediately, too shocked by what the boy had pointed out. After almost a minute had passed, he answered.

"Nothing good. A creature I had never expected to see this far south."

The Captain of the Guard then turned his horse quickly and galloped toward Duke Winborne, yelling at his troops to assume a battle formation. Though the soldiers didn't understand why, they obeyed instantly, responding to the command that had been ingrained into them by hour upon hour of training.

Bryen remained where he was, trying once again to pierce the gloom of the forest but failing. The claw marks in the dirt resembled that of a black dragon, but were considerably smaller, though certainly larger than a human footprint. If he wasn't mistaken, based on his dreams from the night before, it was the mark of a Ghoule.

6

COLLARED

Bryen shifted his shoulders uncomfortably. The soft blue shirt felt strange on his skin, as did the brown breeks and knee-high black leather boots. He had not worn clothes such as this for a very long time, and though they were obviously quite simple and unadorned, they still seemed extravagant to him. He was used to wearing coarse smocks and training shorts, often fashioned from scratchy wool or dirty, stiff cotton.

The chains around his wrists clinked as he stepped into the atrium. The two members of the Battersea Guard standing by the door watched him carefully, having heard of this gladiator, but Bryen had nowhere to go with two more soldiers following behind him. Besides, he was too busy taking everything in. He had never been in such a luxurious room before. The dome-shaped chamber tapered to a skylight, allowing the sun to stream through the colored glass and play its wondrous patterns across the polished marble walls. His new boots sank deeply into the carpet, almost hiding his feet from view. He came to a stop in front of a massive desk with several large chairs placed to either side. But that's not what caught his attention.

Shelves filled with texts and tomes of all shapes and sizes lined the walls and ran from the floor all the way up to where the ceiling began to curve, wheeled ladders connected to steel rods that circled the chamber providing access to the higher ledges. He had never seen so many books in one place. He had read as many titles as he could get his hands on at the training yard, but the supply was limited even with Declan doing all that he could to acquire new volumes when they went off on their weekly trip into the Tintagel marketplace. He estimated that he had read maybe one hundred books in all. But here, in this very room, he was surrounded by several thousand, each one calling to him, beckoning to him, asking him to pick it up and flip through the pages. The temptation was almost too much for him, as reading was one of the few things that gave him pleasure in life. When he lived in the gladiators' stockade, it was the only way for him to escape from the rigors of his existence, if only for a short time. Still, he resisted the urge to get a closer look at the shelves of enticing books and remained where he was. Watch and learn when facing a new opponent, Declan had taught him, rather than risk an unwanted surprise at an inopportune moment.

"You don't look too bad once you've been washed."

Duke Winborne walked into the room, a thin silver collar in his hand. He stopped in front of Bryen and surveyed his latest acquisition. The bath had done wonders for the gladiator, as did the journey of several weeks, allowing the slash on his arm and the burns on his other arm and leg to heal. The boy looked close to presentable, except for the eyes. The feral, almost animal-like quality remained. Kevan doubted that it would ever disappear. This gladiator had been in the Pit too long for his instincts to change now, but he could still serve his purpose.

Kevan leaned back on the edge of his desk, arms crossed, waiting for the questions to begin. But the gladiator -- What was his name? He'd have to ask Tarin again -- stood as still as a statue, his countenance devoid of expression.

"As you may have heard when I bought you," began Kevan, "your purpose here is to serve as a Protector for my daughter. Do you know what a Protector is?"

Bryen maintained his silence, his eyes never leaving Kevan's face, though he had clenched his fists tightly. It was the only visible display of his anger.

"Can you speak, boy?"

"I can speak," replied Bryen in a soft voice.

"Speak louder, boy, I can barely hear you."

"I said I can speak," Bryen said forcefully, his hostility plain.

"Good," said Kevan. "But watch your tone, boy. I have little patience for insolence. You will address me at all times as Duke Winborne." Kevan studied Bryen more closely. He was a young man, yes, but his eyes betrayed him, that and the white coloring his hair and beard. He had aged quickly in the Pit. "I was worried about that. The guards watching over you on our journey said that you barely uttered a word the entire trip." Kevan slipped off his perch and walked behind his desk, settling into his chair. "Now, as I was asking you, do you know the purpose of a Protector?"

"No," Bryen replied quietly, his soft voice not matching his large, wiry frame.

"Duke Winborne," Kevan prompted.

"Duke Winborne," Bryen offered grudgingly, after letting almost a minute pass in silence.

Kevan nodded, not surprised by the small sign of rebellion. The boy would need that fire to perform his new job effectively.

"That's understandable since it's a practice that has fallen out of use in recent years. In short, a Protector is a bodyguard, but there is more to it than that. You will be required to do everything humanly possible to protect my daughter Aislinn, throwing down your life if necessary. It is really that simple. You will protect her and, if need be, you will die for her."

"And if I choose not to?" asked Bryen.

Kevan chuckled softly. "You don't have a choice. You will be compelled to protect Aislinn. You may not want to, you may not want to die, but what you want won't matter. You will do whatever is necessary whether you like it or not. In fact, many of the best Protectors hated their charges, hated them with a passion, in fact. Yet, when it came time to make the ultimate sacrifice, they did. That's why you will be her Protector. Judging from your skills in the Pit, you can do a good job of it. And, in all honesty, you're expendable. Losing your life to protect my daughter is a worthwhile risk from my perspective considering what awaited you in the Colosseum."

Bryen's eyes hardened as Duke Winborne explained the situation, his heart filling with the hopelessness that had troubled him since his first duel on the white sand. He had hoped that leaving the Colosseum would offer him a chance at a real life, a free life, but obviously that was not to be. Bryen turned quickly as the door to the chamber opened with a loud bang, startling the two soldiers standing along the wall. Before they could react, however, a tall man with unruly white hair and a long beard walked in, his mishmash of colorful robes trailing along behind him.

"I apologize for the delay, Duke Winborne," said the

man, nodding a greeting to the Duke of the Southern Marches. He cupped his chin with his hand and began to make a circuit around the room. "But I was delayed by one of my experiments. I've been trying to determine how to meld steel with this strange new alloy that I've discovered. I think this could lead to a much stronger metal, but I can't seem ..."

"Sirius?"

"Yes, Duke Winborne?" asked the old man, halting his wandering at the call of his name.

"Your experiment sounds quite interesting, but if it's alright with you, can we get to the business at hand?"

"Oh, yes. My apologies, Duke Winborne," said Sirius, grinning apologetically, a slight tinge of embarrassment coloring his cheeks. "You know how it is when a problem consumes your attention. It's hard to concentrate on anything else until you have a solution."

Bryen watched the exchange in silence. There was something about the old man that made Bryen look at him twice, initially with amusement, but only at first glance. A quality lurked just beneath the man's harried expression and sparkling blue eyes, a seriousness and hidden danger that wasn't readily apparent. Sirius was not all that he appeared to be.

"Be that as it may, Sirius ..."

"Yes, yes, Duke Winborne. My apologies once more. Now, what can I do for you?"

"This young man has joined our service," said Duke Winborne, nodding toward the boy with his wrists chained who stood in front of the desk.

"Oh, hello there," said Sirius, turning his attention to Bryen, his eyes sparking briefly when he noted the manacles. "My apologies for not noticing you before, but ..."

Sirius lost track of what he was about to say next. He took a long, hard look at the boy, taking in not only his height and broad shoulders, but also the evidence of his recent wounds and his flinty expression. There was a scar on his left cheek that ran down to his neck, and Sirius had no doubt that more battle marks laced the boy's body. A barely repressed violence seemed to radiate from the young man, and he was young. Sirius immediately identified him as a fighter. But why did this young man set him on edge for a brief moment? Not his ability to fight. No, that wasn't altogether surprising or worrying. There was something else to it. For some reason, this young man seemed familiar to him. As if he had met him before. But why that was the case, he had not a clue.

"Sirius, can we get back to the business at hand?" Kevan held out the silver collar. "He is to be Aislinn's Protector. Would you please take care of it?"

The smile dropped from the old man's face, replaced by a look of concern. "Duke Winborne, there are other ways to protect your daughter. We don't need the services of this young man for ..."

"Sirius," said Kevan, as if he were speaking to a wayward child, "I am well aware of the other options that I have for protecting Aislinn. We have certainly talked about them often enough. But this is the one that I have chosen for now. Please take care of it."

Kevan thrust the collar into Sirius' reluctant hands, and the old man stood there for more than a minute, looking down at the circle of silver as if it were a poisonous snake wrapped around his hands.

"Duke Winborne, I understand your desire to protect your daughter, but this path, ancient though it may be, should stay in the past. Affixing this to that young man is no better …"

"Sirius!" Kevan said sharply, struggling to control his temper. He wasn't accustomed to being challenged, and he certainly didn't like it. "You have privileges here that others don't, but in this case, there are no questions to ask, no arguments to be made. Do as I have commanded."

Sirius returned Kevan's glare without flinching. Bryen thought he caught a flash of anger behind the old man's eyes, which changed for just a second from a look of distraction to rare shrewdness, then just as quickly disappeared. Sighing heavily he stared for a long moment at Duke Winborne, then he stepped toward Bryen.

"My apologies, boy. But I can't ignore a direct command. If it must be done, it must be done."

Sirius ran his long fingers over the circular length of the collar. Then he closed his eyes for several seconds, taking hold of the natural magic of the world. Normally, the Magus relished the feel of the Talent, but not now. Not with the task he had been given.

As the silver collar began to glow, Bryen felt a warmth flow through his body as a strange energy surged within him, almost as if he were truly awake for the first time. Unable to look away, Bryen watched as the silver collar in the old man's hands pulsed for almost a full minute before the torque returned to its normal luster.

"It is done," confirmed Sirius.

"Thank you, Sirius." Kevan took the silver collar from the Magus, then approached Bryen. "As I was saying, boy. You don't have a choice. You will do whatever you can to protect your charge, and you can never do anything against her will. You have one purpose in life now, and one purpose only." He smiled broadly, trying to put what would likely be an onerous task in a more positive light. "If nothing else, at least you are free of the Pit."

Before Bryen could protest, Kevan deftly pulled the collar apart, the metal cracking in a single place, then slipped it around Bryen's neck and pushed the silver together until there was an audible click. The collar again glowed a bright white for several long moments, flashing almost angrily, then returned to its normal color.

Bryen's entire body shivered, as if he had been dropped into the coldest lake in the Kingdom. He closed his eyes as an almost unbearable pressure built in the back of his head. The agony increased as Bryen fought back against whatever was rushing through his body. He tried to keep the power out, but each time he thought he had the energy contained, it slipped free, and then he had to try again. As the pressure steadily increased, it became too much for him, the energy coursing through every part of his body, scouring him clean. It was then that he realized that he had lost the struggle. Once the pain subsided, it was replaced by a strange new awareness that initially made him feel off balance.

As a result, he didn't notice the sharpness that had once more replaced Sirius' usually distracted gaze and the shiver that had coursed through the old man's body. The Magus had not expected the boy to have such an intense reaction to the ancient magic of the collar. It was as if the boy had tried to fight the energy and had almost won.

"What have you done to me?" asked Bryen, his eyes showing the slightest trace of fear.

"As I said, you're a Protector," said Duke Winborne, taking a key from his pocket, then unshackling the gladiator and dropping the chains on his desk. "Your sole purpose in life now is to protect my daughter. And that is what you will do. As a Protector, you now have the ability, thanks to Sirius, to know where she is and what she's feeling at all times. Whether she is safe or in danger, well or sick, angry or sad. And you must be near her at all times. You can never be more than a few hundred feet from her. If you fight against this pull, well, you'll understand once you experience it for yourself."

Sirius watched Bryen with renewed interest. He had sensed the charge when Kevan had locked the collar around the boy's neck. The more he thought about it, the more that jolt felt like a natural resistance, of one magic fighting another, though in the end the magic of the collar won out, if just barely. But there was nothing about the boy to suggest why such a contest had occurred. The Magus filed that information away for further consideration, then allowed the unusual sharpness to leave his eyes. Appearing a bit distracted had served his purposes well for years. He would dig deeper into this unexpected discovery later.

The full import of what had just been done to him was becoming clear to Bryen. Suddenly, his mind was filled by a sharper sensory awareness. Someone was coming down the hallway toward the room he now occupied. She seemed content, happy. Even excited. Yet she was thinking about something. What was it? Then shockingly her thoughts actually came to Bryen. She was wondering why she had been called here. How was this even possible? What was happening to him?

Just then there was a knock on the door, and it opened slightly.

"Father, you asked for me?"

A tall girl entered the room. She was the same height as her father, though still a head shorter than Bryen. Her long, auburn streaked hair fell softly on her shoulders, and her quick smile revealed captivating dimples that greatly enhanced her already stunning beauty. Bryen stared at the girl in horror, remembering the dream from just a few nights before. This was the same girl. How was this possible? Then the realization of his fate slowly began to sink in.

"Yes, I did, Aislinn. Please come in."

"Hello, Sirius. How are you today?"

"Aislinn," replied the old man, now struggling to look Bryen in the eye. It seemed as if the weight of Sirius' many years had dropped suddenly onto his shoulders because of what he had just done.

"There's really no reason to beat around the bush," said Duke Winborne. "For several months now, I've been concerned about your safety."

"Really, father, there's no reason to worry," said Aislinn dismissively. "I can take care of myself."

"I know that, Aislinn. But whether you believe it or not, there are some threats that you cannot protect against. Some dangers that might require a different approach. That's why ..." Once again, the name escaped him, but then it finally came to him. "Why Bryen is here."

"Bryen?" Aislinn looked at the tall man standing next to Sirius, acknowledging his presence for the first time. Though his almost white hair and short beard set off his sparkling grey eyes, it didn't fit the rest of his appearance. He seemed to be much younger than that, perhaps only a few years older than she was.

"Yes, the boy is your Protector."

"My what?" replied a stunned Aislinn, her face turning bright red with anger, matching the curls on her head. "I have absolutely no need for a Protector, father. This is ridiculous. How could you do this to another person? A Protector is no more than a slave."

"You do have a need for a Protector, Aislinn," cut in

Kevan, his eyes hardening as his temper threatened to flare once again. He should have expected such a reaction from his daughter. "The boy was a slave to begin with, fighting in the Pit. So at least here he'll have a chance to live a bit longer than he would on the white sand. Besides, there's no point in protesting. The deed is done. The boy is your Protector. There's nothing that you can do about it now."

Aislinn stared at her father in fury, struck by the truth of his words. And then she felt it. She was beginning to sense a presence in the back of her mind. Faint at first, but with each passing second it was growing stronger. A mix of fear and rage. She looked at the tall young man standing to her right, noting the scars on his cheek and neck, his hard eyes, and she knew instantly that collection of emotions was coming from him.

"How could you?" she growled at her father.

Aislinn turned quickly on her heel and headed for the door. One of the guards wisely opened it for her. Otherwise, she may have torn it off its hinges. She stormed down the hallway in a rage, her shouts and curses of anger receding in the distance.

"She took that rather well, don't you think, Sirius?" asked Kevan, having expected a worse spectacle.

Bryen stared at the floor, still trying to come to grips with what had just happened to him. He could feel what the girl was feeling. Everything! Her anger, most of all. But there was also a sense of disappointment, as if her father had treated her like a child rather than as an adult, that he didn't trust her. There was more there as well, but before he could explore it, a sharp pain struck him in the gut, doubling him over with a gasp. He had never experienced anything like it, not even in the Pit when another gladiator had slipped a dagger between his ribs.

"I suggest you go after her, boy," said Duke Winborne. "It will only get worse as the distance increases. Just remember, a few hundred feet. Just a step beyond, and this is what will happen. And don't forget these." Duke Winborne handed him a large dagger and a sword that one of the soldiers had brought with him. "Don't think to use them against me or any of my Guards. Just as you're compelled to protect Aislinn, you can't use your weapons for any other reason than to protect her. If you do, this will also be the result."

Unable to stand it any longer, Bryen stumbled toward the door. Thankfully, as he walked out into the hallway, the pain eased, each step he took in the direction of the girl bringing with it some relief. As he trudged down unfamiliar hallways, an overwhelming despair filled him. All hope had left him, the hope that someday he would regain his freedom. He had simply traded one form of slavery for another. And now, he was certain that there was no escape.

7

WORRIES AND FEARS

K evan stood in the library, his favorite room in the Broken Citadel of Battersea, enjoying the beams of afternoon sun that burst through the skylight, the many colors of the glass dancing across the floor and revealing a three-masted ship slicing through the ocean. With the family name Winborne, the image certainly was appropriate. The Winbornes had ruled Battersea and the Southern Marches since the First Ghoule War, thanks in large part to Arick Winborne, who had served as a general under King Wencilius Roosarian during that terrible time almost a thousand years in the past.

The Ghoules, led by the Overlord and supported by his Elders and a Dark Magic that matched the Talent of the Magii, had swarmed down through the Winter Pass in the Shattered Peaks, catching the Kingdom by surprise. Until then, the Ghoules simply had been creatures of legend, living in the Lost Land and kept from the territories of men by the Trench and the snow and ice that made the treacherous northern mountains impassable for most of the year.

From time to time, adventurers had traveled through the

Winter Pass during the few months that it was open and then across the Shattered Peaks, reaching the very edge of the Lost Land and on occasion catching a glimpse of these beasts from a distance. Yet those accounts were few and far between. Most of these explorers, often driven by stories of gold and precious metals to be found in the Shattered Peaks, never returned, whether because of the weather, the danger of the mountains themselves, or the Ghoules, no one could say. As a result, more often than not such experiences were simply perceived as no more than stories to pass the cold winter nights, having little basis in reality.

So despite an increasing number of reported sightings of packs of these creatures breaching the Winter Pass when the ice and snow had melted and then moving farther south into the Kingdom, as well as regular warnings from the Order of the Magii that these beasts were intent on conquering Caledonia, the Ghoules for most remained myth. Until that fateful late summer when thousands upon thousands of the saw-toothed beasts flooded down into northern Caledonia onto the Breakwater Plateau, so named because the wind coming off the Shattered Peaks often resembled a gale more likely to be experienced when battling the waves of the Silent Sea.

The Ghoules were a head or two taller than the tallest man. They were human in appearance with angular faces and pointed ears, but the resemblance stopped there. Their mottled green skin was covered by scales on their forearms, shoulders, and thighs. These scales formed a natural armor that steel blades failed to penetrate, which made killing the beasts all the more difficult. They wore brown leather armor and favored short swords and axes, yet because their bony, sharp, clawlike fingers were capable of ripping through leather and flesh with equal ease, it seemed as if the weapons they carried were unnecessary. A weaponless Ghoule was just as dangerous as one carrying a sword.

The creatures terrified the people of Caledonia, not only because of their appearance, but also because of their ruthless and horrifying actions. The Ghoules' sharp, serrated teeth tore flesh and ground bone. As wave upon wave of Ghoules came down from the Shattered Peaks, the Caledonians learned quickly that reasoning with these beasts was not an option and that fighting to the death was better than surrender, for at least in death you did not have to fear being eaten alive.

The Magii of Caledonia had watched for and protected against smaller Ghoule raiding parties in the past, however no one but the Magii, those skilled in the use of the Talent, were prepared for the Ghoule Legions that swept over the land that fateful year. The Ghoule Overlord and his Elders understood the danger presented by the Magii. Therefore, the first Ghoule Legions to exit the Winter Pass turned to the east and sought to break through the Northern Spine, a track of mountains that led down from the Shattered Peaks to the Eastern River, and cut off the eastern section of Caledonia from the rest of the Kingdom so that the beasts could focus on destroying the Aeyrie, the ancient tower of the Magii, and cripple the Order at the same time. The Ghoule Overlord had almost succeeded, killing several dozen Magii. Nevertheless, the Magii had held, protecting the Aeyrie and giving King Wencilius time to raise his army and prepare for the Ghoules' expected shift in focus to the west.

Yet even with the additional time provided by the Magii, Caledonia was almost lost. The Ghoules steadily pushed Wencilius' army south until the backs of the Caledonian soldiers were against the Eastern River. During that drive toward the Endless Ocean, the beasts also destroyed

Tintagel, capital of the Kingdom. In a desperate attempt to save Wencilius' troops and allow for the preparation of a final defense against the Ghoule onslaught, Arick Winborne had led a small band of fighters against the Overlord and his Legions, his hit-and-run tactics frustrating the beasts and drawing them into the Dark Forest. With that gloomy wood's massive trees, huge roots crisscrossing the forest floor, and often impenetrable undergrowth, Arick succeeded in bogging down the Ghoules for more than a month. He and his fighters attacked in small groups with lightning speed and ferocity, then faded back into the murk and shadows, knowing that if the Ghoules caught them in a pitched battle they would be annihilated.

When Arick and his Battersea Guard finally emerged from the Dark Forest, they had lost more than half their number. But because of their efforts, King Wencilius had been able to reform his host and position his soldiers at the banks of the land-wrapped sea that was named the Bay of the Dead after the First Ghoule War. More important, Arick's efforts had allowed the Magii who survived the attack on the Aeyrie to connect once more with the Caledonian army. In the end, Wencilius proved victorious, saving Caledonia, though whether the Kingdom's unlikely success resulted more from Arick Winborne's strategy and courage had been a key point of contention ever since. Employing similar tactics as he had used in the Dark Forest, Arick had kept the Ghoule Legions off balance, avoiding a decisive battle for as long as possible so that the Caledonian soldiers could whittle down the overwhelming number of Ghoules.

When that final battle came at the shore of the inland sea, it proved to be the bloodiest in the history of Caledonia. It was said that you could walk across the dead from one side of the bay to the other without getting your feet wet.

The Caledonians had saved themselves, though at a great cost, and the Ghoule Legions were forced back across the Shattered Peaks to be locked away from the lands of man by the Weir constructed by the Magii. And in recognition of his courageous actions, King Wencilius had named Arick Winborne, once a common soldier, a Duke and given his family charge of Battersea and the Southern Marches. The Winbornes had held the province ever since.

Why all this played through Kevan's mind now he couldn't say. Thinking of history and his family's legacy would not help him with the challenge now placed before him. The Southern Marches were sparsely populated compared to the other Duchies and, in some respects, with the Raven Wood, the Deep Wood, and the Waste a part of his province, beside Battersea there was more frontier than farmland. Its people were hearty, self-reliant, and protective of one another, and they didn't take kindly to the Crown's incessant demands for the imposition of higher taxes.

At first glance, why Marden wanted to exercise greater control over Kevan's ancestral lands didn't make sense until you took into consideration Battersea. The only major port on the eastern coast of Caledonia, it was a key connection to the Kingdoms across the Silent Sea and a required stop for merchant ships sailing south to the Endless Ocean. Kevan had no doubt that was what was driving Marden. If he controlled Battersea, Marden would have the eastern portion of Caledonia firmly in his grasp. He could then use that to apply pressure against Cornelius Stennivere, Duke of the Three Rivers and ruler of Ironhill and Trader's Way. Much like Battersea, Trader's Way was a key commercial city and the only major port on the southern shore of Caledonia, while Ironhill produced most of the Kingdom's metals.

So from an economic standpoint Kevan understood why

Marden was pressing him. The political aspect was fairly straightforward as well. Kevan was the strongest of all the Dukes, his friendship with Cornelius increasing that power. Despite Cornelius' irascibility, he was honest, trustworthy, and a good friend to Kevan and the Southern Marches. In Marden's mind, a monarch of only three years, of all the Dukes and Duchesses Kevan was his biggest threat. Therefore, any success at reducing Kevan's power and influence benefited him. Moreover, the King needed to exercise what power he had if he wanted to maintain it. And Kevan was certain that Marden not only wanted to maintain his power, but increase it.

The Duchies had exercised greater autonomy during the last few centuries at the expense of the Crown, and it was clear that Marden sought to change the dynamic of power within the Kingdom. Yet despite Kevan's attempts to assuage Marden's concerns, as he had no desire to seek the throne for himself, all his efforts seemed to have been to no avail. Whether because of Marden's continuing distrust or, rather, Tetric increasing his influence by playing off the young King's fears, Kevan couldn't say for sure. But he had his suspicions.

It was a really simple, obvious gambit. Marden asking for and expecting his daughter's hand in marriage would make Kevan expendable. Once Aislinn bore Marden a child, she too would become expendable. Either way, Marden would gain the Southern Marches, consolidating the power of the Crown and weakening the other Duchies, two circumstances that Kevan wanted to prevent at all costs. But how to do that without provoking the impetuous, young King who had at his command the largest army in Caledonia?

Kevan had ruled the Southern Marches for almost two

decades. The first decade had been a challenge, if only because he had to learn how to govern. His father and mother had died from a fever within days of one another, thrusting him into the unexpected role of immediate responsibility for the lives and welfare of all those living in the province. At the time, King Corinthus Beleron had served as a mentor, offering guidance and assistance whenever necessary. But that relationship had soured once Tetric arrived at the Caledonian court, the devious advisor suddenly appearing as if out of thin air and instantly gaining some sway over Corinthus and his young son, Marden. When Corinthus died under suspicious circumstances, the rumors about Marden only worsened. Tales of debauchery. Unnecessary cruelty. Regular tantrums and tirades. All conducted under the watchful and supportive eye of his Chief Advisor. Yet they were only rumors, the new King often coming across as a cheerful, gregarious young man.

For these and many other reasons, Marden made Kevan uneasy, and he would never allow his only daughter to marry him. But the young monarch wasn't his only concern. There was some facet to Tetric that made him think of a snake hiding in the brush, waiting to strike. The King's Advisor came across as obsequious and always cognizant of his place in Caledonian politics. But Kevan saw through Tetric. He knew who really exercised the power of the Caledonian throne.

Kevan sighed in exasperation. He had thought that circumstances had been difficult when he began his rule so many years before. Or when his beloved wife and Aislinn's mother, Brigid, had died from an illness that even the physicks and then Magii had failed to cure. But now it seemed as if one challenge had piled up on another, and he had few good solutions from which to choose for protecting the Southern Marches and his daughter.

"Are you all right, Duke Winborne? You seem more worried than usual."

Kevan looked up, pulling his eyes from the ship created of color that played across the floor as the sun moved through the sky. He noticed that Sirius' normally distracted appearance, staged so regularly when in the presence of others, had disappeared. The Sirius who stood before him now was focused, sharp, and clear-eyed. This was the Sirius who appeared when matters of great import needed to be discussed.

"You've heard of the King's demand?"

"You mean proposal?" corrected Sirius, his lips twisting into a slight smile.

"Proposal. Demand. It's the same thing," replied Kevan, who began pacing the circular chamber. "It leaves me with little room to maneuver."

"Yes, it was managed nicely."

Kevan stopped in his tracks. "You applaud their efforts?"

"I acknowledge the delicacy of the trap," answered Sirius. "And Tetric's traps are always difficult to escape."

"Always the diplomat, aren't we, Sirius?"

"When necessary. And when not, I am other things."

Kevan studied Sirius' eyes, noting the hard glint. The Magus had served the Southern Marches for the past decade, appearing at Kevan's request when it was time to begin his daughter's instruction. He smiled at Sirius' reply.

"Yes, I know. A man of many talents. All helpful and many frightening."

"You are too kind, Duke Winborne," replied Sirius, pleased by the comment. He could indeed be frightening, if need be, sometimes out of the desire for some fun, sometimes out of necessity, and rarely, but admittedly, sometimes out of spite. He was human, after all. He remembered slights and held onto grudges. He acknowledged that weakness but used it when necessary, often to great advantage.

"Any advice, Sirius?"

"Delay."

Kevan flexed his shoulders, seeking to relieve the tension that had been moving from his lower to his upper back. "I was hoping for something more than that, Sirius."

"I know, Duke Winborne. But for now that is all we have. Marden and Tetric have no power here in the Southern Marches. You have a strong connection to the Duke of the Three Rivers, and for some reason the Duchess of Murcia appears uncommonly interested in you, which helps you as well."

A slight blush came to Kevan's cheeks as he recalled his last meeting with Noorsin Stelekel, Duchess of Murcia. Located south of the Flats, north of the Shifting Desert, and to the west of the Three Tongue River, Murcia was the home of Caledonia's only major university and medical school. The other Duchies tended to ignore the province, as Murcia had little in the way of industry and trade. But for several years Noorsin had corresponded with Kevan and visited several times. A tall woman, she had been described as austere and ascetic because of her interest in books and learning. Yet Kevan had found her unusually attractive when he had met her, her dimples and freckles popping into his mind at the most unexpected or inopportune moments. And the last time she had come to Battersea he had found their final conversation exceedingly uncomfortable as she quite clearly expressed an interest in developing a more personal relationship. He had agreed that he would visit her in Murcia, and the smile and glint in her eyes that he received in return made him think of predator and prey, he being the prey. But that didn't bother him in the least. He had been alone since the death of his wife. With his daughter a confident young woman, he wanted something more now, and perhaps Noorsin could help to provide the connection that he was seeking.

"Yes, well, better to have allies rather than enemies."

"Indeed, Duke Winborne," replied Sirius, deciding to keep the teasing comment that came to mind to himself, staying focused on matters of state. "So my advice, at this time, is to delay, and to continue to delay for as long as possible. Marden's plan is straightforward, though certainly well worked. What worries me more is Tetric. Something else is at work here. Until we have a better sense of this larger construct that the King's Advisor has developed, we must be cautious and vigilant. And, above all, we must protect your daughter."

"I agree with you, Sirius." He began pacing once more, the burdens of his position seeming to weigh him down so much that his feet dragged through the thick carpet of the library. "With the boy Aislinn will have more protection." He stopped and faced Sirius. His doubts about the decision he had made, and the action taken with respect to the gladiator, continued to bother him. "I know you don't agree, but it was my best option."

Sirius responded immediately and emphatically. "No, enslaving a person in such a way was not the way to do this."

"He was a slave to begin with, Sirius. His fate was sealed in the Pit."

"That doesn't make it right."

Kevan waved off Sirius' objection, tamping down his continuing doubts. What's done was done. Once affixed, there was no way to remove the collar.

"Maybe not, but there's nothing to be done about it now. Will he serve his purpose? Will he protect her?"

"You should demonstrate greater confidence in your daughter, Kevan," said Sirius, shaking his head in irritation. Kevan did not miss how Sirius had dropped his honorific. "I wouldn't be surprised if she proved too much even for this Protector, as competent as the boy appears. Forget for a moment her growing ability in the Talent and her training and education to assume your chair at the right time. Aislinn is a warrior. She can handle any weapon with competence and skill, and I doubt that there is any soldier in the Southern Marches who would want to cross blades with her. She can defend herself."

"Yes, but we all need help from time to time. Will he protect her?"

"He has no choice, Kevan. He must."

It was now Kevan's turn to vent his frustration. Conversations with Sirius, though useful, were rarely easy. "You know that's not the question that I'm asking."

Sirius bowed his head for a moment, eyes closed, thinking of how to respond. Of how much he wanted to reveal.

"There is a power within him, Kevan. A strength that's rarely found, whether because of his upbringing or some other reason, I don't know yet. But he can and will protect her. I can think of only one person in the Southern Marches better with a blade than your daughter, and that's the boy. He'll do his duty. He'll protect her. The collar will require it of him. But I have a strange feeling that eventually the boy will protect her, not because he must, but because he wants to, and I find that thought quite unsettling."

8

RESPONSIBILITY CHAFES

Aislinn Winborne knew her place in the world. She knew who she was meant to be. Some day she would become the Duchess of the Southern Marches. Some day she would be responsible for the eastern lands of Caledonia. Some day ...

She wasn't certain that she wanted that day to ever come. When she was a child, upon her mother's death her father had assumed responsibility for her education. Actually, training might be a better word. Her father had changed when her mother had died. He was a loving father, doted on her, but his drive had increased upon his wife's passing, and his drive had been intense to begin with. Aislinn understood what her father was trying to do. He wanted to ensure that she was prepared for any of the challenges likely to come her way as the Lady of the Southern Marches. With that in mind, when she had reached a marriageable age, her training had intensified. Not only in the arts of diplomacy and governance, and of course all her academic subjects, but with weapons as well. Her father sought to protect her from all things, but he recognized that there would come a time when he could not.

That was likely the only reason he allowed her to train with Sirius. One of the few known, remaining Magii -- she had no doubt that there were others in hiding, but how many there were she had no idea -- he had arrived in Battersea when Aislinn had turned nine years old. Her father had sensed something about her, that she was different. She had started to act in ways that other children her age didn't. Strange gusts of wind would swirl in the middle of her room with the windows closed, tearing the sheets from her bed. Or all her toys would levitate from the floor, sometimes for hours. She didn't understand that all the curious occurrences were happening because of her, but her father did.

He had called for Sirius, and the leader of the Order of the Magii had come, traveling from his home at the Aeyrie. It was clear to Aislinn that her father wasn't pleased about this new development. He didn't want his daughter to have this ability, knowing that despite its utility, if the people of Caledonia didn't perceive those with the Talent with suspicion, they usually viewed them with fear instead. But this natural magic was a part of her, so she needed to learn how to control it. And despite his discomfort, her father saw it as another tool that she could use to defend herself. Thus, his decision to bring Sirius to Battersea. Since then, the Magus had become a trusted advisor to her father and a friend and teacher to Aislinn.

Yet if her father had done all that he could to ensure that she could protect herself, why did he feel the need to force a Protector on her? She was improving with the Talent, and she was skilled in the blade, better, in fact, than all the Battersea Guard except perhaps for Tarin. Thinking of what her father had just done to her, she gripped her hands tightly, growling in frustration as she tried to control her temper.

She could feel him, whatever his name was. At that very moment, he trailed her by fifty paces as she stalked through the Broken Citadel. Sighing in resignation, she entered the seventh tower, which stood in the very center of the keep. As she began the long climb to the top of the Broken Citadel's tallest spire, she tried to release her fury. She needed to be focused for what was to come next and allowing her anger to control her would hinder her efforts. With that in mind, she tried to turn her thoughts in another direction.

In her opinion, the Broken Citadel was well named. Six towers anchored the imposing walls of the massive fortress, all hundreds of feet tall. The tower she now continued to trudge up, rising several hundred feet above the others, once served as the workshop of the Magus Orriander, who was one of the greatest members of the Order of the Magii. It was said that a thousand years before he had started to pursue the black arts, arguing with his peers that the only way to protect against the Dark Magic of the Ghoule Overlord was to learn about it and to understand how it worked. Yet Orriander never realized how his studies began to recast him, how the Dark Magic, also known as the Curse, began to worm its way into him, slowly, subtly, until the Magus Orriander was no more. The Curse had corrupted him, and he had become a receptacle for the Dark Magic he had been studying.

Knowing that Orriander had to be stopped before he brought destruction to the Southern Marches and then to all of Caledonia, Sirano, another member of the Order of the Magii, had confronted his former teacher and mentor. The magical battle that ensued between Dark Magic and the Talent shook the very foundations of the keep and could be felt from leagues away. In the end, Sirano had defeated his former master and thwarted the evil that Orriander had unleashed within the Citadel, but not without cost. The battle had destroyed the top floors of the tower. The bodies of Orriander and Sirano were never found, and it was assumed that both had died in the confrontation. The Duke of the Southern Marches at that time, whose name escaped Aislinn, chose not to rebuild the tallest tower of the fortress so that it would serve as a reminder of the danger of man's hubris, and thus the name the Broken Citadel.

Of course, when Sirius came to serve her father, he felt some affinity for the shattered tower, choosing to make his residence the highest floor that remained habitable. After several minutes of climbing stairs, she stopped in front of a large wooden door. She took a few moments to breathe deeply as she sought to calm herself. But she found it to be exceedingly difficult. She could feel her Protector just a few floors below, having no need to look for him. She knew exactly where he was located. He was there, always there, in the back of her mind. He was like a disease you couldn't cure. Struggling to force him from her thoughts, she was about to knock when the door swung open.

"Good evening, Aislinn." Sirius stepped back, allowing her to enter his large chamber. The circular space encompassed the breadth of the massive tower, stretching into the darkened alcoves built into the outer wall. In the very center of the room huge tables made of oak had been pushed together, allowing Sirius to conduct whatever experiments he might be engaging in at a particular time. Pipettes and beakers and other glassware dominated the tabletops, the connected tubing running this way and that, mesmerizing to the eye and a bit sickening if studied too long. "You seem a bit distracted."

Aislinn grunted her frustration. "I'm sorry, Sirius. It's just that ..."

She wanted to strike something, to throw something, to break something, anything. Anything to release the resentment boiling within her. Despite her best efforts she was having a difficult time controlling her emotions.

"You're not happy with your father, I assume."

Aislinn sighed, the anger beginning to flow out of her under her instructor's kindly gaze. "You know me too well, Sirius."

"Aye, that's certainly a possibility," said Sirius grinning. "You do tend to get on my nerves, always demanding to learn more. Always wanting to improve your skills. Always wanting to get stronger in the art of the Talent. In fact, I don't know how I'm to deal with the tediousness of the next few hours as we begin your lesson ..."

"Sirius!"

The Magus' grin had become a full-fledged smile, and then he started to laugh loudly, his eyes sparkling with mirth. Aislinn stood there, arms crossed, her beautiful face scrunched into a furious frown. After a few seconds, Sirius regained control of himself.

"Oh, come now, Aislinn. You are much too serious. You need to have a little fun from time to time. Smile every once in a while."

"How am I supposed to do that when my father, without my knowledge or permission, forces a Protector on me?" She walked toward the circular wall, looking out the window and taking in the lights of Battersea, which extended into the distance, some running all the way down through the port to seemingly touch the Silent Sea. "He doesn't trust me. He doesn't believe that I can look after myself."

Sirius stepped up behind her, a kindly smile on his face. He had grown close to Aislinn during their time working together. She was like the daughter he had never had, though he revised that thought quickly. It wasn't entirely correct. Forcing it from his mind, he turned his attention to the matter at hand.

"Your father loves you. He will do anything to protect you." Before she could protest, he continued. "And yes, he should have spoken to you first, but there's more to this situation than either of us know."

"What do you mean?"

"Your father made this decision when he was in Tintagel. Something must have happened there that made him think that this was necessary."

"But what?"

"I can't say. He hasn't given me all the details. And obviously not to you either. But I will get it out of him eventually."

Sirius felt horrible not telling Aislinn the complete truth, but it wasn't his truth to reveal. Her father would have to do so when he felt that the time was right.

Aislinn sighed again, her vexation finally leaving her. "But what am I to do with whomever his name is? He's always there. Always around. And I can feel him. I know where he is at all times, just like he knows where I am. I can even sense his thoughts when he's feeling a strong emotion, and I assume that he can do the same of me."

"I admit that it is a difficult situation, Aislinn. And until we can learn more from your father, there's little that we can do. All I can offer you is one thought."

"And what's that?"

"Remember that Bryen, for that is the name of your Protector, does not want to be here either. From what I have learned, he has had a hard life, and your father has made it all the more difficult for him. What your father has done affects not only you, but also him. So perhaps a little less woe is me and a bit more focus."

Aislinn took the subtle remonstration surprisingly well, turning away from the lights of Battersea to give what he had just said some thought, thankful that Sirius was there to be more than just a teacher, though she had to admit that he always seemed to be teaching her something.

"I will try to do better, Sirius," she said. "But no promises."

"Excellent. That's all I can ask. Now are you ready for what we are about to do today?"

"Yes, let's get to it."

"Good. We will start from where we left off yesterday."

Aislinn nodded. Closing her eyes she breathed deeply, seeking to center herself and push out all the irritating distractions. As the seconds passed her breathing slowed, and the world around her began to disappear. She knew she was ready when she entered a space in her mind in which all was quiet, all was calm. She was concentrating perfectly on the task given to her. There was nothing outside of the calm space that surrounded her that could hinder or upset her. It was here in this void that she sensed the Talent.

It was like a cool stream that ran through her, containing the natural magic of the world. In her case it was a very small stream, for she had not yet been tested to become a Magus. Instead, as an apprentice, she was limited in what she could do. But once she passed the test to become a full-fledged Magus -- and she would become a Magus, she knew it in her heart and did not fear the consequences of her failing to do so -- that small stream would become a rushing current, opening her up to a much larger world of possibility. But until then, she would make do with what she had.

Raising her hands in front of her, palms close together as if she were holding a large glass bowl, she imagined reaching into the stream of natural magic that passed through her. Gradually she started pulling what she could only describe as strands from the flow, bright white, shimmering threads that she began to twist and turn in her hands. As Aislinn pulled more and more threads from the stream, the light in the chamber grew brighter and more charged.

"Control this, Aislinn. Don't let the power of the Talent overwhelm you."

Aislinn heard Sirius' instruction faintly, her use of the Talent dampening the sound around her. But she sought to obey. Exercising more of her will, she spun the ball of shimmering threads tighter and tighter while at the same time lowering the brightness of the strands. The power remained, but the brightness that had burned away all the shadows in the large chamber diminished so that now it pulsed gently as if the light of the day was about to make way for the evening.

"Good, Aislinn. Well done. Now show me that you can control the size of your creation."

Hearing Sirius' soft instruction, though still muted by the void, she began to manipulate the shimmering strands, pulling on them much as a baker would pull on the dough to stretch it across a pie plate. Slowly the ball of light began to expand.

"Maintain your control over the brightness, Aislinn."

She quickly complied, realizing that as she focused on expanding the ball of light, she had allowed the brilliance to increase again until it was almost blinding. She immediately regained control, dimming the pulsing ball of threads and pulling on the strands until the sphere was larger than a man's head.

"Well done, Aislinn. Now let's see if you can return the energy to its original size."

Aislinn nodded to herself, maintaining her focus. The strength of will required to keep control over just a small stream of the Talent was beginning to tire her. Breathing deeply and evenly, she began to maneuver the ball of energy in her hands once more, pushing and prodding as she tried to compress the threads and make the ball smaller. Slowly her actions began to bear fruit, but something about what she was doing seemed off. With every attempt to make the ball smaller the brightness grew. And she could feel the orb, which was now down to only half of its original size, grow heavier and denser as she compressed it.

A faint tremor of worry settled in her stomach, but she ignored it. Redoubling her efforts, she continued to manipulate the shimmering threads, pushing and compressing until the ball of energy was now a quarter of its previous size. But the problem that she had identified just a few minutes before remained. In fact, it seemed to have gotten worse. The orb, though smaller than what it had been, felt twice as heavy as before. The sphere pulsed erratically now, some of the strands becoming tangled, making the ball spin haphazardly. Still, she was almost there. It wouldn't take much to complete the task. Deciding that one final push should do the trick, she gathered her will and began to compress the strands once more, pushing harder and harder to force them together.

"Aislinn, you need to ..."

She didn't catch all that Sirius said, a huge roar

drowning him out. She felt herself lifted up and blasted backward as the sphere of energy, which had grown as heavy as a solid ball of steel, exploded in her hand. She expected to feel the pain of being slammed back against the stone wall, but instead she found herself floating in the air, protected by a shimmering white globe of energy. Sirius stood next to her, protected by the same type of barricade. Gently he settled her back on her feet, then let go of the Talent. The protective shields dissipated.

Aislinn bent over for a moment. Gasping for air she tried to control the urge to release the contents of her stomach, but she realized almost too late that she was going to fail. Running to a window, she thrust her head outside just in time. She allowed the cool night air to wash over her, and she stood there for several minutes to give her stomach time to settle. Turning back around slowly, she took the cup of water Sirius held for her and with her free hand rubbed at her head because of the massive headache that had erupted.

"Take your time, child. Drink the water. I mixed in some herbs that will help you. It will only take a few minutes."

Sipping at the water, gradually her focus returned as her headache faded and her stomach settled. Finally breathing more freely again, and realizing that she was drenched in sweat, she opened her eyes. She almost dropped the empty cup. The explosion had devastated the chamber, blowing the pipettes, beakers, and other glass pieces off the center tables and against the far wall. If Sirius had not acted as quickly as he had, she assumed that she would have ended up in little pieces as well.

"What happened, Aislinn?" Sirius spoke quietly, seriously, but not with anger.

"I was compressing the strands of energy, pushing them

together, but the threads started to clump and spin erratically. I didn't know what ..."

"No, Aislinn. Think. You're telling me what you did. Not
what happened. Why did your actions lead to this result?"

Tamping down her rising irritation, she thought for a
moment, reliving what she had been doing with the ball of
energy. Then she knew. She was so focused on her task that
she had made a foolish mistake that had destroyed much of
Sirius' chamber.

"When you asked me to expand the size of the ball, I
pulled more strands from the Talent, which allowed it to
grow. But when you asked me to make the ball smaller, I
forgot to pull strands from the ball and return them to the
flow of the Talent. Trying to maintain so much of the Talent
in such a small space made it unstable to the point where I
lost control."

She gritted her teeth in anger because of her failure,
hating that she had made such an obvious mistake.

"Correct."

"I should have been paying more attention. I should
never have ..."

"Aislinn." Sirius' words knocked her from the path she
was about to follow. She looked up from where she had
been staring at the floor before she could continue with the
diatribe she had been about to start on herself. "You are not
perfect. You will never be perfect."

She nodded her head, appearing to not really believe
what Sirius was saying. She had to be hard on herself. It was
the only way to improve. How else was she supposed to hold
her own in the training yard? How else ...

"Aislinn." There was heat in Sirius' voice now, and that
finally caught her attention. "I repeat. You are not perfect.

You will never be perfect. You must accept that you will make mistakes. Do you understand?"

"Yes," she replied reluctantly, nodding her head in frustration. "But I don't have to like it."

"No, you don't have to like it," Sirius agreed. "But you must acknowledge your mistakes, accept them, learn from them, then push them to the side and try again. Do you understand what I'm saying?"

"Yes, Sirius."

Sirius stared at her for several long moments, weighing the truth of her response. Finally satisfied, he nodded.

"Good. I would ask that you try again this evening, but I can sense how tired you are. So ..."

"Sirius, it's all right. I'm not tired. I can try again right now." She stopped talking as soon as she saw the flash of anger cross Sirius' eyes. Normally quiet and composed, and generally appearing to be preoccupied, she had learned through her many lessons with the Magus that arguing with him was not the best course of action. Before saying anything else, she took another deep breath. "I understand. I'm sorry. I didn't mean to destroy your experiments."

Sirius surveyed the chamber, raising his eyebrow at the broken glass and other material that littered the floor. Several weeks' work wasted. No matter. It wasn't Aislinn's fault. He had given her too much freedom. If he had stopped her when he should have, this wouldn't have happened. Of course, if he had stepped in earlier, he wouldn't have this opportunity to teach her this specific lesson either. And, at the moment, this lesson was more important than Aislinn gaining greater skill in the Talent. She drove herself too hard, not realizing that she needed to slow down at times, to relax, to think before doing. Hopefully in some way this failure would help her in the future.

"It's all right, child. We will try again tomorrow evening. In the meantime, think about what you have learned today. Think about what you will do differently so that tomorrow when you do this again, you don't blow apart the walls of the tower."

Sirius said the last with a smile on his face, but Aislinn missed it. Head bowed, she mumbled her apologies once more and then quickly exited the chamber, pulling the door closed behind her and almost running down the steps into the cool of the night. She looked up for a moment at the brightly shining stars, allowing the cool evening breeze to dry the sweat on her brow. And then her brief moment of calm evaporated as the world came crashing back in through her connection to her Protector. She could feel him, just fifty paces away, though she couldn't locate him, try as she might. It was as if he had become part of the darkness that cloaked the Broken Citadel. Unbidden, her anger rose again. At her father for doing this to her, but primarily at herself for tonight's failure.

Snarling in anger she marched off toward her suite, making sure that she would walk by her Protector, whatever his name was, along the way. The fury within her continued to increase. She needed a release, an outlet, and she knew exactly what she was going to do. As she passed the alcove in which her Protector stood, she reached out for the Talent and with a gentle touch took hold of the stream and withdrew a few strands of energy. With a quick flip, the threads shot from her palm and struck her Protector in the chest.

Aislinn had expected him to jump, to shout in surprise or fear, yet no sound came from him. He stood there stoically, calmly patting the area on his shirt that had begun to smolder, smothering the embers quickly, and then his gaze had turned to her after he had ensured that all the sparks were out. His eyes blazed, but not with rage. Rage she could deal with. No, in the place of rage she saw disappointment. She had never expected such a reaction and quickly realized that she had acted like a child, taking her own anger out on someone else. Someone who didn't want to be there, tied to her, but had to be there, nonetheless.

Her own anger disappeared, replaced by shame. She tried to say something, to apologize, but no words came. Lowering her eyes quickly, she ran from the courtyard for her rooms, all the while her Protector trotting behind her, having no choice but to do so if he hoped to avoid the disabling pain in his gut that would follow if he failed to track his charge within a certain distance.

9

EARNING HIS KEEP

Bryen returned to his small room just across the colonnaded hallway from Aislinn's suite, softly closing the door behind him. He stood there for a moment, breathing deeply as Declan had taught him to release the conflicting emotions that surged within him, collecting his thoughts and allowing his eyes to adjust to the dim light provided by the few candles placed around his living quarters. When the girl had flung those sparks at him, he had been surprised by what she could do and then angry, his rage finally turning to disappointment and disdain.

He could understand her resentment, that feeling of being watched, being kept, and needing to lash out in some way. He almost felt for her, and he hadn't felt much in the last few years, but her demonstration of disrespect quashed his budding sympathy. She was in the same position that he was, forced into a situation not of her choosing. But he had expected better from her. You would think that someone trained to rule would think of others before themselves, but perhaps that was simply a fallacy he had been taught.

The sparks that had set his shirt smoking hadn't

distressed him. He had faced worse in the Pit, much worse, so he hadn't been fazed. No, what had stopped him for a moment was the feeling that had coursed through his body when she had used against him what he could only assume was the Talent. He had felt a flare in his chest right then, a strange energy coursing through his body. It had warmed him, made him feel more alive than he ever had before, and he had no clue why that was the case.

The only other times that he had felt something similar was during some of his combats on the white sand. In certain moments, when he believed that he was going to die, that his opponent, man or beast, was too strong, too experienced, or too cunning for him to overcome, he would feel a similar heat build in his chest, as if some mysterious energy was surging through him. In seconds, his focus would intensify, his decision making would quicken, his movements would become faster, and he would know with absolute certainty that in the end he would survive to fight another day. But why would that feeling return now?

He shook his head to clear his thoughts, scrubbing his face with his hands. He stripped off his singed shirt and threw it by the door. He would dispose of it later. Sitting on his small bed, he pulled off his boots and set them neatly to the side near the several shirts and pants that he had placed carefully on the chest at the end of the bed. He had never had such finery while fighting as a gladiator. So he felt somewhat responsible for the few possessions that he had now.

Lying down on the small bed, his feet hanging off the end, he surveyed his domain. He assumed that it was a small room compared to the others in the Broken Citadel, and tight in terms of the space to move around. The bed and trunk barely fit, thus the pegs on the wall for his cloak and weapons. But he preferred to lean his sword against the bed's backboard and place his many knives, usually hidden somewhere on his body, under his pillow or mattress so that he could reach them quickly. A small room, indeed, but it was his own space and really the only place that he could go for some solitude, if only temporarily. And, in all honesty, it was much better than his quarters in the gladiators' stockade.

He was no longer fighting for his life so that rich men and women could bet on his death. So his situation was somewhat improved. But he missed Lycia and Davin, and even more so Declan. Having lived on the streets of Tintagel for almost a year, the Master of the Gladiators had taken him from the slavers' block when he was nine and had given him a purpose, a way of living that he valued. He knew as well that there were worse options. The Watch regularly pulled orphans off the streets, those stealing or begging to survive, and held an illicit auction. The collected children could be purchased, oftentimes for shady or nefarious purposes if they were not hung. The brothels usually acquired such children to meet the needs of their less savory customers.

As a result, though serving as a gladiator was a hard and often short life, he preferred that path to the one offered by the many houses of pleasure located in Tintagel's seedier district. He didn't enjoy the killing, but he had grown numb to it as the years passed, reaching the point where he simply viewed it as a necessity. Kill or be killed. He appreciated the simplicity of it all, and in a twisted way he took some comfort from it. Of course, there was an additional benefit, as taking up residence in the gladiators' training quarters and being pushed onto the white sand within weeks of his arrival had forced thoughts of his murdered parents from his mind. He had no time to think about his loss, about how his life had changed. Though memories of that night and the tall, cloaked creatures who had killed his parents and almost caught him played through his dreams regularly, often forcing him awake gasping for breath with tears running down his cheeks, he felt safe next to the Colosseum, strange as that might seem.

Also, he valued Declan's willingness to teach him more than just how to stay alive. Declan was a slave as well, but he had the freedom to move throughout Tintagel and the surrounding countryside without challenge. On occasion, the Master of the Gladiators would take him into the city and even out beyond the walls to give him a new experience, to see the world, or at least a small part of the world beyond the white sand of the Pit. Often, they would sit at the docks for hours in the evening after purchasing supplies for the gladiators from the marketplaces dotting the city. Declan would point to the ships and tell him where they came from based on their design and sails, sharing stories of faraway lands. Bryen suspected that Declan often mixed the truth with embellishment, but he didn't care. The stories gave him worlds to explore and think about other than his own. Worlds that he desperately wanted to see for himself. Declan also taught him his letters and always had a new book for him. How he obtained them Bryen didn't know. It was almost as if Declan was preparing him for a life beyond the Pit, yet everyone knew that a gladiator only escaped the Colosseum one way. Dead.

He pushed the memories from his mind, turning his thoughts to what had happened that evening while he had waited for his charge. As he had assumed, there was more to Sirius than met the eye. He had seen much the same in the Pit when an opposing gladiator sought to lull him into a false sense of confidence by appearing slower in mind or body than he or she actually was. Sirius did much the same, acting like an absentminded teacher for reasons that Bryen had yet to decipher. As he had stood halfway up the broken tower, hidden in the shadows of the twisting stairs, he knew that Aislinn had failed in whatever task Sirius had set before her. He could feel the event unfold, feel her. Her pride. Her anger. Her astonishment. And then her fear.

That last emotion had jolted him into action. He was almost to Sirius' door, taking the crumbling steps four at a time, when he heard the muffled blast in the old man's chamber, the shaking tower almost knocking him from the circular staircase to the entrance so far below. Finding his balance once again, he realized almost instantly that she was safe. Whatever had occurred during her lesson had not harmed the girl. He had not wished to charge up the stairs, but he had been compelled to do so, the collar around his neck forcing him into action. Angry at his fate, he had stalked back down the stairs and resumed his position. When he heard the door far above him open and close, he had shifted to the alcove outside the tower to wait for his charge.

Tonight's events confirmed some of Bryen's suspicions. Sirius was a Magus. What had shocked him was the power that the old man had exercised. Whatever Sirius had done to protect the girl had sent a bolt of white heat through Bryen's chest. Clearly, the old man was someone to be reckoned with. Yet Bryen could tell that the girl, though not as strong as Sirius, controlled a great deal of energy as well. He found their strength in the Talent somewhat intimidating, and he thought about what it might be like to face a Magus in combat. He had no doubt that his end would come quickly, as he would have no way to defend himself against such a power. But what surprised and disconcerted him even more was his identifying their use of the Talent, that uncomfortable surge of heat that he had experienced. Was it because of the collar and his ability to sense the girl every second of the day? Or was it something else? He didn't know, and that troubled him.

Unable to reach a conclusion that satisfied him, he reached for a book Declan had hidden in his few belongings before leaving Tintagel for Battersea. It was his friend's last gift, a history of the First Ghoule War that followed the travails of Arick Winborne, the general primarily responsible for successfully defending Caledonia. A good choice on Declan's part considering where he was going. He had enjoyed the text so far, not only because of the history, but also because of the long discussion of the strategy that Arick had employed to slow the Ghoule army as it advanced into the Kingdom.

He was only able to read a few pages before he dropped the book on his bed, pushed himself up abruptly, and quickly pulled his sword from its sheath and grabbed a knife from beneath his pillow. He yanked open his door and sprinted across the hallway toward Aislinn's suite. Assuming that the doors would be locked, at a full run he jumped into the air, angling his body and leading with his left foot. Striking the doors perfectly in the center, the force of his kick splintered the wood around the locks and smashed them back against the wall, the one on the left falling off its hinges.

"What are you doing?" shrieked Aislinn. Standing in the center of her antechamber, she pulled the top of her night-gown tight.

Bryen ignored her, charging into the girl's bedroom. Sensing movement to the left of the door, he ducked, barely avoiding the steel blade that would have severed his head from his neck if it had connected. His attacker never had a chance to pull free the sword that had stuck fast in the wooden frame as Bryen drove the dagger in his left hand deep into his opponent's chest. Bryen took in the black leather clothes, mask, and harness the assassin wore as he helped the man slide against the wall and slump on the floor as the light left his eyes. Pulling his dagger free from the corpse, Bryen moved quickly into the room. Two more darkly clothed assassins had stepped through the balcony doors while another was still pulling himself up over the ledge.

Letting his instincts take over, Bryen rushed forward, not wanting to give the attackers an opportunity to dictate the engagement. The two assassins pulled their short swords and tried to separate from one another, which would make Bryen's task all the more difficult if they were able to come at him from different sides at the same time. Fortunately, the girl's massive bed had a canopy of silk that rose to the ceiling and swirled about as the wind gusted into the room through the open doors. One of the assassins became entangled with the material, the killer fighting to extricate himself and preventing the assassin on Bryen's left from moving away from his partner. Even with that bit of luck, Bryen sensed that these men were experienced killers. And with three to fight, he needed to reduce the odds as quickly as he could.

With that thought in mind, Bryen lunged forward, trying to skewer the assassin as he struggled to free himself from the silk. Bryen drove his blade toward the ensnarled assassin's heart, but the man was both skilled and fast, raising his sword just in time and deflecting the strike. But the assassin still wasn't fast enough as Bryen's blade slid off his steel and into the man's shoulder, eliciting a grunt of pain. Pulling his blade out, Bryen raised the bloody sword and dagger at the same time, interlocking the two above his head to take the overhead blow struck by the other assassin in the room, who sought to take advantage of Bryen attacking his companion. Sparks fell onto the carpet beneath their feet as the broadly built assassin's sword met Bryen's crossed blades.

At the same time, the wounded assassin, having disentangled himself from the silk but favoring his left arm, which hung limply at his side, stepped forward to engage Bryen once again. In response, Bryen stepped back, giving himself some much-needed space to maneuver. He took stock of the situation in seconds. The fourth assassin was almost over the balcony's stone railing. The two in the room -- one injured, one not -- had spread out, making it more difficult for Bryen to defend himself. They all appeared to be accomplished fighters. If he wasn't careful, any mistake on his part likely would mean his death.

Although the wounded assassin had his blade in his hand, Bryen could tell that his injury had weakened him. Blood seeped from the wound, trickling down his leather armor to puddle at his feet. To try to even the odds, Bryen decided on a move that he had used in the Pit while fighting five men at once, though these attackers clearly were more adept than those had been. Moving forward with a lightning-fast first step, Bryen feinted an attack on the sturdy, broad assassin who had tried to split him in two, forcing the man to take a step back, then he turned quickly and shot out his left hand. His dagger slid into the already injured man's gut, a groan of agony escaping his lips. Bryen then drove his shoulder into the wounded assassin, sending him tumbling over the bed into the far corner of the room.

Turning faster than the other attacker had expected,

Bryen raised his sword, parrying the strike from the assassin who had fallen for his feint. As they traded blows, the sound of steel striking steel echoing throughout the chamber, Bryen determined instantly that though his opponent was stronger than he was, the assassin was not faster. Wanting to take advantage of that fact, Bryen launched into a mesmerizing assault, sword and dagger moving in a blurred maelstrom of steel as he sought to break through the shorter assassin's defenses.

The assassin often caught Bryen's blade on his own, still, unfortunately for him, several times he missed, Bryen's steel slicing through the black leather armor, blood welling up from every cut, and the assassin having no defense for Bryen's dagger. Despite the growing rage that Bryen saw in his adversary's eyes, he knew that this combat would be over soon. With a final burst of speed, Bryen caught the assassin's sword on his own, then plunged the point of his dagger through the man's left eye with a jab faster than could be seen. Bryen stepped back calmly as the stocky assassin dropped to the floor. Though in constant motion for the last few minutes, Bryen was barely breathing hard.

"Well done, boy."

Bryen turned to face his final threat. The man on the rope stepped into the room from the balcony. Tall and slim, the fighter moved with an animal's grace. Bryen sensed that this last assassin was the most dangerous of the four and that he could have entered the combat more quickly if he had so desired. But it seemed to Bryen that this supremely confident man, only his flashing blue eyes visible beneath his mask, had waited to see how things would turn out before joining the fray. Almost as if he were testing his companions, and allowing Bryen to find them lacking, while studying how the Protector fought.

"You've done better than I expected you would, you being new to the role of Protector. The connection between you and your charge often takes time to reach its full effect." The assassin paused, his gaze sweeping over his fallen fighters. "But perhaps it wasn't you so much as the quality of my men. Let us find out."

The tall man whipped out two short swords from scabbards on his back and lunged forward with a speed Bryen had rarely seen. But seen it, he had. He quickly stepped back and to the side, allowing one short sword to slide past his body with barely a finger's breadth of space, taking the other blade on his sword and punching forward with his dagger, which forced the assassin to stop his initial attack and retreat a step in order to avoid a puncture between his ribs.

"Quick," said the assassin, looking down to his side and seeing the blood begin to trickle down where Bryen's dagger had sliced through the leather armor and across his skin. "Quicker than I expected. But that still won't save you."

The tall assassin began his assault once more, the speed of his attack impressive. Bryen continued to give ground, but stubbornly, assuming a defensive role, not seeking to attack but rather simply blocking the twin blades that flashed in front of him, taking the time to learn the man's patterns and habits. After several minutes the assassin withdrew a few paces, sweat trickling down his brow.

"I must give you credit, boy," said the assassin as he brought a sword blade up to his forehead and nodded toward Bryen in a show of respect. "You are better than I expected. You are to be commended."

It was the nod that gave it away. The assassin believed that Bryen would take the nod as acknowledgement of his prowess, but he didn't. Instead, Bryen had sensed the movement behind him, assuming that the wounded assassin had survived the stab to his gut and was going to attack him from behind, and that the nod from his adversary was directed not to Bryen, but to his conspirator. He was right on all counts. But Bryen was surprised when he heard a deep groan and a body slumping to the floor behind him.

The wounded assassin had indeed found the strength to rise despite his injuries, but he hadn't gotten far. The Lady of the Southern Marches stood behind them by the door, her sword gripped tightly and blood trickling down the blade onto her hand, a look of shock on her face. He caught her eyes for a moment, nodding his thanks, then turned once more to the only assassin still alive and spoke for the first time since the combat began.

"You made a mistake by trying to test me. It's time to end this."

Bryen lunged with his sword, the last assassin surprised to see his companion fall to the girl's blade. The masked man brought his twin blades up in time to catch Bryen's strike, but he had no chance to attack himself. Bryen moved with a deadly grace, Aislinn marveling at his speed and balance as the former gladiator pushed the assassin back toward the balcony, the blood sliding across her hand forgotten. Her Protector looked focused, calm, confident, barely registering what went on around him as he concentrated solely on his opponent.

The clash of metal on metal sounded more quickly as Bryen intensified his attack, the assassin trying to defend himself but finding it more and more difficult as Bryen increased the speed of his assault. Aislinn noticed that the assassin now bled from more than a half dozen wounds and his eyes, once taunting and condescending, appeared frightened. And with good reason. With a final surge of speed,

Bryen attacked, his dagger and sword easily escaping the assassin's twin blades in a whirlwind of steel.

And then it was over. The tall assassin lay crumpled on the balcony, bleeding out on the rose-colored tile.

Quiet settled once more in the room, the only sound coming from the courtyard below as Aislinn heard the shouts of the soldiers as they ran toward her suite. Bryen had stepped over the dying assassin and out onto the balcony, slashing down with his sword to cut the rope and make certain that there would be no more surprises that night.

Walking back into the bedroom, shirtless and shoeless, his scarred body covered in blood, he stopped for a moment and looked at Aislinn with a serious expression.

"Thank you," he said, nodding toward the assassin slumped at her feet. "Training isn't combat, and you know that now. Combat is killing as quickly as you possibly can. Well done."

Bryen then strode out into the main chamber to stand guard, waiting for the soldiers of the Battersea Guard to arrive.

10

UNWELCOME DISCOVERY

"How did the Guard not see this from the inner wall? Four men scaling a rope in clear view?"

Kevan held the large steel claw in his hand, a slim but strong length of rope still attached, cut where Aislinn's Protector had severed it the evening before. He examined it for a few minutes, then handed it to Tarin, Captain of the Battersea Guard.

"Dark Magic, Duke Winborne," came Sirius' reply after he had studied the claw for several seconds upon Tarin handing it to him after his own inspection, turning it this way and that with his hands.

Sirius reached gently for the Talent, sending a few strands of energy swirling around the metal hook. The examination told him nothing that he didn't already suspect. Duke Winborne had looked on with interest as the bright white light engulfed the tool for a short time, Tarin with a twinge of unease. The Captain would stand against any man or beast in the defense of the Southern Marches, but how was he to fight something when he had no way to protect against it? He wasn't afraid of dying. No, his primary concern was failing.

"You did not sense them within the Broken Citadel?" asked Duke Winborne with some irritation.

He had some understanding of the Talent and the abilities of a Magus thanks to his long association with Sirius and his knowledge of the training his daughter had undertaken. He couldn't understand how anyone with Dark Magic could enter his fortress without Sirius' knowledge.

The Magus ignored the complaint, knowing that Duke Winborne's comment came more from fear for his daughter's safety than anything else.

"No, Duke Winborne, I did not. There are remnants of Dark Magic on this claw," explained Sirius. "But faint at best. My guess is that these assassins were cloaked some leagues from Battersea, essentially covering themselves in a darkness that the Guards could not penetrate with their eyes even if they looked directly at it."

"Then how did the boy know the assassins were there?" asked Tarin. "Lady Winborne said that when he charged into her bedroom, the assassins were visible to the eye."

"The Dark Magic likely lasted only so long. The farther the assassins traveled from whomever placed the Dark Magic upon them, the harder it became for this sorcerer to maintain the illusion."

Sirius leaned over the balcony, looking down at the hard cobblestones so far below. He wondered at the truth of his own words for a moment. What he had said was technically correct. The Dark Magic would weaken the greater the distance the ones ensorcelled traveled from the person who cast the sorcery. But in his examination of the claw, the remnants of the spell, though greatly weakened now with all the time that had passed, suggested that during the previous evening the cloak of darkness had remained intact around the assassins well past the time that they entered Aislinn's chamber. He had no doubt that if Bryen had not intervened, the four assassins could have completed their task and left the way they had come with none the wiser, their invisibility still in place. The assassins would have been leagues from Battersea before the spell wore off entirely.

If he was correct in his assumptions, then a key question needed to be answered. How did Bryen, and then Aislinn, detect the deception? He knew that there were some skilled in the use of the Talent who would have the ability to see through a magical subterfuge such as this, though they were few in number. He guessed that was the case with Aislinn. He would engage her in this area during their upcoming lessons to test that hypothesis. But what of the Protector? How did he see through the illusion created by the Dark Magic? He decided to only offer a portion of the truth for now, wanting to think more on the dilemma that rattled through his mind.

"When they arrived on your daughter's balcony, the spell probably was already losing its power," continued Sirius. "The Protector attacking them provided the additional time needed for the sorcery to wear off entirely."

Duke Winborne had come to stand next to Sirius, looking out from his daughter's balcony to the far wall of the Broken Citadel and beyond, the bright sunlight reflecting off the surging waves of the Silent Sea, which crashed against the shore in a regular dull rumble. A beautiful day, but he knew a storm was coming. The sea never lied.

"Where are they?"

Sirius assumed that Duke Winborne referred to the person who had used the Dark Magic for this purpose.

"I don't know. I can sense when someone strong in the Talent or the Curse is close, but after several leagues it becomes more and more difficult. The assassins could have come from the countryside or the sea. There's no way to know. Whoever aided these assassins, I'm sure that they're long gone. I sense no one anywhere near Battersea now with the ability to do what was done last night with the Curse."

"Can we prevent this from happening again?" asked Tarin.

Normally stolid and unflappable, Sirius could tell that the Captain of the Guard was nervous. Tarin had no good way to protect against an attack like this one.

"We can," replied Sirius, noting the breath of relief that escaped from Tarin. "I will set wards around the Broken Citadel and then expand from there into Battersea. Once done, if someone tries to use Dark Magic within the walls, we will know with plenty of warning and can respond accordingly."

Duke Winborne nodded in approval. "Thank you, Sirius. Please make it so as quickly as possible."

Sirius turned to leave, wanting to begin his work, but Tarin's words stopped him.

"There is one issue we have not yet discussed, Duke Winborne," said Tarin, thankful that Sirius would be assisting in the defense of the Broken Citadel and the city. "We keep saying this was an assassination attempt. But what if it wasn't?"

"What do you mean, Tarin?" Kevan's gaze was tight as his mind followed the path that his Captain of the Guard had set before him.

"Yes, these attackers appeared to be assassins. And perhaps they were on other jobs, maybe even members of the Order of the Assassins. But what if their real purpose wasn't to kill Aislinn, but rather to kidnap her?"

"Why would you suggest ..." Kevan stopped himself, taking the time to think instead. It wasn't long before another possibility became clear. Tarin spoke it out loud for all of them.

"Perhaps King Beleron doesn't want your daughter so much as he wants the Southern Marches, and he's decided to speed up his plans. We spoke about this already. If Marden gains control of Lady Winborne and marries her, you, Duke Winborne, become expendable. If he succeeds in eliminating you, then the only thing that keeps Marden from the Southern Marches is your daughter. And if she becomes with child ..."

Tarin felt no need to continue his thought. They all knew what would happen if their assumptions proved correct.

Kevan gazed out at the sea, the blue and grey water swirling and surging as the wind picked up, his face pale and his worry growing. Tarin very likely was correct, but of course with the assassins dead there was no way to prove his supposition. In all likelihood these assassins didn't know who they worked for anyway, so their deaths were of little importance in this regard. But what to do about his daughter? Was she now the primary pawn in what could become a struggle for control of eastern Caledonia? He would have to think about it a bit more and reach out to the Duke of the Three Rivers and the Duchess of Murcia. Perhaps they could work together to slow the King's suspected plans.

"You may be right, Tarin," said Duke Winborne. "But we do not know for sure. We can only suspect. But that does not mean we can't prepare." Duke Winborne turned quickly, stepping off the balcony and striding through his daughter's damaged bedroom, the pools of dark blood having seeped into the carpets. All of this would be repaired within the next few days with stronger doors placed on the balcony. "But I do know one thing."

"What is that, my Lord?" asked Tarin.

Duke Winborne stopped just beyond the entrance to the balcony, turning back to gaze at both Sirius and Tarin before responding.

"That my decision to buy the boy and make him Aislinn's Protector was the right one. He did his job, and he did it well."

11

AN IMPORTANT LESSON

Aislinn stepped back on the hard ground, right foot in front of the left, balanced on her toes, blade held in front of her in a blocking position. She ignored the strands of sweaty hair sticking to her forehead and threatening to drop into her eyes as she turned slowly, watching her attacker. Wary. Waiting. Expectant.

"Eyes always on your opponent, Lady Aislinn," said Tarin, the Captain of the Guard, who circled her slowly and observed her form with a critical eye.

For several years she had been training regularly with the Battersea Guard. Now, Tarin was the only soldier with the quality to match her. So he had become her personal weapons instructor by default.

Tarin lunged forward, his training sword sweeping down in a high arc toward her collarbone. A killing blow if it landed, though not with the dull swords wrapped in heavy cloths that were used on occasion in the training circle to prevent injury. Though Tarin wouldn't have been concerned even if they were using real blades. The girl was fast, perhaps even faster than he was.

Aislinn proved him right, bringing her sword up and allowing the two pieces of covered steel to meet and slide away from each other, then she stepped back immediately to put some distance between her and her opponent. Smart as well, he had to concede. She only needed to see or be told something once to learn it. Two excellent and necessary attributes to succeed as a fighter, but she wasn't as strong as he was. So whenever Tarin tried to profit from his innate advantage, Aislinn attempted to prevent him from getting too close.

Aislinn had been training for several hours every day since the incident with the assassins. When her Protector had burst into her suite, at first, she had been shocked, upset, even outraged. Ignoring her, the former gladiator had charged into her bedroom and demonstrated a competence with the blade that was both fascinating and frightening. He had taken on four trained assassins and won. Yes, she had helped, eliminating the injured assassin who attempted to rise from the carpet and attack him from behind. But she could tell that the assassin she dispatched had little strength remaining, her Protector having already mortally wounded the man.

Still, with barely a thought she had grabbed her sword and finished him, driving the sharp blade into his chest. Her instinctive action had stunned her for a moment, a feeling of coldness seeping into her body. She had never killed anyone before, and even the fact that this assassin was bent on killing her didn't prevent a wave of nausea from sweeping through her. She wanted to become a fighter, a warrior, someone who could protect herself and could be trusted to protect others, yet she didn't seem to have the stomach for what she had done, and that dismayed her.

"Focus, Lady Aislinn!" Tarin shouted at her, recapturing

her attention. "Daydreaming during combat leads to only one end."

Angry at herself for losing her concentration, Aislinn redoubled her efforts. Glimpsing an opening, she lunged forward, blade leading, as she tried to slice across Tarin's right side. She quickly adjusted when he sidestepped her assault, bringing his sword down in a backhanded blow that was directed at her head and would have left her dizzy and on the ground if it had struck. But it didn't. Anticipating how Tarin would react to her attack, she rolled across the hardened dirt, regained her footing, and assumed her defensive posture, ready for Tarin's next assault.

The Guards watching cheered the move, which sent a small bolt of energy through Aislinn. Perhaps all the training was being put to good use after all, as Tarin had yet to score a hit on her. But she was still disappointed with herself. No matter what she tried, she had yet to break through the Captain's defenses on this day or those preceding.

"A good attempt, but not good enough," said Tarin. "You need to put your opponent down quickly. Combat is not a long, drawn-out affair. It has to be fast, because the longer it takes for you to kill your opponent, the more likely it becomes that your opponent kills you." Driving the tip of his practice sword into the dirt, Tarin wiped the sweat from his brow, then walked toward the water bucket. "A short break."

Aislinn growled in annoyance, her frustration plain. Tarin was right, of course. But no matter what she tried, he always evaded her attacks. She wandered over toward the far wall, seeking the little bit of shade to be found in the courtyard. It wasn't until she was leaning her back against the cool stone that she realized that she was standing right next to her Protector. She hadn't even known he was there, as he seemed to have blended into the shadows. That wasn't really true, actually. She didn't know he was right next to her, but she could tell that he was close. He was always close. Always in her head. Her thoughts quickly worked her initial irritation into a burning anger. Feeling the need to lash out, she sought a target for her rage.

"I could have beaten Tarin already. I should have beaten Tarin. But I can't. Not with you here," she said, pointing to her head, "always in the back of my mind. I don't want you there, but you're always there. I want you out of my head. I want you out of my life. I just want you gone. I don't need you. I don't want you here."

As her heated words tumbled out of her, a small voice in the back of her mind kept telling her that without her Protector, she would have died a few days ago, but she chose to ignore that fact.

Bryen stared at her, his eyes narrowing. He didn't feel the need to reply as she vented.

"Always there. No matter where I am, no matter what I'm doing, you're there. Always. I want you gone," she hissed.

Aislinn took a step farther along the wall, sensing in her own mind Bryen's rising fury. His eyes flashed, and his fists were clenched, his body tense. She realized once again just how dangerous her Protector actually was, a sense of barely repressed violence radiating from him.

"I don't want to be here either. I don't want you inside my head either. But you are. And there's nothing that I can do about it." Bryen said it quietly but with a passion that startled her. "We both face the same problem."

"You didn't choose to be here?" asked Aislinn softly, all her anger slipping away as she realized how badly she had been behaving. "You didn't seek this as a way out of the Colosseum?"

"No, I didn't."

Aislinn nodded, making a gesture with her free hand to suggest that she was offering an apology. Now it was Bryen's turn to be surprised as he felt a wave of sympathy emanating from his charge, but he chose to ignore it. He had little forgiveness within him. The silence between them dragged on, and Aislinn began to fidget as she became more uncomfortable. Bryen realized that she didn't know what to say next, so he decided to help her by turning the conversation in a more secure direction.

"Are you done making excuses?"

"I'm not making excuses ..."

Aislinn raised her head, her eyes blazing once more, but then she fought to contain a smile. She detected the faint quirk of Bryen's lips as he looked down at her. She realized that in his own way he was trying to help her in her duel with Tarin.

"You're struggling against his lunges today."

"I am," she admitted reluctantly. "Just as I have every time that we've sparred."

"Before he lunges, what does he do with his feet?" Bryen asked, adopting the same pedagogical approach that Declan had used when instructing him on how to fight in the Pit. Declan never offered an answer. At least not directly. Bryen always had to figure it out for himself. So he waited for Aislinn, who was thinking about his question and trying to recall her time in the training circle that morning.

"His right foot pulls back just a bit."

"It does," Bryen replied, pleased that she had identified Tarin's tell. "He does it every time he's preparing to lunge. It helps him be just a bit quicker than he could be without it."

Bryen stepped closer to Aislinn so that no one could hear what he was about to say. "Now having identified his weakness, what are you going to do about it?"

Aislinn smiled for the first time in days, but this time her grin was wolfish. "Use it against him."

"Let's see it, then."

Tarin had returned to the training circle, sword in hand, beckoning for Aislinn to come join him. Once she stepped across the white chalk, she nodded that she was ready. The combat began again, just as all the other ones had. Tarin began to circle Aislinn, his eyes never leaving hers as he searched for an opening. Aislinn stayed on her toes, keeping her balance, gliding in a small circle of her own to match Tarin's movement. Then she saw Tarin's eyes tighten, and she glanced down for just a fraction of a second. She twisted away from the Captain of the Guard as his sword ran through the space where she had just been standing.

"Well done, Lady Aislinn," Tarin murmured, impressed that she had escaped him.

Aislinn continued to track him as Tarin began circling her once more. She forced herself to stay focused. Then it happened again. Aislinn spun away from Tarin, his blade not even coming close to her this time. She had seen it a second time. Tarin pulled his right foot back ever so slightly before he lunged, every time. For the next few minutes the combat continued, Tarin attacking a half dozen times, Aislinn easily evading each assault. She could see that Tarin was beginning to get frustrated. She had never lasted so long against him without the Captain of the Guard getting a touch on her. So she decided that now was the time to turn the tables.

Her eyes remained locked on Tarin as the big man

stepped around her. But this time when he lunged forward, Aislinn didn't step away. Instead, she turned to the side away from Tarin's blade and allowed his momentum to carry him just beyond her. As he slid past, she brought her sword up and scraped the covered steel across his leather jerkin. For a moment, Aislinn couldn't believe it. But then she saw the look of shock on Tarin's face, and she could hear the hoots and hollers coming from the Guards who had been watching. She wanted to scream with joy. To exult in the fact that she had finally scored a point against the Captain of the Guard. But she pushed down her impulses and simply resumed her defensive stance, expecting Tarin to come at her again.

"Enough," said Tarin, lowering his training sword. He appeared to be pleased and surprised, and perhaps even a little disappointed in himself. "You've been at it all morning, Lady Aislinn. We can begin again tomorrow."

Aislinn nodded her agreement. She was tired, but in a good way. The last week she had spent on the training ground she had wanted to prove a point, more to herself than anyone else. She felt good about what she had accomplished just now, not only holding her own against Tarin, but also finally gaining a touch on him. But something still bothered her from the attack a few nights before, self-doubt circling in the back of her brain.

She had killed the wounded assassin, but the others in the room she had left to her Protector. Yes, he was exceedingly competent and didn't seem fazed by the odds, but should she not have assisted him in some other way? Should she not have joined the fight sooner? Instead, she had watched from the doorway, taking in the spectacle before her, marveling at her Protector's speed and forbearance, before she had engaged at a critical moment.

"Thank you, Tarin, for your time and that of your Guards this morning."

"You're welcome, Lady Aislinn. Remember to stay focused. One slip is all it takes."

"I'll remember, no need to worry about that."

Feeling somewhat annoyed because the Lady Winborne had gotten the better of him, Tarin felt the need to rebuild his confidence and his standing with his soldiers, so he turned his attention to Aislinn's Protector.

Bryen stood in the shade of the wall, able to see the entire training ground and anyone entering or exiting. His eyes were sharp, his hand never far from the hilt of his sword. He looked like he could spring into action like a wolf leaping onto his prey. Though he hated the task forced upon him by Duke Winborne, Bryen took Declan's words to heart: "Everyone dies. Not everyone dies with honor." After the incident with the assassins, Bryen had adopted a slightly refined perspective on his new life. This new task really was no different than what he did in the Colosseum. It was simply a different environment. Kill or be killed. Whatever was to happen, he would honor his former instructor and his teachings.

"The boy seems competent, Lady Aislinn. But is he?"

"What do you mean, Tarin?"

"The boy is a slave from the Pit. Yes, he was successful a few nights ago. But were these supposed assassins truly competent?"

"Tarin, I assure you ..."

Tarin ignored Aislinn, walking toward Bryen, stopping only when their noses were inches apart, though Tarin had to crane his neck to look up into Bryen's cold grey eyes. The Captain of the Guard spoke quietly, but understood that because of the acoustics his voice would carry to all in the courtyard.

"You look like a fighter, boy, but are you? Would you survive a combat with a real soldier? One who knows what it means to kill? What it means to survive no matter what must be done? Or are you just a ..."

Tarin's taunting continued, but Bryen barely heard it. Taller than the Captain of the Guard, he looked down at the soldier. His hand gripped the hilt of his sword tightly, and he had to will himself to remain calm. He knew that Tarin was trying to goad him. But Bryen didn't have to make it easy for him. So he attempted to show absolutely no emotion. As Tarin's taunts worsened, his Guards, arrayed behind him, began to laugh, joining in the fun and offering a few of their own insults. Bryen ignored them, his focus on the Captain, eyes hardening as he fought to control his rising anger. He had faced worse in the Pit, many of his opponents seeking to get his blood up with the hope that he would make a mistake as a result. Responding in any way only benefited his adversary, but he still didn't have to like it.

"But there's nothing that you can do, is there, boy?" challenged Tarin. "Protector in name, you're still a slave. I can see that you want to pull that sword and prove what you are. But you can't, can you? The collar prevents it. Lucky for you, boy. Lucky for you, indeed. I wonder what you would have done if you ever had faced a real fighter in the Pit."

"I grant him permission to spar against you, Tarin," shouted Aislinn, silencing the Guards who had joined in the taunting. She had seen the ire behind her Protector's eyes and could feel it building within him. Though she was not happy that he was her Protector, he had saved her life while risking his own, and he certainly deserved better than this.

Tarin smiled at the announcement, pleased that he had

achieved the result that he wanted. "Well, then. Let's see what you've got, boy."

Tarin stepped backward into the training circle, his own sword now in his hand. Not a training sword. Silence had descended in the yard, the only sound coming from the scraping of the Guards' feet in the dirt as they shuffled away to make a path for the Protector. He looked at Aislinn for a moment. She nodded, hoping that her Protector took it not as permission, but as a show of support. Then, for the first time since arriving in Battersea, Bryen smiled wolfishly. The collar around his neck felt lighter. He felt lighter. Pulling the blade from his scabbard, he strode confidently toward Tarin.

As Tarin watched the Protector approach, taking in the self-assurance of his stride and the sharp focus in his dead eyes, he wondered if he had made a mistake in taking this chance. But he didn't have time to ponder the thought any more deeply, because the boy was on him in an instant.

Bryen attacked with a ferocity that shocked the watching Guards, the speed of his assault astounding them. Many observed with their mouths hanging open, awestruck as Bryen slashed, lunged, and cut, spinning, twisting, gliding around the ring, his movements so compact and smooth he appeared to be dancing across the hard ground as he attacked the Captain of the Guard. It was all that Tarin could do to defend himself, as multiple times he barely got his blade up to parry one of the Protector's strikes in a desperate attempt to ward off the boy's unceasing assault. The sound of steel on steel became a constant, rapid staccato, and through it all Tarin had no opportunity to attack. He had no choice but to focus his full attention on defending himself, and even that was growing more and more challenging.

It was over quickly. In less than a minute, Bryen had

forced the Captain of the Guard to the ground, knocking his sword from his grasp. Bryen stared down implacably at his adversary for just a moment, Tarin seeing not only the anger in the former gladiator's eyes, but also the lack of mercy. Then Bryen swung his sword down toward Tarin's exposed neck. A loud gasp broke out from the assembled crowd of soldiers, stunned first at the ease with which this boy had defeated the best fighter in the Duchy and then as they watched the Protector prepare to deliver the final blow.

"Stop!" shouted Aislinn, fearing that the worst was about to happen, but she had no reason to be afraid.

Rather than bring his sword down onto Tarin's neck, Bryen deftly twisted his wrist and eased the blade back into its scabbard. Then, he reached down with his other hand, offering to help the Captain of the Guard back to his feet. Tarin smiled, glad that he had been right about the boy, though he realized now that he had taken a terrible risk by doing what he had just done.

Tarin stood with Bryen's assistance, then began flicking the dirt from his uniform. "Back to it, lads and lasses," he said to the surrounding Guards. "You've seen what this Protector can do with your own eyes. The stories about the Volkun running free in the Pit don't do him justice."

The Guards responded quickly to Tarin's command, speaking softly as they returned to their stations to continue their training, many eyeing the Protector with a newfound respect. Several quietly howled like a wolf as they walked away, having heard some of the stories about the boy Protector and pleased to now have them confirmed.

Satisfied that he had accomplished what he had set out to do, Tarin turned his attention to Bryen. "Well done, boy. I had my doubts about you coming from the Pit. I didn't think a slave could fight better than a soldier. But I see that in your case I will need to revise my opinion."

Bryen stared at the Captain of the Guard with a hard glare, then twisted his lips into a brief grin before resuming his normally stoic appearance. He nodded to Tarin, who nodded back. They had just reached an agreement, though Aislinn didn't realize it. Tarin was much like Declan, Bryen realized. A hard man, but someone to be trusted if you earned their respect. Bryen understood now what Tarin had done.

The Captain of the Guard wanted to make a point to his soldiers, and his short combat with Bryen had done so quite effectively. The Guards had assumed that the stories about the gladiator and his exploits in the Pit, as well as what he had done to prevent the assassination of Lady Aislinn, had grown with each telling and that this Protector was likely no more than an ornament. All those who had watched the combat with Tarin now realized that, if anything, the tales spreading through the Broken Citadel about this young Protector were more subdued than they should be. Moreover, the stories of what had just happened would spread quickly, much to Tarin's delight. For he had done this with a purpose in mind. It gave Bryen the respect that he deserved and would increase the likelihood that, if it came to it, the Guards would fight with him on equal terms, accepting him as a comrade in arms, and thereby strengthening the protection that Lady Aislinn clearly needed.

Tarin still didn't like the fact that Duke Winborne had brought the gladiator to Battersea, and he couldn't say that he necessarily liked the Protector, but regardless he would use all the tools at his disposal to achieve his mission as Captain of the Guard, something that he viewed as essential after the earlier conversation with Sirius and the Duke about the assassins' use of Dark Magic.

Aislinn stalked over, her eyes flashing with unexpected pride.

"As you have now seen, Tarin, he is not a boy. He is my Protector."

Aislinn stopped in front of the entrance to her suite, the carpenters having strengthened the frame and replaced the doors that Bryen had kicked in so easily with a heavy oak that was several inches thick.

"What were you doing against Tarin?" she asked, turning her gaze to her somewhat surprised Protector. In all the time that they had been forced to spend together since Bryen arrived, this was the first instance in which she had spoken to him directly in a voice that didn't contain condescension or irritation.

Not sure what Aislinn was asking, he responded simply. "Fighting."

"Yes, but I've never seen anything like that before. Where did you learn to fight that way?"

"I had no choice but to learn, Lady Winborne. I was forced into the Pit. If I didn't learn to fight, I would have died. Declan taught me. But I learned from the other gladiators as well. I watched them in training and on the white sand. Anything that would help me survive, I took as my own."

Aislinn nodded in understanding, finally raising her eyes to meet his own. "You could have killed Tarin."

"Yes."

"But you wouldn't have."

"No. He didn't deserve to die despite his insults."

"And is that what it comes down to for you when fighting? Whether your opponent deserves to die?"

"I would like that to be the case, but that's just a wish. That wasn't the case in the Pit. It isn't the case here."

"What do you mean?" asked Aislinn, intrigued by his comment.

"In the Pit it's simple. Kill or be killed. Here, it's to protect you at all costs. Whether I want to or not."

Aislinn was going to say more, but then bit her lip, taking a few seconds to think. "Tomorrow morning, first thing, we will go to the training yard. You're my new weapons instructor. I want to learn all that you know."

Bryen nodded, not really having a choice in the matter to begin with, but at least it would give him an opportunity to do something that he enjoyed. He turned and walked toward his room, but Aislinn's last words before entering her suite made him stop.

"Thank you for protecting me ... Bryen."

12

A NEW BATTLE

Duke Winborne stood under the stone arch leading to the practice ground, the sun slowly stirring in the east, its bright yellows and reds joining with the Silent Sea as if the ball of light emerged from its depths. He had a habit of rising early and wandering the Broken Citadel. It gave him some peace and quiet before the start of his usually hectic schedule. It also gave him a chance to talk quietly with those members of his household who started their work before the day began for most. Yet he had never expected his daughter to be one of them. He had heard that she had begun training with her Protector at the crack of dawn. He found it hard to believe, as she generally took her time in the morning, preferring to sleep in. So watching her dance across the training circle trying to avoid her pursuing Protector first surprised him and then pleased him.

What's more, soldiers filled the training ground, watching the session or working on their own or with their compatriots. Tarin had explained what had happened when he dueled with the Protector and the purpose behind his challenge. From Kevan's perspective, it was a smart move. But neither one had expected this to be the result.

Word of the combat between the young Protector and the Captain of the Guard had quickly spread throughout the Battersea Guard. Those who hadn't been there wanted to see the Protector in action for themselves, and having learned of the early morning practice sessions, had taken the opportunity to discover what this former gladiator could do with a blade. Impressed, many of the soldiers had begun to show up every morning, arriving just before dawn much like the Protector, knowing that the Lady of the Southern Marches would arrive shortly thereafter.

On this morning, Bryen's charge was acquitting herself well. Although they had only been training together for a week, Bryen believed that her movement already was better, faster, and more intuitive than what he had seen when she dueled with Tarin. As Aislinn glided around the training circle, catching her Protector's strikes on her blade or dodging out of the way, he maintained a steady barrage of blows, forcing her to adjust constantly to a new attack, all designed to make her defensive actions more a part of her so that she could rely on her instincts rather than having to think about what to do next. As Declan had explained to Bryen when he had first started fighting in the Pit, the more you had to think about what you were going to do in a combat, the more time you gave your opponent to kill you.

Bryen darted forward, feinting a lunge then swinging low with his blade for Aislinn's legs. Caught by surprise, she almost fell, stumbling at first but regaining her balance and leaping over the strike with barely a whisker to spare.

"Good recovery," said Bryen. "But faster. You must be faster. Don't watch the blade, watch my core. Where my core goes, the blade goes."

Aislinn scarcely had time to register her Protector's instructions as he continued his attack, his sword a blur of steel. She had been on the defensive for almost an hour. Her arms were tired, her legs felt like jelly, yet there was no slackening in her Protector's assault. He wasn't even breathing hard, and that annoyed her. So she dug deep, seeking some hidden reserve of strength that she didn't know she had, to continue in the combat. One sided though it may have been, she refused to falter or surrender. Gritting her teeth and ignoring the exhaustion that threatened to overwhelm her, she lost herself in the clash of steel on steel as she moved around the circle, always keeping her Protector to her front.

Aislinn's swift recovery pleased Bryen. She learned quickly, and she was determined. Continuing his attack, varying his positioning and the angles of his lunges and jabs, he kept Aislinn on her toes, forcing her to do nothing more than defend herself, which was his goal. Though he didn't want to be here in Battersea, he did enjoy his new training ritual, thankful that Aislinn's quarters were so close to this part of the fortress so that he wouldn't experience the disabling pain of the collar if he wasn't within the required distance. And it provided him with the opportunity to watch the sun rise as it turned the sea into a blazing orange for just a few moments before it escaped the water's grasp entirely and took its place in the sky, something that he could never have experienced in Tintagel.

Early morning and late at night were the only times of the day that Bryen had to himself, when he wasn't trailing his charge like a guard dog wary of any threat that might come her way. He understood now after his combat with the four assassins that the threat was real, so he took his responsibility seriously, but the collar chafed, every second of the day, a constant reminder that he remained a slave. As a result, he valued the few moments of his day that belonged to him, the training ground deserted and giving him a chance to work through the daily training regimen that had been a part of his life since he had entered the gladiators' compound.

The work was intense and demanding, and Declan had been a stickler, requiring the very best of him. Admittedly, in the beginning, he had resented the Master of the Gladiators, but Bryen had learned quickly that there was a purpose to his ultimatums, his constant criticisms, his requirement that Bryen perform each movement exactly as instructed. Declan was training him to live, and over time Bryen had come to enjoy his workouts, understanding their value and that they were a gift from his irascible father figure.

But he had not expected what had occurred after his short duel with Tarin. In addition to the Lady Winborne requiring that he assume responsibility for her martial training, Guards had begun to join him on the training ground before she arrived. At first just a handful, then a dozen, and then several dozen. During the first few days they didn't speak to him. They just watched him. For a time he felt like a caged animal, such as those put on display outside the Colosseum before they were forced to fight in the Pit.

It had bothered him in the beginning. But then he realized that after the Guards had watched him for a while, they would pair off and try to imitate his actions. From the corner of his eye he tracked their efforts, some doing quite well, others failing miserably. He could have ignored them, simply left them to it, but despite his bitterness at his fate, he realized that more of Declan had rubbed off on him than he had expected because he had the almost uncontrollable urge to correct their mistakes.

The next morning he had asked if any of the Guards would be willing to spar with him. Silence had descended on the training ground, and it was only lifted when a soldier with an easy smile who was almost as tall as Bryen had stepped forward. Introducing himself as Jerad, a mop of curly black hair on his head, the soldier knew what to expect, having watched the Protector for several days. But he didn't mind the catcalls and laughter as Bryen put him through his paces, Jared laughing it all off. He wanted to learn and Bryen could help him do that.

The next day, several other soldiers asked Bryen if they could spar with him, understanding the value of the experience. The day after, Bryen put all the Guards who appeared in the early morning through a training session, then they broke out into pairs or small groups to practice what they had learned. That approach had continued since then, and each morning more soldiers of the Battersea Guard who were not on duty participated. And every time Bryen asked for his first sparring partner, Jerad stepped forward. Bryen had learned that the curly haired soldier had a fun-loving approach to life, but when it came to matters of the blade, he was deadly serious.

"Stay with me. Stay focused. Do not let your concentration lag."

Aislinn immediately redoubled her efforts, realizing that she was close to slipping. Her Protector's blade continued to move through the air in a blur. He forced her around the training circle, his eyes bright, his mind focused. She sought to emulate him, but her exhaustion increased each time their swords clashed. Despite the length of their contest, he still didn't appear to be winded, and that only escalated her aggravation. She used her vexation to push herself a bit harder.

"You are doing well," said Bryen. "Now let us finish this. Find the opening I give you, then take it."

This is how their sparring always ended. Bryen would provide her with an opportunity to attack, but she had to recognize it first and then take advantage of it. So far, she had not yet succeeded. Thinking back on her failure, she grew even more vexed. But she knew that emotion wouldn't benefit her now. It would only lead to distraction.

Instead, she chose another direction, seeking that calm place as she did when training with Sirius. It was difficult to do, almost impossible with her needing to defend herself from her Protector's unceasing assault, but she willed herself to try. And for a brief moment she succeeded. The calm and focus she achieved when working with the Magus settled over her, and then she saw it. The opening she sought. Twisting her wrist, she turned the blade so that during Bryen's next attack his steel slid off of hers, then she slashed quickly with a backhand cut, trying to take him in the side that he had exposed.

"Yes!" shouted Bryen, pleased that his charge had found the opening, the first time that she had done so. But before the blade could strike him, he turned a half step, bent at the knees, and launched himself over her, spinning in the air and landing slightly behind her. With his free hand he grabbed Aislinn's sword hand, preventing her from turning into him and carrying through with a slash that would have sliced through his stomach.

Shocked by what Bryen had just done, as were many of the Guards watching the combat, Aislinn lost her concentration, slipping away from that place that had sharpened her focus. Jabbing the point of her sword into the hard dirt, she placed her hands on her knees and sucked in as much air as she could. Every muscle in her body burned.

"How did ..." she began, but she needed to take in more air before continuing. "How did you do that? I've never seen its like."

"It was something I learned in the Pit," responded Bryen. Pulling her sword from the earth, he wiped the blade on his pants leg to remove the dirt, then handed it back to her hilt first. "You saw the chance."

Aislinn smiled, too pleased with herself to grow angry at her inability to maintain her concentration. "Yes. I almost had you."

Bryen nodded, agreeing with her. "Remember that there will always be an opening, no matter how skilled your opponent. You found that opportunity despite the fact that you had fought defensively the entire time we were in the circle. I didn't give you the chance to attack. Most other fighters you encounter won't have the patience for such an exercise. So use that to your benefit. Don't be afraid to let a taller or stronger opponent waste their energy in attack. Then, when you see your chance, take it quickly. Finish them."

Aislinn nodded, thankful for the advice. "I didn't finish you."

"No, but perhaps next time." Bryen smiled, then nodded behind her, deciding to walk over to a cluster of soldiers who had broken out into sparring partners. "You have a visitor."

Aislinn turned, surprised to see her father striding across the practice ground. The soldiers he passed paid their respects, then quickly returned to their training.

"Tarin told me what happened," Kevan said, a smile creasing his lips. His daughter's skill with the blade impressed him.

"Tarin brought it on himself," she replied.

"Yes, he did, and other than Tarin who knew this would be the result?" His gaze tracked the many soldiers being put through their paces by a gladiator. The Protector had begun wandering around the training yard, offering advice here and there, adjusting a soldier's grip, ensuring another maintained her balance while attacking. And every one of the Guards, many decades-long veterans, accepted his advice and suggestions without pause or question. All this in a matter of days. "I can understand why you're training with the boy."

"Bryen."

"Excuse me?"

"His name is Bryen, father. He may be my Protector, but his name is Bryen."

Kevan studied his daughter for a long moment, not sure what to make of her correction. Was it a good thing or bad? He didn't know. When he had made the boy her Protector, he understood her anger. But that wasn't his primary concern. He needed to protect her as best as he could. The attack of just a few weeks ago had proven that his decision had been the right one. Clearly since then Aislinn's perspective on her Protector had changed, at least a bit. Kevan viewed his daughter's willingness to correct him as a positive. It took courage, and she would need that if she were to assume responsibility for the Southern Marches at the appropriate time. And it was that question that now played through his mind. Would she have that opportunity? Could he ensure that Aislinn took his place when he was gone?

"What's on your mind, father. I can tell when something is bothering you."

Kevan's smile grew. Aislinn interpreted his moods better

than anyone. "There is something that we need to discuss. Should we return to your quarters?"

Aislinn shook her head. "No. The soldiers like to have Bryen put them through their paces, and there's still time before they need to assume their duties. I'd like to watch for a while. You never know what you might pick up."

"True," said Kevan, impressed by her diligence. He guided his daughter to one of the benches pushed up against the courtyard wall, allowing them to view what was happening on the training ground as well as the slowly rising sun as it made its way above the sparkling sea. "We need to discuss what happened in Tintagel."

Aislinn grunted that she had heard, but her gaze remained locked onto Bryen. He had returned to the training circle, now facing four soldiers who had arrayed themselves against him, each one deciding to take a place at a point on the compass. As the northernmost soldier attacked, Bryen charged forward to meet him, quickly knocking his blade away, before turning and sprinting toward the southernmost soldier, who clearly looked surprised and had not expected such a tactic.

"Marden asked for your hand in marriage," said Kevan, choosing to not beat around the bush.

"What?" Aislinn's shout caught the attention of the soldiers training closest to them. Bemused by the expression of shock that played across her face, and the anger that soon replaced it, they immediately returned to their own tasks.

"You can't say that you haven't considered the possibility," said Kevan. "You know the politics as well as I do."

"I have considered the politics," replied Aislinn. "But I've never considered marrying that pompous jackanapes."

"Be that as it may, he is the King of Caledonia."

Aislinn turned on her father. "Do you expect me to marry him?"

"Of course not," said Kevan. He sighed heavily. "But we are in a difficult position."

Her gaze went back to the training circle. In just a few minutes, the combat was over. Aislinn had a chance to see Bryen disarm the last soldier, the other three already forced to leave the circle, with a quick thrust that deftly became an upward slash, pushing her off balance. Instead of reveling in his victory, Bryen gathered together the four soldiers who had sparred with him, as well as the handful who had been watching, and started to explain how he had approached the combat. He demonstrated the various grips and movements that he had used, and no doubt he talked of his strategy. Several of the attending Guards sought to imitate his movements. Then five more soldiers entered the circle, one defending, four attacking, with Bryen walking around the circumference and offering advice or admonishment once the sparring began.

Aislinn turned her mind back to the issue at hand, concentrating on the politics, on what Marden hoped to gain. Her father had taught her well, so she understood the real implications of the request.

"He's not interested in me, father. He's interested in what I can give him."

"I know."

"If I marry him, he can do whatever he wants. He'll have me. He'll have the Southern Marches and Battersea." She chose not to mention that upon her marriage to Marden, her father would become a liability to the King of Caledonia. She was certain that the thought had already crossed his mind. "And if he gains the Southern Marches ..."

"I know," her father repeated, not needing Aislinn to complete her reasoning.

"How much time were you able to buy?"

Kevan leaned forward, settling his arms on his knees, his eyes taking in the churning waves of the Silent Sea. When he was a child, his father would take him out onto the water, teaching him how to sail, making sure that he understood the dangers of the many hidden rocks that lay in wait near the entry to Battersea harbor, as well as the many sea creatures that could take a sailor to their doom if their boat capsized too far from shore. Though his mother had feared for him every time he went out onto the water with his father, it had been one of his favorite experiences when he was young. The sea air gusting around him, the salt spray covering his face, his father laughing next to him as they battled the waves. And now a new battle approached, one he had not yet identified the right strategy for fighting.

"Until the Fall Council."

"Then what do we do?" asked Aislinn, trying to keep her burgeoning fear from her voice.

"I don't know."

13

A VISITOR

"Duke Winborne."

The Duke of the Southern Marches looked up from the papers covering his desk that he had been reviewing, enjoying the cool breeze from the Silent Sea drifting through the open windows of his library and the play of the sun through the stained glass of the skylight. Jerad, the tall sergeant with the ready smile who served as Tarin's second in command, stood before him.

"Yes, Jerad."

"A message from the Duchess of Murcia."

Kevan went back to the documents spread out before him. "You can drop the note on the table over there. I'll take a look at it later."

"Well, about that, Duke Winborne," said Jerad, clearly uncomfortable. "The message is of a more personal nature."

Kevan removed the glasses that had been perched on his nose, an unwilling but necessary accommodation as he got older, and placed them on the desk atop his papers. He took a deep breath, pushing away his growing irritation. It was early morning, the sun barely up. His favorite time of the day, in fact, when he could get done what needed doing before anyone could bother him with all the challenges and issues that arose unexpectedly on a daily basis and required his attention.

"Personal or official business, it doesn't matter, Jerad. Just place the message over there. I'll get to it after I finish this."

Jerad had been the first to spar with the young Protector, unafraid to take on someone obviously more adept in the martial arts. He knew that doing so would allow him to improve his own skills with the blade, despite the expected embarrassments and mistakes that would occur during the process. That didn't bother him. It was all a part of learning. Moreover, rushing into a skirmish with ocean raiders had never bothered him. During that first charge, before steel met steel, he felt an exhilaration that he had never experienced at any other time in his life. But now, in a library no less, he had begun to fidget, becoming increasingly uncomfortable under the Duke's sharp gaze.

"That's not what I meant, Duke Winborne. When I said personal message, I meant a message personally from the Duchess."

"That makes no sense, Jerad." Kevan's exasperation grew, and he struggled to keep it under control.

Jerad realized that the Duke didn't understand, so he took a different tack. "My apologies, Duke Winborne, for not being clear. What I'm trying to say is that the Duchess of Murcia is here in the Broken Citadel, and she would like to see you."

Kevan's irritation evaporated, replaced by a surprising consternation that also mixed with excitement. "She's here? In the Broken Citadel?"

Jerad nodded. "Yes, Duke Winborne. She arrived just a

few minutes ago with a handful of soldiers. I believe she's waiting for you in the training yard."

Kevan rubbed his hands together, whether from nervousness or anticipation he couldn't say. He had been corresponding with Noorsin regularly, sending at least a letter a week on various issues of concern to both Duchies. He had even invited her to come to Battersea, believing that it was the right thing to do to maintain good relations. And if he was honest with himself, he hoped that his efforts could lead to something more. She had never accepted his invitation formally. Yet now she was here?

The Duke of the Southern Marches, normally imperturbable, jumped up from his chair, knocking it backward in his haste and scattering the papers on his desk, some of them drifting to the floor.

"Lead the way, Jerad."

As Kevan exited the library, he continued to rub his hands together, a manifestation of his fight to control his uneasiness. He was responsible for the welfare of the people living in a large portion of Eastern Caledonia, yet he felt as nervous as a young boy being forced to attend his first dance with his greatest fear the likelihood that he would mess up some of the steps.

NOORSIN STELEKEL STOOD in the shade of the wall, watching the activity in the practice yard. A young lady, tall and slim with long hair streaked with auburn and tied into a ponytail, fought in the training circle against an even taller young man. Wiry, strong, and with a deceptive speed, he clearly knew what he was about. Sometimes he pressed the young woman, forcing her to retreat around the circle, his blade whipping around in a blur. Other times he allowed the girl to press him, deflecting her assault and often requiring her to adjust with a quick counterattack of his own. Throughout the engagement he offered quiet instructions to his training partner.

The Duchess of Murcia had not seen the Lady of the Southern Marches for several years, but her memories of her suggested that Aislinn stood before her now, a beautiful young woman with a knack for the blade, and from what Sirius had told her through their correspondence, perhaps a knack for something else as well. Yet what intrigued her even more was Aislinn's instructor. There was something about him that caught her attention, but she couldn't put her finger on it. Before she could think on it more, her host arrived.

"Duchess Stelekel, my apologies for keeping you waiting. I never got word that you would be visiting, so I didn't expect that you would be arriving so early this morning."

Noorsin turned toward the Duke of the Southern Marches, her brilliant smile leading the way.

"That was the point, Kevan," replied Noorsin, ignoring the hand Kevan offered and instead pulling him into a hug. Clearly, he had not expected it, which made her smile even more. When she finally stepped back, she saw that she had flustered him, which pleased her to no end. "And why the formality, Kevan? We have known each other too long for that."

"My apologies, Duch ..." Kevan caught himself. "Noorsin. It is good to have you here in Battersea. But why no warning?"

"Where's the pleasure in life without a few surprises? Besides, I wanted to travel quickly with just a few soldiers.

Not having to go through the trials and tribulations of orga-
nizing a diplomatic delegation allowed me to do that."

"Of course," said Kevan.

Noorsin's eyes had caught him. Sharp, like the eyes of a
raptor, he found it hard to look away. He wondered if he
really wanted to, the blue swirls captivating him. The
Duchess of Murcia was an exceedingly beautiful woman,
but what really appealed to him was her intelligence.

"Duchess Stelekel, it is good to have you at Battersea."
Aislinn Winborne walked up with a confident step, sliding
her sword into its scabbard with one hand and wiping the
sweat from her brow with the other. "I would offer a better
welcome, but I don't want to impose upon you after my
training session."

"Don't be ridiculous, child. Come here." Despite the
sweat and grime, Noorsin pulled Aislinn in for a hug.
Noorsin had never had any children of her own, but the
time she spent with Aislinn over the years was always a
pleasure and made her wonder whether her decision to not
marry had been the right one. It had proven useful for her
Kingdom, but had it for her?

Noorsin stepped back from Aislinn, maintaining her
grip on the girl's shoulders as she surveyed her from head to
toe. "You have grown, child. And you're even more beautiful
than the last time I saw you."

"You're too kind, Duch ..." Aislinn stopped herself upon
seeing the Duchess shake her head. "Noorsin. Are you
well?"

"I am, indeed, child. And you look exceedingly well,"
said Noorsin, motioning to the training circle where
Aislinn's opponent now stood with several soldiers who
were working their way through various forms and exer-

cises. "And dangerous. I didn't know you were so skilled with the blade."

Aislinn beamed at the praise. "Thank you. I have been working at it. Will you be with us long?"

"I will be staying as long as needed," Noorsin replied cryptically. "We have much to discuss, do we not, Kevan?"

"We do," replied Kevan, having clasped his hands behind his back upon realizing that he seemed to be continuing to act like a nervous schoolboy.

Aislinn was amused by her father's reaction. She had never seen him in such a state before. "Then I'll see you later today, Noorsin. I need to get back to my training."

Noorsin watched the Lady of the Southern Marches jog back to the training circle, rejoining the group and jumping right into the exercises the others engaged in. For a moment, she stared at the tall young man apparently in charge, the one who had sparred with Aislinn. She noticed the sunlight flash against the silver collar around his neck. That discovery set her mind working, not having seen such a device for quite some time.

"Yes, much to discuss, indeed," said Noorsin. "I am tired from the journey, so I shall rest in my chambers until lunch. I suggest the veranda looking out on the Silent Sea. That space remains available, I assume?"

"It does," Kevan replied quickly.

"Excellent. Then I will see you there at midday."

Noorsin stepped toward Kevan, giving him a quick kiss on the cheek, before she turned and strode away. As she walked into the main hall of the Broken Citadel, Kevan took a deep breath, having almost been knocked over by the whirlwind who was Noorsin Stelekel, the Duchess of Murcia.

~

"You are in a difficult position, Kevan."

"I know. I need options, but very few are coming to mind."

Noorsin and Kevan had enjoyed their lunch on the terrace, looking out over the Silent Sea. They had remained there for several hours, mulling Marden's marriage proposal.

"And he expects a response by the Fall Council?"

"Yes, just a few short months from now. Although as you know the proposal is anything but." Kevan tapped his fingers on his crossed knee, seeking to release some of his pent-up energy. "I could simply decline."

Noorsin smiled. Directness was often best when negotiating, but not when the other side held all the cards.

"Are you prepared for war?" she asked.

"Against the Royal Guard? We could certainly hold our own, but the Southern Marches is not the most populated province of Caledonia. We lack numbers. So if attacked we could defend. But it would be a war of attrition." He leaned forward. Clearly, he had already given this scenario some thought. "We could defend Battersea, and I have more ships than Marden so I don't fear what would come from the sea. But if he brought a large force, he would have free rein in the countryside. I would not take him on in a pitched battle as that would play to his strengths. I would cut at his edges and use the Glen, the Raven Word, and the Deep Wood against him."

"A good strategy," agreed Noorsin. "But perhaps one to hold onto until all other options are exhausted."

"Did you have something else in mind?" asked Kevan.

"As you said, a strategy of last resort if ever there was one. I would prefer to avoid a civil war."

"A great deal of information makes its way through Murcia," said Noorsin. "With all the travelers seeking assistance at the Royal Library and the Royal Medical School, it's often difficult to separate the wheat from the chaff."

"But you do," said Kevan. "In fact, it is one of your unique skills."

"Indeed," said Noorsin, pleased by his compliment. She smiled brightly at Kevan, making sure that her sparkling eyes caught his. "We have been hearing strange stories from travelers coming from the north."

"What kind of stories?"

"Ghoules have been spotted in the Northern Spine."

Kevan looked at Noorsin sharply, not expecting what she had just told him, but not really surprised. The news unsettled him, in part because it confirmed some of his own discoveries, but it made sense. Battersea was not that far from the southern edge of the Spine.

"Do you believe these stories?"

"I have no reason to disbelieve them. Then again, I have no reason to believe them. I have seen no evidence to confirm whether they are true."

"Yet you just shared them with me."

Kevan studied the Duchess of Murcia closely. He knew her well, and he knew how her mind worked. Noorsin was exceedingly intelligent, having the ability to work through problems or challenges in ways that he never could. He also knew that she never raised an issue unless there was a reason behind it.

Noorsin nodded. "The Winter Pass is clear at this time of year and likely will remain so for the next several months until late fall. Therefore, the possibility that Ghoules have breached the Weir is certainly a possibility. So I can't ignore the information, particularly since I can't remember the last time that I've heard the same story and so frequently."

"They might be more than stories," suggested Kevan.

"Why do you say that?"

"We found tracks near the Raven Wood."

"But no sightings?"

"Not yet," confirmed Kevan. "Tell me. What do these stories say?"

"Merchants and their caravans seeking to trade with the miners at the southern border of the Shattered Peaks are being attacked and slaughtered."

"And there is no confirmation?"

"Not yet," said Noorsin, shaking her head. "I sent a letter to Marden asking that he send some soldiers onto the Breakwater Plateau to see if we can learn more."

"And I take it by your expression that he decided that meeting your request was unnecessary."

"Yes," she growled in frustration. "But it wasn't unexpected. So I've asked some of the individuals trained at the Medical School and charged with traveling throughout Caledonia to attempt to discover the truth of these stories. Discreetly, of course."

Kevan couldn't help but smile. He valued the service offered by the healers taught at the Medical School in Murcia who were then sent around the Kingdom to apply their skills to the benefit of the many people who lived in places where medical care was scarce. Yet most did not realize the additional service that these individuals provided. Often, they served as the eyes and ears of the Duchess of Murcia, giving her a network of spies that ran the breadth of Caledonia. He decided not to make that point, believing it would likely only irritate his guest.

"And you believe I can use this information to my advantage?"

"If these stories are indeed true, or even if they can't be confirmed but they continue, you could argue that there's a need to delay the betrothal."

"I must focus my attention on the Southern Marches and the east, ensuring that the Northern Spine from the Eastern River to the Aeyrie is clear of Ghoule raiding packs."

"Yes. A temporary reprieve."

"And perhaps during that time circumstances might change that would allow me to extricate my daughter from a fate that I do not wish to impose upon her."

Noorsin nodded. "Yes, but ..."

"You believe this could only serve as a delaying tactic."

"Yes. A few months at best to confirm the truth of the stories. Marden is not a patient man, and he's not a fool."

"No, he is not. He is an impetuous, spoiled, cruel son of privilege who doesn't know the first thing about ruling Caledonia."

"Such fire, Kevan," said Noorsin, the Duchess of Murcia leaning close to him and giving his thigh a pat with her hand. The wicked gleam in her eye set an alarm off in the back of his brain, his face flushing. He quickly sought to change the subject.

"Simply the truth."

"I agree. But we must remember that with Marden we are also dealing with Tetric. That man makes my skin crawl."

Kevan nodded. "He's a plague on Caledonia, but there is nothing to be done about him now. He's done a masterful job of aiding Marden by keeping the Duchies focused on each other rather than taking a closer look at his and the Crown's activities. Tetric would push Marden to ignore my claim, suggesting that Aislinn going to Tintagel would provide her with added protection and me the peace of mind to follow-through on my responsibilities to defend against the Ghoules if there indeed are Ghoules raiding the Kingdom."

"We don't have to agree with Tetric's assessment," said Noorsin. "But we would have to respond to it."

Kevan sighed in frustration. "As I said when we started this conversation, I have few options, Noorsin. If I can buy just a few more months, I will do it."

"Another possibility comes to mind."

"What might that be?"

"Aislinn continues to train with Sirius, and she takes the Test before the Fall Council."

Kevan pushed himself further forward in his chair until he sat on the very edge, a look of worry crossing his face. Noorsin smiled gently, seeking to soothe his consternation.

"Kevan, you know my abilities in certain areas. I've known for some time about Aislinn's unique skills."

"Then why raise this now?"

"Has Sirius explained the next possible step after Aislinn completes her Test at the Aeyrie?"

14

MORE THAN STORIES

"Come in, Sirius. I know you're skulking about out there." Noorsin smiled when she said the words, understanding that they would irritate him, as that was her intention.

"I was not skulking," growled Sirius as he pushed the curtain aside and stepped out onto the balcony that extended along the suite of rooms Kevan had given to the visiting Duchess of Murcia. "I was preparing to announce my presence."

Noorsin laughed, enjoying the game. "So you say. We have known each other for almost two decades, Sirius. I know you know how to skulk."

"I do not know how to skulk," responded Sirius, allowing his irritation to rise until he realized that Noorsin was leading him on and that he had fallen into an old habit that he hadn't engaged in for quite some time. Then he smiled, fond memories flooding into his thoughts. "You're baiting me. Just like when you were my pupil."

"Of course I'm baiting you." She patted his knee after he sat down next to her, both turning their gaze to the Silent

Sea and listening to the crash of the waves against the base of the keep's eastern wall far below. "I need to have a little fun every once in a while. Though I do have to admit that with you it tends to be too easy."

"Too easy. What are you implying, young lady?"

"I'm implying nothing, Sirius. I am simply stating a fact."

Sirius bit back an angry retort, realizing that he was playing into her hands once again. He took a breath to calm himself. "You were always a difficult child. I see that not much has changed since then. How I survived three years with you as my apprentice I'll never know."

"Sirius, I am the Duchess of Murcia. I have to deal with pompous, self-important people every day, all day. I need to have what little fun I'm allowed when I can. And to your last comment, you would not have survived those three years without me."

"Maybe so," answered Sirius as he settled back into his chair and enjoyed the cool ocean breeze. "It's good to have you here, child. It's good to see you."

Noorsin patted his knee once again, giving him the resplendent smile that had worked so often in the past when she served as his apprentice, usually as her first step in extricating herself from whatever difficulty she had caused him. She had enjoyed her time learning from Sirius. In fact, it was likely the best time of her life. Having completed the Test to become a Magus, her parents had suggested that she seek an apprenticeship with Sirius as there was no immediate need for her to become more involved in the governance of the Duchy. They knew their daughter well and, in particular, her love of learning. More-over, they understood the dangers of using the Talent without the proper instruction, and acknowledging that their daughter was headstrong, likely viewed the apprenticeship as a way to ensure that with the increased knowledge she would gain, she would be less likely to use the Talent in a way that could prove dangerous. Noorsin did like to take risks from time to time, so they hoped that working with Sirius would dampen that inclination.

"It's good to see you, as well."

"Kevan revealed what you told him of the stories of Ghoule raids. Now why don't you tell me why you're really here. It's not because of stories."

Noorsin sighed. Sirius always saw right through her, even when she was younger. She had spent three happy years under his tutelage at the Aeyrie and traveling to many of the other Duchies with him. She had explored her knack for healing with the Talent, quickly becoming one of the best physics in all of Caledonia. And she had refined her skill in the Talent in many other ways thanks to Sirius' instruction, but she had yet to learn how to deceive him, if only just a little.

"They may be more than stories," she replied.

"They may, and I wouldn't be surprised if that proved to be the case what with the tracks that were found by the Raven Wood. We'll know more once the patrols Kevan has sent toward the Northern Spine and to the west return. And your other reason for being here?"

"I had heard about Marden's request of Kevan through my sources in Tintagel. We have been corresponding for some time, so I thought I would visit Battersea to discuss it with him. He had invited me, you know."

"All this way for a conversation? Another letter would have been easier and faster."

"Maybe so, but I can be more persuasive in person than through a letter. Remember that what befalls the Southern Marches befalls all of eastern Caledonia. Kevan is the strongest of the Dukes and Duchesses. If Marden gains the upper hand in this Duchy ...”

“Then with time Murcia and the Three Rivers would fall under Marden’s sway as well,” completed Sirius. “And an impetuous, barely competent boy who is really just a King in name only may become more than that.”

Noorsin nodded. “I can’t afford to let that happen, Sirius. All is well in Murcia, all is prosperous. It’s taken me the better part of a decade to make that happen. I need to protect my people, but my people are not fighters. I have an army that’s barely a tenth of the size of the Royal Guard. So I need to protect my Duchy in other ways.”

“If it comes to it, Kevan will stand with you. Of that I have no doubt.”

“Do you believe so?”

“I know so. And not just because he opposes any expansion of Marden’s power. I believe he has a personal interest as well.”

“What are you implying?” asked Noorsin, the color rising in her cheeks.

“I’m implying nothing, Noorsin. I am simply stating a fact.”

“Touché,” Noorsin chuckled. “All right, yes, I am here for Murcia, but just as much I am here for myself. As I said, all is well in Murcia. Is there any cause for not exploring what might be possible in terms of an alliance between Murcia and the Southern Marches based on something of a more personal nature?”

“Of course not,” replied Sirius. “Just be careful. Kevan has been on his own for quite some time, but that does not mean that some aspects of his past aren’t still fresh in his mind, no matter how interested he may be.”

"Thank you for the advice, my friend. Now beyond this being a social call, why did you decide to check up on me?"

"Always to the point," said Sirius, "just like when you were my apprentice."

"Not always," she replied. "But always with you. There were some days that I wondered whether your distracted professor act was more than an act."

"That's a bit harsh, don't you think?" Sirius huffed in indignation.

Noorsin laughed again, enjoying her former mentor's discomfiture. "Always so serious. You need to laugh more."

"I would if I could. There are too many unknowns, too many new variables on the board. It concerns me."

"You believe the stories about the Ghoules?"

"In every myth ..."

"There is a nugget of truth. Yes, I learned that quickly from you. In fact, I said much the same thing earlier today."

Sirius smiled at the compliment. "I've been in contact with several other members of the Order. They've heard the stories as well. A few have begun exploring the Dark Forest, a few others along the fringe of the Northern Spine where it meets the Breakwater Plateau, just to see if they can learn something that might be of use."

"But no definitive proof."

"No, not yet. Let's hope that remains the case. But hoping ..."

"Doesn't make it real," finished Noorsin. "Another of your sayings that's stuck with me over the years."

"I'm glad that you listened to me at least once in a while."

"I listened to you all the time. I just didn't agree with you all the time."

"Ah, child, I've missed you," Sirius chuckled. "You and your sharp wit."

"I needed to amuse myself somehow," replied Noorsin, her keen eyes glowing brightly. "I'm assuming Tetric is another variable that worries you."

"Yes," replied Sirius, his previous look of humor replaced with one of concern. "He has always worried me. I've known his motivations since we were children, and there has always been something off about him. But for the longest time I thought that was simply who he was. The last time I spoke with him he had changed somehow."

"Changed how?"

"Not only did it seem that something was off with him, but I got a very powerful feeling that something was missing within him. Something important. I know, that doesn't make any sense. But it worries me more than it should for some reason."

"You know Tetric better than anyone else. If you're worried, then we should all be worried."

"Perhaps so."

"Do you believe he's behind Marden's grab for power?"

"Yes, but he's only playing off of Marden. Tetric knows what the boy wants. What the boy doesn't know is what Tetric wants."

"And that's part of what's worrying you as well."

"I don't like not knowing what I don't know."

"More words of wisdom," chuckled Noorsin. "Though a bit confusing."

They sat in silence for a time, watching as the shadows lengthened across the balcony, the sun beginning to set in the west. It brought them back to easier circumstances, as this had been their practice when Noorsin served as Sirius' apprentice, taking the time at the end of the day to enjoy each other's company, drifting in their own thoughts.

"You believe Aislinn is a piece on the board as well," stated Noorsin, breaking the quiet reverie.

"I do," Sirius replied. "She has done well with her training. She has a power within her that is uncommon."

"Stronger than me?"

"No. She's likely as strong as you, though her skills lie in directions other than healing."

"Then why do you worry about her? It sounds like she'll have little difficulty passing the Test."

"I don't worry about that. I have no doubt that she will pass. But she is a driven young woman, headstrong, and she rarely listens to advice the first time."

"Sounds familiar."

"Indeed it does," Sirius responded with a grin. "But for her to reach her full potential, she needs to be surrounded by the right people. If she's forced to go to Tintagel ..."

"And falls under Marden's sway, you fear what might become of her."

"Not Marden," said Sirius, his expression grave. "She can handle Marden."

"Tetric!" Noorsin sat forward, surprised by Sirius' comment, her incisive mind having reached a worrisome conclusion. "He's no longer a member of the Order."

"No, he's not. But that doesn't mean he's relinquished the power that he controls. And I've been wondering based on my last engagement with him whether his interests have turned in a darker, more treacherous direction."

"Do you know for sure?" asked Noorsin.

"No, I simply suspect. It might explain my most current estimation of him. Of course, I could be wrong."

"You're rarely wrong about such things," Noorsin admitted reluctantly.

"Thank you, child. I know how difficult it was for you to say that." Sirius flashed a quick smile so that she knew he was teasing her. "But there's another piece that's leaving me even more perplexed."

"Aislinn's Protector."

"You sensed it as well?"

"I did. There's a power in him, a strength that I could feel as soon as I saw him on the training ground this morning."

Sirius nodded. "There is something about that boy that disturbs me."

"How so?"

"When Kevan required that I collar him, trying to do so took more effort than it should have. I felt a power pushing back. A resistance of some sort. I couldn't identify it."

"Collaring him was the wrong thing to do."

"I had no choice. I had no good reason to disobey Kevan. I need him to trust me, now more than ever. If I lose that my larger task will be made all the more difficult."

"So the boy became a slave for the larger good."

"He was already a slave. He survived in the Pit for a decade. This has to be an improvement in his life."

"From your perspective, perhaps."

Sirius took a moment to think before replying. "You're right. From my perspective. The boy has had a hard life. He didn't deserve this, but I understand why Kevan wanted to make him a Protector."

"A poor decision, in my opinion. But there's nothing to do about it now."

"No, there isn't. What's done is done. But perhaps it's an opportunity," suggested Sirius.

"How so?"

"When it comes to our young Protector, clearly there is more to that boy than meets the eye. With you here, we have an opportunity to try to discern what I might be missing."

"For the good of the Order?" asked Noorsin in a derisive tone.

"For the good of the Order," Sirius confirmed with a sigh.

15

ATTACK

"You were outplayed," said Noorsin, who had slid next to Kevan silently. "Quite well, in fact."

Her touch on his arm sent a beguiling shiver through him. Kevan glanced at the beautiful Duchess of Murcia, who had quickly become an accepted part of life here in the Broken Citadel during her visit. Yes, he had been outplayed, he thought, but in more ways than one.

"It would seem so," replied Kevan.

He had opposed his daughter's desire to join the soldiers tasked with patrolling the north road. He believed that it was too dangerous so soon after the assassination attempt. But he had no good argument to stop her since he had forced the Protector upon her, and the boy clearly knew his way around a blade. Besides, Aislinn still had responsibilities to meet. She and her friends visited the orphanage near the Eastern River every month, bringing supplies, trinkets, and toys to the children. With his daughter not facing a known threat at the moment, Sirius having detected nothing of concern within the vicinity of Battersea, he couldn't keep her from doing her good works as the Lady of the Southern

Marches. And with that many soldiers surrounding her, she should be safe from any danger they may face on the road. Who in their right mind would attack a full company of the Battersea Guard?

Aislinn and her friends had ridden at the front of the column with Tarin as they left, her Protector trailing at the very end of the troop with the last of the soldiers who were now making their way through the gates.

Noorsin's usually sharp gaze had narrowed, much like a falcon upon seeing its prey. Though this young Protector didn't seem to be looking at anything at all, she had no doubt that he took in everything going on around him, and his eyes always returned to Aislinn at the head of the detachment, whether because of the collar or some other connection she couldn't say. She had not yet spoken with the boy, but she felt that she should. There was something about him that intrigued her, and she wanted to discover what that might be. As Sirius liked to say, just the other day in fact, she didn't like not knowing what she didn't know.

Noorsin did not agree with Kevan's decision to make this boy a Protector. She had assumed that the ancient practice had died out, not having heard of another Protector in decades, and she believed that knowledge of this disturbing exercise had simply become a footnote in history. But apparently Kevan was worried enough to put it back into play.

As the last of the soldiers ducked under the portcullis, Aislinn's Protector glanced Noorsin's way, their eyes locking for a brief moment. For just a second, Noorsin felt an unexpected spark of familiarity, as if she knew the boy. That shock of recognition jolted her, though the young Protector simply held her gaze for a moment more before disappearing beneath the raised gate. Interesting. Interesting, indeed. She had not expected this twist to the riddle.

"Are you alright?" asked Kevan.

"Yes, I'm fine," replied Noorsin, turning her sparkling eyes back to Kevan. "Aislinn's Protector seems quite competent for one so young."

"He does seem to be," answered Kevan. "So far he's performed his duties better than I had expected that he would."

"Yes, well, I would hope so in that he doesn't have much choice," said Noorsin, offering a subtle dig and making known her displeasure at the arrangement. But she didn't dwell on it, much to Kevan's relief. What was done was done, and once this was done, there was no way to undo it. Although she would be taking Kevan to task at an appropriate time in the future.

"I would like to speak with this Protector," she continued. "From the stories that I've heard, he has quite a riveting background, and not only because of the legend he created for himself in the Colosseum."

"You're welcome to try," said Kevan. "From what I understand he rarely speaks unless he's working with Aislinn and the Guards on the training ground." With the work in the courtyard returning to normal now that the patrol had left, Kevan offered Noorsin a smile. "Now, could I interest you in some breakfast this morning? Perhaps on the veranda with a view of the Silent Sea?"

"That would be lovely," said Noorsin, smiling brightly and hooking her arm with his. "Lead the way."

A warmth filled Kevan at Noorsin's touch. Walking toward the eastern side of the keep, he realized he welcomed it.

Though Noorsin allowed Kevan to guide her away from the courtyard, her thoughts remained fixed on the young Protector. She knew that she had never seen him before, so why did he seem so familiar? Why did he remind her of two of her long-lost friends?

Upon exiting Battersea, Tarin turned the troop to the northern coastal road. Keeping their horses to a slow but steady trot, the soldiers traveled the league down the highway until they caught the edge of the Glen, a small but dense wood that ran the length of the shore road for several dozen leagues before it met the Eastern River, which flowed from the Bay of the Dead far to the west before ending its long journey in the Silent Sea.

Aislinn, Rebeka, and Emilie rode at the head of the column, enjoying the warm sunlight and strong breeze. Rebeka and Emilie had grown up with Aislinn. Rebeka, dark haired and sharp featured, was quiet and bookish. Emilie, on the other hand, was everything that Rebeka wasn't. Tall, blond, and always with a ready smile, she didn't take life too seriously. These two had stayed close to Aislinn because they offered her a balance and grounding, something that she would need as she assumed more responsibility for the Southern Marches.

Often, the three young ladies urged their horses to a faster pace to gain some distance on the troop, and then they would slow down and allow the soldiers to catch up. Each time Aislinn pushed ahead, her Protector had to break from the column and close the distance to her so that the power of the collar encircling his neck didn't incapacitate him, a concern that didn't seem to cross her mind. Rather Aislinn had worried that she would not be able to go for a ride that morning, not because of her father -- she knew that she could get him to agree -- but because of her Protector.

She didn't know if he could ride a horse having spent much of his life in the Colosseum.

"I fought on horseback in the Pit." As always, her Protector's reply had been short and to the point.

Taking that to mean that it wouldn't be an issue, she had moved forward with her plans. Thinking back on the exchange, she smiled. Her Protector was a man of few words, but at least this time his eyes didn't blaze with fury when speaking with her. That was one change that she had noticed in him now that they trained together and her Protector had an opportunity to spend time with the Guards on the practice ground. He appeared more at ease with his surroundings and his fate. Not accepting of his position, of course. She doubted that would ever happen for either of them. But he seemed more settled at least.

He didn't seem to blame her for his servitude, and she, in turn, had released her initial anger at him, or at least most of it. They both had realized that neither had any control over how they had been brought together, but perhaps they could come to some arrangement that wouldn't be too burdensome for either one. She understood why her father did what he did, but she still viewed it as a mistake and as a reminder of his lack of faith in her ability to protect herself, thus her renewed focus on her martial training after the attack by the assassins.

She was still annoyed with herself, though. She had not leapt into the fray with the abandon demonstrated by Bryen, instead hesitating, frozen with fear at the start until she jolted herself into action upon seeing the wounded assassin attempt to attack her Protector from behind. She told herself that she would never permit that to happen again. She would never again allow her fear to take hold as it did. But was she being honest with herself? When next in

a real combat would she step forward? Or would she hold
back?

She had worried endlessly on these very questions for
the last few weeks, acknowledging that it was a useless
internal debate but one that, try as she might, she couldn't
escape. She wouldn't know how she would react until she
faced a similar situation in the future. Bryen had taught her
a great deal during their early morning training sessions,
and not just about the physical aspects of fighting. The
mental training had proven just as useful. She hoped that
when the time came, she would meet not only her expectations, but her Protector's as well. Pushing to the side these
thoughts and worries that plagued her daily, she tried to
focus on other things.

But she found that to be a challenge as she attempted to
make sense of some unexpected emotions. Aislinn could
sense where her Protector was in the column as they trotted
along the coastal road, though strangely instead of feeling
the anger at his presence that she had grown accustomed to,
she felt some small measure of comfort. That disturbed her.
She assumed it was a natural part of becoming more
attuned to the bond forced upon them both, but she wasn't
certain. So just one more worry for her to add to the rest.

When the midday sun had reached its zenith, Tarin
called a brief halt, the small troop coming to a stop where
the road curled around several large sea stacks that jutted
out of the water, the tide currently separating the rock
formations from the beach. The soldiers settled in for a few
minutes of quiet conversation, several turning their gaze
every few seconds to the young ladies accompanying them.

"Aislinn, you need to take your head out of the clouds,"
said Emilie.

"What? What do you mean?"

"You seem distracted," added Rebeka. "Are you alright?"

"Yes, yes, I'm fine," she replied. "I was just thinking."

"So was I," said Emilie. "But I get the feeling that we're focused on two different things." To make her point, she turned her knowing grin to several of the soldiers who sat nearby, catching the attention of a few and giving them a resplendent smile.

Rebeka rolled her eyes at the comment. Emilie's interest in men was notorious. She seemed to have a new love every other week and was always on the prowl for the next one.

"This isn't an opportunity to find your next conquest," said Aislinn. "We have work to do when we get to the orphanage."

"Why can't I do both?" replied Emilie with a cheeky grin. "All these eligible young soldiers all to ourselves for the next few days. We would be derelict if we didn't take advantage of the opportunity."

"You're incorrigible," said Rebeka with a smile, who preferred a good book to flirting with boys. But Rebeka did have to admit that Emilie was right to a certain extent. Several of the soldiers were quite handsome. Perhaps this was a chance that she had not foreseen. "Then again ..."

"You too, Rebeka?" asked Aislinn with a laugh. "You disappoint me."

Rebeka was not deterred. "I'm simply stating that Emilie does make a good point."

"Yes, I am making an excellent point," confirmed Emilie, who had allowed a handsome young soldier to hold her horse's reins as she settled onto a rock to survey what was going on around them. Her back to the waves crashing against the shore, she was clearly more interested in the soldiers at the moment rather than the impressive view. "Tell me, Aislinn, what have you learned about your

Protector? I think we should throw him into the mix as well."

"I can't believe you're ..."

"You must see it as well," interrupted Emilie. "He might not be the best looking of men, but those scars on his face and neck give him a dash of intrigue and danger, and I can only imagine what the rest of him looks like." The last she said with a suggestive laugh. "He has a ruggedness that all these soldiers have yet to achieve and most likely never will. Do you not find that just the least bit alluring?"

"You're terrible," said Aislinn, though she couldn't stop her smile from spreading.

"Maybe so, but you haven't answered my question," continued Emilie, enjoying her friend's discomfort and seeking to make it worse. "Dangerous, deadly even. Do you not find your Protector appealing?"

"I certainly do," interjected Rebeka. Both her friends stared at her in shock. "What? We all have our different tastes. I like the strong and silent type. Besides, there is something about him that ..."

"Gives you an enjoyable shiver," suggested Emilie with a knowing grin.

"That's it exactly," laughed Rebeka. "And I'm not afraid to admit that I quite enjoy it."

"You two are absolutely shameful. I cannot believe that we are having this conversation."

"Indeed we are, Aislinn, and you have yet to answer the question," Emilie pressed. "Do you not find your Protector attractive?"

Both her friends gazed at her expectantly, knowing that she had no way to escape the trap that Emilie had set. "Fine, I will answer your question." She sighed, taking a moment to gather her thoughts. "The answer is no, I do not find him attractive. I am stuck with him every minute of the day. Even at night I know exactly where he is. I can often tell what he is thinking and feeling, and that's way more than I want to know. Thanks to my father, he is simply a burden that I have to manage. He is no more than that."

"Well, if that's the case," said Emilie, "perhaps you could give him to Rebeka for a little while. She seems more than willing to ease your burden for a time."

UNAWARE OF THE conversation occurring at the head of the column, Bryen stood on the very edge of the road that snaked along the cliffs, ignoring the steep drop of hundreds of feet to the sharp rocks and ocean below. Instead, he stared out across the Silent Sea, watching the rough waves surge in from the horizon and pound the shore. Now he understood how they had come to name the capital of the Southern Marches. Battersea certainly made sense. Taking a deep breath, he enjoyed the taste of the salt air. The quiet and calm outside the Broken Citadel appealed to him after living the better part of a decade in the largest city of Caledonia, a place teeming with people and all the noise, smells, confusion, and disorder that accompanied them.

Closing his eyes, he listened to the waves strike the sea stacks, knowing from his lessons with Declan that the water would continue to wear the massive monoliths down over the millennia, giving them a new and intriguing shape as they did so. Concentrating on only what he could hear, the soldiers and horses around him slowly slid away, pushed behind what he imagined to be a solid screen of glass. Still there, but not.

He had taught himself this trick in the Pit, a way to

center his mind, using it to focus his concentration and allow him to ignore the curses and screams for blood coming from the thousands of spectators who attended the gladiatorial games for the weekly spectacle of gore. Learning this skill had served him well over the years. In addition to giving him the required focus he needed for combat, once he had reached this internal place of quiet and stillness, Bryen always felt an accompanying surge of energy that warmed him. The charge also filled him with some additional strength and endurance, a spark of vitality, but he assumed that was simply how he perceived it rather than it being reality.

Having achieved the calm that he desired, Bryen allowed his mind to wander. He replayed their journey up the northern road, images of the rugged and beautiful coast running through his mind, the tall and closely spaced trees appearing to their left as they continued farther north. A strange feeling had bothered him shortly after they had begun riding along the border of the Glen. Though the trees had been cut back from the coastal road a good hundred feet or more in certain places, the tall sentinels appeared ominous and forbidding to him. At first, he had assumed that it resulted from the appearance of this wood and the shadows and gloom that played between the trees, much as he had heard the stories about the silence and gloom that pervaded the Dark Forest northwest of Tintagel. But as time passed, his uneasiness had grown into a sense of disquiet that was almost tangible.

Some aspect of the Glen didn't feel right, yet he didn't know what. It was almost as if the trees harbored a hidden evil, but what it could be he didn't have any idea, and he could offer no evidence to support his escalating worry. Maintaining his concentration, and continuing to keep everything happening around him closed off, he turned away from the Silent Sea and stared at the Glen. The more he examined the forest, the more he felt as if unseen eyes were looking right back at him. The wood was silent. There was no movement. It appeared as if the birds and squirrels and other small creatures one expected to hear and see scurrying about a grove such as this had disappeared ... or gone into hiding.

Bryen released the calm that had settled within him, though the warmth and the energy of the experience remained. The company of soldiers came back into focus. He started to walk the length of the column, his horse following behind him. He ignored Aislinn and her two friends, the dark-haired one whose name he couldn't remember looking at him with a suggestive interest.

"You all right, Bryen." A tall soldier with dark curly hair now matted to his head by his helmet stood before him.

Bryen stopped abruptly, so intent on his task that he had almost walked right into Jerad, Sergeant of the Battersea Guard and always the first into the training circle with him.

"Yes, thanks," replied Bryen, a smile creasing his lips. It was hard not to smile in response to Jerad's always ready grin. "I just need to talk to the Captain."

"Of course," offered Jerad. "He's up the road before it curves."

"Thanks," replied Bryen, starting to head in that direction, but turning back after just a few steps. "Jerad?" The tall soldier looked at Bryen with a quizzical expression on his face. "Eyes sharp, just like when we're in the training circle," he said, nodding toward the silent sentinels. "Spread the word, would you?"

Rather than asking why, Jerad simply nodded and walked toward the closest knot of soldiers. The Sergeant had learned after so many hours on the practice ground with this young Protector that he had a quality that demanded your respect and trust. So he went off to complete Bryen's request, making sure the soldiers were thinking of more than just their lunch. Bryen had used the saying "eyes sharp" many times during their sessions, and always as a way to suggest that danger approached. Better to listen than not. Soldiers, more than anyone else, hated surprises.

Bryen continued up the road to where Tarin stood by himself. The Captain faced the Glen, staring at the trees, his mind seemingly elsewhere.

"Do you feel it?"

Tarin spun abruptly, surprised that Bryen had taken him unawares. Or perhaps he was so deep in thought that he simply was too distracted. "The Glen?"

"The Glen. It doesn't feel right. Something's off."

"But you don't know what," said Tarin, his eyes once again glued to the trees.

"I don't know what. But every time I got this feeling in the Pit, it was because Beluchmel had set some strange beast or creature I had never faced before as my opponent. It was never a good thing."

"So you trust this feeling?" asked Tarin, finally turning his full attention to Bryen.

They had reached a truce of sorts. Tarin still looked down upon gladiators because of his military background, but having seen Bryen in action and having experienced his skill and wrath himself, he had changed his opinion, at least with respect to this one gladiator. Although he still viewed Bryen as a slave, now he treated him more as he would a young soldier.

Bryen smiled. "I'm standing before you now, so yes, I trusted it."

Tarin smiled as well, nodding at the young Protector. "What do you suggest we do?"

"We head back to Battersea instead of continuing to the north. I have no doubt that your troop of soldiers can handle themselves, but ..."

"But with Lady Winborne and her friends our task becomes all the more difficult if we run into any unexpected problems," said Tarin, finishing Bryen's thought.

"Yes, as you said."

"Lady Winborne will not be happy at having to return so soon," Tarin commented. "She and her friends had important work to do at the orphanage."

"In the time that I've spent with her she's rarely happy about anything," replied Bryen. "So what's the risk now?"

"Too true, lad. Too true," confirmed the Captain with a short laugh. "Let's get back to Battersea."

"Jerad, keep the column tight. No stragglers. The two young ladies must keep up. If they can't, they ride behind two of the soldiers. Clear?"

"Yes, Captain."

The young guardsman immediately wheeled his horse and trotted back down the line of soldiers. Aislinn's friends, Rebeka and Emilie, had started the day with high hopes, enjoying the comfortable ride north along the coastal road and hoping to gain the attention of one or more of the soldiers accompanying them before they reached their destination. The return south to Battersea, conducted at a fast trot, was not what either of them had in mind. Unused to the rigor of such riding, they were finding the demand of keeping up with the troop more and more challenging and had begun to flag, drifting to the rear. Jerad settled in next to them, urging both of them on and ready to do what was necessary so that the soldiers could continue at their brisk pace.

"I don't understand why this is necessary, Tarin," continued Aislinn, her exasperation obvious. She had promised her father that she would listen to whatever the Captain of the Guard had to say, but that didn't prevent her from questioning his decisions. "There is no evidence that anything untoward threatens us. I've seen nothing that should cause such worry. Besides, you have a full company of the Guard with us. If brigands appear, I have no doubt that you and your soldiers can manage quite well."

"It's not brigands that I fear," replied Tarin, his eyes constantly scanning the trees that loomed over the road in some places. Mysterious. Imposing. Silent. And perhaps hiding a threat yet to reveal itself. "Something is wrong, Lady Winborne. We heard it when we stopped at midday."

"What did you hear, Captain?" asked Aislinn.

She had hoped for more than a quick ride to the north and then an even faster ride back. Yet what frustrated her even more was the fact that despite her being the Duke's daughter, she had no authority in this situation. Captain Tentillin commanded regardless of her rank, and she had acknowledged that before they had started out. If she really wanted to admit it to herself, that's what bothered her the most right at that moment. Her lack of control.

"Nothing, Lady Winborne. Nothing at all."

"But ..."

"Think on it," said Bryen, who on the way south had chosen to ride right next to his charge. That decision in and of itself she found strange, as her Protector tended to give her some space whenever possible. Whether because of his dislike for her or his continuing anger at the circumstances forced upon him, she didn't know. "When we stopped there was no noise but for the ocean. There was no movement around us. Quiet and still are not natural near a forest. I could feel it as well. Something dangerous is near, it's tracking us, and it's coming from the Glen. Use your ability as you do with Sirius if you don't believe us."

"What do you know of my training with Sirius?" demanded Aislinn.

Her lessons with Sirius were secret for a reason. Talking about what she did while working with him was not to be shared beyond anyone but her father. There were still too many people in Caledonia, and unfortunately also in the Southern Marches, who viewed those select few who could make use of the Talent with trepidation and, sometimes, with disgust and fear.

"The Captain knows what you're about," said Bryen. Aislinn noted that her Protector had spoken with her more in the last few minutes than in all the time that they had been forced together, discounting the training circle of course. "He knows all that's going on in the Broken Citadel. It's his job. And I have no doubt that many of the Guards suspect as well. It's a difficult thing to keep secret."

"Your Protector speaks the truth, Lady Winborne," said Tarin. "I've known since Sirius arrived those many years ago. Most of the Guard know as well. Do what you need to do. They're not afraid of you."

Rather than continue the discussion, she simply nodded, then tried to clear her head. She sought to find the calm that she needed to touch the Talent, attempting to slow her breathing and narrow her focus. But the fast trot and constant jolting while riding her horse made such a task exceedingly difficult.

"I can't do this while I'm ..."

Bryen cut her off, his voice strong, even a bit harsh, and that took her by surprise. "You can do it. Just like when we're in the training circle."

Growling as she bit back the cutting riposte that threatened to escape in response to her Protector's tone, Aislinn tried again, seeking to calm herself and push all the distractions around her out of her mind. After what seemed like an agonizingly long amount of time, but was actually only a couple minutes, she succeeded. She found the Talent. Releasing an internal shout of joy, never having thought that she'd be able to do something like this, she went immediately to her task.

Using the natural magic of the world she began to probe around the troop, pushing her senses out to the west, away from the Silent Sea, and slowly expanding her reach across the open ground leading from the road to the trees of the Glen. Several times she needed to halt her progress so that she could settle her nerves, finding the task she had given herself strenuous and difficult. Sirius had shown her how to expand her senses once, but then it had been a much smaller extension of herself than was required now, and she had done it from the comfort of the Broken Tower rather than from atop a horse.

Sweat broke out on her forehead, the strain of her efforts growing more intense, but she refused to give up. Reaching for more of the Talent, she extended her senses a bit farther, finally making it to the very edge of the Glen, and then farther still as she thrust her consciousness within the dense forest until she could feel all that was around them for almost a mile. She gasped in shock. What she had discovered terrified her, and her fear broke her concentration, the Talent slipping from her grasp.

"A quarter mile up the road and in among the trees! They're trying to surround us!"

"Who?" asked Tarin, still seeking and failing to penetrate the dense and dark foliage with his eyes.

"I thought that they were myths."

Tarin glanced at Bryen, remembering what they had come across at the edge of the Raven Wood when they traveled from Tintagel to Battersea.

"What are they?" asked Tarin again.

"Ghoules. They have to be."

Tarin nodded his head, clearly not surprised. "Ghoules beyond the Shattered Peaks. I never thought that I would see the day. Are you certain?"

"I don't know for sure," said Aislinn, her gaze focused on some point in front of them. "I've never seen one in person since they're supposed to live beyond the Weir. But what I saw among the trees looked exactly like what I've seen sketched in the histories." Aislinn rose in her saddle and pointed. "There! Up ahead!"

Tarin looked to where Aislinn gestured. Several creatures were sprinting from the Glen to block the road. He also could now see movement along the edge of the wood. Large shapes still hidden in shadow but moving faster than any man could hope to were attempting to close the trap.

"Captain, just up ahead before we run into them. Where the road curls."

"Good eyes, lad," agreed Tarin. "Guards, wedge formation!"

The Guards responded immediately to their Captain's order, wheeling their horses on his command to form a wedge that resembled an arrowhead where the road turned sharply south and then coming to a halt. The extra space provided by the curl in the road allowed for the quick maneuver and offered the soldiers the opportunity to limit the direction of an attack against them as they used the cliff drop behind them as a defensive barrier. Without needing any instruction, Jerad had guided Emilie and Rebeka into the center of the wedge for their own protection and to keep them out of the way. The Sergeant then walked his horse forward until he was at the tip of the arrow with Tarin, Bryen, and Aislinn right behind them. What swiftly developed to their front shook him to his very core.

None of the soldiers now arrayed defensively across the road had ever seen with their own eyes these creatures. They ran with an animal's grace and quickly blocked them from reaching the safety of the Broken Citadel. The beasts resembled a man, but they stood taller than the horses the soldiers of the Southern Marches rode. They wore brown leather armor over a mottled green skin, scales showing on their forearms, along their shins and thighs, and across their shoulders. Although they held short swords and battle axes, many of the soldiers concluded that these creatures had little need for such weapons because of their clawed hands. Several of the beasts howled, the high pitch of the sound sending a spike of alarm down many a soldier's spine.

"Ghoules," said Tarin matter of factly, as if this confirmation was of no great import even though these creatures hadn't been sighted in the Southern Marches for more than a century.

Emilie screamed in terror, Rebeka reaching out a hand to calm her friend. Fear rose within Aislinn, threatening to get the better of her. Fighting the urge to bolt, she glanced over at Bryen, who sat his horse coolly next to hers. He held his sword in his hand, his eyes burning brightly. In temperament and posture he looked no different than the creatures now opposing them, a calm, coiled violence waiting to be set free.

Bryen nodded to her confidently, having sensed her unease. "No different than the training circle," he murmured so that only she could hear his words.

Aislinn smiled briefly, buoyed by Bryen's comment. She pulled her sword from the scabbard tied to her saddle and sought the calm that had eluded her when she had discovered what hunted them. Slowly, ever so slowly, she was able to attain it once again, forcing her terror into the very back of her mind so that her only thoughts were focused on what would be demanded of her in the battle to come.

For a moment silence descended over the two opposing forces. Though essentially equal in number, Tarin knew that the Ghoules would have an advantage against his soldiers. Recalling the myths that he had learned as a child, he remembered stories of how it often took two or three warriors fighting together to kill one of these beasts during the First Ghoule War. The creature's size, strength, and speed made it a fearsome adversary, making the task of killing them all the more difficult. He hoped that was simply a myth, but looking across the open space that separated his soldiers from the Ghoules, and recognizing the anticipation that radiated from their sharp, angular faces, he feared that the stories may be more truth than fiction. He knew, as well, the likely consequence for all of them if they lost this skirmish. A quick death for those killed in battle, and a painful, terrifying death for those who survived the fight. Ghoules didn't take prisoners. They ate them.

"Steady, steady," Tarin said, his strong, calm voice carrying to the men and women arranged behind him. "You know the stories as well as I. You know what to expect. We will receive no quarter or mercy, so we will give none ourselves. We fight until there's nothing left to fight against."

Tarin's words energized the Guard, turning the fears that had begun to circulate within their minds at seeing these walking nightmares into a new resolve. They, too, knew the tales of old. They had never expected to confront these creatures from beyond the Shattered Peaks. But here they now stood. Fate had dealt them a difficult hand, but they would fight for their Captain, for their Duchy, for their peers, and for themselves. They were professionals, and they would act as such.

"Everyone dies," Bryen said quietly, so that only Tarin, Jerad, and Aislinn could hear him. "Not everyone dies with honor."

"Well said, lad," said Tarin. "Well said."

Movement at the edge of the Glen brought their attention back to the Ghoules arrayed against them. A Ghoule taller than all the others stepped from between the trees. Although similar in appearance to the creatures blocking the road, this Ghoule wore a brown robe rather than armor, and in the place of a weapon held a bent, crooked staff made of black ash that was taller than him.

"An Elder," gasped Aislinn, her fear now evident in her voice.

"Are you certain?" asked Tarin.

"As certain as I can be," she replied, her voice shaking. "If I'm right and the stories about what an Elder can do are true then ..."

"Then we fight," said Bryen calmly. "Just as we had planned. We simply adjust our strategy a bit. Can you defend against the Elder?"

Bryen knew the tales about the Elder Ghoules as well. They were supposedly the equals of the Magii, yet where a

Magus harnessed the Talent, the clean power of the natural world, for his or her use, the Elder Ghoule employed a Dark Magic that corrupted the user and everything that it touched. If Aislinn was right and an Elder Ghoule now stood before them, the odds of their survival had just dropped precipitously. But that still didn't change what they needed to do.

"Can you defend against the Elder?" Bryen asked again, looking at Aislinn with a composed, assured expression.

To Aislinn, her Protector seemed to relish the fight to come. Perhaps he had never fought against a Ghoule in the Pit, and he saw this as an opportunity to test his skills. That thought alarmed her and almost unnerved her.

"Can I defend against the Elder?" Aislinn turned toward Bryen with a look of incredulity. She leaned across her horse so that she could whisper to him, her voice tight and tense. "You have some idea of what I can do. Do you honestly believe that I have the ability and power to fight an Elder Ghoule with the Talent?"

Bryen grinned, leaning even closer to Aislinn, their fore-heads almost touching, and making sure that he caught her eyes with his own. "Remember our lessons in the training circle. The same rules apply here. When you face a stronger opponent ..."

"Move and seek to turn their strength against them," said Aislinn, completing Bryen's thought for him.

"Exactly," said Bryen. "You don't have to defeat the Elder Ghoule. You simply need to make things difficult for him and buy us some time."

Aislinn nodded, understanding blossoming within her, though it still seemed to be a fool's errand. She had improved in the use of the Talent as her lessons with Sirius continued, but a small voice in the back of her mind kept shrieking at her that she wasn't strong enough to fight the figure just a hundred feet in front of her. And try as she might, she couldn't quiet the shrill, screaming voice that she knew was composed of her many fears and insecurities.

"How much time?"

"I'll let you know," Bryen said with a big grin.

Before Aislinn could ask for more specifics, the Elder Ghoule raised his staff and shouted in a guttural language unintelligible to the Caledonians. In response, the Ghoules surged forward, crossing the open ground with a speed that amazed the soldiers of the Battersea Guard. They had little chance to ponder that discovery as they sought to absorb the initial charge. The point of the Guards' defensive wedge felt the brunt of the assault. The soldiers did well to control their mounts, maintaining their formation and not allowing the attacking Ghoules to slip between their horses. But it was no easy task, as several soldiers spent as much time fighting the Ghoules as they did their mounts, which were terrified by the onrushing creatures.

The Ghoules' strength and speed was obvious from the start. Darting forward like snakes, they sought to overwhelm one or two soldiers at a time, thereby creating a break in the shield wall. Once a Ghoule succeeded in forcing his way into the wedge, what Tarin hoped would be a defensive battle would dissolve into a free-for-all and the unavoidable disintegrating discipline of the Guards would give the Ghoules an easy victory. The Guards realized immediately what was happening as they watched four Ghoules concentrate their efforts at a single point in the defensive wedge with another group of Ghoules doing the same on the other side of the formation.

Bryen likened it to the tactics of a wolf pack when it sought to take down larger prey. The Guards were doing well just a few minutes into the fight, keeping the Ghoules at bay, but Bryen understood that this was just the start. The Elder Ghoule could have set his entire pack against the soldiers at once, but instead the creature seemed to be testing them, watching how the Guards responded, learning their strategies for use at a later time. The Protector sensed that this engagement was more an experiment for the Elder Ghoule than a skirmish. Bryen's scalding rage, what had worked so frequently for him in the Pit when he faced a larger or more experienced opponent, cascaded through him. He didn't like being toyed with. Then he saw what he had expected would happen.

"Stay with me, Aislinn!" Bryen shouted. The Lady of the Southern Marches responded without thinking and followed behind her Protector as he nudged his horse to the left side of the wedge.

The Guards had learned swiftly that their sword strokes were ineffective against the scaled parts of the Ghoule's body. Slashing down with a blade onto a Ghoule's shoulder or forearm was no better than cutting at a steel shield. So they adjusted quickly, seeking to pierce the creature's chest or head, but with so many of the beasts pressing them that proved difficult. The soldiers fought bravely, heeding the words of their commander, but two of the Guard had already fallen, leaving a gap on one side of the wedge. A Ghoule noticed the weakness and leapt forward, slipping into the center of the wedge before the Guards could close ranks.

Fearing that the Ghoule would attack the Guards from behind, Bryen charged toward it. Knowing the difficulty of getting past the Ghoule's natural armor, he feinted an overhead slash with his sword and instead pulled tightly on the reins of his horse so that the large animal swung around swiftly and slammed its large rump into the Ghoule. Taken by surprise, the Ghoule let out a grunt of pain and shock, unable to withstand the blow from the massive war horse. The Ghoule fell heavily to the ground, and Bryen never gave the beast an opportunity to rise, riding his horse over the creature several times, the heavy steel horseshoes crushing the Ghoule's head and chest.

Not bothering to take a breath, Bryen charged toward the other side of the wedge where three other soldiers had fallen and a Ghoule was just about to force his way through the line. Not wanting to give the creature the chance to do so, Bryen pulled his dagger from his belt. Taking the tip in his fingers, he threw the blade while his galloping horse bore down on the Ghoule.

Aislinn followed Bryen as he rode within the wedge, impressed with the intelligence of his first attack and amazed at what he tried to do now. She watched him release the steel dagger, glimpsing only a streak of grey until the blade reappeared once more, the hilt sticking out from the eye of the Ghoule who had almost broken through the wedge. She had never seen the like, astounded that Bryen could prove so accurate while riding a galloping horse.

Bryen's latest exploit astonished even the Elder Ghoule, who quickly barked a sharp command, the Ghoules withdrawing in response.

Thankful for the unexpected respite, Tarin quickly ordered his soldiers to pull the dead and injured into the wedge and to close ranks once again. The Guards did so as quickly as possible, exhausted, terrified, yet happy to still be alive. And angry now. Almost a dozen of their comrades had fallen in the first assault, and as a result their defensive formation had grown inevitably tighter.

Bryen trotted his horse to the Ghoule he had just killed,

hopped down, pulled out his dagger, cleaned it against his pants leg, then slipped it back into the sheath on his belt. Aislinn was taken aback by the nonchalance of his actions, as if what he had just done was nothing more than what was expected.

"How did you do ..."

"Practice," replied Bryen before she could finish her question. "Now be ready. That was just the first act. That Elder doesn't look very happy. If we're going to survive this, it's going to come down to what you can do to buy us some time."

16

BAD MEMORIES

"You seem quite intent," said Kevan, coming to stand next to Sirius on the battlements. "Should I be worried? Pirates on the horizon?"

Kevan's silent approach startled the tall advisor, pulling his gaze from the busy port below and the Silent Sea and its angry waves just beyond the breakwaters. Battersea functioned as the only major port in eastern Caledonia and served as a critical link to the Kingdoms far to the north as well as western Caledonia and the Territories on the other side of the Burnt Ocean. For centuries piracy along the coast was the greatest threat to the prosperity of the Southern Marches, but Kevan's forebears had wiped out the practice for the most part. Every few years an ambitious buccaneer sought to restart the custom, but Kevan demonstrated little tolerance for such behavior. Although the Southern Marches didn't have a large fleet, the captains of the province's ships were exceedingly competent when it came to keeping the shipping lanes free from raiders.

Sirius turned to Kevan with a sheepish grin, flicking his unruly white hair out of his eyes. It was a futile gesture, the strong wind sweeping across the battlements whipping his hair about as if he had just been struck by lightning. Despite his usually distracted appearance, Sirius knew all that went on around him. So it was rare for him to be taken by surprise. While looking out across the sometimes blue, sometimes grey, but always angry sea, the large rocks along the coast upon which the churning water crashed, and the manmade-wall that looped around much of the harbor and guarded against the powerful waves, his thoughts had returned to a time when the Aeyrie, his home well north of Battersea and just south of the Shattered Peaks, stood as a symbol of the power of the Order of the Magii.

A time when the rulers of Caledonia respected the Magii and relied on their aid to protect the Kingdom from the frequent transgressions of Ghoule raiding parties, which came out of the Lost Land and across the Shattered Peaks in search of blood, destruction, and food. If not for the Magii, Caledonia would have been overrun in the First Ghoule War. The Order had barely withstood the Dark Magic thrown at them by the Elder Ghoules, but withstand it they did. They had no choice. For the Ghoule Overlord's primary goal was the annihilation of the humans who dared to oppose him, the greatest threat coming from the Magii.

Sirius had learned through hard experience that the Elder Ghoules were a persistent and crafty lot. The creatures had proved that before the start of the war. Several months prior to the Ghoule invasion, Magii had begun to disappear. It had started quietly with no one suspecting what was happening. A Magus at Roo's Nest, another in Murcia. Then Battersea, followed by Ironhill. It wasn't until word spread that more than a dozen Magii had been murdered that the leadership of the Order realized that they had become targets. After a quick investigation, the Magii discovered that the Ghoule Overlord had sent several assassination squads through the Winter Pass, the easiest route for crossing the Shattered Peaks. The Ghoules had avoided the Watchers placed there by the King of Caledonia to warn of an invasion and made their way to every corner of Caledonia to conduct their deadly missions.

In response, the Magii had banded together, sending several of their own hunting parties throughout Caledonia and eliminating the assassins before the beasts could do even more damage. But Sirius and his peers understood that there was more to this attack than simply an effort to cull the ranks of the Magii, so Sirius and several other members of the Order, including Rafia Riverstone, had journeyed to the Winter Pass after clearing Tintagel and the surrounding countryside of a handful of Ghoule raiding packs. They had discovered what they had feared the most. The Watchers murdered and a massive Ghoule army moving swiftly toward the Breakwater Plateau. Sirius and the other Magii had slowed the advance of the Ghoule Legions. Perhaps most important, they had diverted the Ghoule vanguard toward the Aeyrie, thereby giving Wencilius Roosarian, King of Caledonia, the time he needed to marshal his forces.

Sirius had never liked Wencilius, believing him to be an incompetent ruler who was more concerned with getting his ego stroked rather than ensuring the safety of the Kingdom. If not for the heroic efforts of Arick Winborne and several other generals, who usually ignored Wencilius' ignorant commands and ensured that their outnumbered soldiers fought boldly and well, who knew what would have become of Caledonia? Who knew if there would even be a Caledonia? It was certainly appropriate, he thought, that after all that time he now resided in Battersea and served at the pleasure of one of Arick's descendants.

Thinking about the past made Sirius feel his age. But that was to be expected, wasn't it? He had lived for more than a thousand years and seen Caledonia and the world change so drastically that in some ways he barely recognized it. Yet one truth remained, even after all the centuries that had passed. The Ghoule Overlord wanted Caledonia. And the Ghoules wanted revenge for the terrible defeat that they suffered during the First Ghoule War. Why he had allowed his mind to wander in this direction he didn't know. And why his thoughts had turned to Rafia Riverstone he couldn't say? Their paths had crossed many times since the Ghoule invasion, but he hadn't seen her for more than a decade now. And it was probably better if it stayed that way.

Almost as tall as he was, he wasn't certain if it was Rafia's natural height or her curly hair that could never be controlled that made her appear so imposing. When he first met her so long ago, her strange comments and the sense that she wasn't quite all there, as well as her habit of looking at him as if he were something to be studied, had made him nervous, and that was an uncommon feeling for him. But he couldn't deny that he found her attractive. Her ever-present smile, revealing her dimples, had drawn him in. That and the twinkle in her eyes. Where had she been for the last decade? Was she still the Keeper of Haven? It wasn't her habit to not check in from time to time. A few years perhaps, but usually no more as she tended to appear when he least expected it, and that always led to an enjoyable few months when they shared knowledge about the Talent, news of the world, and often a bit more than that before she went off on her next adventure.

"Sirius, are you alright? You're beginning to worry me."

Sirius came back to himself after a bit of a struggle, trying to hide the slight blush that had come to his cheeks.

"My apologies, Duke Winborne. I was thinking and lost track for a moment."

"Of course," replied Kevan, glancing at his tall advisor with just a little bit more concern showing in his eyes. Sirius came across as preoccupied, but Kevan understood that it was an act for the most part. He knew the real Sirius. The focused and intense Sirius. The deadly and serious Sirius. So his current behavior surprised and disturbed him. "Thinking about what?"

"The past," he replied.

"A dangerous thing to do," said Kevan. "Some memories are better left in the past."

"True. But oftentimes delving into the past is the only way to learn about the present and prepare for the future."

"Is everything a lesson with you, Sirius?"

Sirius smiled, shaking his head. "No, Duke Winborne. My apologies again, but there's a part of me that I often find difficult to turn off." The tall Magus pivoted away from the sea and focused his complete attention on the Duke of the Southern Marches. "You found me for a reason. What can I do for you?"

"I wanted to ask your opinion. I've been speaking with Noorsin."

"Indeed you have, Duke Winborne." Sirius couldn't help but smile. The two rulers had spent a great deal of time together since the Duchess of Murcia had arrived a few weeks before. So much so, in fact, that it was rare to see one without the other.

"Are you implying something, Sirius?" Kevan sought to project the tone of a seasoned figure of authority, but to Sirius the Duke's attempt at hiding his discomfort suggested that his words had struck close to the mark, so much so that

Kevan came across as more like a teenager getting caught with his first love.

"I'm simply stating a fact, and there's no reason to be embarrassed by it. Now, what was your question?" he said with a steely voice. Advisor to the Duke of the Southern Marches Sirius may be, but he was much more than that, and Kevan Winborne knew it. Sirius had found that a subtle reminder of that fact now and again never hurt.

Kevan raised his eyebrows at the tone, realizing that he had almost overstepped and reminding himself that he needed to walk a delicate balance with the leader of the Order of the Magii. There was much more to the man than what appeared in plain sight. Every time he was in the presence of the Magus, Kevan felt as if he were with a barely controlled ancient power.

"It has to do with Aislinn," began Kevan. "Noorsin and I have been discussing how we might delay her traveling to Tintagel in response to Marden's marriage proposal."

"Demand, you mean."

"Yes, demand." Kevan sighed. "I can't accept it. I can't put Aislinn in that position. But to turn the proposal down without good cause would irritate Marden. And I don't have good cause."

"It would do more than that," replied Sirius, turning back toward the frothing water of the Silent Sea. "He would view your refusing his marriage proposal as a slap in the face. Knowing that boy's petulance, he would take it as an act of war."

"That's the problem," said Kevan. He stepped closer to Sirius, leaning his elbows on the parapet and gazing out at the waves pounding against the sea wall. A pod of orcas swam not too far off the shore, the younger whales bursting from the waves and crashing back down, seemingly without a care in the world. Unlike him. "Aislinn can't go to Tintagel. If she does, she'll likely never return to Battersea. It just brings Marden one step closer to what he wants, and I can't allow him to attain it."

"The Southern Marches. And if he has Aislinn, the rest of the pieces of the puzzle fall into place for him."

"Yes. If he marries Aislinn, then it would just be a matter of time."

"Have you spoken to any of the other Dukes and Duchesses?"

"Besides Noorsin, Cornelius of the Three Rivers has similar concerns. He understands where a marriage between Marden and Aislinn would lead. But the others?"

"Focused primarily on their own interests as usual. It's not unexpected, but I can't believe that so many would be so short-sighted."

"Indeed. They likely believe that Marden focusing his attention on the east rather than the west is good for them. It means they don't have to worry about him, at least not yet. They don't seem to realize that once Marden gains what he wants in the east, the west is next."

"Not an unexpected perspective, but still disappointing."

"Agreed," said Kevan. "And also a dangerous one."

Sirius nodded. "So you're looking for a way to keep Aislinn from Marden's grasp. And despite the cunning of the Duchess of Murcia you have yet to come up with a good solution."

"Correct. Except for one possibility."

"Apprenticeship," said Sirius.

"Yes," answered Kevan. "Noorsin explained that a new Magus normally is apprenticed to a master for a period of three years. During the centuries some of these new Magii have come from the ruling classes. By tradition ..."

"But not by law," interjected Sirius.

"By tradition," continued Kevan, "while serving their apprenticeship they were free from the demands of their born position. For those three years their primary allegiance was to the Order of the Magii, having relinquished their secular power during that time. No demands could be made upon them other than by their mentor."

"I know how apprenticeship works," growled Sirius. "I've had several apprentices during my time in the Order. Some more difficult than others."

"I understand that." Kevan sighed again, ignoring Sirius' flash of annoyance. "It may be the only way. Nothing else comes to mind."

Sirius shifted his gaze away from the sea, leaning his back against the battlements and taking in the Broken Citadel, his tower rising above him. "You realize that Marden may ignore the traditional demands of apprenticeship. He seems to care little for the practices of the past. The only thing that seems to drive that scoundrel is the desire for more power."

"I know. But what other possibilities do we have? This is the strongest option that came to mind. Do you have a better solution?"

"No," admitted Sirius with some reluctance. It always bothered him when he couldn't come up with a better solution to a problem than the one that had been presented by someone else. It made him feel powerless, and that was another uncommon feeling for him. "No, I don't."

"Would you be willing to take Aislinn on as an apprentice?"

"You're getting ahead of yourself and asking the wrong question, Kevan," answered Sirius. "She can't become an apprentice until she's become a novice Magus. She would need to pass the Test first at the Aeyrie."

"Is she ready?" Kevan asked, some trepidation creeping into his voice. He knew the dangers for those not prepared for or those too weak to pass the Test.

Sirius shook his head in weariness. Kevan's concerns pressed upon him, filling him with an unwanted but real sense of urgency. Sirius agreed with Kevan. He could not allow Aislinn to go to Tintagel, having no doubt of how events would play out once she was under the Crown's control.

"I would like more time to train her ..." began Sirius.

"As would I," interrupted Kevan. "But there is little time. Marden expects a response by the Fall Council."

"I know," said Sirius. "I know. If worse comes to worse, we can accelerate her training. I would prefer several more months but if that's not possible ..."

Sirius pushed off the parapet and shot up to his full height, his eyes glazing over as he turned toward the north and the road leading away from the city and winding along the coast.

"Sirius?" Kevan stared at the Magus with worry, thinking that perhaps the Magus' earlier distraction was a larger concern than he had let on.

Sirius didn't hear Kevan's question. Taking hold of the Talent, he expanded his senses, searching for the disturbance that had pushed against the edge of his consciousness. After more than a minute, he finally found the source of his worry. There! Less than an hour up the road. Aislinn had reached out for the Talent, drawing in more than she ever had before. And for good reason. She battled an Elder while the Guards defended desperately against a pack of attacking Ghoules. He came back to himself, a deadly rage surging through him.

"Go! Ghoules on the northern road. Aislinn is in danger!"

Kevan didn't bother to ask Sirius how he could have known such a thing, fear for his daughter flooding him. He ran from the wall while calling for the Guards. He could only hope that he could get to her in time.

"Hurry!" yelled Sirius. "I will do what I can for her from here."

17

STANDING FAST

"Stand fast!" ordered Tarin, as he rode his horse around the inside of the Guards' now smaller defensive wedge. "We've only gained a brief respite. We'll have another chance to defeat the beasts soon enough."

Several of the veteran Guards chuckled at their Captain's humor. They had cared for several of their severely injured comrades and covered with cloaks those who had been killed during the first attack. The men and women of the Guard could do the math. They knew that if the Ghoules could cause this many casualties with just a few focused assaults on their defensive formation, the Guards stood little chance if the Elder Ghoule ordered all of his beasts to attack at the same time. So they appreciated their Captain's bravado.

Bryen remained close to Aislinn's side, having already assisted those Guards in need of medical aid as best as he could. Having fought in the Pit for more than a decade, he had learned how to care for the many injuries and wounds that he and his fellow gladiators had received there. As the soldiers around him prepared for the next attack, Bryen turned his attention to the Elder Ghoule, knowing that whatever happened next would be decided by him. The creature stared directly at Bryen, apparently having concluded that the Protector offered the greatest threat after watching two of his Ghoules die at his hand in a matter of minutes.

His face a stony mask, Bryen stared back at the Elder Ghoule. He didn't mind the attention. Many of his opponents had tried the same when he fought in the Colosseum, seeking to get into his head and intimidate him. Admittedly, his nerves were on edge, but not because of the Elder Ghoule. Bryen felt the need to take action, believing that the only chance they had at survival, slim though it might be, was to do the unexpected. But there was only so much that he could do. His primary responsibility was protecting his charge, and he didn't lead the Guards. Then he realized that he was out of time.

The Elder Ghoule had summoned what Bryen only could assume were his captains, giving them instructions in that harsh, guttural language that he couldn't understand. The creatures ran to their troops in that deceptively fast gait to carry out their new orders. As one the Ghoules formed into a curved line that draped itself across the Guards' arrow-shaped formation. Bryen's fear was about to be realized.

"They come!" shouted Tarin. "For the Southern Marches! For the Guard!"

The Elder Ghoule spat out a raspy command and the Ghoules charged toward the soldiers, their clawed feet ripping into the dirt, their screeches and shrieks filling the air.

The Guards could focus on nothing more than defending themselves. The attack struck against every soldier forming the wedge at once. Thankfully, the tightness of their formation aided the defenders, allowing them to rely on their comrades to protect their flanks. Moreover, the ferocity of the charge pushed the soldiers back, crushing the two wings of the arrow closer together, which served to prevent the Ghoules from bringing their greater dexterity and speed to bear. The Guard fought with a controlled desperation, the tighter space aiding them.

The Elder Ghoule realized his mistake too late. Having all the Ghoules attack at once proved less effective, as more often than not their brethren got in the way of their own attempts to break through the humans' defense.

"Fight, damn you!" shouted Tarin as he regained his position at the point of the arrow. "Fight as if your lives depend on it!"

The Guards needed no encouragement. They understood what was at stake. For several minutes, the soldiers put up a frenzied defense, but soon cracks began to appear. One Guardswoman fell from her horse on the left wing, a Ghoule spear in her side. A Guardsman on the right soon followed, a bone knife protruding from his throat. The remaining Guards pulled together more tightly, desperate to maintain the integrity of their shield wall. Another soldier fell on the left, and then another. Sensing weakness on that side of the formation, several of the attacking Ghoules rushed forward, one pushing between two horses that had lost their riders, another of the beasts jumping over the animals in a single bound to land in the middle of the wedge.

"Aislinn, with me!"

Bryen didn't hesitate, urging his horse toward the two Ghoules before they could attack the Guards from behind. He was pleased to hear the pounding hooves of Aislinn's

horse behind him. Bryen's action had caught Aislinn by
surprise. But she ignored the steadily growing fear within
her and followed after her Protector, sword in her hand. She
saw that the two Ghoules had turned to face them, standing
only a few feet apart from one another, and because of the
constricted space within the wedge were hindered in their
movements, making them more vulnerable. Bryen had realized it as well, and he hoped that Aislinn could intuit what
he was about to do, otherwise he rode to his death.

Charging toward the Ghoule on the left, the creature just
a few steps in front of his brethren, and ignoring his snarl
and the sharp teeth revealed, Bryen feinted an overhead
strike across his horse, instead whipping his sword lightning
fast backhanded so that the blade slashed across the back of
the Ghoule's neck on his right, the steel digging deeply into
the flesh just above the beast's armored shoulders. The
Ghoule on his left had dodged out of the way during the
Protector's charge. The beast had seen how the boy had
used his horse to kill one of his comrades just minutes
before and didn't want to fall victim to the same tactic.

The wounded Ghoule, having been caught by surprise,
raised his clawed hand to the slash across his neck, which
now seeped a blackish blood down his back. Aislinn took
advantage of the diversion, following right behind Bryen
and driving the tip of her sword into the chest of the
wounded Ghoule just as it turned toward her, the beast realizing his mistake as the light left his eyes. The Ghoule
collapsed in the dusty road, but Aislinn's sword went with it,
stuck in the creature's ribcage. She turned her horse
sharply, narrowly avoiding a slash aimed for her thigh by
the Ghoule who had escaped Bryen's charge. She was
thankful for her training with Bryen. Without the time that
she had spent with her Protector in the training circle, she

didn't think that she'd have survived the attack. But the fight wasn't over.

The Ghoule sprinted toward the unarmed Aislinn, grinning evilly in anticipation as the beast leapt into the air well above her horse to swing down with a crushing stroke that would split her in two. A bolt of fear shot through her as Aislinn realized that she couldn't evade the blow in time.

The end was barely a second away when Bryen appeared, deflecting the Ghoule's strike with his sword and maneuvering his horse's rump into the descending creature at the same time, giving Aislinn an unexpected and much appreciated reprieve. Knocked to the ground, the Ghoule hissed in anger as he pushed himself up from the crushed grass at the side of the road and slowly began to circle Bryen and Aislinn, ignoring the Guards who continued to fight against his enraged and hungry companions. Although a handful more Guards had been forced from the wedge, either dead or wounded, as the perimeter shrank, the surviving Guards continued to gain some small benefit, reducing the number of Ghoules who could attack at one time.

The Ghoule in the middle of the wedge had eyes only for Bryen. The beast circled calmly, studying his opponent, his black eyes revealing no emotion. Suddenly the creature barked out a series of undecipherable utterances. Bryen assumed that they were curses or an attempt to unsettle him. He didn't understand the language. He didn't care what the Ghoule had to say.

"Can you reach your sword?"

Aislinn looked to where her blade was, hilt pointing to the sky, stuck in the chest of the dead Ghoule near the edge of the cliff. She thought about making a run for it, but realized that the Ghoule facing them was probably faster than

she was. She'd never make it even with her horse. Without
something to defend herself with, the Ghoule could kill her
before she reached her weapon.

"No, it's too far away."

"Then stay close. Take my dagger." He handed it to her
while he kept his eyes on the Ghoule. "If there's a need or an
opportunity, use it."

Aislinn nodded, though she realized that Bryen couldn't
see it. A disturbance in the air, a surge of energy much like
she experienced when she practiced with the Talent, pulled
her gaze away from the circling Ghoule. The power was
similar in its application, but different in its formation. It
brought to mind a rotting decay. Trying to locate the cause,
her attention immediately went to the Elder Ghoule. The
beast had become frustrated as he waited for a break-
through, and she watched a small black orb form just above
the top of the Elder's staff. In an instant, Aislinn compre-
hended what was about to happen.

"Tarin, to the front!" shouted Aislinn.

The Captain of the Guard, still at the tip of the wedge
and fighting desperately against the Ghoules pressing
against him and his soldiers, glanced up quickly at Aislinn's
yell, glimpsing the black orb that shot toward him from the
Elder Ghoule's staff. He nudged his horse out of the way just
in time, but the Guard next to him wasn't so fortunate,
taking the full brunt of the Elder Ghoule's Dark Magic. The
young man, barely in service to the Duchy for a year, didn't
even have a chance to scream as the corrupted power of the
Elder Ghoule consumed him, turning his body to ash in
seconds.

Sickened, the first tendrils of fear licked at Tarin's heart
upon seeing the young Guard's gruesome death and him
powerless to stop it. Tarin mercilessly crushed that debili-

tating emotion and immediately returned to his position at the point of the wedge, his soldiers moving backward in good order to bring the sides of the arrow closer together once again. But now Tarin had to keep his eyes not only on the Ghoule who attacked him, but also on the nasty beast gesturing with that damned staff.

Bryen saw what had happened with his peripheral vision, unwilling to take his eyes from the Ghoule who tracked him. Bryen and Aislinn had continued to turn their horses in response to the stalking Ghoule, so that now Aislinn was directly behind Tarin, though in the wider part of the wedge.

"You must go to Tarin and do what you can to defend against the Elder Ghoule's Dark Magic," said Bryen, feinting a quick charge forward with his horse to push the Ghoule back a few more feet.

"How am I supposed to help him?" Aislinn replied, holding Bryen's dagger in one hand and the reins of her horse in the other. "I don't know the first thing about Dark Magic. I can't even ..."

"Aislinn," Bryen said quietly, the Lady of the Southern Marches hearing him despite the shouts and screams of the battle going on around them. "That doesn't matter. You're the only one who can try to do something to protect against the Elder Ghoule. You may not succeed, but you must try. If you don't, we die for sure."

Aislinn stared at Bryen's back, the truth of his words making her sick to her stomach. She was about to turn her horse toward the front of the wedge when her Protector's words caught her, and she realized what he had in mind.

"Before you go, please give me a small distraction."

Without another word, Bryen drove his heels into his horse's flanks, the animal trained for war leaping forward.

The Ghoule began to lift his short sword to defend himself, but the creature wasn't able to raise it as high as he wanted, Aislinn having thrown Bryen's dagger at the beast, the sharp steel slicing across the Ghoule's upper arm and cutting through his leather armor and skin.

More an annoyance than anything else, the brief diversion still served its purpose, allowing Bryen to avoid the overhead swing the Ghoule had aimed at him. Dodging beneath the slash, he leaned down toward the ground on the right side of his horse and slashed behind him, cutting across the Ghoule's right hamstring. The beast screeched in pain, but did not fall. Bryen had hoped to disable the creature. Yet despite the fact that the Ghoule could no longer put weight on that leg, the beast still turned slowly as Bryen now circled, the prey having unexpectedly become the predator.

Normally in such a situation, Bryen would have taken his time, respecting the abilities of his opponent. But he saw that Aislinn now sat her horse right behind Tarin. She was attempting to ward off the Elder Ghoule's Dark Magic, and he didn't know how long she could last. He needed to end this duel quickly.

"We are coming," hissed the Ghoule, the beast struggling to say some of the syllables clearly. But Bryen understood the creature, nonetheless. "We are coming. This is just the beginning."

Initially surprised that the Ghoule could speak the language of Caledonia, Bryen strengthened his focus as he continued to move around the beast, looking for an opening. Then the Ghoule stumbled because of his injured leg, and immediately Bryen put heel to horse, leveling his sword like a lance and aiming the blade at the creature's head.

UPON REACHING the front of the wedge, Aislinn struggled to calm herself. She found it difficult to ignore the fighting raging around her, just feet away. The cries of anger, the screams of pain from her soldiers; the hisses, grunts, and incomprehensible words escaping from the Ghoules. As a result, finding the inner calm that she needed to grasp hold of the Talent took longer than she would have liked. For a terrifying moment, she worried that she'd fail to reach the familiar warmth of the world's natural magic, but after what felt like hours, yet actually was less than a minute, she exulted in sensing the Talent flowing within her, giving her a strength and a confidence that she wouldn't have had otherwise.

Looking beyond Tarin and the other soldiers putting up a brave resistance at the very point of the wedge, she saw that another black orb had formed above the Elder Ghoule's staff, spinning rapidly with a darkness blacker than the night. With a flick of the creature's wrist, the orb shot from the staff, once again aimed directly at Tarin, the Elder Ghoule likely expecting that once the leader of the humans fell, their resistance would collapse. The Captain of the Guard glimpsed the dark energy streaking toward him, but this time he had no place to go. The space where he fought was so compressed that his soldiers were crushed against him on both sides. He could do nothing but continue to fight, to keep the creatures from breaking through the line, knowing that his death was all but certain when the sphere constructed of evil sorcery struck in just a few seconds.

Recognizing Tarin's deadly predicament, for a split second Aislinn lost touch with the Talent, her concentration consumed by her fear and worry. But as the black orb shot through the air with a sizzle that brought to mind the charged atmosphere of a lightning storm, she instantly regained control of the Talent, forcing herself to ignore the consequences of her possibly failing at what she was about to try. Instead she focused on the moment and nothing else. With barely any time to think, she did the only thing that came to mind. Several strands of white light appeared, dancing across her palms as she deftly wove them together into a wider net made of energy. Aislinn then flung the webbing with her right hand at the orb of Dark Magic that raced toward Tarin.

The blazing strings of white light, fashioned into a simple latticework, shot forward and collapsed on top of the black orb with a clap as loud as the thunder that crashed during a summer storm, startling both human and Ghoule. For just a moment the fighting stopped, but the silence only lasted a few seconds as the Ghoules surged toward the soldiers once again. The white energy of the strands didn't have the power to destroy the tightly massed power of the orb, but it had just enough strength to divert it from its path, forcing the sphere up and over the Guards to fall harmlessly beyond the cliff and into the Silent Sea.

Aislinn stared across the trampled grass that led away from her, noting the malicious grin that appeared on the Elder Ghoule's face, his sharp teeth sending a shiver of terror through her heart. But then her anger grew. She interpreted the beast's expression as one of amusement, as if a child had entered a space better left to the adults and, in consequence, the child needed to be taught a lesson. Another orb of virulent energy instantly formed at the top of the Elder Ghoule's staff, the power spinning faster than the eye could track so that the threads of corrupted Dark Magic created the appearance of solidity.

This time when the Elder Ghoule flicked his wrist the orb shot directly toward her rather than the tip of the wedge, and this time she was better prepared. Aislinn's confidence had sparked after she had defended against the first attack. As the sphere sped toward her, Aislinn flicked her wrists, hurling several short bursts of threaded white energy at the oncoming orb. Still not strong enough to stop the dark energy's progress entirely, what she did was enough to deflect it once again. The strands of the Talent nudged the Dark Magic off track and to the side. Much to Aislinn's unexpected delight, the ball of corrupted energy struck a Ghoule who had stepped back from the attack because so many of his brethren were in his way.

The Elder Ghoule watched in surprise and dismay as the dark energy consumed the Ghoule, the creature emitting a high-pitched scream of agony as his body burned to ash. The Elder Ghoule's expression hardened, his anger plain. Aislinn realized that she may have reached the limit of her abilities as another orb of Dark Magic appeared above the Elder Ghoule's staff and shot toward her, followed by another, and then one more.

Not knowing what else to do, she decided to follow the instructions her Protector had given her while training in the circle. Trust your instincts. If you think too much, you die. She drew in even more of the Talent, more than she ever had before, and began flicking her wrists and directing the blazing white threads of energy toward the spheres of darkness that hurtled toward her. Each time the threads of white struck, the orbs were knocked off course, although the last one almost killed her. The final sphere was so close when she defended herself that the strands of white energy barely touched the orb before the Dark Magic slammed into her, but touch it they did, just enough to allow her to duck to the side as the inky sphere passed by her. She could feel the icy coldness as the Dark Magic shot past, slamming into the grass and leaving behind a charred hole several feet around and just as deep.

The Elder Ghoule nodded his head, almost as if he was acknowledging that he may have misjudged her. But then he raised the staff above his head, yelling in the harsh Ghoule language that she didn't understand. A dark cloud of jet-black energy began to swirl slowly above the Elder Ghoule's head, then faster and faster as the power gained speed to the point where Aislinn could barely see the Elder Ghoule through the twisting and turning mass of shadows. Not knowing what she would need to defend against, all she could do was maintain her control of the Talent. But she feared that she had come to the end. She was just learning. She didn't have the experience or knowledge to battle an Elder Ghoule for long. She didn't have the strength to defend against the attack her adversary was about to release upon her.

"*Have no fear, child. You are strong enough.*"

"Sirius? How?" Aislinn responded upon hearing Sirius talking to her, realizing his voice was softly whispering in her mind.

"*Time to answer that question later,*" Sirius replied. "*Let's focus now on how you can defend against the Dark Magic to come.*"

"I can't keep doing this, Sirius. I barely survived the last attack. I don't have the knowledge or ability to fight an Elder Ghoule."

Sirius' voice lashed out, much like a teacher displeased by a student's lack of effort. "*You have more strength and knowledge than you know,*" he said stridently. "*This is not the* time for self-pity. Your soldiers are depending on you. You must do all that you can, and there is so much more that you can do."

Aislinn nodded, castigating herself privately for lacking confidence and failing to demonstrate it when so many depended upon her. She didn't know how Sirius could see her reaction, but he seemed to be mollified by her renewed determination.

"*Now do as I instruct,*" Sirius said. "*Reach more deeply into the Talent and take in more of the power offered by the natural world.*"

"I've already taken in more than I've ever controlled before."

"*Be that as it may, you have the strength to take in even more. Do it. Your life and the lives of the soldiers around you depend on it.*"

Aislinn followed her teacher's instruction, pulling in more and more of the Talent, the white strands of energy growing and swirling within her, until she felt as if she were about to burst. The feeling was intoxicating, but she knew that she had to be careful, otherwise she ran the risk of destroying herself by taking in more of the power than she could control.

"*Good, good,*" said Sirius, pleased with her progress. "*Now start to guide the flow. Open your hands and allow the strands to stretch out in front of you and to the sides as if you were building a wall. Allow the threads to reach out far and wide. Remember, the Talent responds to your command. Think what you want the natural magic to do, envision it in your mind, and the Talent will respond accordingly. But do it slowly. Do it well.*"

Aislinn didn't respond, instead seeking to maintain her concentration and follow Sirius' instructions. Soon a smile appeared on her face. It was working. The energy flowed swiftly from her hands, the white strands blazing brightly and beginning to swirl and extend beyond her Guards. As the Talent drifted through the fighting, the attacking Ghoules jumped back in alarm, giving the soldiers a needed break as the blazing energy expanded across the defensive wedge.

"*Excellent, child. Excellent. Now that you have the shape that you want, allow more of the Talent to flow into your creation, as much as you can control before you lose yourself. But do not allow the energy to become solid. Keep it flexible, so that it can bend but can't break.*"

Aislinn understood now what Sirius was teaching her to do. The white light of her shield grew brighter as more energy surged into it. The construction now covered the Guards' entire perimeter. And just in time, she realized.

Once again, the Elder Ghoule directed his staff toward her, streaks of black energy sizzling through the air and taking on the shape of sharpened stakes. Aislinn cringed when the Dark Magic struck her glowing shield, fearing that the spears would pierce the barrier. But she breathed a sigh of relief when she realized that her defense had held. As Sirius had predicted, the shield had bent where struck, but it had not broken, allowing the Dark Magic to burn itself out against the energy of the shield.

"*Well done, child,*" said Sirius, seeing what was happening through his pupil's eyes. "*Maintain your hold on the Talent. That's it. Keep feeding in more power where you see gaps in your shield and allow the energy to subside where the shield is already strong so that you can maintain the balance of your defense. Remember, something that is solid is more likely to crack or break than something that gives a little. As you saw, the Dark Magic of the Elder Ghoule will spread across the shield, but won't be able to break through so long as you continue to feed more of the Talent into your defense. Keep it up. You are doing well.*"

Sirius watched as Aislinn did as he instructed, offering gentle instructions and guidance as she continued to withstand the Elder Ghoule's magical attack. He was proud of her. She was doing better than he expected, but his worry increased as each minute passed. Although Aislinn had mastered this new skill, she was pulling from an immense pool of the Talent that she had never managed before, which meant that she would grow more and more tired as her own energy diminished. Eventually, without aid, her defense would fail, because her body would fail. And there was nothing more that he could do as he sought to assist her while standing on the battlements of the Broken Citadel. He could only hope that her father reached her in time.

TEETH GRITTED, a resolute expression on her face, sweat dripping down into Aislinn's eyes, the strain of her maintaining control of the brightly glowing shield was wearing on her. But she couldn't release her hold on the Talent. Her soldiers had no defense if she did. So she continued to follow Sirius' instructions, constantly scanning the shield, moving the strands of energy to and fro, filling the gaps that appeared as needed, and then releasing excess energy in those places where the shield threatened to solidify, all the while pulling from the unending stream of natural magic that flowed within her as her strength wavered.

She stared across the battlefield, barely noticing the Ghoules who stood motionless in front of her, the creatures watching the battle between Dark Magic and the Talent. Instead her gaze remained fixed on her opponent, the Elder Ghoule, who continued to pound at her shield every few seconds, a new surge of Dark Magic striking in the form of spikes or lances with annoying regularity, but still failing to shatter her barricade. The Dark Magic crackled as it slid across the brightly glowing barrier before it was consumed by the sizzling energy of her shield.

She noticed that the Elder Ghoule didn't appear to be angry as he had been the first time she had defended against his attacks, and that worried her. After she had succeeded in holding back the beast's assault for several long minutes, she soon realized that the Elder Ghoule's perspective had shifted once again. Intrigue, perhaps. Wonder at how she had withstood his attacks for so long? No matter. She used the surprise and doubt that he displayed openly as motivation, taking the Elder Ghoule's interest as an insult, her resulting anger giving her the little bit of extra strength that she needed to maintain control of the Talent.

And then it was over, at least for the moment. The Elder Ghoule released the Dark Magic that swirled around his staff and beckoned to his captains, likely to plan the next stage of the assault. Taking advantage of the pause, she released her hold on the Talent, feeling completely and utterly exhausted.

"*Excellent work,*" whispered Sirius in her head. "*Rest, be ready for the next attack. It will come soon. Hold as long as you can. Help comes.*"

With that last communication, Aislinn realized that Sirius had left her mind. She wanted to lie down on the grass at the edge of the road and rest, but she couldn't. She couldn't show weakness. Not now. Not with the Elder Ghoule preparing another attack just a hundred feet away. Instead, she gulped thirstily from the water pouch Jerad handed to her, acknowledging his nod of respect and silently thanking him for it. Surprised by his action, she glanced around, pleased to see so many Guards still alive, though in her opinion far too many had been killed or wounded. Every time she caught the eyes of one of her soldiers, he or she nodded as well, their admiration obvious.

Aislinn took some satisfaction from her efforts. Perhaps she had accomplished more today than she had expected, and not just with the Talent. But what to do next? She was bone-tired and what strength she retained was flagging. When the Elder Ghoule attacked again, and she had no doubt that he would, she didn't think that she could defend against his Dark Magic for very long.

"Sirius says help is on the way," Aislinn said as Tarin moved his horse next to hers.

"How did you speak to ..."

Tarin let the comment go. After watching the exhibition put on by the young Lady of the Southern Marches, who was he to question what she could or could not do. She had put on a truly impressive display, yet more would be required of her.

"If that's the case, then we could try to hold a bit longer and hope that help arrives in time."

Aislinn shook her head, her weariness making it hard to think, but she knew that what she was about to say was the truth.

"I don't know how much longer I can hold back the Elder Ghoule. I've reached the limit of what I can do. And I don't know how much time we have."

Tarin grunted in reluctant understanding. He could see just how much effort it was taking Aislinn to simply stay on her horse.

"We need to attack," said Bryen, the tall Protector appearing next to Aislinn, thick black blood oozing down his blade, and several streaks of red coloring his scarred arms. Through his connection to his charge, Bryen could feel how tired she was and understood that any defense she could provide from this point forward would be short-lived despite her best efforts. "We don't know how long it will take help to arrive, so we can't count on that possibility. Our position is untenable. If we don't change our circumstances, the Ghoules overwhelm us in the next assault."

Aislinn glanced behind her, taking in the Ghoule lying dead in the trampled grass. Any soldier willing to challenge a Ghoule on his or her own virtually guaranteed themselves an early death, as such audacity gave the Ghoule all the advantages. The task of killing a Ghoule was much more manageable if several soldiers worked together to complete the task. Yet her Protector had killed several already without assistance. And he was right. The Ghoules would overwhelm them during the next attack. With no other options coming to mind, she nodded in agreement.

"What would you suggest?" she asked.

Bryen quickly explained his plan, Tarin nodding more and more as he listened. At the end of the Protector's explanation, a wolfish smile had spread across the face of the Captain of the Guard.

"You are one crazy bastard," Tarin said, shaking his head. He meant the statement as a compliment. "I like it."

"Everyone dies," said Bryen. "Not everyone dies with honor."

Tarin actually laughed at that. "Well said, Protector." The Captain of the Guard turned his horse and called out. "Jerad! To me!"

The Sergeant trotted his horse up to the small group, sword still in hand. There were a few small slashes across his arms, but beyond that he was none the worse for wear.

"Captain?"

"Rally the Guard and form ranks. If we are to die this day, it will be on our own terms."

"Yes, Captain." Jerad nudged his horse away, relaying Tarin's instructions.

Tarin trotted his horse back toward the point of the wedge. "I'll see you on the other side, Protector. One way or another."

"I'll see you on the other side," replied Bryen with a respectful nod.

~

"I DON'T KNOW if I can do this," whispered Aislinn.

"You can," Bryen answered calmly. "You've already done it."

"Yes, but I don't know how long I can hold it."

"Do the best you can," said Bryen softly, turning his attention away from the Elder Ghoule, who had just finished talking with his captains and seemed to have reached a decision on what the Ghoules would be doing next to break the Caledonians. As the former gladiator expected, they were out of time. "That's all anyone can ask."

Aislinn glanced over at her Protector, catching his faint smile. His eyes blazed fiercely. Clearly, he was in his element. Then she realized something else that had not occurred to her before. Her Protector trusted her, as did the Guards. That realization sent a bolt of energy through her that burned away some of her weariness.

Closing her eyes for just a moment, she found the Talent in an instant, allowing the warmth of its touch to lift her spirits. She smiled. This time she had no problem whatsoever reaching for and taking hold of the natural magic of the world. She barely had to think about what she wanted to do.

With even greater confidence, she took in more and more of the Talent, the glowing white strands of energy appearing in her hands. Then, she began to mold the threads much as she did the last time she trained in Sirius' chamber. Satisfied with her work, she looked at Bryen and nodded. She was ready.

Bryen then turned his keen gaze to Tarin and nodded. The Captain of the Guard smiled, apparently looking forward to what they were about to do. It seemed that Bryen wasn't the only crazy bastard.

"We are the Battersea Guard!" yelled Tarin, raising his sword into the air, the steel catching the bright sunlight of the day. "We ride for the Lady of the Southern Marches!"

A shout rang out from the soldiers as they put heel to horse, swords outstretched like lances, and charged toward the Ghoules who milled about in front of them. The attack completely surprised the Elder Ghoule, who had not thought that the humans would ever willingly leave their defensive formation. Even worse, the creature had no time to rally his troops as a tightly wound ball of white-hot energy shot toward him. The beast raised his staff quickly, calling on his Dark Magic to craft a makeshift shield of swirling energy, which deflected the orb just before it struck.

The Elder Ghoule wanted to renew his attack as the Guards galloped toward him, the tip of the wedge having slammed into his Ghoules, the soldiers using the weight of their horses to their advantage and pushing back the beasts. But the creature had no chance to do so. Another ball of white light shot toward the Elder Ghoule, and then another, followed by a third.

The Caledonians had stolen the momentum, but for how long?

"I CAN'T DO this much longer," shouted Aislinn, continuing to craft spheres of glowing white energy as quickly as she could and then throw them toward the Elder Ghoule, who was now focused solely on defending himself. She didn't care if she hit her adversary. She just wanted to make sure that he was fully occupied and couldn't do anything to thwart the charging Guard.

Bryen scanned ahead of them. The Guards' attack had caught their adversaries unprepared, their initial charge trampling more than a dozen Ghoules as the soldiers used their horses to excellent effect. Tarin continued to lead the Guard forward, Jerad right behind him, the men and women of the Southern Marches seeking to force their way past their enemies to the Elder Ghoule. But Ghoule resistance had stiffened, the initial shock of the rush having worn off, and their assault had slowed inevitably. If it became a slog, the Caledonians were finished. The faster and stronger Ghoules would surround the soldiers quickly and then slaughter them. It was time to move.

"Just a few more throws and then we ride forward," Bryen said.

He knew that she was exhausted. He could feel the strain his charge was under through the magical link they shared through his collar, and he worried that she might burn herself out if she continued much longer. But the risk had to be taken. The lives of all the Guard depended on her.

Aislinn nodded, crafting three more balls of flaring energy and flicking them toward the Elder Ghoule before releasing her hold on the Talent.

"Stay with me," Bryen yelled to Aislinn as he urged his horse to a gallop. "We fight together."

Bryen turned his horse directly toward the tip of the Guards' wedge, which still remained intact despite the increasing pressure being placed on it from both sides by the Ghoules. He realized that Tarin's assault was beginning to falter, several of the Guards at the back of the wedge fighting for their lives as the Ghoules tried to flank them. Time was running out quickly. Knowing that Aislinn would be safer within the wedge, he pushed his horse on to an even faster pace. Bryen needed a little bit of luck for what he planned to try next, and then much to his pleasure chance favored him.

A small opening appeared between Tarin and Jerad as the two soldiers were drawn to opposing sides by the attacking Ghoules. Bryen guided his horse into the gap and rushed through just before the two Guards came back together to close the small opening. Two Ghoules sprinted toward him, gliding across the grass, reminding him of some of the creatures that he had been forced to fight in the Pit. Holding his sword at the ready, he lined up his mount directly with the first Ghoule. The creature hadn't expected such a tactic, thinking the human would try to escape instead, and with the Ghoule moving so fast, the beast had no chance to change course.

Bryen took advantage of the opportunity, allowing his horse to do his work for him as his mount shouldered into the Ghoule and then trampled the fallen and dazed beast with its steel-shod hooves. The second Ghoule skidded to a stop in time and avoided the war horse, but in his effort to do so, the beast forgot about its rider, which proved to be a costly mistake. With a deft slice, Bryen caught the Ghoule across the neck and then used his horse's momentum to finish the task of cutting through the flesh and bone, the beast's head popping up into the air as his body slumped to the grass.

Bryen then shifted his gaze to the Elder Ghoule as he maintained his charge. With Aislinn ending her attack with the Talent, the creature now had the opportunity to begin his own assault once more. Knowing that the Guards were finished if he gave the Elder Ghoule the chance to use his Dark Magic again, Bryen patted his horse on its straining neck, encouraging his mount as the tired and lathered animal galloped toward the three Ghoules who had placed themselves in front of the Elder Ghoule as a protective guard. This new development would complicate what he was about to do next, but it wouldn't stop him. Bryen loosened his grip on the reins, trusting the horse to stay on its course. Then he slipped his boots from the stirrups and pushed himself up so that he stood on his horse's back in a crouch, still holding the reins lightly in his hands.

When his horse was just about to smash into the Ghoules, he pulled back on the reins, his horse's front hooves digging into the soft grass as the back hooves came up from the ground. Bryen used his horse's kick to propel himself off his mount, flipping through the air and above the Ghoules arrayed against him. Landing deftly on his feet, Bryen sprinted toward the Elder Ghoule, who stood rooted in the long grass, stunned by what he had just seen. The Elder Ghoule brought his staff down just in time to parry Bryen's sword as the steel missed his neck by the breadth of a hair. Forced to defend against this dangerous human's blistering attack, the Elder Ghoule had no choice but to release his hold on the Dark Magic he had been about to launch at the Battersea soldiers.

Bryen maintained his ferocious assault, swinging his blade in a blur, pushing the Elder Ghoule back and closer to the trees. His steady stream of slashes, cuts, and lunges chipped into the Elder Ghoule's staff, the creature yelling and cursing at him in its unintelligible language.

Bryen knew that he couldn't falter. He couldn't stop. He had to maintain the pace of his attack. He needed to give the Guards time to fight without the threat presented by the Elder Ghoule's Dark Magic, but he also expected at some point soon that he'd feel the steel of a blade or the sharp claw of one of the Ghoules assigned to protect the Elder rip into his back.

Realizing the danger of his predicament, the Elder Ghoule began to call on his Dark Magic with his staff again while also trying to defend against Bryen's vicious assault. Bryen recognized the danger of what was likely to come next, so he feinted a slash, then gripped his sword in both hands and brought his blade down with all the force that he could muster onto the Elder Ghoule's staff, attempting to destroy the tool that his adversary depended on for manipulating his power. Much to the former gladiator's surprise, the steel blade broke in half, leaving just a foot of its length above the hilt. But Bryen still breathed a sigh of relief. Even though he had lost most of his blade, he had achieved his goal.

The Elder Ghoule screamed in rage upon seeing his staff broken in two. In his fury the creature let go of his control over the Dark Magic that he commanded and lunged for Bryen, stabbing the piece of his broken staff that he still held in his claw into Bryen's side. The Elder Ghoule, who stood no more than a foot away, stared down at Bryen with his cold, remorseless eyes. Smiling with a wicked pleasure, the Elder pulled the broken staff free from just beneath Bryen's ribs. The Elder Ghoule believed that he had finally vanquished his opponent, the boy responsible for the deaths of so many of his Ghoules. The creature expected the human to collapse to the ground, unable to bear the injury just inflicted upon him, but then the Elder Ghoule began to understand his mistake as waves of increasing pain spread through him. The creature could feel his strength fading, a splotch of black blood now appearing on the front of his robes before spreading down the length of the rough fabric.

Bryen's eyes blazed brightly as he gave his broken sword a final twist deep within the Elder Ghoule's chest. He had seen his chance and taken it when the Elder Ghoule stabbed him with the splintered wood, driving what was left of his sword into the Elder Ghoule's heart. As Bryen's hand slipped from the hilt of the broken blade, the Elder Ghoule collapsed onto his back, the light seeping from his eyes as his thick, black blood tarnished the grass around him.

Turning quickly to defend against the attack that he expected from the Ghoules tasked with protecting the Elder Ghoule, he slipped to one knee, realizing that he was more badly injured than he had thought, his vitality draining away. He eased himself down onto the soft grass, stretching out onto his back as his free hand went to the wound in his side. Bryen tried to roll onto his other side and then push himself up as he heard the thundering hooves approaching, but to no avail. The seriousness of his wound was dawning upon him. Looking toward the sky he saw that Tarin, Jerad, and several other Guards had eliminated the three Ghoules who had tried to defend the Elder Ghoule. Bryen's charge had invigorated the soldiers, giving them that last spark of purpose and energy needed to finish their attack and vanquish their enemy.

"Like I said," Tarin said, looking down at the Protector as Bryen settled himself on the grass. "You are one crazy bastard."

"Of course he is," confirmed Jerad, who rode his horse next to Bryen on his other side. "He's the Volkun. The Wolf. He has to be crazy to pull a stunt like he just did and still be alive."

Bryen could only smile, not having the opportunity or the energy to reply as Aislinn pulled her horse to a stop just a few feet away, jumped down from her saddle, and ran toward her Protector, her own weariness forgotten.

"What were you thinking?" Aislinn demanded, kneeling down where Bryen lay on the trampled grass. She pulled off her riding scarf, bundled it up, and pushed it down onto her Protector's wound, stanching the flow of blood that exited from below his ribs on the left side.

"I wasn't," replied Bryen, trying to raise himself onto his elbows.

"Clearly not," Aislinn said, her anger obvious in her voice as she gently pushed him back down to the grass and let the pressure she applied do its work. "Stay with me. We fight together, you said. You didn't say anything about engaging in death-defying acrobatics and trying to be a hero."

"It was the only way," said Bryen. "If the Elder Ghoule attacked us again ..."

"Just because you may be right doesn't make me any less angry with you," Aislinn said in a tense voice.

Pulling up Bryen's shirt, she saw that the wound in his side had not gone through to his back, which she took to be a good sign. But she noticed that several long splinters of wood from the Elder Ghoule's staff had been lodged in the wound, burning the skin and muscle where the shards cut into his flesh. Not knowing what else to do, she grabbed a dagger and cut off a long length of her riding skirt. She then wrapped that around the wound, the scarf, which had quickly become wet with blood, still in place, and tied it off.

"We need to get Bryen back to Battersea."

"Yes, we will," replied Tarin. "As well as all the other Guards who need medical attention."

The Captain of the Guard surveyed the battlefield, counting more than three dozen Ghoules dead and, unfortunately, a similar number of Guards as well. Still, he took heart. Reliving the battle minute by minute in his own mind, he knew that they had been exceedingly lucky. And if not for the Lady of the Southern Marches and her Protector, by his own estimation they would all be dead.

18

LESSON LEARNED

Tall trees grew densely on one side, a sheer drop of several hundred feet to a small beach and jagged rocks that lined the shore on the other. Large waves pounded the coast in a powerful rhythm. When some of the bigger breakers struck, clouds of salty spray drifted up above the crest, becoming a shimmering mist in the bright sunlight.

Nibli, gripping his staff of black ash tightly between his claws, had stood at the edge of the forest for the better part of an hour. Watching. Waiting. Making sure that no surprises awaited him after having observed the debacle that had occurred just hours before.

Finally satisfied that he had nothing to fear, the Elder Ghoule walked out from the wood, his long, crooked staff hitting the rough ground every time the towering beast took a step. The creature had pushed the hood of his robes back, enjoying the play of the warm sun across his face. But he didn't enjoy the sight that spread out before him.

The soldiers had taken their dead and wounded with them, leaving the Ghoules who had fallen in battle along the side of the road. Nibli walked slowly down the line of the dead, the creature's anger rising as he passed each one. This should not have happened. Krazak, the Elder Ghoule in charge of this war pack, had argued that he had the strength to destroy the column of soldiers. He had been arrogant, and he had been wrong. He underestimated the humans and that error had cost him and his Ghoules dearly.

The Elder Ghoule continued to walk down the long line of fallen Ghoules until he came to a stop where Krazak's body lay. Staring down at his former friend, he admitted to himself that the fault was his. Nibli led all the Ghoule war packs in the Northern Spine and the Southern Marches. He could have overruled Krazak and sent another war pack with him. But he hadn't, and because of that the Ghoules with Krazak had paid the ultimate price. He didn't mind that Krazak had died because of his overconfidence. It would be a good lesson for when the Legions swept down from the mountains. Still, he felt responsible for the Ghoules who fought under him. They shouldn't have had to die for Krazak's mistakes, but such was the price of hubris. In this case, his own.

The Elder Ghoule gazed at Krazak a moment more, taking in the sightless eyes that stared up at the sky and then examining the wound in his chest. He had decided to watch the fight from within the wood to get a better sense of the adversaries that he faced. He could have aided Krazak during the battle, but he had chosen not to, his other purpose more important. Since he had entered the Southern Marches, he had seen nothing from the soldiers of this land that had worried him, that would suggest the humans could withstand the coming onslaught. Until now.

He knew that the Order of the Magii survived, despite the Ghoule Overlord's many attempts during the last few centuries to destroy it. But he had not expected to find a Magus here on a remote coast road. The girl had been strong and perhaps more than a match for Krazak, but he would never know. Not with the boy who had decided to end the clash on his own terms. The boy was the first human he had seen who could hold his own with one of his Ghoules. He was just as fast if not more so. Fearless. Relentless. Remorseless. If not for the boy, Krazak likely would have killed the Magus, and then his Ghoules would have taken the humans who survived. Krazak and his war pack would have feasted that evening on their former opponents, rather than finding themselves rotting in the hot sun by the side of the road. All because of a young Magus and a boy.

He had learned a great deal after watching this defeat, and he would adjust his strategy accordingly. But he would put off the task that he dreaded for as long as possible, at least until he had found a way to accomplish his mission here in the south. Then, and only then, would he inform the Ghoule Overlord of what had occurred. The Overlord never looked kindly on failure, and he didn't want to be held responsible for Krazak's mistake if he could avoid it. The Overlord needed to know, just not right away. And not until Nibli found what he was searching for.

19

THROUGH THE GATES

Kevan led Aislinn, her friends, and the soldiers who had survived the attack by the Ghoules south down the coastal road to the safety of Battersea. He and his column of the Guard had met them a short distance from the attack, what several soldiers were already calling the Battle of the North Road. Once he was certain that his daughter was safe, he and a small troop of the Battersea Guard had gone farther north to examine the site of the skirmish. He wanted to see things for himself, to apply some truth to the stories already being told.

What he had discovered had shocked him, and not only because the mythical creatures from the Lost Land were made flesh and blood. The Ghoules killed by the Guards lay where they fell, and it wasn't until he had walked the small battlefield that he had the soldiers accompanying him place the creatures along the side of the road. He would send a larger detachment on the morrow to remove the beasts and scout the Glen. No, what also caught his attention was that what Tarin had reported of the fight had not been embell-

ished, including the actions of his daughter and her
Protector.

He had never come across a Ghoule before, knowing
them only from the tales that he was told as a child. Their
size and strength from the stories didn't do these creatures
justice. Moreover, Aislinn's Protector had told him that one
of the Ghoules had spoken a rough version of the Caledonian language, hissing out the words between his serrated
teeth. None of the stories going back to the First Ghoule
War had ever said a word about that possibility. The histories had been fairly accurate regarding the Ghoules' capa-
bilities, something that his soldiers who survived this
encounter had quickly confirmed for him, but there had
been no reference to their ability to communicate in the
common tongue.

He would set that significant discovery and huge worry
to the side for the moment, asking Noorsin to take on the
task of trying to learn more through her extensive knowledge and network of resources. But what worried him even
more was the fact that this Ghoule raiding pack had gone
undetected. To have this many Ghoules so close to Battersea
with no warning being given, having made their way
through the Winter Pass in the Shattered Peaks and then
across and down the Northern Spine and into the Southern
Marches with not a single word being said, sent a tremor of
fear through him.

Kevan nudged his horse over to where the Elder Ghoule
lay, the grass around the beast soaked in a black blood that
now resembled tar. Aislinn had told him all that had
happened during the battle, but she had done so quickly in
a nervous stream of consciousness that he could barely keep
together in his own mind. He had been pleased to hear that
she had acquitted herself well, as she explained how she

had made use of the Talent to protect against the Elder Ghoule's attacks. Now that so many soldiers had seen her use the Talent openly, at least he had one less worry.

Clearly, these men and women had accepted her, not caring but rather appreciating her arcane skill, which had helped them during the fight of their lives. With the word out, and likely to spread as soon as they returned to the Broken Citadel, there no longer would be any cause to keep this knowledge secret. And perhaps he could, indeed, use it to address his other concern, the danger coming from the Caledonian capital. He would talk to Noorsin to get her perspective when there was a free moment upon his return to Battersea.

As he continued to slowly walk his mount among the Ghoule dead, trying to get a feel for how the skirmish played out based on his daughter's hurried description, more and more he felt justified in his decision to give Aislinn her Protector. Obviously, the boy had done his job well. He would need to check into Aislinn's report on what her Protector had done during the battle, supposedly charging and killing the Elder Ghoule while avoiding the creature's personal guard at the same time. It seemed a bit too much to believe, but perhaps there was some bit of truth to the story. Perhaps more truth than he believed initially upon surveying the carnage.

As Kevan turned his horse, his men following behind so that they could catch up to the main force as it made its way south toward Battersea, the image of the Protector's broken sword, the blade thrust deep into the chest of the Elder Ghoule so that only the hilt was visible, stayed with him.

When the Guard finally rode through the gates of the Broken Citadel, they were a somber lot. The soldiers had lost many comrades, and they worried for those who had been seriously injured. Yet many of the men and women who had survived the clash against the Ghoules felt some measure of vindication as well. Almost all had trained with the boy gladiator in the early morning for the last several weeks, and their efforts to improve their skills had proven effective and useful on the battlefield. Many of the soldiers believed that they remained alive now because of that training.

Several of the Guards nodded to the Protector when they passed him on the way to the stables, demonstrating their respect for what he had done for them, both prior to and during the battle. They knew that their final charge against the Ghoules was a desperate action, and one that suggested that their deaths were all but assured. But thanks to the magical power of the Lady of the Southern Marches and the martial skills of her Protector, they would be returning to their homes and families tonight rather than being lowered into their graves or worse ... eaten. And for that they were exceedingly grateful.

Bryen appreciated the nods from the soldiers as they passed. Living in the Colosseum and fighting weekly in the Pit, he had found it not only difficult, but also prudent to keep his distance from many of the other gladiators. When he trained with them in the yard, he knew almost immediately who would survive for at least a time on the white sand and who would not. So he had become friends with only a few of his fellow fighters, those who he believed would survive the Pit for more than just a few bouts. He had appreciated that comradeship, especially the friendships he had developed with Lycia and Davin, even needing that camaraderie at times despite the fact that he tended to keep to himself. Now, after spending so much time in the Southern Marches, he was beginning to feel a similar connection with these soldiers who had trained with him and now fought with him.

Extending his leg across his horse's back with some difficulty as he slid from his saddle, the wound in his side sending shooting pains through his body, Bryen stood next to his horse for a minute, holding on to the pommel to support himself. He patted and rubbed the animal's neck in gratitude for all that his mount had done for him.

"Thank you," whispered Bryen into the horse's ear. "You fought like a true warrior today." The horse tossed its head at Bryen's words, apparently pleased by the compliment, then sought to nuzzle his rider's hand. Bryen chuckled softly.

A stable hand quickly appeared to lead the horse away, bowing in respect to Bryen, who was somewhat surprised by the action. Since he had arrived in the Broken Citadel, most of the servants and other inhabitants had simply ignored him. What astonished him even more was that when he next opened his eyes, he lay on the hard cobblestones of the courtyard looking up at a clear, blue sky, the sun moving farther and farther to the west.

"Father!" shouted Aislinn.

When they arrived at the keep, the Lady of the Southern Marches had made sure that her friends were all right after such a frightening experience, only to turn and watch her Protector collapse to the ground. She rushed to him, noting that the wound in his side had begun to bleed once again, the length of cloth she had torn from her riding skirts and wrapped around his waist now soaked in a dark red blood.

Kevan was there in an instant, carefully pulling free the improvised bandages that had been applied, then pressing gingerly at the edges of the wound, which had begun to turn a nasty black with veins of the same color beginning to spread up Bryen's chest and down his hip, bringing to mind a spider's web. Taking one look at the boy's injury, he knew that there was only one recourse.

"Sirius!"

The Magus came bounding up, having first checked on Aislinn to ensure that she was all right before examining several of the more seriously injured Guards. He had been pleased and relieved to discover that all would survive.

"What happened to you, young man?" asked Sirius, tearing Bryen's shirt by the wound and folding it out of the way in order to get a better look. After poking and prodding at the edges of the gash for almost a minute, he grunted in worry. The inky tendrils had spread farther out from the wound in just that brief period of time and a thick, pungent, black pus seeped from the gash.

"Just give me a moment," whispered Bryen, his eyes unfocused. "It's just a scratch. I just need to lie down for a bit." With that his eyes rolled backward, and he promptly passed out.

"I have not seen something like this in a very long time," said Sirius as he shifted his attention to Aislinn, who kneeled next to him, her face a mask of worry. "Tell me what happened."

"Bryen fought the Elder Ghoule and broke the beast's staff in half. Before Bryen killed him, the Ghoule stabbed a piece of the broken staff into his side."

"Step back, Sirius. Allow me to take a look." Noorsin had hurried down to the courtyard to assist, drawn to the small group now hovering over Aislinn's Protector and gliding up silently, having overheard Aislinn's explanation. She knelt down next to Bryen, tearing away more of his shirt so that she could conduct her examination. Murmuring to herself, she gently touched the skin around the wound, clearly not liking what she saw. "Leave this to me, Sirius. This is my area of expertise."

Sirius nodded. "I'll see to the soldiers." He moved away quickly, trusting in the abilities of the Duchess of Murcia.

"Wait," said Aislinn. "Sirius is our best healer. He needs to help Bryen." Tears had formed in her eyes, threatening to cascade down her cheeks.

Noorsin glanced up at her, smiling kindly. "I know you want the best care for your Protector, child. And he shall have it. I promise you that. Sirius is very skilled in the art of healing, but I am even more so. Have no fear. Your Protector will be well looked after."

Aislinn nodded, comforted by her words and her promise, though still uncertain. Her father knelt down next to her, grasping her shoulder to offer his silent support.

Noorsin bent back to her task, kneeling more closely to Bryen's wound and tracing the black tendrils with her fingers. Confirming her initial suspicions, she explained what she had learned.

"The slivers of wood from the Elder Ghoule's staff are poisoning the boy. They hold the residue of the Dark Magic the Ghoule practiced. If the splinters remain, he dies."

"I wasn't aware of your knowledge and skill in this area, Noorsin," said Kevan. For him it had been a day of surprises, this discovery just the latest.

Noorsin looked at the Duke of the Southern Marches, her eyes sharp and bright, as she was refreshed by the challenge that she faced. This was a woman of quick decisions and action and not the one said to be quiet and demure, as was her reputation. Obviously, there was more to the Duchess than Kevan had expected, yet he had suspected as much having spent so much time with her during the last few weeks.

"There is much you don't know about me," replied Noorsin.

She stood quickly, wiping the dirt and dust of the courtyard from her dress. "Bring him to the medical ward immediately," she commanded. "If he's to live beyond the afternoon, we have little time."

20

DESPERATE DECISIONS

"Will Aislinn's Protector live?" asked Kevan.

The Duke of the Southern Marches stood at his favorite spot in the Broken Citadel. His private terrace jutted out from the keep's battlements, giving him an excellent view of the Battersea harbor below and the seething waves of the Silent Sea beyond.

"Do I sense worry for that young man's health?" asked Noorsin.

The Duchess of Murcia had stopped in her suite to change her clothes and refresh herself. After caring for Aislinn's young Protector, she had assisted Sirius with the Guards wounded during the battle with the Ghoules. She was tired, but she was also energized. She had trained in the Royal Medical School in Murcia when she was younger, and this was the first time in years that she had been able to put that training to good use. She had forgotten just how much she had enjoyed that time in her life, before the demands of ruling Murcia had taken over.

Kevan turned to face her, marveling again at her beauty. It had been years since he had spent so much time with one woman, thinking back to before Aislinn's mother had died. At first Kevan had thought that Noorsin's unexpected appearance would lead to an awkwardness or tension within the Broken Citadel, yet Aislinn had taken to the Duchess immediately. Perhaps he was the only one who felt a bite of nerves every time Noorsin appeared. Still, a small part of him admitted that his unease also made him feel more alive than he had felt in quite some time.

"Concern for my daughter, actually," he replied. "From what I've learned in speaking with Tarin and several other members of the Guard, the boy protected her well today. I'd like her to continue to have that protection."

Noorsin studied Kevan for several long moments, his discomfort growing. Her gaze reminded him of Sirius, the sharpness of her eyes and the uncomfortable feeling that she saw more within him in that single glance than she had a right to know. He began to fidget, so he clasped his hands behind his back in an effort to control that impulse.

"Say what you will, Kevan, but I think that there is more to it than that. After caring for Bryen -- your daughter made sure that I knew his name, by the way -- I assisted Sirius as he aided several of the wounded Guards. To a man, they all said the same thing. If not for the Protector, the Ghoules would have wiped them out before you arrived with your relief column."

"The boy was simply doing what was required of him," countered Kevan. "What the collar requires of him."

"That boy protected your daughter as he should, but the collar does not require him to aid others. I spoke with the Captain of your Guard. He says that Bryen is a born leader. His tone implied a measure of respect, the Captain even admitting that he had his reservations upon first seeing the boy gladiator, but no more. His men and women spoke the truth. This boy not only protected your daughter, but he also killed a handful of Ghoules before charging the Elder Ghoule on his own. He protected your daughter, and he fought for your people. Those soldiers saw it. They know it now."

"Know what?" asked Kevan, not understanding where Noorsin was leading him.

"That this boy is not all that he seems."

"Perhaps there is more to this boy than I originally had thought," Kevan admitted with a heavy sigh. "It hasn't taken him long to find his place here."

"Perhaps there is," agreed Noorsin. Then she shifted her focus, wanting to make a point. "It was wrong to collar him. He didn't deserve it."

Kevan sighed again, turning back to the Silent Sea as the sun began to touch the western horizon, enjoying the play of the day's last rays of sunshine across the now increasingly rough water.

"I have heard enough about this from Sirius," answered Kevan. "I do not need to hear it from you, as well, Noorsin."

"You enslaved the boy, Kevan."

"I did. I know that." Kevan gripped the railing running along the terrace, his anger rising. But his anger wasn't directed toward Noorsin. Rather, it was directed toward himself. "Yes, it was the wrong thing to do. Looking back, I would not have done it. I should not have done it. But I was …"

"You were desperate," Noorsin finished for him, reaching out a hand and placing it on top of Kevan's. She knew that he was becoming agitated, and her touch calmed him.

"Yes. I didn't know what to do. With Marden's demand, I had to do something. Based on what happened today, she is well on her way to becoming a formidable young woman. But she still needs to be protected. There are some threats that she won't see on her own and won't be able to handle on her own."

"That she is," said Noorsin. "And from what I understand, Bryen has proven you correct more than once."

"Yes, this attack and the assassins of a few weeks ago." Kevan put one hand on top of Noorsin's, surprising the Duchess as his fingers intertwined with hers. "Believe me, Noorsin, if I had to do it all over again, I would not have done this. But it's too late now. There's nothing that I can do."

"Yes, once collared, always collared." She was about to suggest that Kevan talk to Bryen about what he had done to him and why, but she didn't get the chance.

"Will you be returning to Murcia soon?" asked Kevan, seeking to change the subject.

"Are you trying to get rid of me, Kevan?" Noorsin asked with a smile, giving his hand a squeeze. "Have I reached the end of my welcome here?"

"No, no, not at all. I simply thought that after this attack, you might want to return to Murcia to ensure that all is well there. We have not had to deal with Ghoules for a hundred years or more, but now we are."

"I appreciate your concern, Kevan. But I think not. Your Guards have just begun to pursue the surviving Ghoules who attacked your soldiers this morning. And who knows if there are other raiding packs still in the Southern Marches that we're not yet aware of. My guess is that where there is one Ghoule war pack there are others. I came with a small guard and can't ask you to provide additional soldiers with all that's going on now. Besides, I know that all is well in Murcia, and I can do more good here now that our ancient enemy has returned. So I will stay a bit longer. With your permission, of course."

"Of course," replied Kevan, secretly pleased that he would be able to spend more time with her. "It would be our pleasure to have you stay."

"Our pleasure?" asked Noorsin, eyebrow raised, recognizing that Kevan had switched to a diplomatic dialogue with the use of the word *our*.

"My pleasure," corrected Kevan.

"That's better," said Noorsin, giving his hand a squeeze. Her dazzling smile sent a jolt of energy through him. "Besides, once Aislinn's Protector has recovered, I would like to talk to him."

"I'm sure that won't be a problem." Kevan decided to broach the subject that had been playing through his mind once he had learned of the skirmish on the north road. "Do you think this will give me the opportunity to delay?"

Noorsin's smile faded, her thoughts turning in another direction. "You mean Marden's proposal?"

Kevan nodded. "Do you think it will give me more time?"

Noorsin took a moment to gather her thoughts. "Yes, I think you can use it to your benefit. Once Marden receives word that Ghoules have attacked beyond the Northern Spine, and that you need to focus your attention on the Southern Marches and ensure that any remaining raiding packs are eliminated, I think he would be hard pressed to make any demands right now."

"That's what I was thinking as well," said Kevan. "The reemergence of the Ghoules can't be ignored. But do you think he will accept that explanation?"

"For a time," replied Noorsin. "But not for long."

Kevan nodded. "A reprieve, but likely just a brief one."

"Unfortunately, yes," agreed Noorsin. "You've talked to Sirius about my other recommendation? The role your daughter played in the fight today certainly suggests that you could follow that path as well."

"Yes, but we didn't have an opportunity to complete the conversation. How did you know about that possibility?"

"I am not just a healer, Kevan," answered Noorsin. She raised her hands from his and in an instant several blazing white strands of energy danced from one palm to the next, and then just as fast the threads disappeared as the Duchess of Murcia released her hold on the Talent. "After passing the Test I apprenticed with Sirius for three years."

"How did you keep it a secret for so long?" Kevan wasn't surprised by the revelation. He had suspected that there was something unique about Noorsin, a power hidden within her.

Noorsin smiled before she began. "I was young, no older than Aislinn when I first began learning how to touch the Talent. My parents wanted to keep it a secret, so they wove a web of stories that kept away prying eyes. They said that I was a studious girl, more interested in books than in people. I spent a lot of time in the private rooms of Murcia's library. So people believed what was said. What most didn't know was that Sirius had come to Murcia, not only to use our library for his experiments and projects, but also to teach me. Then after passing the Test my parents began spreading the rumor that I would be visiting several other Duchies to broaden my education in preparation for assuming a larger role in governing Murcia. And I did do that with Sirius as my guide, but we also visited the Aeyrie several times to continue my training with him and a few other Magii."

Kevan nodded, appreciating the lengths to which Noorsin's parents had gone in order to protect her.

"Aislinn has revealed herself today. All of Battersea will know before tomorrow, and the rest of the Kingdom not long thereafter."

"True, but they will know as well that the Lady of the Southern Marches fought with the Battersea Guard, using the Talent to defend her soldiers against a pack of Ghoules," said Noorsin. "The story will spread and grow. If anything, it will only strengthen her stature here and her connection to the people. Not only a Duchess in training, but also a fighter, and a dangerous one at that."

"So you don't think that she'll have anything to fear because of her nascent ability in the Talent?"

"From the people of the Southern Marches? No. But with respect to the King of Caledonia, possibly. Rather than weakening his ardor, he might view this new development as an opportunity."

"That's what I feared. He may insist on the marriage occurring as soon as possible. To be married to a Magus would give him even more power than he originally expected to obtain."

"Agreed," replied Noorsin. "All the more reason to talk with Sirius again. Based on tradition -- and admittedly this hasn't happened very often, but it has happened -- when someone in line to rule a Duchy has discovered their ability in the Talent, and they pass the Test, they are granted the opportunity to master that ability through their apprenticeship. That might be the delay you need. In fact, that might be the only tactic now that could not be construed as a slight."

"But Aislinn would need to pass the Test to make that claim."

"Yes, and the sooner the better," confirmed Noorsin.

"Then I will speak to Sirius tomorrow. After Aislinn's

display today, he may have adjusted his initial assessment as to whether she was ready to go to the Aeyrie."

"He likely has," said Noorsin with a devilish grin. "You know, Kevan. I was just thinking."

Kevan chuckled. "Why do I have this terrible sense of foreboding?"

"As I just mentioned, once Marden learns of Aislinn's ability with the Talent, he may view his marriage to Aislinn as having an additional advantage," continued Noorsin, ignoring Kevan's attempted humor. "If you play your cards right, you may have the chance to gain the same advantage."

"How do you mean?" asked Kevan, his chest tightening and his body feeling a slight burst of heat as he realized where Noorsin had unexpectedly turned the conversation.

Noorsin grasped both of his hands, her sparkling eyes capturing his own. "Think on it, Kevan. You'll figure it out eventually."

21

A NEXT STEP

Aislinn had slept into the late morning the day following the clash on the north road. Although the extra sleep helped her body recover from her extensive use of the Talent, she still felt exhausted when she woke. But she chose to ignore that fact, focusing instead on her renewed confidence and strengthened sense of responsibility. Just a few weeks before she had failed during her lesson with Sirius, destroying a good portion of his chamber. Yesterday, she demonstrated that she could manipulate the Talent with a skill that she had never imagined. And she did it to help people who had depended on her.

But she was jittery, and she had to force her hands to her sides rather than allowing them to twist the fabric of her skirts. She stood just outside the medical ward. Aislinn didn't understand why she was so tense and anxious as she snuck a peek around the open door and saw Bryen sleeping soundly in a bed by the window at the back of the chamber. His side was bandaged, but other than that there seemed to be no lasting effects from the wound that he had received from the Elder Ghoule.

So what was the cause of her discomfort? She didn't want to have anything to do with him when her father thrust them together, and she knew that he felt the same way about her. But he had handled his fate better than she had. He'd earned the respect of the Guard, including Tarin, training with them and making them better soldiers. He could have easily kept his distance. His only duty required by the collar was to protect her. Yet he hadn't. He had done more than was required of him. If circumstances had been different, maybe they would have formed a friendship, but the damn collar took away their freedom, their choice, the connection between them serving as a constant reminder of a forced servitude.

Gritting her teeth in irritation, and refusing to explore the uncomfortable path that had opened up in her mind, she strode resolutely into the medical ward. The several physicks there nodded respectfully, and several of the soldiers wounded in the attack actually saluted her from their beds. She stopped to speak a few words of thanks and encouragement to each one, and what she thought would be a visit of just a few minutes in the infirmary led to several hours of her spending time with her Guards.

They wanted to talk about what had happened on the north road, many still coming to grips with the fact that the mythical Ghoules of the Lost Land were, indeed, real. That news had spread through the Broken Citadel and then Battersea in a matter of hours yesterday, and the stories of what had happened were becoming more fanciful by the minute. That, in itself, was not unexpected. What surprised her was that the soldiers wanted to talk with her, and it took her some time to realize that it was because she had been there, she understood what they had been through, she knew how many of their friends had been lost, and she had fought with them. She was no longer just the Lady of the Southern Marches. The soldiers now saw her as one of their own, which she understood was the greatest compliment that she could receive from the men and women of the Guard. As the hours slipped by, she realized that these soldiers appreciated the time that she gave them, and even more so she valued the conversations.

When she finally made it to Bryen's bedside, he had awakened, pushing himself up against the wall so that he could look out the window to his front, his gaze fixed on the deep blue sea surging far below. His eyes had a faraway look to them.

"Where are you?"

Bryen glanced at Aislinn. She looked uncomfortable, and he could tell through his connection to her that she was nervous.

"Not here," he replied softly. "I was just watching the waves and thinking about where they could take me. Someplace where I could be ..."

Bryen's voice trailed off, his eyes returning to the whitecaps that crashed against the base of the Broken Citadel's eastern wall.

"Could be free," said Aislinn, finishing her Protector's thought for him. The comment increased her discomfort, but she offered it, nonetheless.

Bryen, turning his penetrating eyes back to her, took in everything about the Lady of the Southern Marches in an instant. She was different today. Nervous, yes, but more confident. More certain. More comfortable in who she was.

"Yes, in part," he replied. "Though, to be honest, even if I were free, it's been so long that I don't know how I would handle it." He flicked a finger against the silver collar around his neck to accentuate the point.

A silence settled between them. At first, they were both ill at ease, but then as the minutes passed neither seemed to mind. Aislinn sat on the very edge of the bed, her weariness from the previous days' exertions still bothering her.

"I wanted to thank you. For what you did yesterday. If not for you," motioning to the soldiers around them, "we wouldn't be here. We have you to thank for that. I, and they, know that. We owe you our lives."

"You give me too much credit. I played just a small part."

"You give yourself too little credit," replied Aislinn.

Bryen smiled briefly. "You gave us the time we needed to fight. Only you could have taken on the Elder Ghoule and his Dark Magic. If not for you, we would be dead. I simply took advantage of the opportunity you gave me to finish him."

Aislinn blushed at Bryen's words, not used to such compliments. "Well, I don't know about that ..." she stammered.

"Lady Winborne," said Bryen, the use of her formal title stopping her short. Her Protector barely used her name as it was. In fact, he seemed to make every effort not to. "That's all the Guards in here have been talking about. I'm sure you sensed it when you spoke with them. They're proud of you, and they're proud to serve you."

Aislinn was caught unprepared by his words, unaware that she had gained such a high regard that was usually reserved for her father or Tarin. All she could manage in response was a quiet "Thank you."

"You don't get many compliments, do you?" asked Bryen. "You don't seem to know what to do with them."

Aislinn thought for a moment as to whether she wanted to answer her Protector's question. She had not expected the conversation to head down this particular, personal road.

Rather, she had thought that she would have already left the ward upon offering her thanks, but she seemed to have taken up residence on the edge of Bryen's bed.

"No, not really. Just Sirius from time to time."

"But not your father."

"No, not my father."

"He seems a hard man," said Bryen, gesturing once more to the silver collar.

"He can be," Aislinn replied. "Not that I'm offering excuses for what he did to you with the collar, but he had his reasons."

"He fears Marden. That's why he brought me here and gave me to you."

Aislinn looked at Bryen in surprise, not expecting such a naked comment from her Protector. "What do you mean?"

Bryen chuckled softly. "I may only be a gladiator at heart, but I'm not stupid. The only currency that's truly valuable in the capital is gossip. Rumors circulated throughout Tintagel about Marden's ambitions and his constant struggles to maintain his sway over the various Dukes and Duchesses who sought to challenge him. I can understand your father's concerns. The Southern Marches was a frequent topic of conversation even in the Colosseum."

"You discussed politics in the Colosseum?" asked Aislinn, unable to contain her surprise. She had never thought that any of the gladiators were very well educated or had any interest in anything beyond their survival.

"We couldn't train all day," answered Bryen. "We needed to find other ways to pass the time."

"So how is my patient this morning?" asked Noorsin, the Duchess of Murcia having strode through the center of the medical ward to stand at the end of Bryen's bed.

Aislinn pushed herself up from the mattress, stepping back to give Noorsin more room. The Duchess of Murcia smiled at Aislinn before turning her attention back to Bryen.

"Thank you for helping me," replied Bryen. "I am in your debt."

"It was the least that I could do," replied Noorsin. "I wanted to check your wound. See how it's healing."

Bryen pulled up his shirt to reveal the clean, white cloth beneath. Aislinn turned to leave, giving Noorsin and Bryen their privacy. But Noorsin's words forced her gaze back to her Protector.

"Aislinn, this is something that you must see," she said. "You're learning about the Talent, but you also need to learn about the Dark Magic of the Ghoules, what I prefer to call the Curse. The two magics are distinct, obviously, but they function similarly."

With a practiced hand, Noorsin quickly unwrapped Bryen's bandage, Aislinn watching intently, but her eyes often drifted from the wound on Bryen's lower abdomen to the many scars that laced his chest. She assumed that they all came from his time in the Pit. She was able to identify those caused by a slash of steel and those that were puncture wounds, likely from a dagger or an arrow, although there was one scar that ran along his side that she couldn't determine what kind of weapon may have caused it.

"Good, very good," commented Noorsin. She ran her hand softly along the edge of the wound in Bryen's side, Aislinn's Protector barely flinching at her touch. "If you remember, Aislinn, yesterday the wound had filled with a thick, black pus, and the edges were raw and an inky black. The poison from the splinters of the Elder Ghoule's staff had begun to spread, after just a few hours, which was obvious from the spiderweb of black that appeared on your Protector's chest and hip. Now we have healthy skin, and the wound is healing nicely."

Noorsin studied the wound more closely, her face scrunching up with interest. She had to look twice just to confirm, as the ragged gash from yesterday was almost completely closed. She had never seen anyone recover so quickly from such an injury before. In fact, few people had ever survived such a wound. Intriguing, to say the least. She wondered what the cause could be.

"You had mentioned yesterday and again just now that the wood from the Elder Ghoule's staff was poisoning Bryen," said Aislinn.

Aislinn's comment brought Noorsin's wandering thoughts back on track. "Yes. Those slivers of wood that stayed in the wound after Bryen was stabbed immediately began to fester. The pus, of course, was an obvious sign, as were the black tendrils that extended from the wound. Once the poison takes hold, it spreads quickly. And that's not unexpected. Any weapon used or touched by an Elder Ghoule will contain the residue of the Dark Magic that they practice. The corruption of a blade, or in this case a staff, will naturally transfer to the person harmed with that weapon."

"So did removing all the slivers of wood stop its spread?" asked Aislinn, her curiosity piqued. "Or was there more to it?"

"That's an excellent question," said Noorsin, nodding in approval. "In part, yes. The slivers had to be taken out, otherwise we could never eliminate the poison. But doing just that isn't enough. Normal healing methods won't work against the Dark Magic of the Ghoules. The poison would have continued to spread even if I was able to heal the wound with conventional medicine."

"So you used the Talent."

"Yes, child," answered Noorsin with a kind smile. "It seems that both our secrets are now out in the open. The Talent is the only way to fight an infection such as this. Much as you saw on the coastal road, the Talent is the only way to balance the evil and corruption of the Curse."

"How did you do it? That's not something that I've learned yet."

"I'll show you another time," answered Noorsin, pleased by Aislinn's interest. "When you've regained your full strength. And with Sirius' permission, of course. For now, simply remember that there is little difference between the Talent and the Dark Magic of the Ghoules. Both function in a similar manner, and that, in itself, is a danger."

"How so? When I fought the Elder Ghoule, the Dark Magic seemed to give off this stench of decay."

"It connects to the legends about the Ghoules. No one knows where they came from. But there is a myth that they were once human. Supposedly, several millennia ago, a people to the north began using the Talent in a way that went against the principles of the natural world."

"What do you mean?"

Satisfied by the progress of Bryen's recovery, and in fact still a bit mystified by its speed, Noorsin began to wrap the wound with a new bandage.

"As you know, the Talent represents the magic of the natural world, of the world around us and everything in it. It is a neutral power in that how it is used is determined by the person able to master it. It is much like a sword. It's a tool, though a dangerous one. Yesterday your Protector used his sword to defend you and the Guards. I would suggest that was a good use for the blade, though we must always understand that perspective is essential to such a conversation, as the standpoint of the individual when examining the blade always comes into play. I'm sure that the Ghoules had a different view when facing this young man's steel."

Bryen grunted softly as Noorsin tied the bandage off tightly before speaking. "You're talking philosophy. Essentially the argument that everyone is biased, and as a result their standpoint on any issue is biased as well. Therefore, in order to reach agreement through dialectic, the individuals must first acknowledge their biases, their standpoints, and move on from there. Failing to do so means they'll simply be talking at one another rather than with one another."

Noorsin stared intently at Aislinn's young Protector. The young man was full of surprises. "Correct. As a gladiator, you seem to have learned quite a bit more than simply how to survive in the Pit."

"I made good use of what little free time I had," replied Bryen, pulling his shirt back down over his injured side.

"Is that so? Tell me, young man, what would you argue regarding the concept of truth?"

"That would depend."

"On what?"

"Two arguments could be made," Bryen answered. "We could pursue the search for absolute truth, which was so important to philosophers such as Pilatus. Or we could pursue the teachings of the Solistics, who argued for the contingent nature of truth, in that truth is not absolute but rather socially constructed."

"Aren't you full of surprises," said Noorsin. She was obviously pleased by his answer, patting him on the knee before rising from her perch on the bed. "Very good, indeed."

"This is all quite interesting," interrupted Aislinn. "But perhaps we could return to our original conversation?"

"My apologies to you both," Noorsin said with a smile, using her hands to smooth the wrinkles from her dress. "When I was younger, I spent a great deal of time in the Royal Library in Murcia, reading on all subjects of interest and engaging with some of the best tutors in Caledonia. Your young Protector allowed me to return to more carefree times when the greatest argument I had was philosophical and had no real impact on life. Now, in my position as Duchess, I have no time for philosophy, only reality. But this has been an enjoyable diversion."

"A single reality or multiple?" Bryen asked with a grin, valuing the intellectual engagement.

"You are a lively one, aren't you?"

"You were talking of the Ghoules?" asked Aislinn, trying once again to bring the conversation back to the topic that interested her the most.

"Oh, yes, my dear. As I was saying, we know that the Talent has always existed in the world. In fact, the assumption is that without the Talent, we would not have a world. That the world comes from the Talent. But that's a philosophical discussion for another day. Specific to the Ghoules, there are several myths that I was able to dig out of the ancient texts and scrolls that most scholars no longer study. Though the myths differ to a certain extent, there are specific strains that run through them consistently. They all suggest that the Ghoules many millennia ago were men and women from another Kingdom on the far side of the Shattered Peaks. Much like a sword, the Talent could also be viewed as a tool. These people sought to use the Talent for their own benefit rather than for the benefit of those around them. As a result, they used it for darker and darker purposes."

"They became corrupted," said Bryen.

"Yes, that's what the myths seem to suggest. They couldn't help themselves. They pushed continually at what can and should be done with the natural magic of the world, moving the boundary closer to evil and farther away from good. Such power, once tasted, is hard to let go. And they couldn't. As they continued to use the Talent for their own selfish purposes, the power itself began to change. It was no longer the clean, natural energy of the world, but rather became something darker. Something more sinister. The people practicing it began to change as well. Fearing those from other Kingdoms would seek to steal the power that they had learned to control, they sealed their borders."

"Perhaps the cause for naming the territory beyond the Shattered Peaks the Lost Land," offered Aislinn.

"I had much the same thought," confirmed Noorsin. "With anyone not of that Kingdom prevented from entering, the people there were left on their own. My best guess is that over the centuries the Dark Magic these people had unleashed or created -- who knows which term is correct -- continued to change them, and that over time they became the Ghoules that apparently still threaten us today."

"If correct, that would explain a great deal."

"Yes, it would," said Noorsin. "But again, simply a myth, and not necessarily a truth."

"In every myth there is a nugget of truth," said Bryen.

"Protagius the Elder," replied Noorsin. "As well as Sirius, who seems to enjoy that saying quite a bit. Well done, young man. As I said, you are full of surprises."

"Although we're not certain of how the Ghoules came to

be, do we have any idea why they've chosen now to come across the Weir?" asked Bryen.

Neither Noorsin nor Aislinn could miss the intensity of his gaze. They assumed his interest resulted from yesterday's skirmish, not realizing that the Protector had a more personal interest regarding the Ghoules.

"Yes, I was wondering the same thing," said Aislinn. "Why here? Why now? And how could so many come through the Weir at once?"

"All excellent questions," replied Noorsin. "Unfortunately, I have few answers for you. Duke Winborne, Sirius, and I believe that the Ghoule Overlord still wants to conquer Caledonia, but if there is more to it than that, we have yet to discern it. So more work is required to find answers to the questions you've raised."

Aislinn seemed satisfied by the Duchess of Murcia's response, at least for now. But Bryen wasn't. He didn't think that she was lying, but he was certain that she wasn't telling the whole truth. Before he could pursue his suspicions, the Duchess turned to go.

"There are several things I would like to discuss with you, philosophical in nature, of course," said Noorsin to Bryen. "But you need to rest now. I shall return tomorrow to check on your wound, and we can continue our conversation then."

Noorsin then swept from the room, Aislinn and Bryen watching her go. He sensed that the Duchess of Murcia had several reasons for wanting to speak with him -- when she looked at him, he felt more like a specimen to be studied than anything else -- philosophy being the least of the reasons why. Perhaps she sensed his dissatisfaction with her response.

"Quite an impressive woman," said Bryen. "To the point of being intimidating."

"Yes, she is," agreed Aislinn. "You learned philosophy in the Colosseum?"

"That and many other topics," answered Bryen, shifting on his bed to find a more comfortable position.

"Is that where you learned to ride a horse? Or I should say, learned how to stand on top of a galloping horse? I've never seen anything like what you did yesterday."

Having grown tired, Bryen settled his head against his pillow, though his mind still worked furiously on the questions that Aislinn and he had raised. He felt good, better than he expected to feel after his exertions and injuries of the day before -- in fact, he hadn't expected to survive his wound, so he thanked his luck that the Duchess of Murcia had been there to help him -- but his body was still recovering, and he needed to rest.

"There were several gladiators in the Pit from Dumeria, a land far to the north," explained Bryen. "They told me that they rode their horses on steppes that went on for thousands of leagues with endless grass that stretched to the horizon. They knew their horses as well as they knew themselves. Beluchmel used this knowledge to his advantage."

"Beluchmel?"

"The Master of the Colosseum. He had the Dumerians fight on horseback against man and beast. These gladiators were kind enough to show me a few things before they were gone."

"Gone? You mean people can leave the Colosseum?"

"In a manner of speaking," Bryen replied with a sardonic twist of his lips.

"Sorry, dumb question." Aislinn cursed herself silently for misunderstanding.

"It's nothing. When you fight in the Colosseum, the only exit is death. At least for most of the gladiators. I should be thankful for my current circumstances."

Bryen's tone didn't suggest that he was, indeed, thankful.

"Well, as I said, the reason that I came here was that I wanted to thank you," she began. "I know you have no choice when it comes to protecting me. But you didn't have to assist the Guards. So I wanted to thank you for that."

Bryen looked at Aislinn for a long moment, his eyes boring into hers. She knew that he was only a few years older than she was, but the white that liberally colored his light brown hair and beard made him appear so much older than he really was. That and the hardness of his grey eyes. Even when he smiled, his eyes never changed. Aislinn thought that she should feel uneasy under her Protector's gaze, yet she didn't. It was almost as if she wanted him to see her for who she really was. Not just the Lady of the Southern Marches, but as something more than simply a title.

"You're welcome, Lady Winborne."

22

POPPY ROOT

"Enter."

With some reluctance, Tetric, Chief Advisor to the King of Caledonia, pushed the wide doors open. Time was wasting, and there were other matters that he needed to address, much more important matters. But he couldn't avoid what he had to do next. It was expected of him as a servant to the Crown, and he needed to continue to play his current role, at least for a little while longer, because it was the only way to reach the point where he could focus solely on serving himself.

The Royal Guards standing to each side of the entrance ignored him entirely, used to his coming and going at all hours of the night. The soldiers' gazes were fixed on the long hallway that connected the King's private chambers to the rest of the castle. Tetric imagined that these soldiers wished to do something more important as well, rather than guard a profligate king with loose morals who had little inclination to leave Tintagel for any reason whatsoever. Marden apparently believed that the whole of his responsibilities to Caledonia existed solely in the capital city.

Then again, perhaps not. Maybe the soldiers viewed this task as an easy assignment, one that did not require them to risk their lives for a King they probably did not respect, let alone fear. Maybe there would come a time when there would be a need for a new king, and then these and the other soldiers of the Royal Guard would know what it was like to be led by a true king. A king who knew how to exercise power deftly and who understood that fear could be employed just as effectively as compassion or trust.

But that would have to wait. The time was not quite right. Pulling his thoughts from the future, Tetric stroked his short, oily beard a few times to ensure that it ended in the perfect point that was so important to him, his actions serving to calm the agitation that continued to run through his veins. He reminded himself that he needed to discuss the matter that had brought him to the King's quarters with a careful delicacy, and thus a calm disposition was essential.

As he walked into the shadowy chamber, Tetric stepped carefully, seeking to avoid the rumpled clothing that littered the floor. Finding the far wall, he took hold of the drapes and pulled them open, allowing the bright sunlight to reveal even the darkest recesses of the bedroom. Turning reluctantly toward the bed, Tetric shook his head in disgust. He and the King had put in place a plan of cunning that demonstrated a subtle brilliance, at least in Tetric's opinion, one designed to enhance the power of the Caledonian throne in a way not seen since the First Ghoule War. Yet rather than focusing his full attention on the task at hand, Marden had succumbed once again to his greatest weakness.

The overturned pitcher of wine and the few remaining flower petals that lay next to it on the table by his bed confirmed Tetric's fear. Obtained with great difficulty and risk at the very edge of the Shattered Peaks where those towering mountains touched the Trench, the poppy root was the drug of choice for the rich and privileged, because they were the only ones who could afford it. The illicit trade had high costs, not only in terms of the work that went into acquiring the poppy root, but also in terms of men, for with every work group that traveled to that forbidding landscape some inevitably never returned. Whether because of black dragons, some other deadly beasts, or the harsh terrain, Tetric didn't know or care. It wasn't relevant to his larger design. But he did care about his accomplice's lucidity, at least at this moment. At other times allowing Marden to fall within the grasp of the poppy root often served his purposes, just not now. Not when so much depended on the cunning but flawed King of Caledonia.

"My King, we have grave matters to discuss." Tetric's sharp voice came out as a whisper.

Marden opened his eyes for the first time that morning, then rubbed at them as he tried to clear the fog that clouded his mind. He pushed himself up in the bed, then settled himself against the headboard and squinted at the bright light streaming into his room.

"We always have grave matters to discuss, Tetric," croaked Marden with some exasperation, his throat exceedingly dry from his activities of the night before. "Move over there so I can see you."

Tetric kept his lip from curling at the command, then stepped to the left and out of the sunlight, complying with Marden's wishes.

"Yes, my King. But this cannot wait and needs to be dealt with now. Privately."

Marden stared at his advisor for almost a full minute, trying to express through his gaze his annoyance at having been pulled from his dreams. But he failed miserably, flinching at Tetric's shrewd, intense black orbs, his own bloodshot eyes watering because of the brightness of his chamber. Though shorter than himself and physically not very imposing, his bald, bearded advisor exuded a sense of power that Marden desperately craved for himself. It irritated him to no end, but he hoped that the plan he had set in motion would allow him to achieve his goal. Acceding to Tetric's wishes, he slapped gently at the naked buttocks of the two servant girls who had spent the night with him.

Still feeling the effects of the wine they had drank the night before, the girls lifted their heads groggily. Tetric wondered if Marden had offered the wine with or without informing them that it contained the poppy root. He pushed the unneeded distraction from his mind. What did he care about Marden's proclivities if they kept him occupied and out of his way?

"Off with you," he said. Marden nudged the girls, both finding it difficult to gain their bearings. It didn't take long for their slow and unsteady movements to annoy the King. "Off with you, I said!"

The girls responded immediately to the command, one sliding off the bed, the other falling, both reaching quickly for their dresses, which had been strewn about the floor.

"Out!" shouted Marden, not caring if they left with or without their clothes. "Now! Or running through the halls naked will be the least of your shaming on this day!"

The girls took what few pieces of clothing that they had gathered, leaving the rest on the floor, then stumbled out of the room in tears. The guards shut the doors quietly, unperturbed by the young women scurrying down the hall and struggling to put on what few garments that they had in their possession. The soldiers assigned to protect Marden's private rooms had seen far worse during their time with him.

"We have received word from the Duke of the Southern Marches, my King."

The news brought a smile to Marden's thin lips. He had maneuvered that rigid, pompous, self-righteous lord into a corner with no avenue for escape. He would gain a great deal from the arrangement that he had proposed. Moreover, the thought of his stunningly beautiful daughter taking the place of the two scullery maids who had just left his bed aroused him. Tetric threw Marden's nightshirt to him as the Advisor endeavored to hide his distaste.

"When can we expect the Lady of the Southern Marches to join us here in Tintagel? There is so much I have to show her." Marden grinned, amused by his own wit, while Tetric ignored the crude attempt at humor.

"He delays, my King. We received a letter this morning."

"He dares to oppose me?" laughed Marden, still lounging on the bed. He was certain that he had not given Kevan any room to maneuver. "My marriage proposal was not a request. It is not something that requires discussion."

"Yes, my King. As you may recall, he said as much when we spoke to him in the Colosseum those few short months ago. But he claims that he and his daughter won't be able to attend the Fall Council. He reports that recent events require that he focus on the protection of the Southern Marches and the eastern territories."

Marden shook his head in disbelief. "He's using the excuse of piracy? That's ridiculous. We haven't seen pirates along the eastern coast of Caledonia for years."

"No, my King. Not pirates. Rather, he reports that the Battersea Guard has engaged a large Ghoule raiding pack on the road to the north of the city."

Marden's eyes narrowed, his ire rising. Ghoules? Did the Duke of the Southern Marches actually expect him to believe that? Ghoules hadn't come down from the Shattered Peaks for centuries and measures had been put in place to keep it that way.

"He's dissembling, Tetric," said Marden. "I authorized the use of the men you suggested. They failed to kidnap the girl. But even that should have been enough for the Duke to see that his daughter would be safer here. Ghoules? Even if Kevan is telling the truth about the Ghoules, and I find that hard to believe, that should simply serve as an additional incentive to bring his daughter to me, where she would be safe."

"Yes, my King," Tetric agreed amiably, though he knew that no woman or girl was ever truly safe around the King of Caledonia. "Duke Winborne believes that his daughter can be protected best in Battersea. Apparently, he has acquired a Protector for the girl. From what I have discovered, this Protector handled with ease the men that we sent. So the Duke likely believes that his daughter will be safe with her Protector by her side."

Marden laughed with a snort, then lay back into his pillows. "You overplayed your hand, didn't you, Tetric?" Marden turned his sharp, unforgiving gaze on his Advisor. The King was many things, but he was not a fool, and his mind worked quickly despite the still fading poppy root. "What did you do, Tetric? It was to be only the Order of the Assassins. I did not give you permission to contract with the Elders."

Marden pushed himself up quickly. "Because of you, Kevan now has a legitimate excuse to delay. He must defend his Duchy. Moreover, stories of the Ghoules will spread rapidly, complicating matters."

"But now we have a larger problem," continued the King. "Although I find this story of Ghoules to be a bit farfetched, I doubt that the Duke of the Southern Marches would lie to me." Marden's eyes blazed with a fervid anger, the last effects of the poppy root burned away. "So I have no choice but to believe that Ghoules have, indeed, entered through the Winter Pass. And I have no idea why they might be here, Tetric, unless, perhaps, they were invited."

"My King, we can use this to our advantage ..." Tetric began, but he never had a chance to complete his thought.

"You gave Kevan the excuse that he needed to delay, and you did so without my approval!"

Marden's eyes burned even more brightly, his face turning red with rage. Tetric bit back the sharp retort that begged to escape his lips, understanding that his position in Tintagel remained haphazard, at least for a little while longer. Until he could solidify his plans, he would need to tread carefully around Marden, who despite his many failings still retained the loyalty of most of his Guard and clearly had a sharper political acumen than Tetric had given him credit for.

"He disrespects you, my King," Tetric hissed.

"He fears for his daughter, you fool," Marden replied calmly, who had pushed his anger to the side so that he could focus his calculating mind on this new challenge. "For his Duchy as well, and rightly so."

"The Duke's concern for his daughter is not relevant to this matter, my King. This is about Caledonia, not a girl. She must do what is best for Caledonia. What she wants is of no concern."

"Maybe so, Tetric. But what would you have us do now that you have upset our carefully laid plans so grievously?"

"Push the Duke of the Southern Marches, my King.

Force him to send the girl now. If he refuses, then we view it as an insult and take immediate action. If he accepts, we can move forward with our plans that much faster."

"And what would you suggest that I do now? I can make no legitimate claim on him with his attention focused on an attack that I did not authorize!" Marden's explosive fury threatened to overwhelm him. Normally, he controlled his rage, knowing that it distracted from what he hoped to achieve. But now, Tetric had thrown a piece onto the game board that shouldn't be there, at least not yet. "And need I remind you of the Ghoules? Once those stories spread, they will complicate my strategy in ways that worry me."

"Send me to Battersea, my King. I am sure that I can convince the Duke to make the right decision."

"And if he doesn't?"

"Then I will take other steps to ensure that our plans are no longer delayed."

Marden took a few minutes to consider the request. "So be it," he finally replied. "Go. Now."

"Yes, my King." Tetric turned on his heel, but before he could take a step Marden's cold voice held him in place.

"But first you will tell me the truth about the Ghoules."

B ryen sat on one of the many large couches in the center of the Broken Citadel's library, feeling distinctly out of place. He breathed in deeply, enjoying the smell of the old books and scrolls that lined the shelves encircling the chamber. This new space, now available to him, gave him a much-needed sense of escape. He now had one more place, other than his small room, where he could break away from the demands of his life, if only for a few hours.

Having learned of his interest in history and philosophy, Aislinn had suggested that he use the library whenever time permitted and there was no one about. He had done so readily during the last few weeks, spending several hours late into the night roaming the stacks and reading after Aislinn had completed her lesson with Sirius and returned to her suite for the evening. Best of all, the library was situated just a stone's throw away from Aislinn's chambers, so he could remain close to her and still enjoy, and make the best use of, the offerings of the library without experiencing the potentially painful tug of the collar.

But Bryen's time in the library wasn't just an opportunity

for his mind to take him somewhere else. He had work to do. Bryen believed that time was of the essence, and that he needed to understand more about their adversaries. It was one thing to hear stories about Ghoules and think the creatures the stuff of legend. It was quite another to meet the beasts in the flesh. And thinking back to Declan's many lessons, he knew that the best way to defeat an opponent was to learn everything you could about them, and then use that knowledge against them. Because he had no doubt that he would be crossing swords with the Ghoules again sometime soon.

As he sat there, pausing from his reading and research, gazing at the leather-bound covers of several books he had already pulled from the shelves and placed on the couch next to him, his mind drifted to the Lady of the Southern Marches. His charge perplexed him. She was extremely intelligent, even bookish at times, yet she seemed to measure herself based on her fighting skills and what she was learning from Sirius. He could understand in part why she drove herself so hard. He need only look at her father to understand why. Yet despite everything that she did to improve herself, no matter what she might accomplish, such as hold her own against an Elder Ghoule, she never seemed to be satisfied. She always needed to be better.

He thought back to their time in the training circle earlier that morning. He had driven her hard as they practiced with daggers. Clearly, this was one of her strengths, as she had learned rapidly and competently. In fact, based on his experience training the Duke's soldiers, who now regularly attended their early morning practice sessions, Bryen could say with complete confidence that Aislinn was a better fighter than almost all the soldiers of the Battersea Guard except for perhaps Tarin and Jerad. He had told her as much, but that didn't seem to matter to her. Because of their connection through the collar, he had sensed her frustration, as if despite her work she had not reached some unattainable expectation that she had set for herself. He could sympathize. He had felt much the same way when training for the Pit. But he also understood that such a demanding perspective on life could also work against you.

Bryen pushed himself up from his seat quickly, hand on the hilt of his dagger, sword within easy reach, having sensed movement just outside the library, though he didn't believe that it was a threat. The door opened on its silent hinges and two shadows entered.

"Why on edge, young man?" asked Noorsin, who walked into the faint light offered by the handful of lit wall sconces, Sirius right behind her. "Are you worried about another attack on Aislinn?"

"No, Duchess Stelekel. Simply a force of habit."

"That I can understand."

"If you're here to look at my wound, Duchess Stelekel, there's no need. I removed the bandage several days ago. My thanks to you for your help. It has healed well."

"It's healed faster than I expected," replied Noorsin, sitting on the couch across from the one Bryen now stood in front of. "Sit down, young man. I have no desire to get a crick in my neck while speaking to you."

Bryen stared at the Duchess of Murcia for a moment more, trying to discern why she had any interest in talking with him. Failing to reach a conclusion, he then did as requested, perching on the edge of the couch so that he could rise in an instant if needed. Noorsin noticed, but did not comment, smiling to herself instead. This was going to be an interesting conversation, and she had been looking forward to it since she had first seen this young Protector working with Aislinn on the training ground. Sirius sat down next to her, his normally distant expression replaced by a keen and incisive gaze.

"It really is remarkable how quickly you healed from that wound," began Noorsin. "In fact, in my time at the Royal Medical School and with the Order, I've dealt with wounds of a similar nature a few times, corrupted in much the same way. In all those other cases, if the individual didn't die, and I must admit that despite my skill in healing almost all of them did die, the unfortunate patient would still be in their sick beds for weeks after the injury, barely able to raise their heads as their bodies fought the infection."

"I've always been a quick healer."

"Indeed," responded Noorsin, her intense stare catching Bryen's eyes, which flashed briefly with an innate defiance.

He would speak with her and answer her questions. He owed her that much. But her curiosity in him made him uncomfortable. It felt much like the last time she had examined him in the infirmary, as if he were more specimen than person. She wanted to learn something from him, that was clear, but he didn't know what that might be, and he didn't have the patience for anything but a direct conversation.

Sirius chose to interrupt at that moment. "Actually, young man, we are here for a different reason altogether. Although Noorsin remains quite intrigued by your unique healing abilities, we wanted to discuss something else with you."

Bryen sat there quietly, not feeling the need to respond. Having spent more time around Sirius during the last few weeks, he had come to understand how the Magus approached matters of import. He would begin the conversation when he was ready. So there was no point in making it easy for him. But Sirius appeared to be uncomfortable, and not sure how to start, which was very unlike him, so Noorsin decided to jump in.

"We would like to test you, young man," said Noorsin, breaking the awkward silence.

"Test me?" asked Bryen, not understanding. "Test me for what?"

"You know of the abilities that both I and Sirius possess, the abilities that Aislinn has as well and is currently learning to master. We believe you might have those same abilities."

"You mean the Talent?"

"Yes," answered Sirius finally. "As Noorsin just said, we are curious as to whether you have some skill in the Talent."

Noorsin studied the young Protector carefully following Sirius' admission. She had expected some reaction from the young man. Shock. Surprise. Fear. A chuckle of laughter. Instead, Bryen's response for quite some time was only silence and an expression that she was unable to interpret.

"Are you all right, young man?" Noorsin finally asked with some concern. Usually when it was suggested that a person might have some skill in the Talent, they were either excited or terrified, and more often than not the latter. This was not the reaction that she had expected.

Bryen nodded. "I'm fine. Why do you believe I should be Tested?"

"As Noorsin just explained, she's never seen anyone heal so quickly from a wound such as yours," said Sirius. "She believes the reason might be your ability, if you have it, to touch the Talent, even if only subconsciously. It's rare, but it has happened in the past."

"You're basing your hypothesis on a single premise," replied Bryen. "That's really not much to go on."

"I would like nothing better than to engage in a philosophical debate," said Noorsin. The more she spoke with this young man, the more she liked him. There was a fire within him, an obstinance that required him to question everything around him, and that appealed to her. He reminded her of herself at his age. "But Sirius offers further possible evidence to support his request and argument."

Sirius nodded. "When I affixed the collar of a Protector to you ..."

"You mean when you continued my enslavement." Bryen's eyes flashed dangerously. It was not something that he would ever forgive or forget. That was clear.

"I had no choice, young man. I could not refuse the Duke of the Southern Marches in his own study, despite the fact that I did not agree with his decision."

"Everyone has a choice."

"Be that as it may," continued Noorsin, hoping to regain control of the conversation. "When Sirius affixed the collar, he sensed a natural resistance."

"What do you mean by resistance?" asked Bryen.

"As if the magic of the collar struggled against some other magic," explained Sirius. "At the time, I didn't understand why that would be the case."

"But now you suspect something," said Bryen.

"Yes. And I would like to determine if my suspicions are correct."

Bryen stared at Sirius for a long time, the shadows created by the few candles in the library dancing across the walls and elongating as the minutes passed. He tried to manage his anger at what Sirius had done to him, but it was a difficult struggle. He should have reserved his fury at being made to serve as a Protector for Duke Winborne. Nevertheless, Sirius served as a key accomplice in the affair, and that still bothered him. His nod was barely discernible, but it elicited a sigh of relief from the Magus. If the two Magii were correct, maybe this would prove advantageous, and he could discover some way to remove the collar.

"What would you need to do?"

"Nothing complicated or intrusive," said Noorsin. "Sirius would simply place his hand on your forehead and with the use of just a tiny stream of the Talent ascertain if you demonstrate a reaction, a connection I should say, to the ability within you. If there is, then ..." She allowed her words to trail off.

"No more than that, correct?" Bryen's hard words were directed toward Sirius.

"No more," the Magus replied. "You have my word."

"Go ahead."

Worried that Bryen would change his mind, Sirius quickly rose from his seat and gently placed his hand on the young Protector's forehead. Reaching for the Talent, Sirius felt the energy of the natural world flow within him. For just a moment, he reveled in the power that it availed him, but only for an instant as he set about his task. Sending a tiny stream of the Talent into Bryen, probing into the boy's consciousness, Sirius opened his eyes and smiled before sitting back down.

"I take it by your expression that you confirmed your suspicions," said Bryen evenly, his voice emotionless, hard. Noorsin assumed that Bryen's gladiator persona, so much a part of this young man for so long, was revealing itself once more.

"I did," replied Sirius. "You clearly have the ability to touch the Talent. I should have realized that the first time I met you. You have a potential strength that I have rarely seen before. Only a few current Magii could manage as much of the Talent as you can."

"Which would explain why you healed so quickly from your wound," continued Noorsin. "Whether you knew it or not, your connection to the Talent aided you. It helped you heal. And having seen the scars of the wounds you suffered in the Pit, I believe your innate connection to the Talent has aided you in that regard as well. It might very well be why you're still alive today, as that long scar on your left side suggests that you should be dead."

Bryen's mind drifted back a few years at the mention of that particular injury. He had fought a Giant Scorpion, the creature towering above him, its sharp stinger perpetually poised to strike down at him. And strike down it did. Dozens of times. He had killed the creature by sliding through the white sand of the Pit on his back and dragging his sword through the animal's soft underbelly, but not before one of the Giant Scorpion's dozens of strikes had hit home. However, rather than being impaled, the creature's stinger had sliced down his rib cage instead.

Afterwards, he had hovered near death for several days because of the poison released into his bloodstream by that single hit. There was no cure for the venom. Declan, Davin, and Lycia had stayed with him night and day, expecting the worst, just not knowing when it would come. Yet much to their surprise and pleasure, one morning he had awakened feeling fresh and renewed, the corrupted wound having healed and leaving just the long scar that gradually had faded with time. Somehow his body had fought and won against a poison of which one drop normally would kill a person in minutes.

"May I ask you a few questions, Bryen?" asked Sirius.

Bryen came back from his memories reluctantly. He nodded his permission.

"From what Tarin told me, you had been a gladiator for

quite some time. That you were an orphan before entering the Colosseum. Correct?"

"Yes, my parents died shortly after we reached Tintagel."

"Where are you from? Do you remember?"

"Somewhere to the east. I don't remember much about it since I was only a child. I believe it was on the eastern side of the Northern Spine because my mother always warned me to never go too far from our home. 'The Waste is near,' she liked to say. She didn't want me wandering into it by mistake. At least that's one of the few things that I recall."

Sirius gave Noorsin a meaningful look, a twinge of anxiety adding to his discomfort, then continued with his questioning. "What happened to your parents?"

"They were murdered," he replied quietly.

Noorsin closed her eyes for a moment in sympathy, then picked up where Sirius had left off.

"This may be difficult for you, and it may not be something that you want to answer, but could you tell us how? Or at least what you remember?"

Bryen pushed himself back into the couch, staring up at the circular skylight at the very top of the chamber, the etching barely visible in the darkness. He had tried to push those memories from his mind many times. But they always returned, usually in the nightmares that plagued his sleep every night.

"I'm not sure why their deaths would concern you," Bryen sighed. "Wouldn't our time be better spent focused on more important matters?"

Sirius and Noorsin sat across from him quietly, staring intently.

"I believe this is an important matter," Sirius replied.

"Please," added Noorsin.

After a time, he began speaking in a monotone, seeking to keep the emotion from his voice.

"We had just arrived in Tintagel, and I remember my parents were looking for an inn for the night. My father was talking to my mother, saying something about how we were supposed to meet someone the next morning. A friend. Someone they had never mentioned before."

Sirius sat straighter upon hearing Bryen's words, bringing back memories of his own that he had sought to keep locked away. Rather than interrupt, he closed his eyes and bowed his head, fearing that he already knew much of what Bryen was about to say.

Bryen began speaking in clipped sentences, as if he was simply reporting on the terrible event rather than having lived through it.

"It was late. The street was deserted. My father said the inn was just up the hill. That it would offer some protection. I never understood why he said something like that. About an inn, no less. It didn't make sense. We were almost there when several cloaked figures appeared around us. It was dark and had begun to rain. I didn't get a good look at them. They were taller than anyone I had ever seen. They wore cowls so I couldn't see their faces. They attacked us. My parents fought back. Right at the start, my father engaged one of the cowled figures. He saved me. He pulled me to the ground and sent a flash of something right back at the attacker. My father never pulled a sword or dagger, so I'm not sure what he had done. But once he had gotten me to the ground, he couldn't get up.

"I crawled out from under him and rolled him over. His chest was charred black. Whatever the figure on the other side of the street had done, it had killed my father, and he had died saving me. I wanted to help, but I couldn't. It was like I had been placed in a protective bubble. Streams of energy, some darker than the night, some brighter than sunlight, streaked down the street. But I wasn't afraid. My mother had done something so that even though I was right there, the streams of black couldn't touch me. The fight seemed to last forever, but it was only a few minutes. My mother charged toward the same creature, the bolts of energy still shooting down the street. But she fell to her knees, a bloody wound in her side. One of the creatures had surprised her. He was going to stab her again, so I charged him. I stabbed him in the back with the dagger my father had given me for my birthday.

"The creature knocked me back into the mud. He couldn't reach the dagger, so he left my mother alone. Then one of the figures on the side of the street snuck up on her. He drove his blade into the back of her neck. When she died, whatever was holding me, protecting me, disappeared. I wanted to go to my parents, to help them somehow, but I couldn't. One of the creatures came toward me, and I ran. I barely escaped, finding a garbage pit not too far away. I dug into it and stayed there until the morning. When I finally emerged from my hiding place, I went back to the street where we had been attacked. My parents' bodies were gone. It was like what happened the night before had never occurred. As if my parents hadn't even existed."

Bryen shifted his gaze away from the skylight, fixing it now on Noorsin and Sirius.

"I had no one to turn to, nowhere to go, so I lived on the streets of Tintagel for almost a year, surviving by my wits alone, stealing food, no different than many other orphans," he continued. "Tintagel does have a few orphanages, but you learn quickly to avoid them like the plague. Better to be on the street. But as I became hungrier, I took more risks.

Eventually my brazenness caught up with me. The Watch arrested me when I was trying to steal some fruit in the market. It was then that Declan saved me, taking me to the Colosseum to serve as a gladiator rather than being hung or sold to a pleasure house."

"Save you?" proclaimed Noorsin. "Gladiatorial games are nothing short of barbaric."

"True," replied Bryen. "But the Watch could have sold me to a worse fate."

Sirius had yet to raise his head, still staring at the carpet, his arms leaning against his knees. "Bryen, what were your parents' names?"

"Alana and Loren."

Sirius finally raised his head and looked at Bryen once more, his eyes brimming with unfallen tears. He could barely breathe out his next few words, but he needed to confirm what he already knew.

"And your family name, Bryen?"

"That name hasn't meant anything to me for a long time. When you're in the Pit, your name doesn't matter. The only name that matters is the one given to you by the crowd."

"What name did the crowd give you?" asked Noorsin, noting Sirius' impatience at wanting his question answered, but the Duchess of Murcia ignored him, taking her time because she understood the delicate nature of their questioning.

"Volkun," Bryen replied. "After my first fight in the Pit, the crowd serenaded me with it, and the Master of the Gladiators told me that it fit my fighting style perfectly."

"Volkun in the Old Tongue means the Wolf," said Noorsin.

"Yes, Declan told me that once."

"And Declan is?"

"The Master of the Gladiators in the Colosseum. He's the one who took me in, saved me from the Watch."

"And made you a gladiator," said Noorsin, her disapproval clear in her voice.

"No, the King did that, or at least the King's supposed justice," countered Bryen. "Declan didn't have any choice. It was all that he could do to save me as he is a slave himself, and he knew that the only way to protect me was to teach me. So he did. He taught me how to fight, how to protect myself."

Noorsin nodded. "He certainly did an excellent job. I've watched you train Aislinn. And I've heard the stories of your encounter with the Elder Ghoule. You do move like a wolf. The name given to you is most apt."

"Bryen, having seen you fight, Declan clearly knew what he was about," interrupted Sirius, his impatience getting the better of him. "But still I need to ask again. What is your patronym?"

For a long moment, Bryen simply stared at the Magus, and Sirius feared that the Protector wouldn't answer. Then the name came out in a whisper.

"Keldragan."

Sirius abruptly rose from his seat, wiping at his eyes as he turned away and walked into the shadows. Noorsin understood why, but it wasn't her place to explain it to the stoic young man sitting before her.

"That's a strong name as well," said Noorsin, continuing the conversation in order to give Sirius the time that he needed to master his emotions and regain his focus. "In the Old Tongue that translates to *Dragon Warrior*. The Wolf and the Dragon Warrior. I doubt that there are but a handful of people in all of Caledonia who could make a claim to such a heritage."

"They're just names," protested Bryen. But as soon as he said it, he regretted it, because he didn't believe his own words, remembering a conversation with King Corinthus Beleron five years before on the same topic.

"Names have power," said Noorsin strongly but not harshly. "Never forget that."

Bryen stared at Noorsin. Her eyes were sharp, intense, as if she were trying to force a hidden meaning into him, yet he wasn't sure that he quite understood what she meant. Hoping to relieve himself of her gaze, he nodded.

Sirius finally returned from the gloom, having regained his composure. "Bryen, do you come to the library every evening?"

"Yes, once Aislinn goes to her rooms after she trains with you."

Sirius nodded. "That's good. I will meet you here tomorrow evening. We will begin your training in the Talent after I am done working with Aislinn."

Quiet descended for a few moments, Bryen sensing that this was an important moment. The unexpected turn in the conversation had surprised him.

"Why do you want to do this for me? I'm just a Protector. A slave by any other name."

"What do you mean?" asked Sirius.

"Why teach me the skills and knowledge of a Magus? So I can defend Aislinn more effectively?"

Sirius stared at the young Protector for almost a minute, the old man's expression shifting from sadness to anger to resolve as he thought about how to respond. Bryen saw that the Magus' perpetually distracted look had slipped away, the real person beneath appearing. There was power there, belief, and an ancientness that startled Bryen.

"I failed some very close friends some time ago and

never thought that I would have the chance to make amends," said Sirius. "But I see now that I may be able to do something after all."

Sirius leaned in close to Bryen, his eyes blazing with a fire that Bryen had never expected to see.

"I will train you in how to use the Talent, young man, so that you learn how to fight in another way, and so that you can protect yourself, not just Aislinn. I will see you tomorrow night once Aislinn returns to her rooms, and every night thereafter."

With that, Sirius stalked from the room. Noorsin rose and nodded to Bryen, silently following after.

As the quiet once more settled within the library, Bryen tried to push the conversation from his mind so that he could go back to the book that he had been reading. Yet every time he tried, he failed. With the scab removed, his thoughts naturally drifted back to that terrible night so long ago on a deserted street in Tintagel.

But this time his perspective had changed. His thoughts now centered on the green scales he had glimpsed on the forearm of one of the attackers. And he knew in his heart, though he couldn't explain why, that the reappearance of the Ghoules was connected to his parents' murder. But he still didn't know why.

So many questions and so few answers. Yet Bryen was certain of one thing. Both Sirius and Noorsin were holding something back, and he meant to find out what.

24

A STRONG NAME

"Do you believe this wise, my King? These gladiators are nothing but scum. They are condemned. They have nothing to lose. They can't be trusted."

Marden Beleron, King of Caledonia, turned his crafty eyes toward Killen Sourban, but he could hold the gaze of the Captain of the Royal Guard for only so long. Killen's icy blue eyes made him nervous. There was an emptiness there. It seemed that whatever humanity might have existed in the man had been removed long ago, and his eyes confirmed it.

"It is not your place to question me, Killen. Remember that."

"Yes, my King." Killen bowed his head in acceptance of his monarch's rebuke, though that's as far as his subservience would go. "I simply worry for your safety."

Marden couldn't help but chuckle as he flipped a hand behind him to acknowledge the full company of Royal Guard at his back, several dozen of whom had already entered the gladiators' training ground to prepare the way for him. He then glanced upward, taking in the staggered walls upon which Caledonian soldiers bearing crossbows stood at regular intervals before peering at the outer façade of the Colosseum, which rose behind the enclosed dirt field and ancient barracks.

"I doubt I have anything to fear, Killen, but thank you for your concern." Marden then stepped forward through the gate with an unwavering confidence. "Now come along, Captain."

Killen and the company of Royal Guard trudged after Marden, who was trying to put some distance between himself and his soldiers, perhaps to make a point to the gladiators he was walking among that he didn't feel any fear being in their presence, though Killen guessed that his action was more to make that point to himself. Of course, the gladiators paid barely any attention to the monarch who had deigned to visit them this morning. As Killen followed Marden around the practice yard, he saw that every one of the fighters in the compound cared little about their illustrious visitor, remaining focused on their practice.

The Captain watched in astonishment at how the gladiators trained. Some gladiators charged across thin beams of wood while dodging sword thrusts from their peers, who were stationed along the way. Others practiced their archery, shooting steel-tipped arrows in a constant stream toward the targets set against the far wall, while a few did the same with spears instead. Not striking the center of the target was the exception. And those were just a few of the activities going on around him.

It was all movement. There was no idle chatter. No standing around. Killen assumed that those who had been sentenced to fight in the Pit had concluded that their ability to stay alive rested solely on their own shoulders, so they set about improving their odds for doing so with a will. Or perhaps the man that Marden now strode toward had something to do with it.

The Captain of the Royal Guard didn't doubt that this man could best every gladiator training in the Colosseum with little effort, and then just as easily turn his attention to the soldiers of the Royal Guard who had entered the practice yard. When the man's eyes finally turned to take in the approaching King and then him, Killen's hand drifted down to the hilt of his sword, recognizing the coiled violence that could spring from the man at any moment. Killen was certain that he could best the gladiator, but he acknowledged reluctantly that it would be a close thing.

"You are Declan, Master of the Gladiators."

The man ignored the King for a moment, his eyes shifting back to the combat currently playing out in the training circle. Killen followed his gaze. Two gladiators stood back to back. Both were tall. Both had flaming red hair. The man allowed his hair to run free; the woman's was braided down her back. Brother and sister, he assumed, and clearly dangerous, as they appeared to be having little trouble keeping the six gladiators circling them at bay.

"I am, King Beleron." Declan had waited as long as he could before responding, wanting to make the point that the King was now in his domain without stepping too far over the line and actually insulting him. "And to what do we owe the pleasure of your visit?"

Declan's focus stayed on the fight that was taking place before him. Two of the six gladiators were now down in the dirt on their backs, knocked unconscious. They had gotten too close to the woman. With the long spear that she spun slowly from her right hand to her left and then back again, she had taken out one and then the other with the butt of her weapon faster than a person could blink. The remaining four gladiators had shifted their positioning to fill the gaps and keep the two surrounded, but if what Killen had just seen was any indication, their effort was wasted. The combat was already decided, the circling gladiators just didn't know it yet.

"I require a few minutes of your time," said Marden, who was trying to determine if the Master of the Gladiators was simply distracted by the combat or was purposely trying to disrespect him. He settled on the former, unable to comprehend that a slave would take such a risk. "I would like to speak with you about a gladiator."

Declan nodded, his gaze never leaving the training circle. Two more of the gladiators were down now. The young woman had feinted an attack at the two fighters on her side, forcing the two larger combatants back, and the two gladiators on the far side had thought to take advantage of her movement, trying to come at her from behind. But they had realized too late that her feint was actually a trap. When the two gladiators behind her moved forward, the young man drove into their flanks, his spear a blur as he knocked the first gladiator unconscious with a hard strike to his helmet and then used the shaft to sweep the feet out from under the other fighter. At the same moment that the gladiator slammed onto the ground, the young man jabbed the butt of his spear into his throat. Not hard enough to kill him, but certainly with enough power to disable the man and take him out of the fight as the fallen combatant struggled to breathe.

"Which gladiator?" asked Declan. "I have many here."

With four of their opponents eliminated from the combat, the young man and the young woman separated from one another, pairing off with the two remaining combatants. Their expressions were unreadable. To Killen they appeared to be focused entirely on the task at hand, their eyes never leaving the men who tried to stay within the bounds of the training circle but still keep their distance from the twin gladiators' twirling spears.

"The one called the Volkun," replied Marden.

The name the King offered finally caught the attention of the Master of the Gladiators as his right eyebrow rose just a bit, the only sign that he had heard.

"Finish this," ordered Declan.

The two red-haired fighters responded immediately to the command. The young man shot forward, his spear point aimed for his opponent's throat. Then, at the very last moment, he pivoted, bringing the haft of the spear down on the helmet of his opponent. The man collapsed into the dirt with a groan, unable to rise. The young woman took a similar tack, feinting a lunge and then with remarkable speed swinging the haft of her spear up between her adversary's legs. After that strike, she didn't need to do anything else but watch as the gladiator dropped his spear, grabbed for his midsection, and collapsed to his knees, barely able to breathe as an unimaginable pain wracked his body. The brother and sister nodded to each other, then leaned against the hafts of their spears as they turned their attention toward Declan and the King.

"What would you like to know about the Volkun, King Beleron?" asked Declan, his piercing gaze settling directly on Marden. For a moment, Marden experienced the desire to turn away, but he forced himself to keep his eyes locked on those of the Master of the Gladiators. He refused to back down. His pride was at stake, as well as his reputation.

"The name itself seems a bit pretentious, does it not?" Marden asked with a laugh, trying to establish a rapport with the older man. "The Wolf? A bit much for one likely no older than I am."

"He didn't name himself. The crowd gave him that name. He earned it."

"Why the Volkun?"

"I can't speak for the crowd, King Beleron. Who can? The crowd does what the crowd desires. There generally is little rhyme or reason to their decisions."

Marden waited for more, but clearly the Master of the Gladiators had nothing else to say. His deep, grey eyes twinkled, as if he was enjoying the opportunity to irritate his master.

"If you had to guess?" Marden prompted.

Declan smiled, but it was more predatory than a sign of pleasure. "If I had to guess, the crowd likely picked up on his movement and his ferocity. The Volkun was fast, faster than any other gladiator whom I've had the privilege of training. And he never quit. Once the combat started, he fought with a savagery that only a few others have exhibited on the white sand of the Pit. I can only assume that the crowd believed that because of that, he resembled a wolf."

"Just so," replied Marden. He had only seen the Volkun fight twice, against the Champion of Sharston and then the black dragon, and in his opinion the crowd had named the gladiator appropriately, though he refused to admit it. "And the Volkun's real name?"

"Bryen," replied Declan. He had hesitated to offer it, but if he didn't respond to the King's question, someone else would.

"A mundane name," said Marden.

"A strong name," corrected Declan.

Marden looked at the Master of the Gladiators and realized that though the man continued to smile, his eyes were hard and unforgiving. A shiver of fear shot through the King, something that he was unaccustomed to. He felt the urge to step back from Declan, but he held his ground, comforted by the fact that Killen stood at his back and his soldiers had formed a circle around him that included the Master of the Gladiators and the two red-haired fighters in the center, both of whom now stared at him with an intensity that sent another shiver of fear up his spine. He was unused to the feeling that threatened to set his limbs trembling, but he had to admit that he found it oddly exhilarating.

"Why did the Duke of the Southern Marches buy the Volkun?" asked Marden.

Even though his soldiers were close at hand, the King of Caledonia was beginning to feel uncomfortable. He had little desire to try to continue to banter with a man who clearly had no desire to do so and was enjoying so obviously his discomfort.

"I can't say," responded Declan.

"You can't say, or you won't say?" interrupted Killen. The Captain of the Royal Guard gave the Master of the Gladiators his flintiest glare, yet it had little impact on his target, who simply ignored him.

"I can't say," Declan replied again. "Duke Winborne didn't take me into his confidence."

"But if you had to guess?" prompted Killen harshly.

Declan finally acknowledged the Captain of the Royal Guard, apparently measuring him in a matter of seconds and determining that the man wasn't worth his time, before turning his attention back to the King of Caledonia.

"If I had to guess, I expect it's because Bryen survived in the Pit for a decade. He's one of the best fighters I've ever trained, if not the best. If that's what Duke Winborne was looking for, a fighter such as that, then that's what he got."

Marden nodded slowly as he considered Declan's response. "How would the Volkun compare to these two?" he asked, gesturing toward the brother and sister still leaning against their spears. "Could he best them?"

"Who can say?" replied Declan. "Anything can happen in the Pit."

"You know, Declan, I was thinking that if Duke Winborne has purchased a gladiator, perhaps I should acquire one as well."

Declan simply stared at Marden, not bothering to respond, though his expression suggested that he was less than pleased by the idea.

"What of these two?" asked Marden, motioning to the two gladiators who had just demonstrated their skill in the training circle. "Perhaps the girl? I expect that she's quite attractive once you wash away the dirt and grime covering her, and she seems to have a great deal of experience handling a spear."

The young woman's cheeks flushed red, and her eyes blazed the same color as her hair, her anger at the King's insinuation barely controlled. The young man's strong hand on her forearm kept her firmly where she stood, though her brother's eyes suggested that he would more than welcome the opportunity to drive his weapon through the King's chest, and the tall gladiator wouldn't bat an eye doing it.

"Better watch your tone, King Beleron. The Crimson Devil could break you in two without breaking a sweat."

Killen bristled at the veiled insolence the Master of the Gladiators offered the King. "You better watch your tone. You're speaking to your King."

"Or what?" Declan replied quietly. Killen had taken a

step closer to his master, a foot of steel now showing from the Captain of the Royal Guard's scabbard. "You'll make me a slave? Throw me into the Pit? It's too late for that. There's nothing that you can do to me that hasn't already been done."

Marden stared at the Master of the Gladiators. He could kill the man for his impertinence right there without any consequences. But he would wait. He would gain his revenge when it would really matter.

"Careful, Declan. I understand that you're not afraid of me." Marden stepped in close so that he could whisper into the older man's ear, and also demonstrate his lack of fear at being so near to the trained killer, though it was more show than reality, because the Master of the Gladiators did, indeed, unsettle him. "That you don't really care about what happens to you. But you might want to think about your gladiators." He nodded toward the brother and sister. "Perhaps you'll care about what I can do to them."

25

A NEW UNDERSTANDING

"Is everything all right, Lady Winborne?"

Aislinn had pushed the door halfway open on its silent hinges and was about to peek around the door frame, but she froze when she heard her Protector's voice. She stopped for a moment, steeling herself.

The last few nights she had paced in her suite of rooms, a nervous energy flowing through her as the fight on the north road played continually through her mind. She still couldn't believe that Ghoules were in the Southern Marches. She wanted to know why, but she had made little progress in finding an answer, her father, Noorsin, and Sirius unusually tight-lipped. She needed to change her routine, to do something that would give her an opportunity to step back, even if just for a moment, and be something other than what she was -- heir to the Southern Marches -- in order to gain a different perspective. So not knowing where else to go, now she was here.

"Yes, Bryen," replied Aislinn, stepping silently into the library and closing the door behind her. "But you need to stop calling me by my title when we're alone. Aislinn will do when it's just us."

Her Protector had risen from the couch on the other side of the room, the only light filtering dimly through the large chamber cast by the handful of candles arrayed around him. He studied his charge for a brief moment. Aislinn wore her nightgown and a robe. Nothing revealing, of course, but in that instant Bryen saw the Lady Winborne in a way that he never had before, as a beautiful young lady rather than the girl he was required to protect. He pushed that thought from his mind, concentrating instead on the weight of the collar pressing down on him. Her father owned him. Despite his new privilege of visiting the library, he remained a slave with little control over his life.

Aislinn sat down in the chair across from him, her blue eyes sparkling in the candlelight, and motioned for him to sit as well.

"What are you reading? It looks like that book is falling apart."

"*The Legend of Arick Winborne*," he answered as he regained his seat.

"That would explain its sorry state," nodded Aislinn. "If I recall correctly, it was written shortly after the First Ghoule War."

"Yes, it was," Bryen replied.

Aislinn expected Bryen to say more, but apparently his limited loquaciousness, and by that she meant speaking more than two or three sentences together at the same time, was restricted for the most part to their early morning training sessions in the circle. "I didn't know you were interested in ancient history."

"That and more."

Aislinn gritted her teeth. She had come here hoping to

regain her focus, to settle her nerves and attain a calm she sorely wanted, but at the moment all she felt was a building exasperation. Rather than let her temper get the better of her, she tried a different approach with the hope of initiating a meaningful conversation.

"Why this book out of the thousands on these shelves? From what I remember of my lessons when I was younger, that text was more fable than history. I'm not sure it will explain the Ghoules we faced the other day. Are there any texts more recent rather than one focused on folklore?"

Bryen stared at Aislinn silently, watching the flickering candles play across her smiling face and twinkling eyes. His mind started to wander in a direction that it shouldn't, one that he had never considered before. He needed to move his thoughts to a different path, knowing that if he wasn't careful his charge would be able to decipher them.

"I was taught that the foundation for every myth was truth."

"You didn't get that from, Sirius, did you?" asked Aislinn with a grin. "He says something much the same quite frequently."

"No, from Declan," replied Bryen. "Perhaps he and Sirius were friends when they were younger."

Aislinn smiled. "If I didn't know better, I'd take your last comment as an attempt at humor."

At first Bryen thought Aislinn was criticizing him, but the sparkle in her eyes told him otherwise. "A lame attempt, apparently."

"Even so, a day for us to remember," she said with a husky laugh. "But again, why this particular tome?"

"As I said, I was taught that every myth contains a grain of truth," said Bryen. "Keeping in mind, of course, that the argument could be made that if a myth is repeated often enough and becomes an accepted part of a society's culture, that myth inevitably will then become truth."

"The contingency of truth," interrupted Aislinn. She should have been surprised that she was having this conversation with her Protector, but she wasn't. Not after the discussion that had occurred in the medical ward when Bryen was recovering from his wound. Clearly her Protector was better educated than anyone had expected. "I can't remember the philosopher's name, but I remember the argument. And this applies to this text how?"

"It applies marginally," answered Bryen. "I'm simply making the point that there may be some truth somewhere within the story of your founding forebear. I thought to read more about him because of what happened on the coastal road."

Finally it all began to fit together for Aislinn. At first, she had thought that Bryen was simply trying to irritate her, and if so, he had been doing quite well at accomplishing his task. But now she realized that he had simply been seeking to explain in his own, admittedly roundabout, fashion.

"You're interested in the Ghoules just as I am."

"Yes."

Once again Aislinn expected more from Bryen, but he sat there silently. She closed her eyes, willing herself to be patient. She continued their conversation, hoping to draw him out some more.

"You're seeking to learn more about how to fight them? After what happened a few weeks ago, it would seem that you've already mastered that ability."

"Fight them, yes," said Bryen. "But not in a small skirmish. I want to learn the tactics that were used during the First Ghoule War to push them back beyond the Shattered Peaks."

"You think there will be more raiding packs?"

Initially Aislinn hoped that it was a happenstance that they had come across the Ghoules, but the more she thought about it, the more she concluded that the beasts were there for a reason. But what? There were few reasons for the Ghoules to brave the Winter Pass, and none of them good for Caledonia. And why now?

"Yes, I do. Moreover, why that raiding pack there?"

"What do you mean?"

"Why was that raiding pack on that section of the north road the very same time that we were?"

"My father seems to think that it was our own bad luck. We were at the wrong place at the wrong time."

"Did you believe him?" Bryen asked. "Your father also sent out more than a dozen companies of soldiers to search the countryside for any surviving Ghoules and any other packs that may be out there. In addition, he increased the Guard around Battersea as well as the Broken Citadel. And he increased the Guard specifically in that section of the Citadel where you have your quarters. Just because your father told you he thought that it was bad luck doesn't mean he believes his own words. Moreover, Tarin says that weeks can go by without a single traveler on the north road. Yet the one time we ride it, we're attacked by a Ghoule pack. Putting all that together, I would suggest that there was more to this engagement than just happenstance. Your father knows it, and he is responding in a way that confirms it."

Aislinn stared at Bryen. In just the last few seconds he had said more in a single breath to her than he'd likely said during his entire time in Battersea. Pushing that fact to the side, Bryen's words resonated with her as she had been thinking much the same. She hadn't paid much attention to what had occurred after the attack, how her father had reacted, yet her Protector had. In fact, nothing had escaped him.

"I agree with you that the Ghoules were there for a specific purpose." Aislinn sat back in her chair, the fingers of her right hand tapping a rhythm on the wooden armrest. Deep in thought, she examined the situation from a strategic perspective. "But what could the reason be?" she asked, her mind still working on the problem.

"You know," Bryen replied simply.

Her fingers stopped tapping when she leaned forward. "You think that the Ghoules were there for me."

Bryen nodded, not feeling the need to say anything more. He could see that the conclusion she had reached rattled her. He understood that she needed time for that realization to settle.

"But why me?" she finally asked. "Why would an Elder Ghoule have any interest in the heir to the Southern Marches?"

"Two excellent questions," replied Bryen. "And I have no answers for you. At least not yet."

"I had come here to try to find answers to why the Ghoules have reappeared," complained Aislinn. "Yet you give me even more to ponder than when I first arrived."

"The privileges of being the heir to the Southern Marches."

Aislinn snorted at Bryen's response. "Not humor, but rather sarcasm. Will wonders never cease this evening?"

For several minutes they settled into a comfortable silence, neither feeling the need to talk. Bryen focused on the moonlight streaming through the stained glass and avoided looking at Aislinn, not wanting his mind to drift too far down a certain, uncomfortable road.

Every once in a while, Aislinn's eyes fell upon him. The

more time she spent with her Protector, and the more she learned about him and from him, the more confused she became. She had never felt the need for a Protector. She had never wanted a Protector. And as a result, at first, she had been angry. Angry at her father for doing this to her, for not trusting her. Angry at Bryen for always being there, for always being a presence in her head, for never giving her the space she craved. Yet it was only recently that she realized that she needed to consider Bryen's standpoint. If anyone had a right to be angry, it was her Protector. Not yet ready to retire for the night, she sought to move the conversation down a brighter path.

"You come here every night?"

"I do."

"Why?"

"Because I can."

Aislinn thought for a moment before responding, finally beginning to understand a little bit more about her Protector. "You have a choice."

"I have a choice. One of my few choices."

Aislinn stared at Bryen, taking in everything about him. He confused her, and she didn't know why. Perhaps it was because he was so different from anyone else that she knew. Many of the people she interacted with wanted something from her, whether a favor or recognition or a privilege or even her. But Bryen didn't want anything from her, because the one thing he wanted she couldn't give him. That thought pained her. She closed her eyes for a moment, nodding in understanding.

"I'm sorry. I didn't ask for this. Maybe there is something in these old books that can tell us how to remove the collar."

"I don't blame you," he said. Then a small smile played

across his lips. "At least not anymore. And if there is some-thing here, I haven't found it."

This time when Aislinn looked at Bryen, their eyes met, her Protector's gaze holding her own. She couldn't look away even if she wanted to, yet she felt a loss when Bryen finally broke the connection. They nodded to one another, having reached an unspoken agreement, one in which they acknowledged that the circumstances that had brought them together were out of their control and that all they could do was make the best out of what they had.

When Aislinn finally stood to leave, Bryen stood as well. Their movement brought them close together, no more than a finger's breadth away. Not knowing why, Aislinn reached up with her hand, touching Bryen's collar, feeling the cool metal and the energy that it contained, a spark of recogni-tion surging within her. She withdrew her fingers slowly. Aislinn stared into her Protector's eyes for just a moment, then turned quickly and walked out.

After Aislinn left the library, Bryen stared out the open door, not understanding what had just happened. The only thing that he did know was that for the first time since arriving in Battersea, he felt like he was where he was supposed to be. And that thought scared him in a way that his combats on the white sand of the Pit never had.

26

THREADS OF ENERGY

"Are you ready?"

Sirius had entered the library just a few seconds before, having completed his evening lesson with Aislinn. He was pleased with her progress. During his many years as an instructor in the Talent, all his pupils had followed a similar progression. In the beginning, they would improve slowly, much like they were pushing a large boulder up a hill, but then once they became more comfortable in the art, and their understanding of how the Talent functioned increased, they would progress rapidly, as if they had pushed the boulder to the top of the hill. But then they would hit a wall, essentially plateauing for a time until they were ready to take the next step with the Talent, to push the boulder up the next hill, because there were always more hills.

Then the cycle would begin again as his students learned to master the more difficult and complicated aspects of the Talent. Inevitably, this often stilted progression annoyed his pupils. He would tell them to let the frustration go, knowing that it was simply a part of the process. What had pleased him the most in working with the Lady of the Southern Marches these last few weeks was that she had not only pushed the boulder up the hill, but she had avoided any plateaus and had simply continued up the next hill, and then the next, expanding her ability in the Talent every night.

Since the attack on the North Road, Aislinn had blown past many of the walls that his previous students had been forced to overcome, as if her contest with the Elder Ghoule had given her a certainty and belief in her abilities that few attained at such a young age. For what she had been doing with the Talent the last few nights was usually only seen in someone who had already passed the Test and completed their apprenticeship. If that was the case, then all the better. She needed to be ready, because time was running short for her.

He pushed that thought from his mind and turned his attention to the young man who had been waiting for him. Bryen stood there calmly, seemingly at peace. But Sirius knew better. There was a wariness about his new pupil, a natural distrust, that suggested that he had already seen more of the world and its less savory and dangerous aspects during his short life than he should have. The boy was always on his toes. Always ready to move. Always scanning his surroundings for the next threat. He doubted that this part of his personality came from his brief time serving as Aislinn's Protector. Instead, he guessed that his many years fighting in the Pit had inscribed it within him, making it a part of his very identity. Taking Bryen's silence as acquiescence, he plowed forward.

"Good. Then let's begin."

In a flash, blazing white threads of energy appeared

around Sirius. He pulled more and more of the glowing strands from the Talent and began directing the flow. The threads responded, circling around Sirius, and then as more and more joined in the swirl, he expanded the small circle until it extended to the walls of the turret. The strands of energy spun faster and faster around the chamber in a dazzling, blinding display.

"Did you see what I did there?" asked Sirius. "How I reached for the Talent?"

"The Talent is where the energy came from, correct?" asked Bryen.

"Yes. The Talent contains all the natural magic in the world, and the Talent is all around us. But only some of us have the ability to not only sense the Talent, but also to make use of it. It's from this reservoir of energy that a Magus obtains his or her power. Or rather, I should say that a Magus accesses his or her power by learning how to connect to the Talent and then pull a fraction of that natural energy into them. They can then apply the Talent to whatever task they have in their mind."

Bryen nodded. "Yes, I saw what you did."

"You need to understand that it may be a struggle at the start," continued Sirius, not really listening to Bryen. None of his students during their first lesson had ever reached out and grasped the Talent successfully, much less perceived how he manipulated the flows of energy. The Magus expected that today's instruction would be much as it had been in the past, a frustrating experience as the Protector struggled to touch the natural magic of the world. "Simply finding the Talent can be a challenge, to say nothing of the difficulty of touching it for the first time. Wait. Did you say that you saw what I did?"

Bryen smiled gently, not wanting to irritate his new instructor. "Yes, I saw what you did."

Closing his eyes for just a moment, Bryen centered himself much like he did before a contest in the Pit. Declan had taught him how to do it, how to focus so intently on one thing that the rest of the world fell away until there was only silence and stillness. And, in that moment, Bryen perceived the Talent. Imagining that he was reaching out to touch a stream of water, he became immersed in the Talent, the threads of white energy flowing through him, building within him, filling him with a warmth that he had experienced before.

He wasn't surprised. Several disconnected memories formed into a theory that led him down the road to this unexpected but correct conclusion. It would explain how he healed so quickly, even from his most ghastly wounds acquired on the white sand of the Colosseum, or why he felt a heat in his chest every time Aislinn touched the Talent. He realized that it wasn't because of his connection to her through the collar, but rather it came from him. When she touched the Talent, apparently it awakened his link to the Talent as well. He just hadn't understood what was really going on.

Opening his eyes, several small strands of power danced across his palms. A large grin replaced his normally reticent countenance, which only grew when he saw Sirius' expression of amazement. Feeling confident in his control, he reached more deeply into the stream of energy. More threads appeared, and now they jumped from one palm to the next. Smiling even more broadly, Bryen felt an exhilaration that he hadn't experienced since he was much younger, when he had first started training with Declan in the Pit and the newness of it all had excited rather than terrified him, before the years of killing had eaten away at him and deadened his soul. Thinking about what he wanted to do next, the Talent responded, forming into a shimmering circle that spun in front of his chest.

Sirius was shocked by the ease with which his new student had taken to the Talent. In all his time he had never seen anyone accomplish what Bryen was doing so fast and so adeptly. But then again, why should he be surprised? He knew who the boy's parents were. That thought saddened the Magus, but only for a second. There was nothing he could do about the past. Yet there was something that he could do in the present that would prove useful, perhaps critically so, in the future. Realizing the opportunity that he had before him, not only to teach Bryen, but also perhaps to make amends in some small way for his failures, his spirits lifted, if only just a little bit.

"Well done, lad," said Sirius, releasing his control over the Talent so that he could focus his attention on his student. The streams of energy speeding around the tower's wall blinked out. "What are you trying to do?"

Bryen had continued to pull in more of the Talent, seeking to mold the rough circle that he had created, but was struggling to craft the energy into the object that he had in his mind.

"When Lady Winborne fought the Elder Ghoule, she created a wall of energy in front of us to protect against that creature's Dark Magic. I was trying to do the same thing, but instead of expanding the Talent laterally to craft a wall, I wanted to concentrate it into a shield."

Sirius liked this young man's initiative, though his lack of apparent fear, not only with respect to the Talent but also his approach to fighting, worried him. "A good idea. The next time you decide to make a suicidal attack on an Elder Ghoule, you can have the shield in place to protect yourself from a counterattack."

"Right," responded Bryen, ignoring the sarcasm in Sirius' remark. "And it wasn't suicidal. I didn't die. For it to be a suicidal attack, I would need to die. Let's call it an exceedingly brave and legendary assault that proved successful in the end."

"Humor at a time like this," muttered Sirius. "Will wonders never cease." But he couldn't help but smile himself when he saw Bryen's grin, and he realized that there was more to this young man than just the hard glare and frightening stare of a skilled warrior. "Watch what I do and then try it yourself. Just don't release your hold on the Talent."

Sirius reached out once more, touching the Talent, taking in the natural magic of the world, and shaping it as his student had been trying to do. Bryen followed along, and in just a few seconds both had perfectly formed shields of blazing energy spinning before them.

"Well done, lad." Sirius nodded his approval. "Now let's try it again. Release your hold on the Talent."

Bryen did as Sirius commanded, feeling a brief sense of loss when the last of the natural power left him.

"All right. On my command, form your shield again. Ready?"

Bryen nodded, looking forward to the challenge.

"Shield!"

Bryen reached for the Talent. In just a few seconds, the spinning disc of white energy appeared once more in front of him.

"Excellent!" beamed Sirius. "But you can be faster. You need to be faster. Release your hold on the Talent."

Bryen did as Sirius bid, ready for the command to come. "Shield!"

"Even quicker than the last time," crowed Sirius, clapping his hands together with pleasure and clearly enjoying himself. "But you can do better. We will continue with this and then move on to some other things you can do with the Talent that would benefit you as a fighter so that the next time you take on an Elder Ghoule you'll know how the contest will end before it even starts."

Once Bryen had mastered forming his shield so that the process was more instinct than thought, Sirius gave him several other exercises to work through. The speed with which Bryen learned how to use the Talent thrilled the old Magus. He became so consumed by his instruction that he didn't realize that they had been training for hours and that it was well into the early morning. Sirius was exhausted, yet Bryen looked to be none the worse for wear. In fact, he appeared refreshed and energized.

"Enough for tonight, lad. I need to rest." He patted the Protector on his shoulder in a fatherly way. "You have a huge reserve of the Talent within you. The challenge will be learning finesse. But you will. Of that I have no doubt."

"Thank you, Sirius. I appreciate what you're doing for me."

"You're welcome, young man."

Bryen remained standing in the center of the library, his gaze fixed on his new instructor. Clearly there was something else on his mind.

"You're experienced in keeping secrets, aren't you?"

"As a Magus, sometimes you have no choice," said Sirius, not expecting the question.

"When I told you about what happened to my parents, it affected you in a way that I hadn't expected," continued Bryen, pushing gently with his words. "A personal way."

Sirius' expression saddened and then quickly hardened. He was not yet willing to discuss what he considered over his long life to be one of his greatest failures, even if it was directly relevant to the young man standing before him.

"We all have our secrets. Some may be revealed. In time."

"I am not asking you to tell me everything you know. I have only one question right now."

Sirius nodded, demonstrating his willingness to answer though not promising that he would.

"The creatures that killed my parents. They were Ghoules?"

For a moment Sirius simply stared at him, then nodded. Bryen easily read the pain that flashed behind the old Magus' eyes.

"I suspected as much. I caught a glimpse of what looked like a scaled forearm and claw for just an instant that night, but I had no idea what it was. I finally put it together during the skirmish on the north road."

Bryen thought that Sirius was going to say more, but then the Magus' expression changed once again, a touch of worry in his voice.

"You need to go," said Sirius, glad for the unexpected interruption. "Duke Winborne comes. Your being in the library would not raise any questions, but both of us being here would."

His eyes hard as flint, Bryen studied Sirius for a moment longer. "We'll talk more of this when the time is right," he said before nodding his thanks once again and slipping from the room with barely a sound, closing the door softly behind him.

Sirius stood in the library, body still, head bowed, thinking back to that day a decade in the past. He had failed his friends. He had known the danger that they faced, yet he hadn't taken the necessary precautions. He had been a fool, and as a result they had paid for his lack of understanding with their lives. Shaking his head in sorrow and then determination, he promised his long-lost friends that he would not make the same mistake with their son.

Deciding to step out into the corridor, Sirius almost collided with Kevan, the Duke of the Southern Marches stopping short.

"We need to talk, Sirius."

"It seems to be a night for difficult conversations."

"I'm sorry?"

"My apologies, Duke Winborne. I was thinking about something that has bothered me for quite some time."

Kevan let the comment go. "I just spoke with Tarin. A rider has arrived."

"Tetric is on his way here."

"Yes, he'll be here tomorrow, no later than midday." Kevan looked at him strangely, feeling as if the Magus had read his mind. "How did you know?"

"I have my ways, Duke Winborne."

"Yes, how could I forget," replied Kevan with some exasperation.

"Allow me to take Aislinn to the Aeyrie for her Test. There is more to Tetric than just his service to Marden. There is something lurking just beneath the surface, something dangerous. Better that she's not here when he is. Then, regardless of Tetric's demands, with her absence and the continuing threat presented by the Ghoules, you have a good excuse to delay."

"Is she ready for the Test?" asked Kevan, his worry plain.

"Yes, Duke Winborne."

Kevan turned away from Sirius, then started walking along the corridor, seeking the fresh air of the courtyard just beyond.

"If she fails ..."

"Then she pays a terrible price," finished Sirius. "That can't be denied."

Kevan closed his eyes, allowing the cool breeze to waft over him. After several minutes, he finally made up his mind. "Keep on with your instruction, Sirius. I don't want her to go just yet."

"Kevan, this is the only way to keep her from Marden. Tetric can't force our hand if Aislinn is not here."

"I understand, Sirius. But there is a value in having my daughter here for now. And you as well."

Sirius worried over the Duke's logic. He tried one more time. "Kevan, I understand your fears. But remember that Noorsin is more than qualified to manage Tetric. If I take Aislinn tonight, we could be a day's ride to the north before Tetric even reaches the Broken Citadel."

"Sirius, I have made my decision," said Kevan, his voice hard.

The tone immediately set Sirius' anger ablaze. He had watched over Caledonia for centuries. He controlled a power that few could even comprehend. Yet he had to listen to the commands of those who didn't fully comprehend what was truly at stake? Who didn't understand what they all stood to lose if they didn't succeed? It took him several seconds to push down his rising arrogance. The conversation he had just had with Bryen reminded him of the danger of allowing his ego to reign. It had cost that young man his parents ten years before.

"Of course, Duke Winborne. I will see you tomorrow morning."

Sirius strode away, head down, his thoughts immediately turning to Tetric's arrival. Perhaps his having to remain here could prove fortuitous. He just needed to figure out how.

27

BEFORE THE STUMP

Kevan sat uncomfortably on the roughly carved wooden throne that had served as the seat of the Lord of the Southern Marches for a millennium. Arick Winborne, the first to rule the Duchy that ran the length of the eastern coast of Caledonia, had ordered its construction from an ancient tree that had collapsed during a storm in the Deep Wood, the almost impenetrable forest that lay to the south of Battersea. The massive throne sat on the stone floor and spread behind Kevan like the roots of the tree from which it was carved, and then flowed up the wall almost to the ceiling, spreading out to the left and right, which thanks to the intricacy and skill of the craftsmanship, gave the appearance of a grove of trees situated at the back of the hall. His ancestor, with his predilection for avoiding pretense, aptly named the chamber the Hall of the Stump.

It was an impressive piece of workmanship, the carving knotty, complex, and beautiful. But it wasn't the most practical design. He shifted once more on the smooth, hard wood, seeking to find a more comfortable position but failing to do so. Kevan rarely used the audience chamber, usually meeting diplomatic delegations in his library. But today was different. Today Kevan needed to remind his unwelcome visitor that he ruled the Southern Marches and that in this Duchy his word was law.

Noorsin had offered several suggestions to assist him in making that point. She stood beside him to the left, Sirius towering above him on his right, while Tarin, the Captain of his Guard, stood at attention at the base of the steps. Soldiers from the Battersea Guard lined the walls of the long hall from the bottom of the dais to the doors. Aislinn positioned herself to the right of Sirius, and agreeing with Noorsin's advice, Kevan had placed Aislinn's Protector just slightly behind her and to the side.

It wasn't long before the herald walked into the audience chamber, slowly and with a stately grace. Standing in the middle of the path that led to the Stump, the herald called out in a loud voice, "Duke Kevan Winborne, Lord of the Southern Marches, Overseer of the Aeyrie, Defender of Eastern Caledonia, may I present to you Tetric, Chief Advisor to his Highness, King Marden Beleron."

Noorsin grinned, pleased that the herald had remembered her request to focus more on his lord than the visitor. But her smile faded quickly. Tetric stalked into the room, his billowing black robes trailing behind him. Every time she met the King's Advisor, and she readily admitted that she avoided that burden whenever possible, her skin crawled. Though not very tall and appearing slight of frame, the intensity of Tetric's gaze could prove unnerving, something that he used to full advantage whenever required. The soldiers of the Royal Guard who had served as his escort since leaving Tintagel followed behind him.

Bryen examined Tetric as the man strode purposefully toward the Stump. Of course, this wasn't the first time that he had been in the presence of the Advisor, and now, as then, he experienced a wave of animosity combined with fascination when their gazes locked for a split-second. It was as if there was some unfinished business between them, but what it was Bryen couldn't say. There was a power in this visitor that Bryen didn't fully comprehend, which he found more curious than worrisome, in part because of his experiences in Tintagel.

Bryen's gaze went to the Royal Guard that trailed the King's Advisor. The score of soldiers appeared to be hard men, one and all, their eyes quickly taking in the Battersea Guard lining the walls and calculating the odds if this diplomatic mission turned into something else entirely. Several tried to intimidate with their eyes and their postures, a few even placing their hands on the hilts of their swords, yet it seemed to have little effect on the watching, alert soldiers of the Southern Marches.

Based on Bryen's time with the men and women of the Battersea Guard, he believed that Jerad and the other fighters in the room would be more than a match for Tetric's escort. But he doubted that it would come to that. He figured that Tetric's guard was simply here for show, a suggestion of the power that Marden Beleron could wield. But Bryen guessed as well that the real power of the Caledonian throne was manipulated by the man who had finally made his way to the base of the steps leading to the Stump.

"Duke Winborne, thank you for receiving me," Tetric said in a voice that oozed insincerity, nodding his head to the Lord of the Southern Marches and offering the least amount of respect that he could without his action being taken as an insult. Noorsin frowned at the calculated affront, but Kevan ignored it. He had expected much less.

"I had no choice, did I not, Tetric?" asked Kevan with a

smile, making light of the reality of the situation. "I couldn't turn away an emissary from our King."

Tetric was at a loss for words for just a moment, trying to determine whether his host had employed humor or insolence in his reply. Since he was not in a position to act on the latter, he gritted his teeth and chose the former.

"Quite right, Duke Winborne," chuckled Tetric. "Quite right. My Duchess of Murcia, I had not expected to see you here, though from what I understand you have been visiting with the good Duke for much longer than anticipated. I would think that you would be more concerned with what's occurring in your own Duchy rather than one far to the east of the center of the world."

Tetric's barbed comment was not only an attempt to belittle Kevan and the Southern Marches, but also to relay to the Duchess and the Duke that he knew more about their activities than they might expect. The strong tie between the Southern Marches, Murcia, and the Three Rivers was well known. But Tetric hadn't realized just how strong those relations might be. It added another, perhaps difficult, dimension to the puzzle that he had been working to solve since he had first appeared in Tintagel in service to Marden's father.

"And I had not expected to see you here," replied Noorsin, her voice carrying strongly throughout the throne room. Her tone suggested that she was less than impressed with Tetric's veiled comment. "It's a rare pleasure to have the opportunity to spend time with just you. Normally, you are chained to the King. Where he goes, you suddenly appear. I'm surprised he let you off your leash to make the long trip here."

Tetric forced himself to keep in place a polite smile to prevent Noorsin from knowing her barb had struck home.

An almost uncontrollable rage swept through Tetric at the impertinence, yet he controlled his fury. He wanted to strike out, but he knew that he could not. Not yet. His upper lip curled into a sneer as he strove to maintain his composure, which became all the more challenging when he glimpsed the spark of amusement that he identified in Sirius' eyes. For several long moments the two stared at one another, apparently having their own private conversation without the need for words.

Bryen watched the silent battle with interest. Based on their tight expressions and the tautness of their frames, the two had a history, and it likely involved a great deal of bad blood. Why that would be the case, Bryen didn't know. But he would find out.

Tetric's hands formed into fists that tightened as the seconds passed. For a time, it seemed that there was no one else in the hall but for him and the Magus. Several memories of past interactions with Sirius played through his mind, none of them good. Fighting to control his boiling rage, he forced himself to pull his gaze away from the man who had harried him for so long. He closed his eyes for a moment as he sought to regain his calm. When he opened them again, Sirius was no longer the only person in the chamber.

Tetric reminded himself that he was here for a reason. To perform a specific task. A task that needed to be completed if he was to have any hope of gaining his overall objective. Therefore, patience was needed now just as before. With patience he would achieve his goals. And then? Then he could allow his desire for revenge to come to the fore. Ignoring the tall Magus, Tetric turned his attention back to the Duke of the Southern Marches.

"Indeed," replied Tetric, ignoring the Duchess of Murcia's jibe. "I am here at the request of the King."

"We expected as much, Tetric," replied Kevan, who tried to keep his increasing irritation under control.

Tetric waited for more, expecting Kevan to continue, then pushed his own annoyance to the side when he realized that the Duke had little desire to help him get to his reason for being there. So be it. The Duke of the Southern Marches felt the need to put on this show of strength in his Broken Citadel. He would allow it. He would let him enjoy it for just a little bit longer. Then he would break him just like the stones of that cursed tower for which the fortress was named.

"Yes, well allow me to get to the point."

"We wish you would, Tetric," offered Kevan, who tapped his hand impatiently against the Stump.

Tetric gripped his hands tightly once again, willing himself to maintain his poise. He continued as if he hadn't been interrupted though he would have liked nothing more than to strike out and put this ungracious fool in his place.

"The King asked me to come because he fears for you."

"Fears for me?" chuckled Kevan. "That I had not expected. Why does our good King fear for me?" The Duke of the Southern Marches' scorn dripped from his words.

"When he received your missive and learned of the attack on Lady Winborne," said Tetric, directing his gaze to Kevan's beautiful, young daughter, "he grew concerned. The Ghoules have not raided for centuries. So, of course, he feared for your safety but, even more so, he feared for the safety of his future bride. He couldn't just sit by and do nothing. So he sent me to you."

Through the collar, Bryen sensed the anger simmering within Aislinn at Tetric's last words. He glanced at her and noted that she had formed her hands into fists as she did when she was working with the Talent. He took the stance of her body to mean that if she had a dagger available, she probably would have gone after the King's Advisor. Good for her, he thought. The same thought had already passed through his mind.

"I feel safer already," replied Kevan, his voice hard and not amused. "Thank you for your concern, Tetric. But as you can see, we are well though we seek to eliminate the threat. My soldiers continue to hunt the Ghoules and to ensure that the Southern Marches is free of these raiders."

"Excellent news, Duke Winborne. I am glad to hear it. I had no doubt, nor did the King, that you would manage these dangerous circumstances as was required. But still, King Beleron asked me to come here to offer his services. The Southern Marches, just like all the other Duchies of Caledonia, remains his responsibility after all."

Kevan's eyes turned to flint. The fury that had been building within him threatened to explode. Noorsin's gentle touch on his shoulder reminded him that now was not the time to lose his temper. Nodding briefly in thanks, he pushed down his anger.

"And what services might those be?"

"Clearly you have much to worry about right now," began Tetric, his oily voice drifting annoyingly throughout the audience chamber. "His Highness thought that he could lighten your load so that you could focus your full attention on the crisis at hand. Based on our last conversation, he understood that your daughter would be joining him in Tintagel by the time of the Fall Council so that their engagement could be announced officially. The wedding would then follow shortly thereafter in the presence of all the nobility of the Kingdom as they celebrated the merger of the two greatest houses in Caledonia."

"I remember that conversation quite well, Tetric," said Kevan, leaning forward on the Stump, his hard gaze fixed on the King's Advisor with a needle-like focus. "With the Ghoules raiding in the Southern Marches, the King's plans, though certainly appealing, must be delayed. I must focus on the safety of the Duchy before I can think on more personal matters. For as you know, as a Duke of Caledonia, I must serve my people first above all else."

Tetric bit back the sharp retort that he wanted to offer, understanding quite well the hidden meaning of Kevan's last comment but deciding to let it pass.

"Quite so, Duke Winborne. Thus the reason that I am here. His Highness, in all his wisdom, has suggested that the lovely Lady Winborne return to Tintagel now with me, where she would enjoy the protection of the King. In fact, King Beleron has sent the best of the Royal Guard," Tetric nodding toward the soldiers behind him, "to get her safely to the capital. You could follow after Lady Winborne once you've eliminated the Ghoules plaguing the Southern Marches. Moreover, with your daughter in Tintagel, it would be one less thing for you to worry about. You would have no distractions and could marshal all your forces to stamp out this current affliction of beasts."

"I will not be thrown about as if I were a toy," Aislinn protested, her anger finally breaking free, but her father's raised voice drowned her out.

"Your suggestion is appreciated and noted," responded Kevan, his voice strong and barely controlling his rage. He was not surprised by Tetric's suggestion, as this audience was playing out exactly as he and Noorsin had expected that it would. But knowing that they had been right didn't fill him with any satisfaction. He glanced quickly toward Noorsin. Her expression matched what he was hiding inside. "We will take it under advisement."

Tetric waited for almost a full minute, expecting something more from the Duke of the Southern Marches, but he realized that as the silence continued to drag on that he had pushed as far as he could for now. He had not expected this gambit to be easy, nor quick. But in the end, he would achieve what he had set out to do. He simply needed to remain patient and slowly increase the pressure that he could apply to the recalcitrant father.

"Thank you, Duke Winborne. I have one final task, and this one much easier to complete. If I may, I have a token of the King's affection to give to the lovely Lady Winborne."

Tetric reached into his robes for the gift that he had procured for the girl and supposedly was from the King. The gold bracelet shined brightly in the light as he placed his foot onto the first step of the dais in order to approach the Duke's daughter. The gift served multiple purposes, one of which was the opportunity to get a bit closer to the girl so that he could gain her measure. He had heard the stories about her skill with the Talent and how she had battled an Elder Ghoule, and that had intrigued him for numerous reasons. But his progress was impeded before he could take a second step.

The young man standing silently behind her had glided in front of the Lady Winborne faster than Tetric thought humanly possible, his hand on the hilt of his sword with several inches of steel already free from its scabbard. The young man's movement was so quick that no one else in the throne room had yet moved, but that didn't last long. Several of Tetric's guards placed their own hands on the hilts of their swords, quickly followed by the Battersea soldiers lining the walls, who stood ready to follow whatever command their Captain gave them. The already tense situation had become explosive in just seconds, and Kevan sought to defuse it.

"Perhaps another time," suggested Kevan, before events got out of hand.

Tetric stepped back until he was closer to his guards. "Perhaps so."

The King's Advisor stared at the young man who stood before Kevan's daughter. There was a strength in him that he found surprising for one so young, and to be made her personal guard he found quite astounding. Then he recognized the lad and the silver collar around his neck, and his interest became more acute.

"A Protector," said Tetric. "I did not know the practice continued."

"As you mentioned earlier, the Lady of the Southern Marches has need of protection against all manner of threats," replied Kevan.

Tetric understood quite well that Kevan's response had more than one meaning. But once again he chose to ignore it. This Protector could prove to be a nuisance, but the boy also presented an opportunity.

"Indeed," replied Tetric, finding it difficult to take his gaze from the formidable young man standing before him. Not only did he appear more than competent, the scars on his cheek and neck testifying to the fact that despite his age he likely had a great deal of fighting experience, but he sensed something else about this Protector. There was a fortitude within him that he had not seen in others, though why he thought that he couldn't say. He had no doubt that this young man would be a formidable opponent and a deadly enemy. After several seconds had passed, finally he turned his attention back to the Duke of the Southern Marches. "With your permission, I will take my leave for today. My thanks for your kind hospitality. I'm sure that we can continue this conversation once I've had a chance to recover from my long journey here."

With that, the King's Advisor nodded once more then glided from the room, his men following quickly after him. Yet to those who remained in the Hall of the Stump, it felt as if Tetric's hidden malevolence had settled within the audience chamber much like a noxious smell.

28

WHAT'S DONE IS DONE

K evan stood on the wall that rose behind the training ground, the sun just about to emerge above the eastern horizon. He watched with great interest, several times shaking his head in disbelief. Despite the early morning hour, Guards filled the yard. Many worked on their own as they ran through various fighting forms with blades, daggers, and spears slicing through the air. Others trained in pairs, such as two soldiers who fought with staves, the rapid staccato of wood striking wood heard even over the shouts and grunts that echoed around the enclosed space. Still more practiced in larger groups, oftentimes one side having fewer in number than the other in order to learn how to fight when at a distinct disadvantage. Regardless of approach, all sought to improve their fighting skills, and from what Kevan could see with his practiced eye, it was working.

In fact, the Captain of his Guard had joined in as well. Rather than leading the many soldiers who had rolled out of their beds before the sun was up, instead Tarin had deferred to Aislinn's young Protector and engaged in the training himself. Kevan found that quite intriguing, as Tarin was not one to cede authority easily or willingly. Why the change of heart, he meant to find out.

Kevan was distracted for a moment as he observed Jerad, the Sergeant of his Guard, his curly black hair unmistakable, sprint toward a ten-foot wall, then plant his right foot on the wood as far up as he could, using his momentum to launch himself higher into the air, which allowed him to grasp the top with his hands and pull himself over, all with arrows slamming into the wall behind him and chasing him up the obstacle. He knew that at the boy's request, Tarin had put several of the Citadel's carpenters to work building the equipment for these training sessions. The structures had been placed at various locations around the dirt field, ranging from what looked like a thin balance beam that gradually reached several stories in height to a series of ropes and rings that could be used to circumnavigate the practice yard without having to set foot on the ground. All were currently in use, as his soldiers went through the exercises with a will, their compatriots cheering them on or offering some good-natured digs when their efforts didn't achieve the success they sought.

Kevan shook his head once more, this time in wonder. He never expected peace to be achieved between Tarin and the boy after the Captain's less-than-pleased reaction to Kevan selecting the gladiator for his current task. But obviously Tarin's opinion of the Protector had changed, so much so that there now seemed to be a mutual respect between the two.

That, in itself, was an accomplishment. But what impressed him even more was the impact that this boy had had on his daughter. He watched with pride as she danced around the training circle in a contest against three Guards, her Protector watching closely, taking in every move she made, every good decision, every mistake. He barely said a word to her, yet with every nod or gesture by the boy she adjusted her approach just a bit, and each time she did it put additional pressure on her opponents. Kevan had asked Aislinn about the boy's approach to training and why, during these bouts, he never shouted instructions at her, as his instructor in arms had done to him so many years before. Her reply had surprised him, though it had also made sense.

"Bryen says that there is no point in telling someone what to do while they are in the training circle. Once the advice or criticism is given, it no longer applies, the situation having changed already. Everything moves so fast that any instructions provided are irrelevant a second later. So better to have a conversation afterwards."

Kevan had brought this former gladiator to Battersea for a single purpose, and he had already proven his worth in that regard. Yet he had not expected the boy to offer so much more than that. Kevan had decided on this course of action because at the time he had felt that it was the best way to protect his daughter. That, for him, would always be his primary consideration. How he had forced the boy to come here worried his conscience from time to time, but he was used to making such difficult and sometimes unpopular decisions. His daughter always had to come first.

"Aislinn is doing quite well."

Kevan didn't bother to turn his gaze from the yard as Noorsin came to stand next to him, their bodies close, their hands almost touching as they both leaned on the parapet. He had caught the scent of lavender a few seconds before she appeared, bringing a smile to his face. Knowing that she was about to join him had pleased him.

"She is," he replied, allowing his small smile to grow larger as he watched his daughter more than manage the three attackers who tried but failed to penetrate her defenses. She was quick, decisive, composed, and she clearly knew what she was doing, not only holding the three off, but also preventing them from getting an assailant behind her. If that occurred, the contest would come to a quick conclusion. Instead, she kept them off balance, attacking one, then dashing away to attack another on the far side of the circle before the three could coordinate their actions. Much to their chagrin, she'd even gotten several good strikes in on her opponents. "Since she began participating in these training sessions, she's excelled. Her skills have improved, and her confidence has soared. That can only help her in the future."

Noorsin smiled and nodded, then placed her right hand on top of his left. He made no move away from her, enjoying the contact. "Do you regret it?"

Kevan watched the contest for just a few minutes more in silence. His daughter had done exceedingly well, keeping the three soldiers at bay for fifteen minutes with nary a scratch. When the boy ended the combat, Aislinn thanked the soldiers who had competed against her, and then she went off to the side of the training ground and spoke to her Protector about her performance. She seemed to be doing most of the talking, the boy offering just a few short responses. Their conversation complete, she started to walk the training yard with her Protector as he offered suggestions and words of encouragement to the soldiers, all of whom appeared to value the personal attention and particularly the presence of his daughter.

Turning away from the training yard, he crossed his arms across his broad chest, not really wanting to have this conversation but seeing few options for escaping it. When Noorsin had something on her mind, there was no good way to divert her attention.

"That's a difficult question for so early in the morning."

"Maybe so," she replied, her eyes shining with intensity. "But still a good one."

Kevan nodded noncommittally. "In all honesty, no." Before Noorsin could question his response, and clearly, she was about to, he continued. "Placing the collar on the boy was the wrong thing to do. I admit it, and I understand that. But at the time I had no other choices. No other way to protect her. Since he's been here, he's saved her life twice. If not for him, she, Tarin, and the other Guards with them would have been slaughtered by that Ghoule pack. So do I regret my decision to make the boy Aislinn's Protector? No. Do I wish there had been another way? Yes. But there's nothing for it now. What's done is done."

"What's done is done," repeated Noorsin, nodding in understanding. "No truer words have ever been spoken." She reached for Kevan's hand again, this time her fingers playing across his lightly in what was now a familiar gesture. "But what if what's been done could be undone?"

"You can release the boy from the collar?" After learning of Noorsin's skill as a Magus when she helped heal the Protector, Kevan found her more willing to reveal pieces of her past to him. He had been honored to be taken into her confidence in such a way. "I have never heard of it being done."

"Nor have I," she replied. "I spoke with Sirius about it. Even he had no knowledge of anyone ever successfully freeing a Protector from their service."

"What do you mean by successful?"

Noorsin turned away from the practice yard as well,

pleased to see that the soldiers who had accompanied her from Murcia also had joined in this morning's training. She took a final, appraising look at the young Protector as he continued to walk the yard, Tarin and Aislinn now both at his side and speaking with the soldiers and among themselves. The boy's skill with a blade was beyond doubt. Yet who could have suspected that his influence would spread so quickly and in so many ways. Finally, her thoughts returned to Kevan's question.

"Sirius did a bit of digging for me. Apparently, there were two occasions when Protectors were brought to the Aeyrie and the Order of the Magii attempted to release them from their magical bond."

"What happened?"

"They failed to remove the collar, and in the process both the Protector and their ward died. It seems that the collar, once affixed, begins the bonding process immediately, and as time passes that bond only grows stronger. In these two cases, the Protectors had worn their collars for so long, and the bond had grown so strong, that severing the connection had deadly effects for both."

"What's done is done," repeated Kevan fatalistically. Although he was not of a mind to release the boy at that very moment, he had considered the possibility of making the attempt at some point in the future. But after listening to Noorsin, there was no way he would put his daughter at risk in such a way. He shook his head in resignation. "Thank you for looking into it."

"Of course. And I'll research the issue a bit more. There are resources in Murcia that are not available here. There may be more information that could be of use in the future. It's just a matter of locating it."

Kevan nodded his head. "Thank you. But my priority is

Aislinn. Right now, I need the boy, and apparently not just to protect my daughter."

Noorsin nodded, her sharp gaze catching Kevan's eyes. "You do realize that there are certain dangers that he won't be able to protect her from if she goes to Tintagel. Certain threats that even he can't defend against."

"I know," he admitted reluctantly. "I'm well aware."

"And where is your esteemed visitor today?" Sarcasm dripped from Noorsin's voice.

"After he cornered me earlier this morning to reiterate Marden's proposal, Tetric rode off with several of his men toward the north. He said that he wanted to explore the countryside, perhaps even see for himself where the skirmish occurred on the coastal road."

"Perhaps he'll run into what's left of that Ghoule pack," she said suggestively, a hint of anticipation in her words.

"We can only hope."

Noorsin smiled, pleased that despite all that weighed on Kevan's shoulders he could still offer a little humor. Then she turned serious. "You know that Aislinn has to go. It's the only way that you can continue to delay. Beyond just a few more months, at least."

"I know. I'm just not …"

"I've spoken with Sirius," said Noorsin. "He believes that she's ready. He knows that she's ready. You can trust his judgment. He Tested me."

"I know. He said as much to me last night. I will speak with Sirius later today."

"I know it's a hard decision for you, but it's the right one." Having touched on one of the topics that she wanted to raise with Kevan this morning, she moved on to the next one. "You do realize that this pressure from Marden will not lessen. He wants more power. He wants the Crown to be as it once was, the Duchies subservient rather than equal. The only way to obtain that power is to reduce the power of the Duchies."

"Yes, but why the Southern Marches as his first target? Why not the Coves or Sharston for that matter? Militarily, those western Duchies are more isolated and have fewer men to call to arms than the Southern Marches. Marden consolidating his hold on western Caledonia first would limit our options in the east and make it that much more difficult for us to oppose him."

"Yes, a good question. Perhaps he thinks that weakening you will make it easier for him with the other Duchies. Once the Southern Marches falls in line, the other Duchies will have no choice but to do so as well. Or perhaps he's a fool, though I doubt that. Cruel and senseless he may be, more prone to listening to his urges rather than common sense, but he's not stupid. His political acuity has served him well the last three years."

"Perhaps it's not Marden who's piloting the vessel," suggested Kevan.

"Tetric?"

"Year after year, ever since he wormed his way into the good graces of Corinthus, Tetric has exerted more influence over Caledonia than any Chief Advisor has a right to. Perhaps there's more to this than just Marden's desire for my daughter. Perhaps Tetric is using Marden's game to play his own."

Noorsin took several minutes to consider Kevan's suggestion. "That certainly would explain a few things. But not everything. We need more information, yet there is very little to be had. I'll contact my sources in Murcia and see what they can discover."

"Thank you." Kevan nodded his appreciation, knowing

that if anything more could be learned, it would be through Noorsin's network of physicks and instructors that stretched to the farthest corners of Caledonia and beyond and served as the Duchess of Murcia's private intelligence network.

"Kevan, there is something else that we should consider that might benefit us with the current situation."

Kevan frowned with suspicion, noting the suggestive glow of Noorsin's eyes as she turned her full attention on him.

"What might that be?"

"An alliance between Murcia and the Southern Marches."

"We already have several alliances in place," responded Kevan, somewhat perplexed. "The last one we concluded I think provides us with what we need militarily. If one Duchy is attacked the other comes to its aid. Moreover, the Three Rivers signed that agreement as well, giving us an even stronger position."

"I'm well aware of that alliance and the others that we've put in place," said Noorsin, stepping closer to Kevan so that he could see only her sparkling eyes and feel her soft breath on his cheek. "I was thinking an alliance of a more personal nature."

29

HUNTED

"I know you disapprove of what we're doing," said Aislinn. "I can feel it through the collar. Riding in the Deep Wood helps me think, so I hope that you understand. And there have been no reports of Ghoules. A patrol was through here just the other day."

She glanced over at Bryen, her Protector riding his horse alongside hers. He hadn't said a word since they had left the Broken Citadel after the early morning training session. In fact, he had barely glanced at her, focusing most of his attention on the countryside as they headed south upon riding out through Battersea's gates. He seemed to be more vigilant than usual.

"I need to clear my head. My father is keeping me in the dark. I have no idea what he's planning. With everything going on with Tetric and Marden, I had to get out of Battersea. My father has barely spoken to me about the proposal, and it affects me. My life. My future. He should talk to me about it. Not Sirius. Not Noorsin. He won't even give me the chance to share my thoughts."

She looked over at her Protector again, who was

currently scanning the line of trees to their front, the Deep Wood now no more than a mile away.

"It appears my father is not the only one who chooses not to listen to me," she sighed, not expecting an answer.

Bryen finally shifted his gaze to her, his unreadable grey eyes fixed on hers. "Yes," he replied simply, then looked once more to the south as if he hoped to decipher what was going on among the trees that they were riding toward.

"Yes? Yes, what? Why do you have to be so irritating?" Aislinn mumbled the last questions, not expecting him to hear her. But he did.

"Lycia told me once that it was a gift," he replied, his smile finally breaking out, though it was only a small one. His eyes never left the trees shrouded in gloom.

So he was listening, she thought to herself, and she saw that Bryen was now looking at her with a broad grin.

"Well, she got that right. Who is Lycia?"

Bryen waited a few moments before responding. Something was bothering him the closer that they rode toward the Deep Wood. He had never entered this forest, but he had heard the stories from Jerad and some of the other soldiers of the Battersea Guard. They had said that unlike the Dark Forest, in which the roots of the massive trees formed a tangle across the forest floor, there was nothing to block their passage once they set foot in this wood. The detritus of the Deep Wood was clear with few if any shrubs and a thick layer of dark loam, but the trees were so tall and the foliage so dense that a perpetual dusk imbued the grove.

Jared also had said that sound didn't travel in the Deep Wood, and many found the quiet and the darkness oppressive, making it seem as if any bold enough to enter were always being watched. Perhaps that feeling extended beyond the edge of the Deep Wood, thought Bryen. But then again, perhaps not. Perhaps there was something more to the unease that afflicted him. The patrols sent out to scour the province for any sign of more Ghoule packs had yet to report any additional evidence of the beasts, but who knew what a forest like the Deep Wood could be hiding. Understanding that continuing to think about it would only frustrate him, he turned his attention back to his charge.

"A gladiator in the Pit. A friend. She was always looking out for me."

"So she was a better gladiator than you," Aislinn suggested, ribbing him just a bit. "Sounds like she took your measure."

"In more ways than one," he said, his comment catching Aislinn's attention in a disquieting way, but she didn't have a chance to pursue it. "We spent a lot of time together. I thought that she was the most beautiful woman in the world."

When Aislinn looked over at her Protector again, she couldn't tell if he was telling her the truth or simply playing with her. His next words surprised her.

"I do understand."

"Understand what?" asked Aislinn, still thinking about Lycia, who she could be, and what Bryen's life was like in the Pit with this female gladiator.

"I understand why you might want to get away," said Bryen. "And you don't need to ask my permission."

"I wasn't asking your permission," she replied.

"Of course not," he replied with a smile. "But it seemed like you just were."

She shook her head in exasperation. "Why did this Lycia put up with you?"

"She enjoyed our conversations."

Aislinn looked at her Protector in surprise, then seeing his smile, she broke out into a laugh.

"Be careful, Protector. If anyone else learns that you have a sense of humor, they might see through the threatening mystique you've crafted for yourself."

"I'll try not to do it again," Bryen said with a smile and a tilt of his head.

Aislinn laughed again, feeling lighter for the first time since they had left Battersea.

"Come on," she said as she urged her horse into a trot. "Let's see what the Deep Wood has to offer us."

"This can't be more than an hour old," said Jerad. "The vultures haven't even had a chance to get into it yet."

It was the vultures circling in the air that had drawn the Sergeant of the Battersea Guard to this cart track at the northern border of the Deep Wood. Once he and his company had completed their work here, the massive birds would enjoy a feast, and when they were done the other animals of the forest would emerge for whatever had been left for them. Several oxen that were pulling the wagons filled with timber had been slaughtered, and Jerad's soldiers had dragged the beasts to the edge of the forest. The handful of woodcutters who had chopped down the trees and loaded the carts were already being buried farther off the path.

"Ghoules," said Duke Winborne. "It has to be."

He was kneeling at the edge of the track, dozens of large, four-taloned claws visible in the muck. He and the Duchess of Murcia had decided to tag along on Jerad's patrol south of Battersea that morning, both wanting to get a better sense of what was going on in the countryside. They had arrived at their current location just after midday, and it was their first piece of evidence that confirmed the increasing number of reports that Ghoules had been sighted not only to the north of the capital of the Southern Marches, but also to the south.

"There are a lot of tracks," said Noorsin. "But I expect that no more than a handful of Ghoules took part in this attack."

"What makes you say that?" asked Kevan.

"They were doing something here," replied Noorsin, pointing off to the side. "The long grass is crushed down, and there's a lot of blood."

"But what could they have been doing?" asked Jerad, who had walked up behind the two. After checking on the progress of the soldiers given the task of burying the dead, he had confirmed that the rest of his troops had established a perimeter around the site that would ensure that they would not be surprised if the Ghoules appeared once again.

"How many bodies were found?" asked Noorsin.

"A half dozen," replied Jerad.

The Duchess of Murcia nodded. "A half dozen dead, yet we have four carts stacked with timber. That's a lot of wood."

"And not enough men to cut it," offered Kevan.

"Correct," said Noorsin. "I would expect that there were likely twice as many woodcutters than we found."

"So the Ghoules left what they didn't need," concluded Kevan.

"What do you mean?" asked Jerad, having some difficulty tracking the conversation. "Somehow I don't think that I'm going to like the answer."

Noorsin turned toward the sergeant, her eyes sharp and angry. "Ghoules eat what they kill. Animal or human, it doesn't matter to them. After they killed the woodcutters, they slaughtered a half dozen and left the ones they didn't need here."

Jerad's face took on a green cast, and he had to swallow the bile that rose in his throat before he could speak again. "But why slaughter the woodcutters? Why not just cut up the oxen?"

"Who can say?" answered Noorsin. "Perhaps they wanted to make a point. Perhaps they prefer the taste of man."

"Are you certain that it's no more than a half dozen Ghoules?" asked Kevan.

"That's simply a best guess," answered Noorsin. "I'm not certain of anything. And there could be more Ghoules farther into the Deep Wood. I wouldn't be surprised if there were."

Kevan stood up, then stared into the gloom of the murky forest. He could see no more than a few dozen feet into the grove before the shadows made everything indistinct.

"You mean to go after them, Duke Winborne?" asked Jerad.

"I do," replied Kevan. He had thirty soldiers at his back, which by his calculation should be more than enough to handle a half dozen Ghoules, if Noorsin was correct. "Would your company be up for that, Sergeant?"

"Absolutely, Duke Winborne. Of that, I have no doubt."

"Get them ready, then. We'll track the Ghoules into the Deep Wood and see what we can find."

"Do you sense that?" asked Aislinn.

She and her Protector had entered the Deep Wood less

than an hour before. She knew that many people felt that they were being observed when they walked among the huge, oppressive trees. But this had an altogether different air about it. One of menace. Not only did it feel as if they were being watched, but she thought that they were also being tracked.

"Use the Talent," suggested Bryen. "See what you can find."

Aislinn glanced at her Protector. His eyes moved across the gloomy landscape without stopping at any one thing as they rode their horses among the towering trees. She realized that he was looking for any sign of movement, as that would be the only hint of an attack in this world of shadows. She sensed that he already knew what it was that was worrying them, but she still did as he suggested. Reaching for the Talent, Aislinn extended her senses into the surrounding forest. She didn't like what she discovered, though she couldn't say that she was surprised.

"Ghoules," she said, trying the keep her growing concern from her voice.

"How many?"

"Four."

"To our left?"

"Yes," confirmed Aislinn. "How did you know?"

"I didn't know the number, but I could sense their movement. Are they coming closer?"

"No, they're moving with us," she replied. "Stalking us."

Bryen nodded, beginning to understand what might be going on. "Extend your search. Are there any other Ghoules near us? Perhaps on our other side?"

Aislinn reached out for the Talent once again, identifying the four Ghoules who continued to follow them on their eastern flank, then extending her search as Bryen had requested.

"There are four more Ghoules coming in on our right. No more than a mile away. And also from behind. Three Ghoules." Aislinn was proud of herself for preventing the fear that had replaced her concern from creeping into her voice.

"They're herding us," said Bryen. "Once we're a bit deeper into the forest, they'll take us."

"Why not just attack? There are only two of us."

"I don't know," said Bryen. "I would have thought that they would have come for us by now. Maybe they want something."

"What could they possibly want?" asked Aislinn.

Bryen shrugged. "Maybe they want you," he said casually. "Maybe they remember you from the north road. Maybe there's another reason." But if that was the case, how did the Ghoules know that she would be here? His charge didn't decide to leave Battersea until this morning.

"Why would they want me?" protested Aislinn, a chill settling within her. "It doesn't make sense?"

"I'm very likely wrong," replied Bryen, trying to help settle her nerves. "But these Ghoules are acting strangely. They should have attacked by now. There are only two of us. They'd see us as an easy kill."

"We can't keep riding into the Deep Wood. That will only give the Ghoules the advantage."

"Those Ghoules coming at us from the west. They're close?"

"Yes, less than a quarter mile away now."

"And the Ghoules coming behind us. There's still a gap between them and the ones to our west?"

"Yes, but it won't be long before they connect with one another."

"That's what I'm worried about," said Bryen. "Once they link up, the trap is set. That's when they'll try to take us."

"We need to find that gap between the two groups of Ghoules coming toward us, and we need to get through that opening before they can close the vise."

Bryen pulled his sword from the scabbard across his back. "Then we ride as fast as we can for the border of the Deep Wood. You focus on the Ghoules coming behind us. Do whatever you need to do to keep them off us. I'll take care of the Ghoules coming at us from the west. Agreed?"

"Agreed," replied Aislinn, pulling her own sword from the scabbard across her back.

"Whatever happens, you head northwest, and you don't stop until you're free of the forest. Are we clear?"

"But what if ..."

Bryen cut her off harshly, his eyes flashing. "You don't stop."

Aislinn had never seen her Protector like this before, as if he knew something that she didn't, and she nodded reluctantly.

"Then let's go!"

"WHAT WAS THAT?" asked Kevan.

He and his soldiers had moved farther into the Deep Wood, tracking the Ghoules who had slaughtered the wood-cutters. But they hadn't gotten very far when a series of muffled explosions rumbled through the forest to the southeast.

Noorsin took hold of the Talent and extended her

senses. It didn't take her long to determine the cause, and it didn't surprise her.

"The Talent," she confirmed. "Aislinn is riding toward us. There are Ghoules chasing her."

"Aislinn!" exclaimed Kevan. "What is she doing ..."

"Later, Kevan," interrupted Noorsin. "She'll be here in minutes and the Ghoules are right behind her. It will be a close thing."

Kevan growled, then shifted his focus to the problem that was rapidly coming their way. "Jerad, Ghoules from the southeast. Form a wedge!"

Jerad and the soldiers of the Battersea Guard quickly obeyed, getting into position just in time.

Aislinn burst from between the trees, her horse galloping as fast as the animal could, yet even so two Ghoules were no more than a few steps behind her. She was surprised to see the soldiers in front of her, but also relieved by the turn of events. She didn't stop, steering her horse through a gap between two of the Guard, who moved their horses out of the way for her.

The two Ghoules, so intent on their prey, realized the danger too late. The beasts slammed into the two soldiers, taking both them and their mounts to the ground. But the soldiers around the fallen warriors recovered faster than the Ghoules did as they drove their spears repeatedly into the creatures before they could regain their feet. The soldiers then returned to their positions in the wedge. The two who had been taken down were a bit battered, but still able to fight.

"Where is your Protector?" asked Kevan, his daughter pulling tight on the reins and bringing her horse next to his.

"He was right behind me," she gasped, struggling for air.

"But I don't know where he is now. He told me not to stop no matter what happened."

"Kevan, later!" shouted Noorsin. "We have more Ghoules approaching."

As if to make her point, a ball of white fire shot from her palm, streaking over the heads of the soldiers in front of her and slamming into the chest of a Ghoule who had just emerged from between the trees. The Ghoule was knocked backward, dead before he hit the dirt, but then several more Ghoules burst from the gloom of the Deep Wood, moving faster than any animal possibly could. The Battersea Guard held as the dozen Ghoules slammed into them, but the fighting was desperate, several of the creatures almost breaking through if not for Aislinn and Noorsin, who both crafted several more spheres of scorching energy that blasted into the creatures who threatened to overwhelm the soldiers.

Kevan also stepped forward to help. As the battle raged for several minutes, the Duke of the Southern Marches placed himself in the thick of the fighting. Each time that a Ghoule was about to take down one of his soldiers he was there, his steel forcing back the creature or sliding into green flesh. Even so, he knew that the tide of the melee was shifting. Several of his soldiers were down and more Ghoules had appeared out of the shadows. Using the Talent, Aislinn and Noorsin had kept them in the fight, but if something didn't change soon, they were going to be butchered.

A quick flash of movement right behind the attacking Ghoules proved to be the catalyst that the Battersea Guard needed to regain the momentum and stop the Ghoule advance. A Ghoule who had just materialized from between the trees collapsed to the ground, his body falling to the right, his head to the left as a horseman charged through the space that the creature vacated. The rider struck again, driving his sword into the chest of a Ghoule who had turned to face him, and then he guided his horse behind the Ghoules attacking the soldiers, slashing and cutting deftly with his blade. If he couldn't kill a Ghoule, he aimed his strikes for an arm or a back of the leg, trying to injure or distract the beasts and give the Guard a better chance to take down the creatures.

Bryen! Aislinn immediately focused her attention on him. Several spikes of blazing energy burst from her palms, ripping through the Ghoules who had pivoted to face this ghost who had emerged from behind them. Doing so was a mistake, as it created space between the Ghoules and the soldiers, giving not only Aislinn, but also Noorsin more of a chance to engage without having to worry about whether their use of the Talent would harm their own soldiers. That small but critical shift in the skirmish was all that was needed. After several more of the Ghoules fell to the turf, their chests torn apart by the Talent, the devastating wounds smoking, the remaining creatures broke off their attack and faded back into the murk, silence finally descending once more over the Deep Wood.

"Should we pursue them, Duke Winborne?" asked Jerad. He and several other soldiers seemed to be raring to go, wanting to avenge their fallen comrades.

"No, it's a trap," said Bryen, who had ridden up and now sat his horse next to his charge. "There are more Ghoules out there than those who attacked us. We need to get clear of the forest as fast as we can."

"What happened to you?" whispered Aislinn. "You were right behind me, but then I lost track of you."

"I had to double back," answered Bryen quietly. "Several

Ghoules were coming at you from the other side. I caught them before they could catch you."

Her Protector said it as if killing multiple Ghoules was a fairly simple matter. And perhaps for him it was. But even he had limits. If he had fallen ...

"I knew what I was doing, and it needed to be done," said Bryen, sensing her concern and irritation.

The fact that her Protector knew exactly what she was thinking only made matters worse. "Protecting me does not mean that you should take unnecessary risks that put your own life in danger."

"Actually it does," he replied evenly.

"Even if you're required to protect me," she hissed, "that does not mean you should be reckless."

"Aislinn, he's right," chided Noorsin. "The collar compels him to protect you above all else. Now get your head in the fight. There is nothing to be done about this now." The Duchess of Murcia used the Talent to search around them once again. Her next statement prevented Aislinn from continuing to upbraid her Protector. "This was just the first attack. More Ghoules are massing less than a league away."

That last bit of information made Duke Winborne's decision for him.

"No," he replied, turning his gaze to Jerad. "See to the wounded and the dead. We make for the edge of the Deep Wood in three minutes."

Jerad nodded and then nudged his horse toward his soldiers, who had already started to care for the wounded and carefully placed those who had died in battle across the back of their horses for the ride back to Battersea.

Kevan then turned a furious gaze toward his daughter.

"What are you doing out here?" he demanded of Aislinn. "This is no place for you to be, even with your Protector."

"Father, can we talk about this later?" she asked calmly, her self-possession impressing the Duchess of Murcia. "There are more important things to deal with right now."

"She's right, Kevan," interjected Noorsin. "Besides, having Aislinn and her Protector join us may have been a stroke of good fortune. Without them, this could have been a much harder fight with a much different result."

Kevan conceded the point. "This conversation is not over." He still planned to pursue the issue with his daughter once they had reached the safety of the Broken Citadel. His thoughts then turned to more curious matters. "Why would the Ghoules be drawn here? Are they simply hunting? Trying to cause as much confusion as possible?"

"It could be that," replied Noorsin. "Or it could be me or Aislinn. We won't know for sure."

"You and Aislinn?" asked Kevan.

"We don't know why the Ghoules forced their way through the Weir, and until we can learn more about their intentions, we can likely assume that they're hunting Magii. The Ghoule Overlord gave his Legions that task after the First Ghoule War and that instruction has remained in place since then."

"Aislinn is not a Magus," protested Kevan.

"Not yet," replied Noorsin. "But after her fight with the Elder Ghoule, they've probably marked her."

Kevan accepted her reasoning, which Noorsin was thankful for, as she wasn't prepared to share all of her thoughts. Yes, the Ghoules had hunted Magii since their first failed invasion, but for so many of the creatures to have broken through the Weir, and to have so many Elder

Ghoules die to make that happen, suggested that some other strategy was in play.

Was the Weir weakening to the point where the Ghoules could force their way through the magical barrier with fewer casualties? Was the Ghoule Overlord simply seeking to eliminate more members of the Order of the Magii? And if he was, did that mean that he was planning to invade Caledonia in the near future?

So many questions, and she didn't have enough information to answer them. But she was certain of one fact. The Ghoule Overlord and his Legions were stirring, and that was not a good thing for Caledonia. She would need to reach out to Rafia as soon as possible. Perhaps she had a better sense of what was going on, because if Noorsin's suspicions were correct, then these Ghoule raids were just the beginning of a larger assault.

30

FAILED SEDUCTION

B ryen stood calmly at the base of the shattered tower, hidden in the shadows provided by one of the many alcoves dotting the surrounding gardens. He enjoyed the darkness and the quiet of the early evening, when the constant daily activity in the Broken Citadel began to slow down. Aislinn had been training with Sirius for several hours, so he knew that she would be coming down shortly. Once she returned to her rooms for the night, he could go to the library and read for a bit before Sirius appeared to guide his instruction.

Much like his time in the Colosseum, his life had adopted a rhythm that had become comfortable for him, and he did prefer having a routine. He couldn't say that he enjoyed his time here in Battersea, but it had become some-what more bearable. He readily admitted that not having to fight in the Pit every week was a major improvement. And in several other ways, he had come to appreciate some aspects of his new life, such as training in the circle in the early morning, his evening lessons with Sirius, and then his time to explore the library. His hand drifted to the silver collar that encircled his neck, a habit that he had been trying to break. Yet no matter his best efforts, he couldn't keep himself from scratching beneath the torque at least a dozen times a day. Yes, life was tolerable in Battersea, but it was not what he wanted.

Stepping out of the pall, Bryen placed himself in front of the entrance to the steps leading up to Sirius' chamber, his hand on the hilt of his sword.

"You have nothing to fear from me, boy."

Tetric emerged from the darkness of the courtyard, striding purposefully toward him. He radiated a power that exceeded his stature. Bryen viewed Tetric as someone perpetually poised to strike. There was also a weakness to the King's Advisor that Bryen sensed, though he had yet to identify it. He guessed that the man with the intense gaze preferred to work from the shadows. So he assumed that if you turned your back, Tetric wouldn't hesitate to drive a dagger between your shoulder blades if it served his purpose. Because that's what it was all about with the King's Advisor. What he wanted.

"I doubt that," Bryen replied quietly.

For a long moment Tetric stared at Bryen, apparently trying to divine something about him that wasn't readily apparent, his black eyes meshing with the darkness surrounding them. Then he laughed in a startling cackle. "You don't mince words, boy. I like that."

Just then Aislinn Winborne pushed open the door leading into the Broken Tower with so much strength that it slammed against the stone wall with a resounding thud. That was followed by a string of muttered curses that would have made a seasoned soldier blush.

"A difficult training session this evening, Lady Winborne?" asked Tetric, his mocking voice carrying on the gentle, cool breeze of the evening.

Aislinn stopped short, locking away her irritation and taking in what was going on around her. Tetric stood no more than ten feet away, blocking her path toward her chambers. Her Protector had positioned himself in front of the King's Advisor, his hand resting comfortably on the hilt of his sword. Outwardly Bryen appeared to be completely at ease, but the bond that they shared through the collar suggested that he was anything but. In fact, if she was reading him correctly, she sensed that he was in the same frame of mind as when he prepared to enter the Pit for a duel. Looking across at the King's Advisor, his discordant grin sending a shiver down her spine, perhaps her Protector was right to get ready for a fight.

She decided to ignore his question. "A wonderful evening for a stroll, is it not, Tetric?" asked Aislinn. "Though I would recommend the gardens on the western side of the Broken Citadel. Even at night the color is quite impressive."

"Thank you for the suggestion, Lady Winborne. But perhaps another time."

Tetric's smile only deepened. He was impressed with how quickly the young Lady of the Southern Marches adjusted to his unexpected appearance.

Aislinn nodded, having anticipated that she would need to deal with Tetric at some point during his visit to Battersea, just not having thought that it would be so soon after his arrival. She stepped a bit closer until she stood next to her Protector, but she went no further than that, and she made sure that she came up on Bryen's left side so that if he needed to draw his sword, she wouldn't get in his way. Her

Protector gave her a wink at that, but his gaze never wavered from the King's Advisor.

"You wish to speak with me."

"I do, Lady Winborne," replied Tetric. He stared at the young woman with a newfound respect. She may be young, but she was shrewd, and the tone of her voice suggested that she was not easily intimidated. "I thought that perhaps a private conversation could smooth over any of the issues that would keep you from going to Tintagel with all possible haste."

"You have already spoken with my father," she replied. "Why would you expect that a conversation with me would help you?"

"Because young women sometimes choose not to listen to their fathers," chuckled Tetric, his laugh a rasp that reminded Bryen of the sound that Lycia used to make when she ran her fingernails across the chalkboard that Declan used when he was instructing gladiators in tactics. "Sometimes they choose to do what they want when they want."

"You forget yourself, Tetric. I am not just any young woman. Nor am I a silly girl fresh out of the classroom. I am the Lady of the Southern Marches and heir to the Duchy."

"I have not forgotten that at all, Lady Winborne. I am well aware of the power that you will wield at some point in the future, of the responsibilities to Caledonia that you will bear."

"I do not need a reminder of my responsibilities, Tetric." Aislinn chewed out her words. "I am well versed."

"Of that I have no doubt, Lady Winborne. I simply ask that you consider that any delay in meeting your responsibilities could affect you and your Duchy negatively."

"You mean with respect to Marden's marriage proposal."

"I do, Lady Winborne. King Beleron is a patient young

man. He understands that a young woman such as you may hesitate at first. But he also understands that you will make the right decision in the end."

Aislinn's eyes narrowed as she stared at the King's Advisor. "Is that a threat, Tetric?"

"No, Lady Winborne. Of course not."

However, she noticed that his words didn't match his expression, which instead suggested that he had little patience for a young woman quite happy to delay his plans.

"And tell me, Tetric. What happens if I don't make the right decision?" Her gaze was challenging, strong. Clearly, he did not intimidate her, which pleased Tetric all the more. Once she was in Tintagel, he would enjoy breaking her.

"Then the decision likely will be made for you, Lady Winborne. As I said, King Beleron is patient. But you can only expect so much from him. He is young as well. Sometimes his emotions can get the better of him. There is much he must deal with as the ruler of Caledonia. Acceptance of his proposal and you going to Tintagel would take one huge worry from his shoulders, for as I said, he fears for your safety. Besides, sometimes we must do what we must, not what we like. I'm sure you're well aware of your duty to do what is right for the Kingdom."

Aislinn nodded, listening as much to what Tetric left unsaid as to what escaped from his lips. "You know, Tetric, I don't respond well to ultimatums. Nor does my father."

"I would expect as much, Lady Winborne. But as I said before, nothing that I have said is a threat. I am simply stating facts. Your father cannot ignore King Beleron's proposal. He cannot say no. He can simply delay, and that benefits no one. Perhaps if you had a quick word with your father, we could move this business along to its inevitable conclusion. If it continues for too long, then who can say what might happen?"

"Another threat, Tetric?"

"No, Lady Winborne," said Tetric silkily. "I apologize. My concern for your welfare is getting the better of me. Much like King Beleron, I fear for your safety, what with these reports of assassins and Ghoules running rampant in the Southern Marches, your adventures in the Deep Wood just a few days ago simply another reminder."

"I thank you for your concern, Tetric. But I have no need of it. My father will deal with Marden's proposal when he deems the time appropriate. And I'm well aware of my duty to do what is right for the Kingdom. I hope that you and King Beleron don't forget that." She then swept past the King's Advisor, heading for her chambers. "I bid you good night, Tetric. I can't say that this has been a pleasant conversation, but it certainly has been an enlightening one."

With a final glance at the retreating Lady of the Southern Marches, Tetric settled onto a bench across from Bryen, arranging his robes just so. Bryen studied his movements. He could only describe them as sinuous, confirming his initial impression of the King's Advisor as someone who could escape the tightest of space with the greatest of ease.

"May I ask why you're here? It's not just to irritate Lady Winborne."

"You may," replied Tetric. The moonlight reflected off the man's bald pate, which appeared to give off a strange glow. The robed figure waited a few seconds before saying more, staring at the Protector and shaking his head in annoyance. "Not one for dry humor, are you?"

"I'm not one who likes to waste time in useless conversation. If you're here to see Sirius, I doubt he'll want to speak with you at this time in the evening."

"Oh, I'm not here to see Sirius," chuckled Tetric, the raspy laugh giving the man a sinister quality. "In fact, I'd prefer not to speak with Sirius right now. He'd only vex me, and I don't feel like being irritated at the moment." He looked at the Protector with a serious expression. "Don't you find Sirius a bit unsettling?" The question seemed to be more of a test rather than an attempt at gaining information.

"There's something about you that unsettles me."

Tetric's laughter ended just as quickly as it had begun. "And there's something about you that intrigues me. That's why I'm here this evening. I remember you from the Pit. I remember your combat against the supposed Champion of Sharston, that now deceased mountain of a man Stil Sheldgard. You should not have beaten him, yet you did. That's why I'm here. You should have died that day, yet here you stand, and I still don't understand how you did it."

The King's Advisor stared at Bryen for quite some time. Others likely would have wilted under his gaze. Bryen found it no different than when he fought in the Pit and another gladiator sought to intimidate him. He simply ignored the intense stare and stood there calmly, revealing nothing with his expression. He was curious now about what Tetric had to say, but knew that the unwanted visitor would reveal his intentions when ready, so there was no point in giving in to him. Bryen didn't have to wait much longer.

"I've only been here a few days, but I've learned quite a bit more about you. You lasted almost a decade in the Pit, fighting and defeating men and beasts that you had no right to beat. Then upon your arrival here you defend the Lady Winborne from four assassins, apparently cutting through these hardened killers much like a knife through butter. And from what I understand after having spoken with several of the Guards, these assassins were not men to trifle with. They were professionals. They knew what they were about." Tetric shifted on the hard stone of the bench, seeking a more comfortable position. "Then what happens next? Our intrepid Protector saves his ward once more, as well as a troop of soldiers, from a Ghoule attack." Tetric chuckled again, Bryen realizing that it was the Advisor's way to control his nerves. "At first, I thought that it could only be exaggeration, as it seemed as if a legend of old had come to life. So I went to the site of the skirmish this morning. Having pieced together what was said to have happened, I must admit that I was somewhat suspicious, thinking that the story had been embellished."

Tetric settled into silence for a few seconds, expecting Bryen to cut in and offer his thoughts on what had occurred. He knew that soldiers liked to share their exploits, usually stretching the truth as much as they could while still retaining some level of believability. Yet the boy offered nothing, maintaining his hard gaze. His hand continued to rest on the hilt of his sword. If Tetric's information was correct, if need be, the boy could have the sword at his throat before he could take another breath. Tetric nodded to himself, having gained another useful nugget that potentially could be put to use in the future. After all, Tetric understood one gained just as much knowledge from what was left unsaid as from what was said. He filed away what he had learned and continued.

"Yet if that's not enough, you take it upon yourself to charge an Elder Ghoule. Not only do you avoid his personal guard during your assault, but you kill the creature, suffering a wound that should have killed you. And here you are, somehow standing before me in good health. Truly remarkable. Just retelling it now, I still find it hard to believe.

But every soldier who has told me that story has said much the same thing, so it must be true."

"What's your point?" Bryen had tired of the monologue, hoping that Tetric would leave so that he could enjoy the quiet of the night for just a little bit longer. But he realized that it wasn't meant to be.

"My point? My point? My point is that there is something about you that, as I said, I find quite fascinating. Something about you that has nagged at me since I first saw you in the Pit those many years ago. You have martial skills and an inner strength that are unmatched. And yet here you stand, protecting a young woman who likely doesn't need your protection, serving as no more than a glorified guard."

Tetric stood up quickly and took a step toward Bryen, but then had to stop or run the risk of cutting his own throat. The Protector's blade had appeared at Tetric's neck faster than he thought possible.

"Put that away," said Tetric. He tried to keep his voice calm, confident, but the lack of feeling in the boy's eyes frightened him. "If I meant you harm, you would be dead already. That is a certainty you can believe."

Bryen stared into Tetric's black eyes, noting the swirling darkness, realizing that he would be lost if he didn't do something quickly. So he forced himself to look away, not wanting to be captured by the Advisor's gaze. He knew in his heart that Tetric spoke the truth. There was some aspect about the man that insinuated a terrible power that few, if any, could stand against. Bryen immediately changed his opinion of the Advisor. He knew that he was dangerous, but he had not expected him to be so deadly.

"Why are you here, Tetric?"

"You know why, boy," said Tetric harshly. Bryen kept his blade at the Advisor's neck, refusing to give ground, so Tetric was forced to step back. It wasn't until several feet separated them that the Protector brought his sword down to his thigh. "I'm here for the girl. King Beleron plans to make her his queen, and there is really nothing her father can do about that except delay. Eventually, he will have no more excuses and will have to accede to the wishes of the King. The Duke, as arrogant and stubborn as he may be, will not risk the wrath of the Royal Army even for his daughter."

Bryen sighed with exasperation. "I know that. Everyone here in the Broken Citadel knows that. Why are you here standing in front of me?"

"Straight to the point. I like that." Tetric's eyes took on an evil glint. "As I said, I've learned quite a bit about you. I believe that you could be of use to me in the future."

Now it was Bryen's turn to chuckle, flicking the silver collar that sparked when it caught the faint light of the moon.

"You forget my position. I am a Protector. I must protect Lady Winborne, and I cannot raise a hand against anyone else here."

"I do not forget your position," said Tetric. "You are a slave. Protector you may be, but you are still no more than a slave. Just as you were when you fought in the Pit."

Bryen's eyes narrowed. He didn't like how Tetric could read his innermost thoughts so easily. He didn't like how Tetric could find the anger and humiliation that Bryen had struggled so hard to control and use it against him. Bryen regularly grappled with the fact that for the last decade he had lived a life that had never truly been his own, and Tetric had found that weakness in an instant and already begun to make use of it.

"Slave. Protector. You're right. There is little difference.

But I have no way to change that. I am what I am, and I must live with what fate has given me."

Yes," replied Tetric. "I can understand your stoicism. It's to be commended, in fact. But what if I could change your current circumstances? What if I had the knowledge to free you from the collar? Think on that Protector. Think about what you would do for me if I could free you and allow you to live whatever life you desire."

31

MAKING A POINT

Bryen relished the movement as he spun and danced around the training circle. This was his time in the morning, the sun just peeking over the walls, the quiet of the dawn giving way to the building sounds of activity within the Broken Citadel. Granted, it was only an hour or so during the day when he could feel free of the responsibilities that he carried, but he would take what he could get. Aislinn had returned to her chambers after her practice session to prepare for her busy morning, which meant that he could spend just a few minutes more with the Guards before he, too, needed to get cleaned up and be ready for when his charge emerged from her suite.

Stave in hand, the piece of wood that was longer than he was tall felt as if it was a natural extension of his body. The continual clacking of wood on wood soothed him, bringing him back to his time training under Declan. In the Colosseum there was little to take pleasure in, so he had found it in the rhythm of the training circle, in the sounds and motions that he was so familiar with and that had become a part of him. He glided around the circle, avoiding the blows of four members of the Battersea Guard who, try as they might, had yet to gain a hit on him.

But the same couldn't be said for these soldiers. They had been struck numerous times by Bryen. Never hard enough to disable, but rather just hard enough to make a point, and every time the Protector connected, he offered a quick word of advice on what he had done to penetrate their defenses or how they could respond to shift the combat back in their favor. The Protector was younger than all of them, but his knowledge of and skill with the weapons available to the soldiers of the Battersea Guard had been proven time and again, so they pushed their egos to the side and valued what they could learn from him.

"Perhaps it would be more of a challenge, boy, if you fought soldiers with more skill. It appears that these fools are sadly lacking in that regard."

The combat in the circle came to a stop, the four soldiers with Bryen turning their stony stares to the men who had just entered the practice yard. Killen Sourban, Captain of the Royal Guard, stood arrogantly at the edge of the ring, a dozen of his soldiers with him. They were unperturbed by the fact that all of the activity in the courtyard had halted, and that all of the soldiers of the Battersea Guard stared at the unwanted visitors with undisguised contempt.

"Your men would like to test their luck, Captain?" asked Jerad, the Sergeant stepping in front of Sourban. "You won't like the result if you do."

"My men are hardened soldiers, boy. Real soldiers, unlike these men and women playing at them." How he stressed the word *women* made clear to all his less than generous perspective on whether the "fairer sex" should be equal members of any Duchy's Guard. "They have little to fear from what the Southern Marches might offer them, particularly a gladiator."

Jerad ignored the insult. Killen's icy blue eyes seemed to have little effect on the Sergeant. Glancing expectantly at Bryen and catching the subtle nod, he smiled.

"Then by all means, Captain. Go right ahead. Pick four of your best fighters. But it'll be staves, not blades. We don't need any unfortunate accidents this morning. We'd hate to have to explain the loss of your soldiers to your master. He appears to be the unforgiving type."

Killen nodded, accepting the terms and ignoring the slight. He then motioned for his four largest soldiers to enter the training circle. As they did so, the soldiers who had been sparring with Bryen dropped their staves, making the members of the Royal Guard pick them up. The Battersea soldiers murmured a few words of encouragement to Bryen as they positioned themselves outside the ring, but Bryen's attention was caught by the shadow that had appeared on the eastern wall. He assumed that Killen was doing Tetric's bidding, the King's Advisor wanting to test the Protector. Nodding to Tetric with an impudent grin, Bryen then turned his focus to the four hulking soldiers arrayed against him.

"Don't kill him," ordered Killen. "We don't want to upset Lady Winborne, which will only make the long journey back to Tintagel with her more unbearable. But some reminders of what it means to stand against the Royal Guard are certainly in order."

The four soldiers of the Royal Guard smiled arrogantly as they began to circle Bryen. All the other soldiers in the practice yard crowded around the ring, wanting a good view of the combat.

"I would tell you not to harm his face," offered Killen, "but he isn't much to look at, is he? I doubt that the Lady

Winborne would be able to tell the difference if anything happened to him in that respect."

The soldiers standing around Killen laughed at his joke. The soldiers of the Battersea Guard ignored the Captain, eyes intent on what was about to happen in the circle. They knew that this was more than just a training exercise, that more was at stake not only for the Protector, but also for them, as their reputations now were tied to his.

Bryen stood calmly in the center of the ring as the four soldiers walked around him, keeping their spacing from one another, trying to gain his measure with a few jabs and thrusts that they pulled back before they struck just to see if they could make him flinch. But the former gladiator simply ignored them, his eyes locked on Killen's. To Jerad, it appeared as if the two were engaging in a private duel as they stared at one another, but it came to an end when one of the soldiers in the ring stepped too close to Bryen, thinking that he could crack him across the head with his stave and end the fight before it even began.

Bryen swiftly ducked down and swung his stave up with as much power as he could muster between the man's legs. As the soldier collapsed to his knees and clutched at his groin, Bryen smacked him on the back of the head with the hardened wood, sending him to the dirt unconscious. The three remaining soldiers stopped circling him for a moment, stunned by the speed displayed by this gladiator and the fact that one of their fellows had fallen so quickly.

They didn't have long to think about what had just happened, as Bryen set upon them with a vengeance. Pivoting to his right, Bryen feinted a swing at the soldier behind him, then brought the point of his stave back around, slamming it hard into the chest of the soldier who had been standing in front of him with so much force that he knocked the wind from the man. As the injured soldier bent at the waist in an attempt to draw in the air that his lungs so desperately demanded, Bryen smacked him hard underneath his chin, sending the man onto his back.

Sensing the soldier who had stumbled backward when he had feinted in that direction now coming toward him, Bryen rolled to his left, the man's stave swinging harmlessly through the air. The attacking soldier now off balance, Bryen took full advantage when he completed his roll and came back to his feet, hitting the man four times in quick succession with his staff, first in the right side just below his ribs, then in the left side, followed by a smack on his right hand that forced the soldier to drop his stave, and then the final knock across the back of his head that dispatched him in a jumble to the ground.

Before the last soldier standing knew what had happened, he found himself on his back as well, seeing double, Bryen having swung his stave behind him with just one hand, smashing it into the man's forehead. Four men down in less than a minute. Bryen looked at his handiwork for just a moment, a little disappointed in himself that he hadn't been faster, then returned to his position in the center of the training circle, ignoring Killen, his eyes locked instead with Tetric's, the glare of the King's Advisor revealing that he was less than pleased by what he had just witnessed, but perhaps not entirely surprised.

"If this is what it means to stand against the Royal Guard, I'm terrified," said Jerad, his sarcasm bringing laughter from the soldiers positioned around the training circle, a laughter that enraged Killen and the men who stood with him.

Killen's eyes flashed, his ego clearly getting the better of him as he stepped into the training circle himself, picking up a stave from the dirt and stepping over one of his fallen men to approach Bryen, whose calm expression and seeming lack of concern that the Captain of the Royal Guard approached fueled his rage even more. This boy had made a mockery of his soldiers. He had made a mockery of him, and that needed to be corrected. Now.

Killen launched himself at Bryen, swinging his stave over his head and aiming for the boy's neck. Bryen didn't move his feet, simply dodging the blow by twisting at the waist, and then again when Killen tried to catch him with a backhanded uppercut. Incensed by his opponent's nonchalance, Killen swung again, this time aiming for the boy's chest, but the former gladiator was already gone, having moved faster than anyone he had ever fought before.

That should have registered as a warning to the Captain. Still, Killen allowed his fury to drive him as he chased the boy around the training circle. His anger threatened to consume him as every one of his attacks missed their mark, the boy stepping cleanly out of his way, not bothering to fight back, apparently having no need for his own stave as he easily avoided Killen's onslaught. Simply moving, dodging, staying out of Killen's way as the Captain made himself look the fool, which only infuriated the Captain of the Royal Guard all the more.

"You're not a Protector," huffed Killen, trying to spit out the words as he continued his attack and finding that he was out of breath. "You're a slave. No more than that. And you will always be no more than a slave."

That last comment finally seemed to strike home with the boy, his grey eyes flashing with specks of green, but not in the way that Killen had expected. In an instant, the Captain of the Royal Guard was on the defensive. The boy was a blur of motion, his stave flashing in front of him faster than the eye could track. Killen caught the first few strikes with his own staff, but that was all that he could do as his body began to absorb hit after hit. Ribs. Kidneys. Gut. Chest. Back. Blow after blow, the boy never letting up, until Killen found himself on his back with the tip of the boy's stave wedged against his neck.

"I am a Protector, and I am a slave," confirmed Bryen, as he looked down coldly at the Captain of the Royal Guard. "But I am also a gladiator. If this were the Pit, you and your men would be dead. Count yourself lucky."

Embarrassed and infuriated, the soldiers who had been standing with Killen made to enter the training circle to aid their fallen leader, several pulling sword blades free from their scabbards. But they got no more than a few steps before Jerad and the soldiers of the Battersea Guard got between them and Bryen, swords, staves, and other weapons at the ready.

"I suggest you step back," Jerad said, his normally mirthful eyes now hard and unforgiving. "Your Captain was bested by our Protector. Accept it. If you take another step, all of you will be joining him on the ground, and some of you likely beneath it."

Jerad's statement stopped the soldiers of the Royal Guard for a moment, and then the harsh words of the Duke of the Southern Marches halted them for good.

"Get those fools out of the training circle!" shouted Duke Winborne, gesturing toward Killen and his fallen soldiers. "I'll have none of this nonsense. You can either return to your quarters or you can leave the city. But I will not have bloodshed in the Broken Citadel."

Jolted by the appearance of the Duke of the Southern Marches, the soldiers of the Royal Guard did as he commanded, helping up their fallen comrades. They were about to assist their own Captain, but Killen had already risen to his feet on his own, though it had been more of an effort than he would have liked thanks to the many blows his body had absorbed.

"That boy is a menace!" Killen shouted at Duke Winborne. "I demand that he be arrested for striking a soldier of the Royal Guard."

"You demand?" asked Duke Winborne in a deadly quiet voice, his flinty eyes now turned toward Killen.

"I demand that the boy be arrested!" repeated Killen, but then he realized that he may have overreached. The Duke of the Southern Marches was almost as tall as the Protector and had slightly broader shoulders. Killen didn't grasp just how intimidating the man could be until he had stepped in close to him.

"You demand nothing. I suggest that you and your soldiers leave now with what little dignity you still have intact."

Killen appeared to be about to offer a few more choice words, but then he glanced up at the wall in front of him and saw that the King's Advisor was nowhere to be seen. Realizing that he was on his own, he bit back the angry retort at the tip of his tongue and stalked away, his men following after him and helping those who had been injured in the training circle.

Duke Winborne then turned his harsh glare onto his daughter's Protector. "What do you think you're doing?" he demanded. "Matters are difficult enough as it is, and you decide to make them worse? Think, boy. What good could possibly come from you challenging soldiers of the Royal Guard?"

Bryen stared at Duke Winborne, locking down his emotions, his expression turning to stone. He could tell that the Duke was going to have his say one way or another, so there was little point in trying to defend himself.

"Duke Winborne, permission to speak?" interrupted Jerad.

Duke Winborne shifted his hard gaze toward Tarin's second in command, surprised that the man had spoken up, but curious as to what he had to say. He nodded for him to go ahead.

"What happened here this morning wasn't Bryen's fault. The Captain was seeking to embarrass the Battersea Guard. Bryen didn't seek a fight, but he did finish it. And in so doing, he upheld the honor of the Southern Marches."

"That's really what happened?" asked Duke Winborne.

As his gaze traveled across the assembly, he saw that all of the soldiers around Jerad were nodding, backing up what he had just explained. He took one more look at Aislinn's Protector. The boy was an enigma to him. Obviously more than competent, but he revealed little about himself or what he was feeling, his steely expression keeping all that hidden. Even now after the tongue-lashing that Kevan had given him, the boy stood there calmly, as if it had had little effect upon him. And upon consideration, Kevan decided that it likely hadn't affected him at all after all that he had been through before his forced arrival in the Southern Marches.

Duke Winborne nodded himself, satisfied by Jerad's explanation, and secretly pleased that his soldiers had not only backed up their Sergeant, but also supported his daughter's Protector. That was something that he hadn't expected, but it was a welcome surprise.

"Training is done for today," ordered Duke Winborne. "To your posts." He then marched out of the practice yard, needing to speak with Sirius.

Once Duke Winborne had turned his back, Bryen

nodded to Jerad in thanks. Jerad returned the nod with his usual grin.

"It's the least that I could do," the Sergeant said. "You made fools of the Royal Guard and their Captain. Who knew that we were going to have so much fun this morning?"

"For the Marches," Bryen said quietly.

"For the Marches!" shouted the soldiers around him.

The roar from the Battersea Guard echoed within the courtyard, the noise traveling throughout the Citadel. As Kevan made his way to his library, he couldn't stop the huge smile that broke out when he heard the cheer. For the Marches, indeed.

32

BROKEN

"Come in, Tetric. There's no point in hanging around in the hall."

The deep voice carried through the thick door, and though he tried to prevent a smile, Tetric couldn't avoid it. He had heard the same instruction countless times, and it brought him back to a time when his worries were fewer and his ambition had yet to be fully realized.

The King's Advisor pushed the door open and stepped through silently, taking a moment to look around the huge circular chamber, the highest floor in the Broken Tower that was not actually broken. He found what he expected. Organized chaos.

Sirius stood on the other side of the workspace, his hands leaning on the edge of the table, his eyes bright as he studied his former pupil.

"You had little to say when I met with Duke Winborne," began Tetric. "I was expecting a warmer greeting from you."

"You've always expected something from me," answered Sirius.

"Yes, yes I have," confirmed Tetric, his raspy voice barely

a whisper. "And usually you have failed to meet my expectations."

Sirius ignored the dig. He instead continued to examine the King's Advisor, taking in the physical changes that had occurred since he had last laid eyes on him. There was a tightness to Tetric's features that surprised Sirius, as if his skin had been stretched across his bones. His pallor had never been good, but now it appeared a ghoulish grey. And his eyes. All black, the hint of any color somehow removed, the swirling pools of ink not only unsettling, but hypnotic. What worried Sirius the most was what he found when he looked a bit deeper. Or rather, what he didn't discover. When studied with the Talent, his former student was an enigma. He knew that Tetric had great strength in the natural magic of the world, but Sirius couldn't sense it now from no more than ten feet away. And if he couldn't discern that, what else was Tetric hiding from him? And how was he doing it?

"Are you here to rehash your past grievances, Tetric? Because if you are, the night is only so long. I doubt that we'd have the time to make it through your list."

Tetric disregarded Sirius for a moment, instead finishing his survey of his former instructor's living and working space. "Quite right, Sirius. My list is long and getting longer."

Sirius snorted, but more from contempt than any sense of humor. "Not much has changed, has it? You always expect more to be given to you. You never considered the fact that you might have to earn whatever it was that you wanted, and that sometimes what you wanted came with a price that couldn't or shouldn't be paid."

Tetric stepped farther into the room until he was standing on the other side of the table from Sirius, his black eyes seeming to suck in the light from the chamber. "You're right, Sirius. We don't have the time to relive our past disagreements. Neither of us will change our perspective. We are both too certain that we are in the right."

"That's the truest thing I've heard you say in decades."

Tetric took no notice of the jibe. "I'm not surprised that you took the Broken Tower for your own. Even when we were children you liked broken things. Trying to fix them."

"Yes, though with the benefit of time and experience I have learned that some broken things cannot be fixed."

Tetric smirked, knowing that the last comment was directed at him. "You can only fix what wants to be fixed, Sirius. Otherwise, you're wasting your effort."

"Perhaps," replied Sirius, his expression thoughtful. "Though I believe that in your case it was worth the effort. I would have regretted not trying."

"Do you regret failing?" taunted Tetric, trying to get a rise out of the Magus but failing to do so, as Sirius' expression remained unchanged, his tone even and tempered.

"No, I don't regret failing. I was not so foolish as to think that I could fix what was broken within you, Tetric. I had assumed that you were too far gone by then."

"Then what do you regret?"

"Not having the strength to do what was necessary when I determined that I could not help you."

Tetric nodded, his gaze thoughtful. "And for that, Sirius, I am forever grateful."

The King's Advisor had hoped to put the Magus on edge and off balance, but he was disappointed by his efforts. For several long seconds they simply stared at one another from across the tables.

"You came here for a reason, Tetric. Let's get down to

business. I have only so much patience, and it's wearing thin."

"Some things never change."

"Most things never change," corrected Sirius.

"Perhaps so," agreed Tetric. "Tell me. How is your instruction with the Lady Winborne going? A good pupil, I take it?"

Sirius thought at first to deny that the Lady of the Southern Marches was training in the Talent with him, but he realized that it would be foolish to do so. Tetric likely saw her leaving the tower this evening and her strength in the Talent was a beacon to anyone skilled enough to sense such things, to say nothing of the stories regarding her fight with the Elder Ghoule.

"A better pupil than you, I'll grant you that."

Tetric smiled, though his eyes suggested that he didn't find the last statement humorous. "That's not saying much."

"It actually says a great deal," replied Sirius.

"You will never let this go, will you, Sirius?"

Sirius shook his head. "I can't let it go, Tetric. You betrayed me in a way that I had never imagined. It was personal. It has always been personal between us."

The sharpness of the Magus' words struck home in Tetric. An unwelcome and unfamiliar sadness swept through the King's Advisor, but he quickly quashed it, replacing it with the anger that he was more accustomed to, the controlled rage that gave him the fire that he needed to achieve the objectives that he had set for himself.

"We can't change the past, Sirius. But we can change the future."

"Meaning?"

"Meaning we have an opportunity, Sirius."

Sirius stared at Tetric with a gaze that suggested that he

couldn't quite believe what he had just heard, then he burst out laughing. "You think that I will help you in your efforts to send Aislinn to Tintagel?"

"Laugh all you want, Sirius. But it will happen regardless of what her father or anyone else tries to do to stop it. She will marry Marden. There is no way that she can escape that sentence. So why make things more difficult now? And she is strong in the Talent. She can do much good in Tintagel. Once the Southern Marches is tied more tightly to the Crown, once we've achieved greater stability in Caledonia and these rumblings of rebellion have been muted, we can focus on more important things."

"What more important things, Tetric?"

"You know quite well, Sirius. The Ghoules are stirring. From what I understand that Protector of hers played a key role in keeping the Lady Winborne alive. If not for him, the Ghoules would have killed her and the troop of soldiers with her."

"He did what was required of him," answered Sirius.

The shift in the exchange worried Sirius. There was something else going on here. Sirius felt as if he and Tetric were engaging in two distinct conversations at one time, and that he was only privy to the most obvious discussion.

"He did, indeed," agreed Tetric. "But who can say what could happen in the future. I expect that the Ghoules will become more of a problem what with the increasing number of sightings and attacks east of the Northern Spine. If we don't take action now, this might just be the beginning of some larger strategy that could put all of Caledonia at risk ..."

"Yes, let's talk about the Ghoules. Why a reappearance now?" asked Sirius, immediately on guard. He continued to feel as if he was missing something essential in this conversation, and that irritated the Magus to no end.

Tetric realized that he may have overstepped and perhaps revealed too much, so he attempted to backtrack. "It stands to reason, does it not? The Ghoules have crossed the Weir on a few occasions since the First Ghoule War, but not in such numbers as we have seen recently. I'm simply suggesting that Caledonia must demonstrate its strength right now. It's unity. If the Ghoule attacks continue, then we must all be prepared to work together."

"And having the Lady Aislinn in Tintagel is the best way to achieve that desired unity?"

"Quite so," replied Tetric. "With her safe in Tintagel, it would give King Beleron one less thing to worry about."

"It would give him more than that," corrected Sirius. He examined Tetric one more time, then shook his head in disappointment. "Did you really think that you could get me to do what you wanted? Did you really think that I would go to Duke Winborne and argue your case for you? After everything that has happened between us?"

"No, actually I didn't," replied Tetric.

"Then why did you come here? What did you hope to gain?"

"Confirmation."

"Confirmation of what?" demanded Sirius, his tightly controlled irritation finally getting the better of him.

"Confirmation that our differences are irreconcilable. That we have both chosen our paths and that the two can never meet. Confirmation that at some point in the future, we will likely stand across from another as we are doing now, but after that encounter, only one of us will walk away."

33

IT'S TIME

"It is time, Duke Winborne. Aislinn needs to go to the Aeyrie for the Test. We can't delay any longer."

Well past midnight Sirius had appeared in the Duke of the Southern Marches' chambers, the guards standing outside the door having no clue he had entered.

Kevan was still awake, studying ancient texts on the Ghoules, trying to puzzle out their reemergence, attempting to determine if the appearance of these creatures had to do with something other than the weakening of the Weir. He certainly couldn't sleep. Not with Tetric's presence in the Broken Citadel weighing on him, making him think that his decision to keep his daughter in Battersea had been a mistake. He had not forgotten his conversation with Noorsin earlier in the day and his promise to speak with Sirius, but other matters had demanded his attention. By the time that he had thought to find the Magus, the day had passed. As fate would have it, Sirius had found him instead.

"Sirius, why now? What has changed?" Kevan tossed the book aside, the irritation clear in his voice.

"Some new information came to light this evening," replied Sirius.

Kevan stared at the Magus, who was as tight-lipped as always, never revealing any more than he thought necessary.

"I need more than just that in order to make a decision, Sirius. What information came to light? How did you acquire it?"

"Tetric visited me just an hour past."

"He visited you? Why would he visit you?"

"Because we have a history."

Kevan stared at him once more, then motioned with his hand, suggesting again that the Magus needed to provide more detail.

"Tetric was once my apprentice. At one time he was a member of the Order of the Magii."

"He has skill with the Talent?"

"Yes. As I said, he was a member of the Order of the Magii. He had some skill in the Talent, great skill in fact, but he started going down a path that should not be explored. We had no choice but to expel him."

"I assume this path is dangerous?"

"Dangerous, deadly, and corrupt, Kevan. Once you tread upon this path there is no way to come back to what you once were."

"You are just telling me this now?" exploded Kevan. "I was worried enough as it was."

"You should be more than worried, Kevan. You should be afraid. We all should. Marden's plans move forward whether we like it or not. Tetric's patience is wearing thin, I'm sure. I expect that if Aislinn remains here and we do not accede to Tetric's demand that she go with him to the capital, even with her Protector she will simply disappear.

Weeks later, we will hear that she is now in Tintagel. We need to remember that Tetric is a dangerous and driven man. He is capable of more than just kidnapping to achieve his objectives."

"He wouldn't dare!" Kevan jumped up from his seat, his face flushing with anger.

"Why wouldn't he?" answered Sirius. "If he were to take her, what consequences would he face? She's already all but committed to that incompetent child playing at king. You did not refuse the marriage proposal."

"I could not refuse the marriage proposal. You know that. And tell me, Sirius, if Tetric is so dangerous, why didn't the Magii handle him as they should have?"

Sirius ignored the jibe and focused on Aislinn. "Although you have not accepted the proposal, you have not turned it down. We have already discussed this. Your daughter is essentially already betrothed to Marden. Once Aislinn is in Tintagel, no matter what protest you might offer, who would listen? Who would care? The other Dukes and Duchesses? Most just want that foolish boy to leave them alone. Only Murcia and the Three Rivers would offer any assistance, and even that would be muted because they understand the Crown's larger designs. If Marden is at odds with the Southern Marches, then all the better for them. Even if you issued a call to arms, you would not have the strength to defeat the Royal Guard in a pitched battle. The Crown's forces are simply too many. We both know that, just as all the other Duchies know as well."

Kevan sat back down, his hands curled tightly into fists. He wanted to strike out. But at what? His anger remained. At Marden and Tetric, of course, as well as Sirius. His habit of only revealing some of what he knew infuriated him, and he didn't like feeling as if he were a puppet dancing to the tune of the Order of the Magii. But now it was joined by a mounting frustration and fear. He was the Duke of the Southern Marches, one of the most powerful men in all of Caledonia. Yet at the moment he simply felt impotent. There was little that he could offer his daughter in the way of protection, and she was now no more than a political pawn.

"Think for a moment, Kevan. We thought the initial attack on Aislinn was an assassination. What if it wasn't? What if it was an attempted kidnapping instead? We had discussed this, I know, and we had discarded the theory. But now it makes more sense. The assassins appear and attempt to take Aislinn, stopped only because of the timely intervention of her Protector. With that plot thwarted, several weeks later the King's Advisor appears to reiterate Marden's demands and suggest that she go to Tintagel now, even though you had agreed originally to respond by the Fall Council. Something has changed though I don't know what. Marden wants your daughter in Tintagel as soon as possible. Tetric isn't here to negotiate with you. He's simply playing a game. Once he has an opportunity, he'll take it, and that means he'll take Aislinn. He's tried to get your daughter alone with him several times already, but if Tarin and his Guards aren't there, Aislinn's Protector always is. In fact, that boy is probably the only reason she's still here."

Kevan's mind started to turn, following the trail that Sirius had laid out for him. They could be wrong, there were other pathways to consider, but everything that had occurred in recent weeks pointed in this direction.

"Once Tetric has Aislinn out of Battersea and in Tintagel, Marden claims that she is safe," said Kevan. "Whether the Ghoule attacks are connected to the Crown's schemes, we can't say for sure, but we can't ignore that possibility. As you said, we have no way to refuse Marden's proposal. So he simply marries her. She becomes a hostage in the capital, limiting our options. Marden begins to exert even greater influence over the Southern Marches. Marden is getting what he wants. Once he has the Southern Marches under his thumb, he can focus on Murcia and then the Three Rivers. And if the Ghoule attacks do continue, and I expect that they will, it gives all the Duchies greater incentive to bow down to Marden. Once one or two more acquiesce, all the other Duchies will fall in line."

"I agree with your assessment," replied Sirius, knowing that Kevan would find his way through the fog of Marden's machinations. "Some guess work, yes, but based entirely on facts. The only outlier is the Ghoules. Are the beasts here for themselves or for someone else? The timing of their recent attack seems a little too convenient, but we have no proof."

"What of Aislinn's Protector? If she remains here, could he not defend her as he did before? Tetric would think twice about taking that boy on."

"Kevan, that boy has proven his worth time and again. And no doubt he would do what is required of him. He has no choice after all. But both Noorsin and I believe that there is more to Tetric than meets the eye. If he must face off against the King's Advisor, I don't believe he stands a chance."

"Yes, it comes back to Tetric. It would have proven quite useful if you shared what you knew of him sooner."

"There is a power within him," replied Sirius hesitantly, once again ignoring Kevan's reprimand. "I can sense it, if only barely. But it doesn't feel as it should. The Talent gives off a certain signature. When I'm close to an individual able to wield the Talent, I know that he or she has some skill in the natural magic of the world, and I know how strong they are. With Tetric, the strength of his ability is hidden. Neither Noorsin nor I can get a clear reading."

"Which means what?"

"When I trained Tetric to become a Magus, I was stronger than he was. Now I can't tell if that's still true," Sirius admitted reluctantly. "The Talent that I sense within him feels wrong, as if it has been corrupted or consumed. If my and Noorsin's suspicions are in any way correct, Tetric is more treacherous than we imagined. As you said, Bryen would defend Aislinn, and he would likely die. Noorsin and I would try to stop Tetric as well, but I don't know that we would succeed either."

"You had better not be hiding anything else from me, Sirius. You're not filling me with confidence."

Again, Sirius ignored the jab, concentrating only on Aislinn. "No, Kevan. I'm simply trying to be realistic. Better for us to go now. Distance from Tetric will give Aislinn the safety that she needs. The safety that can't be provided here."

Several other excuses for keeping Aislinn in Battersea ran through Kevan's mind, but he pushed them aside. He had been looking at the issue from the perspective of a worried, overprotective father, and taking that standpoint likely had increased the danger now faced by his daughter. Now he had to view these difficult circumstances from the standpoint of the Duke of the Southern Marches. Aislinn was his daughter, but also his heir. He needed to not only protect her, but also his Duchy. Sirius was right. He had been right for quite some time, but Kevan had allowed his emotions to get in the way of making a good decision.

"I'll send a message to Tarin and make sure that he and a troop of soldiers are prepared to accompany you," Kevan sighed reluctantly. "They can do so quietly, and you can be gone before first light."

"It would take too long, Kevan." Sirius looked down at the Duke with some sympathy, understanding the internal struggle that roiled within him, the father and the lord fighting for dominance. But what Kevan wanted now was no longer important. Sirius had to think of larger matters first. "Despite Tarin's best efforts I'm certain that Tetric would catch word of what we were trying to do. Even if we made it out of Battersea, Tetric and his soldiers would catch us on the road. Besides, we can move faster with a smaller group. I will take Aislinn and, of course, her Protector will come as well. We'll be gone within the hour. If you manage things correctly here, you could give us a full day on the road before Tetric is any the wiser of what's going on."

Kevan nodded. "So be it. Keep her safe, Sirius. She's all that I have."

34

IRRITATION AND DELAY

"What can I do for you, Tetric?" Kevan already knew why the King's Advisor had requested the audience, but he chose to play the gracious host instead, at least for a time.

It was late afternoon, the sun beginning its descent in the west. Kevan and Noorsin had retired to the veranda, their favorite spot for that time of day, giving them a wonderful view of the harbor and the eastern ocean. Today proved to be one of those rare occasions when the Silent Sea chose to mimic its name, as the placid water was as smooth as glass and stretched as far as the eye could see.

"You know quite well, Duke Winborne," replied Tetric in a testy voice, his black eyes flashing and barely containing the anger that raged within him. "I have been here for almost a week. I admit that the Southern Marches is an impressive landscape, but I can spend only so much time wandering the countryside as I wait for your response. King Beleron can only be expected to be patient for so long. There are other issues that he needs to address and delaying the inevitable is simply a waste of time. His bride must be protected, and Tintagel is the best place to achieve that goal."

"We understand the Crown's concern," replied Kevan evenly. "And we appreciate his interest. But as I've said, Tetric, Aislinn is quite safe. There is no need to rush the King's proposal. Before I can release her, I must ensure that the way is clear of danger. The Captain of my Guard manages that responsibility even now. It's simply a matter of time before the next step can be taken."

Tetric looked at the Duke of the Southern Marches with a quizzical eye, seeking to discern some hidden meaning in his words, but failing in his efforts. He decided to return to the tack that had yet to gain any traction.

"Duke Winborne, if I may, as we both know, Lady Winborne is not safe in Battersea. The assassins of just a few weeks past prove the threats that she faces. Surely you can see that. Even with her Protector, she is in danger. I have no doubt that the boy will do all that is required of him, but there is only so much that can be expected of him. He managed four assassins. What if there are instead six or eight? Or that many Ghoules, for that matter? Even a former gladiator would struggle against such odds."

The Duke of the Southern Marches' face had turned to stone, his eyes unyielding, as his hands gripped the armrests tightly. Was that a veiled threat? A light touch by Noorsin brought him back to the task at hand.

"We reached much the same conclusion," replied Kevan.

Tetric was about to continue with the same argument that he had offered for the last several days, but the Duke's words stopped him short. At first, he thought that he had misheard.

"You agree?"

"We do," answered Kevan. "I understand that Marden

and I both have the same objective, to keep my daughter safe." Kevan struggled to get out the last sentence without releasing the scorn that threatened to emerge at the same time. "I would simply ask for a bit more patience. Before you travel back to Tintagel, I would like to ensure that the way is clear of Ghoule raiding parties. The Captain of the Guard should complete that task in a few days. Then, he and the Battersea Guard can escort you and your men to the border of the Southern Marches."

Once again, Tetric searched for the hidden meaning behind Kevan's words. He had no doubt that the Duke of the Southern Marches would like nothing more than to expel him and his soldiers from his Duchy, but that was just a fleeting dream. Tetric would leave the Duchy when he was ready, and not until he had the girl with him. He took a moment before responding in order to ensure that the tone of his voice was appropriate.

"Duke Winborne, I appreciate your concern and your desire to be thorough. But from what I understand your patrols have not found any other Ghoules near Battersea and for several leagues around. Those you found in the Deep Wood have likely gone back to the Shattered Peaks. Moreover, I can assure you that I and my men can offer Lady Winborne the protection that she would need if, in fact, Ghoules were foolish enough to attack us. My men are more than a match for your own Guard."

Kevan allowed the insult to slide by, although he expected that if he gripped the armrests of his chair any more securely the wood would crack.

"I don't doubt your abilities, nor that of your soldiers," Kevan replied. "In fact, I've heard rumors of exactly what they and you can do. I believe the Captain of your Guard offered just such a demonstration in the practice yard the other day." Tetric scowled at Kevan's reference to the Protector's success against his soldiers, and the Duke was pleased to have taken the Advisor down a notch. "But, again, just a few more days. Perhaps the way is clear now, perhaps not. As a father, I would simply like to make sure that I've done all that I could to protect my daughter. I'm sure you understand." The Duke's hard eyes suggested that he really didn't care if Tetric understood or not.

Tetric smiled, his lips curling into a sneer as he deciphered the concealed meaning. He realized that once again Duke Winborne had won their daily engagement. So be it. His patience was at an end. He would need to take more drastic measures if he wanted to move his plans forward.

"I understand entirely, Duke Winborne. Just a few more days then."

Tetric turned on his heel, his robes billowing around him as he walked quickly back into the keep without a look back.

"You handled him quite well," said Noorsin, having enjoyed the conversation. "Though he did look a bit angry there at the end."

"Quite so," replied Kevan. "May I ask if your network of sources has turned up any additional information on the King's Advisor?"

Noorsin gave Kevan a tentative smile, relieved that his earlier coolness to her had dissipated somewhat. When he learned that she and Sirius had kept information from him, he had taken her to task, his distrust plain.

"I've received several messages in just the last few days. There was nothing in them that we didn't know already. But I have received some tidbits that are beginning to suggest that my and Sirius' concerns may be justified. Rumors.

Innuendos. That's all. But my people will continue to dig. Once I have something more tangible, I'll let you know."

Kevan examined Noorsin closely. He had not heard of any messengers arriving at the Broken Citadel in the last few days, so he could only imagine how she remained in communication with her network. But he had a good idea now that he knew that, like Sirius, she was a Magus. And he could comprehend now how, having been in Battersea for several weeks, her distance from her Duchy had no impact on her ability to rule Murcia and gather the information she desired. A unique skill, the Talent, and one that obviously proved quite valuable to her.

"How long before Tetric suspects, do you think?" he asked. "I believe his patience is coming to an end."

"Two days at best," she replied.

Kevan nodded. "Two days should be more than enough."

35

PULLING TEETH

"Try again, Aislinn. Focus. You can do this. Do not let your concentration waver."

"Easier said than done," she muttered in response, shooting daggers with her eyes at Sirius.

The Magus had said something about how the task that he had given her was more about honing her concentration rather than applying the Talent. But how she was supposed to master the Talent while riding a trotting horse, she didn't know. Every time her mare's hooves struck the uneven ground, a discomfiting jolt shot from her toes up through her spine to her neck, making any effort to focus on the Talent difficult at best. Nevertheless, Sirius had insisted that she master the skill, believing that it was essential that she do so before she took the Test. She had hoped that perhaps Sirius could offer some advice on how to achieve the objective that he had set for her, but he seemed to be more than happy to allow her to figure it out for herself, which only served to increase her irritation and make the assignment all the more difficult.

She, Sirius, and Bryen had entered the Waste just that morning, having made good progress since sneaking out of Battersea two days before in the early morning hours. When the journey began, she felt lighter with the constant pressure that Tetric had been applying to her and her father on behalf of Marden left behind at the Broken Citadel. She was finally doing something, instead of being kept in the dark by her father. But her perspective had changed after just a few hours on the first day, as Sirius had decided that they would use every available minute to ensure that she was prepared for what she would face when they reached the Aeyrie.

Frustrated by her failure, Aislinn took a moment to center herself once more, taking a deep breath and surveying their surroundings. Not much had changed in the last few hours. She found the Waste to be unsettling and almost intimidating. It was a desolate land, a rough terrain of rolling hills to their west and to their east those knolls transformed into massive sand dunes that fell away to the coast. Desert more than anything else with but a few lonely, withered trees and scattered patches of shrubs and bushes, there were few travelers in the Waste and no homesteads or villages. Because of its proximity to the Aeyrie, some said that the land had once been green and verdant, but that the experiments of the Order of the Magii had harmed the environment, making it what it was today. Aislinn had asked Sirius about that rumor, but he had no knowledge of it. He explained that the land was dry and dusty simply because there were no rivers and just a few watering holes dotting the Waste. They wouldn't even find a stream until they got closer to the forest that surrounded the Aeyrie, which would take several days at their current pace.

He was likely right Aislinn surmised, as they hadn't seen

so much as a trickle of water since they had left the cover of a small grove that morning. Aislinn had grown worried, as they only had their canteens and a few extra water bags for themselves and their mounts. But Sirius didn't seem concerned. He had said that there were several places that they could stop for water along the way, all of which only he and a few others who traveled the Waste frequently knew how to find.

Yes, a desolate land. Yet as they traveled deeper into the Waste, she had discovered a strange beauty within it. A red flower would peek out from the rocks in the least expected place, or near the coast she would glimpse a twisted but mesmerizing tree, its white blossoms swaying in the breeze, that had somehow learned how to survive in this barren landscape.

Shaking her head to clear it, she turned her attention back to the task given to her. Reaching for the Talent once more, she took hold of the natural magic of the world, savoring the feeling as it flowed within her. Her first touch proved to be a struggle again, the energy slipping between her fingers as her horse struggled to find the best route through the loose rock and grasping sand, but heeding Sirius' advice, she fought to maintain her concentration as they worked their way through a gorge that resembled the dozen other fissures they had traveled through that morning.

"Good," said Sirius, keeping a close eye on her and sensing that she touched the Talent. "Now as before."

Sirius flung a handful of sand off to the side. For just a second, Aislinn watched it sparkle in the bright sun. Then she directed the threads of the Talent that she held toward the swirling crystals that danced in the air, turning the cloud into a dazzling display as the sand melted and formed into small pieces of twisted glass that shattered when they struck the rocky ground.

"Well done," said Sirius. "Much better than your previous efforts. Now again."

The training went on for the next twenty minutes, Aislinn using the Talent to turn the sand into glass, though with each throw Sirius increased the level of difficulty until on the final toss Aislinn used the Talent to mold all the sand crystals thrown into the air into a single piece of glass that blazed briefly in the light before shattering against the rocks strewn across the path. Aislinn grinned with some satisfaction.

"Excellent," said Sirius. "As you likely have discovered, trying to maintain your concentration when preoccupied is a difficult challenge. Your ability to focus must become second nature, something that you don't even need to think about, so that you don't have to worry about whether you can call on the Talent when you most need it. It'll simply be there, ready for you to use it." Taking in the sweat dripping from Aislinn's brow, the Magus decided that a break was in order. "I think that's enough for now."

Aislinn nodded, taking a long swig from her leather canteen. "I'm exhausted and it didn't even seem like I was using that much of the Talent."

"Rightly so. Using the Talent is difficult enough. Having to use it when your focus is being pulled in multiple directions even more so. Remember, you are using your energy not only when you are reaching for the Talent, but also when you are shaping the Talent so that you can accomplish whatever task you've set for yourself. The more Talent you pull in, or the more complicated the way in which you apply the Talent, the more tired you will be."

"Are you worried that I won't pass the Test?" she asked, trepidation seeping into her voice.

"No, child," replied Sirius with a smile. "I wouldn't allow you to take the Test unless I believed that you were prepared to pass it. Besides, you demonstrated that you were ready for the Test when you battled the Elder Ghoule on the north road. Let's call what we're doing now fine-tuning. It's simply an opportunity for you to enhance and refine your skills one last time before we reach the Aeyrie."

Aislinn nodded, satisfied, and she felt her worry dissipate somewhat. She had trained for years for this opportunity to prove herself, in fact ever since Sirius had arrived in the Broken Citadel and she learned that she had the ability to become a Magus. But she also knew the potential cost if she failed. She had been worrying about that ever since they had left Battersea in the middle of the night and that fear, small though it may be, likely wouldn't leave her until she had completed the Test.

"For someone raised in a city, your Protector seems quite at home," said Sirius, having taken a long drink of water as well. Fixating on the challenge that awaited her, as Sirius knew she would, wouldn't help Aislinn, so the Magus sought to direct her attention to other matters at least for a time.

Aislinn twisted around in her saddle and looked behind her, watching Bryen trail them by several dozen yards, riding his large horse quite comfortably. The unevenness of the terrain didn't seem to bother horse or rider one bit. When they had snuck into the stables just after midnight a few nights before, her Protector had selected the same animal, more a draft horse than a war charger, that had served him so well against the Ghoules.

From his perch, Bryen's eyes constantly scanned the

surrounding countryside. She didn't know if his roving gaze was simply a habit, ingrained in him since his time in the Pit, or he feared or sensed that danger was near. From where they were now, riding close to the coast along a hilly crest that allowed her to take in the Waste stretching westward to the very base of the Northern Spine and the massive sand dunes dropping off into the Silent Sea to the east, she could see for several leagues around. Nothing seemed to be moving except the sand and the gritty, soft dirt that spun up into small dust devils when touched by the constant, salty breeze that flowed up from the ocean.

"He hasn't always lived in the city," replied Aislinn. "So I'm not surprised. When he was a child, he lived in a small cottage in the forest, so he's probably enjoying the opportunity to get out of Battersea. To see more of the Southern Marches than just stone walls."

"How do you know all that?"

Aislinn gave Sirius a sly smile. "We do talk, you know. Although it's often like pulling teeth. Bryen prefers to not say much unless pressed."

Sirius was going to ask more, but then he stopped himself, taking a moment to think about what Aislinn just said. Obviously, the collar forced a closeness upon Aislinn and Bryen that was unavoidable, interaction between the two a must if they were to figure out a way to manage the thoughts and feelings that would naturally move across the bond that they now shared. And clearly, based on how they had been behaving the last few weeks, they had reached some kind of truce, both allowing their anger at the situation they had been forced into to dissipate.

Yet had their compelled engagement led to something else? Sirius wanted to get a better sense of Aislinn's connection with Bryen, what it meant and how deep it had become since he had affixed the collar around the boy's neck, but he wasn't sure how. He wondered if the link between the two was no longer based solely on Bryen being her Protector. And if he was correct, what did that mean? Did it bode well or ill for the future?

36

THE NEXT STEP

"**D**uke Winborne, I can't believe you have allowed this to happen," hissed Tetric, his black eyes blazing with fury as he fought to control his rising anger.

Though the King's Advisor spoke softly, his voice carried throughout the library. After his last attempt to gain the Duke's agreement that it was time for his daughter to leave for Tintagel, he had left with his men for several days, explaining that he had business to attend to in the west. It had also given him the opportunity to prepare for the likely eventuality that he would need to take the girl out of Battersea without her father's permission or knowledge. Yet now, upon returning to the capital, he had discovered that the Lady Winborne and Sirius were gone from Battersea. The Duke had strung him along for more than a week and had then played him just as he had been planning to play the Duke. The thought that he had been bested at his own game enraged him, and Tetric's always short temper threatened to explode.

"You forget yourself, Tetric," said Noorsin sharply. The

Duchess of Murcia stood to Kevan's side as he sat at his desk, fingers drumming regularly against the wood. "The Duke of the Southern Marches may do as he deems best. Aislinn is his daughter, and this is his Duchy. In the Southern Marches, he answers to no one but himself. Do not forget that." Noorsin bit off the last as if she were upbraiding a wayward child.

Tetric clenched his hands into fists as he struggled to master the anger that surged within him. And as his fury engulfed him, the delicious, intoxicating power that he controlled tempted him, called to him, sought a release. But no matter how much taking control of that power appealed to him, he knew that now was not the time. He had heard of what the Duchess of Murcia had done when healing the gladiator wounded by the Elder Ghoule. She clearly was a member of the Order of the Magii, but how powerful a Magus she was he couldn't determine. Starting a fight at this very moment would not serve his purposes, so he forced the magic so desperate to be employed into the back of his mind, locking it away for the time being. He had tried to deal with this situation in a respectful manner. Obviously, that had been the incorrect approach.

"The King will be most displeased, Duke Winborne," said Tetric in an even voice, though he desired nothing more than to rant and scream. To make his real displeasure known to these two who dared to challenge the tremendous power that he exercised in the name of the Crown. "When do you expect Lady Winborne to return to the Broken Citadel?"

Kevan smiled as if he didn't have a care in the world, though the constant tapping of his fingers upon his desk suggested otherwise. His casual posture didn't fit with his hard eyes, which failed to disguise the tension that ran through him.

"Who can say, Tetric? We took your advice and that of the King, taking into consideration Aislinn's safety. The fewer who know her location or how long that she will be gone, the better. Sirius agreed to accompany her, believing that it would be a good way to broaden her learning. There is only so much that can be taught in a library, after all. And with Tarin having confirmed that there has been no sign of Ghoule raiding parties close to Battersea, I'm sure she's safe." The Duke of the Southern Marches leaned forward and rested his forearms on his desk. His flinty eyes caught Tetric's. "That is your and the King's primary concern, is it not, Tetric? Aislinn's safety?"

Tetric bit back the harsh words that rose to his lips, realizing that for the moment he had been caught in the same trap that he had sought to weave around the Duke and the girl. That realization annoyed him more than he cared to admit, but he would deal with it later. His patience was at an end. He would not allow himself to play any more of the Duke's games. It was time to implement the more drastic measures he had been preparing in order to achieve his mission.

"Of course, Duke Winborne. The Lady Winborne's safety has always been my primary concern and that of King Marden's." Tetric spit out each word as if he were chewing leather.

Tetric turned sharply on his heel and strode out of the library, his barely controlled rage threatening to devour him as Duke Winborne continued to get the better of him. But Tetric took some solace from the fact that he believed that Aislinn's overprotective father had made a mistake. He had allowed the girl to leave the Broken Citadel with only the Magus and the boy to protect her. That was an error that he could make use of and that he was certain the Duke of the Southern Marches would come to regret.

37

QUIET CONVERSATION

Aislinn settled herself uncomfortably against a large boulder, one of several that at some point in the last few centuries had rolled down the hillock and come to a stop at the edge of the sand dune. Wanting to remain hidden as evening fell, Sirius had suggested that they leave the crest that they had been riding along for most of the day and find a safe place for the night. Bryen had located this particular spot. The boulders had settled into a formation that resembled a small fort. The space among the boulders was large enough for all three and their horses, offered protection on all sides, and gave the added advantage of blocking the incessant wind that whipped between the rocky crests and the sand dunes that bordered the cut they currently were traveling through.

Taking a moment for herself, she looked up at the dazzling evening sky. The stars were crisp and clear, and the full moon provided a dim glow that illuminated the dark of the night. She adjusted her position on the rough ground several times, struggling to ease the aches and pains that came awake every time she moved. She had ridden her horse from before first light to well beyond the last, having stopped only when Sirius began to worry that one of the horses would break a leg on the uneven ground.

Thinking back just a few days before, when she had left Battersea after she had been awakened in the dead of night, her excitement and relief knew no bounds. Finally, she was off to the Aeyrie to be tested as a Magus. But the last few days had worn her down, and her initial excitement had transitioned slowly into a grim determination. The constant riding was bad enough, but the lessons in the Talent had, for the first time in her life, become more of a burden than a delight. She was completely and utterly exhausted and wanted only to close her eyes and rest.

"Are you ready, child?" Sirius stood over her, his eyes shining in the moonlight. "Your Protector will see to our dinner. Let's continue with your lessons. We will reach the Aeyrie soon and need to make use of what time we have left before we get there."

About to argue that she needed to lie down for just a little longer, Aislinn bit back her reply. Her irritation came from her exhaustion, but Sirius was right. Better to ensure that she was as prepared as she could be for the Test to come. So she simply nodded and forced herself back to her feet, pushing herself up with the help of the massive rock at her back. She then followed after her instructor, her feet dragging in the dirt and loose scrabble.

As she walked past Bryen, who had built a small cooking fire but in a way that would keep the flames hidden among the boulders, Aislinn envied the simple task that he now performed. Her Protector kept his head down as he added herbs and vegetables to the pot that he had set over the flames, but she could sense what was going through his mind when she passed. He could tell how tired she was, and he felt for her. For someone as hard as he was, she never thought that he could have such an emotion. Her discovery surprised her and also warmed her heart.

It wasn't until well into the evening that Aislinn had the opportunity to drag herself back to the fire and eat the simple but filling meal that Bryen had cooked for her and Sirius. The tall Magus sat with his back against a boulder, using what little light remained from the dying flames to page through a book that he had brought with him. His constant muttering suggested that he was looking for something in particular but had yet to find it. Even though the two hours of additional training with Sirius had drained her of energy, and the thought of rolling into her blankets appealed to her more and more with each passing minute, she couldn't. At least not yet. Her body was tired, but her mind was still awake. She felt edgy and unable to calm her thoughts. She needed to do something.

Walking out between two boulders she peered into the darkness of the night, the only light coming from the brightly glowing full moon. After checking on the hobbled horses, Bryen had left their campsite while she was still training with Sirius. She had no idea in which direction. Using the connection that the collar created between them, she focused her thoughts on her Protector and found him not too far away. But, not unexpectedly, as far from her as he could be without experiencing the debilitating pain of going beyond the limits set by the magical artifact.

Aislinn walked into the darkness, allowing the moonlight to guide her steps. She turned to the left, careful where she walked on the rocky ground. It wasn't long before she saw the tall figure standing next to another large boulder. If not for the connection between them, he would have appeared as no more than a shadow, and she likely would have walked right past him without even knowing that he was there. He didn't turn toward her when she approached. He didn't have to. He knew that she was there. Instead, his gaze remained fixed on the crest of the ridge far above them.

"Tired from your lesson?" asked Bryen in a quiet voice, though he was stating exactly what she was feeling.

"Exhausted," she replied. "It's been a long day."

"That I can understand," Bryen said. "Sirius is pushing you hard."

"He just wants to make sure that I pass the Test. He says that I'm ready, but he's still worried."

"Are you worried?"

Aislinn took a moment before responding. "No. I'm ready."

"I'm sure you are," Bryen replied sincerely. "With the focus that you've shown during the last few days you remind me of a gladiator about to set foot in the Pit." Aislinn bowed her head at the compliment, hiding her blush at the unexpected comment. "You know, a touch of nerves isn't a bad thing."

"I assume you can tell through the collar."

Bryen looked at Aislinn quickly with a bright smile before turning his attention back to the crest of the knoll that loomed above them. He swept his gaze across the top of the hill and then to the encircling countryside that disappeared into the darkness.

"No. I mean, yes, the collar does allow me to not only sense where you are, but also what you're feeling. But I've learned in the last few weeks how to block the emotions that flow through the collar." Bryen turned his penetrating gaze back to his charge, taking in how her eyes sparkled in the dim light. He immediately focused once again on their surroundings, hoping that she didn't sense the unexpected spark that shot through him when he caught her eyes for that brief instant. "Block might not be the best word. The emotions are still there, just much more muted, less distracting."

But Bryen had nothing to fear, as Aislinn's thoughts were elsewhere. She wondered whether she could do the same as her Protector, blocking the emotions that flowed naturally through the collar so that she could regain some measure of privacy. She placed that possibility in the back of her mind. She would speak with him about it tomorrow when she wasn't so tired. She returned to his original assessment.

"I guess nervous is the right word," she confirmed, then attempted to lighten the conversation. "Probably not something that gladiators experience all that often."

"Sirius says that we'll be at the Aeyrie the morning after next, if all continues to go well. You've been training to become a Magus for almost half your life. In a few days you have the opportunity to achieve that goal. It's no different than when I walked out onto the sand of the Pit. I believed that I would survive. Well, most of the time I believed that I would survive. But I was always just a little bit nervous as well. It kept me from being ..."

"Overconfident."

Bryen nodded, Aislinn having completed his thought for him. "Yes. I learned that next to incompetence the easiest way to die in the Colosseum was to be overconfident. Better to keep a little bit of fear with you to ensure that you stay sharp."

"Thanks, Bryen. I appreciate that you are trying to put me at ease -- with conversation, no less," Aislinn said in a teasing voice.

"That wasn't my intention," said Bryen. "You seemed to want to talk, so I was just trying to oblige. Clearly, I'm not very good at it. I don't have much experience making conversation."

"No, you're not very good at it," said Aislinn with a smile. "But that's all right. I still like you."

Aislinn closed her eyes, gritted her teeth, and held her breath. She couldn't believe that those last few words had just come out of her mouth. Thankfully, Bryen didn't seem to attach any significance to what she just said, so she was able to breathe again.

"So once you become a Magus, what will you do?" asked Bryen. "Noorsin is a Magus, and she's hidden that fact quite well. It hasn't affected her ability to rule in Murcia. In fact, I expect her skill in the Talent has helped her in that regard. I know you have certain responsibilities as Lady of the Southern Marches. Have you thought about where you might go as a Magus? From what I understand, it's common for a new Magus to apprentice to a more experienced Magus and perhaps travel around Caledonia or beyond."

Aislinn had concentrated so much on becoming a Magus that she had never considered what that might mean with respect to the choices she would need to make once she attained her objective. She stared at Bryen, her face revealing the surprise that she was feeling. She was absolutely certain that that was the most that her Protector had ever spoken to her at one time. Usually his comments, especially in the training circle, were direct and to the point. An economy of words to match his economy of movement on the practice ground. And how did he know so much about what a new Magus might do after passing the Test?

"I haven't really thought about it," Aislinn replied quietly. Catching the sharp glint of the moonlight on the collar encircling his neck, she decided to ask Bryen a risky question. "What about you? What if you weren't my Protector? What would you do?"

"If I wasn't your Protector, I'd still be in the Pit," said Bryen, his voice barely above a whisper.

"No, I mean what if you weren't in the Pit? What if you were no longer a gladiator and you didn't have to wear the collar?"

"You mean what would I do if I were free?"

"Yes, what would you do? Start a life somewhere else doing ... what?"

"I don't really think about it," said Bryen, who tried but failed to keep the resentment she could sense within him from his voice. Despite having learned how to keep his emotions hidden from her to a certain extent, at that moment he was failing miserably. "When Sirius snapped the collar shut around my neck, he said that it could never be removed."

Aislinn was silent, feeling responsible even though it was her father who was to blame. She didn't expect her Protector to answer and was preparing to walk back to their makeshift camp when Bryen's voice stopped her.

"I would travel," said Bryen quietly. "For ten years I saw nothing but the Colosseum. White sand and white stone. Blood. Pain. Tears. Sweat. The very worst of what humanity had to offer, and rarely the very best. I was required to do what others wanted me to do. I want to do what I want to do. I want to see more of the world. I want to go where I want when I want. I want to go where no one can tell me what to say or what to do. Somewhere far from Caledonia. That's what I would do."

Aislinn bowed her head for a moment, suddenly ashamed, never really having considered what her Protector might be thinking about the experience of being shackled to her.

"I'm sorry," said Aislinn. "I didn't mean for this to happen to you."

Bryen nodded, but chose not to say anything. Though he apparently had the ability to read her emotions, she still needed to learn how to read his. Not knowing what to say, she chose to say nothing at all.

They stood in silence, side by side, for quite some time, each retreating to their own thoughts. When Bryen spoke again, she almost jumped.

"Something doesn't feel right."

His eyes once again scanned the crest of the knoll that towered above them, then he tracked the path that they had followed to get where they were now before peering in the direction that they would be going in the morning.

"Were we followed?"

"No, I don't think so." He grimaced for a moment, as if he had a bad taste in his mouth. "But I can't say for certain. It feels as if we're being watched. That's the best way to describe it. But I know that no one is about for miles around us."

Having spent so much time with Bryen over the last few months, Aislinn knew to trust his instincts. "Let's return to Sirius. He needs to know."

38

NOT ONE OF US

Sirius and Bryen sat across from one another. The small fire continued to spark and dance as the breeze slipped between the rocks separating them. They had settled into a comfortable silence for a time after Bryen had reported the strange feeling that he had experienced when he had wandered out from the rocky enclosure that served as their campsite.

The former gladiator had expected the Magus to dismiss it out of hand. But he had not. Instead, for the last several hours Sirius had used the Talent multiple times to search around them for any hint of a threat. Each time he had expanded his search, going farther and farther out until he was at the very border of the Waste, but Sirius had found nothing. That, in itself, hadn't surprised him. They were, after all, in the Waste, and there were few people who would brave the harsh environment without having a reason for doing so.

No, what bothered the Magus was that every time he searched around them, he had found absolutely nothing. No sign of life, no movement, and that wasn't normal at night in the Waste. Deer often came out to forage, as did smaller animals such as badgers, squirrels, and foxes. Owls would hunt the lizards, snakes, and mice that would appear when the sun went down. All this activity naturally attracted larger predators as well, such as the solitary mountain lions known for making the caves on the western edge of this barren landscape their dens.

But there was nothing. No animals at all. It was much like when a predator was about, and a forest went deathly silent in response. No, Sirius didn't doubt Bryen's instincts. What he discovered, or rather didn't discover, only confirmed for the Magus that he should pay attention to what the Protector had told him. That conclusion naturally led him to the possibility that whatever was out there, and he was certain now that there was something out there, had the capacity to mask themselves from the Talent. That unsettling fact could mean only one thing.

As a result, Sirius was on edge. He felt the need to take action, to sniff out whatever it was that was causing him such worry, but he couldn't leave the Protector and Aislinn on their own if his suspicions were correct. So he needed to occupy himself some other way since sleep would remain a challenge for him.

"You've been doing well with your lessons in the Talent. I hadn't expected that you would progress so far so rapidly."

"Yes, you did," corrected Bryen.

Although the Protector's eyes had been closed, Sirius knew that the boy was wide awake. As they had spent more time together due to his training, the Magus had gotten used to the Protector's directness.

"You're right, I did," Sirius admitted.

He caught the tight grin that Bryen gave him, the boy's grey eyes now open and shining brightly whenever the flames touched them. Before continuing, he glanced over at the sleeping form not too far away from the boy. Aislinn had lain down in her blankets close to her Protector and fallen asleep immediately, her constant work with the Talent during the day tiring her. That was to be expected. He hadn't expected that she would stay so near to her Protector. From what he had seen, she preferred to keep her distance from him, and he from her, whenever possible. But something had changed the relationship between them, or at least made it more manageable, and he was curious as to what it was.

"Why did you really take on the task of teaching me the Talent?" asked Bryen. He had pushed himself off the rock that he had been resting against and now leaned toward the fire, his eyes intent.

"As I explained before," replied Sirius. "Learning the Talent will help you with your responsibilities with respect to the Lady Aislinn. Mastering the natural magic of the world will help you protect your charge, and it will help you."

"That may be," answered Bryen. "But I think there's more to it than that. I think that there's something that you're not telling me."

"Are you always so suspicious?" Sirius asked with a tight laugh.

"Yes, I am. I've found that being suspicious is the best way to stay alive."

Sirius nodded. He could understand that as he considered how the Protector sitting across from him had spent the last ten years of his life fighting in the Pit for the pleasure of others.

"Why did I take on the task of teaching you to make use of the Talent?" mused Sirius, almost as if to himself. The

Magus wondered how he should reply. As several possible responses ran through his mind, as he almost always did in situations such as this, he decided to offer part of the truth, while keeping the guilt and pain that he experienced every time that he looked at the tall Protector to himself. "To keep you alive."

Sirius pushed himself off the rock he had been leaning against and studied the young man staring at him from across the fire. "As you know from our first lessons, throughout history the Talent has been called many things, although it seems that what we call it now has gained prominence over the other names. It has also been called the Power, the Light ... there are so many I can't remember them all. Magii prefer the term the Talent, because it suggests the need for agency on the part of the individual who can make use of the natural energy of the world. A natural energy that most can't connect to, can't touch, can't feel or sense, but the Magus can. Those who know nothing of the Talent call it sorcery, but it's not. It's a matter of restructuring, reengineering, redirecting the flow of the world's organic power."

"You still haven't answered my question," interrupted Bryen.

"I was getting to that," the tall Magus replied testily. "You have little patience, lad."

"I have little patience for long-winded responses that skirt the question raised."

Sirius bit back the sharp retort that instantly sprang to his lips. "I was getting to that. May I continue?" The last was said with barely controlled irritation.

Bryen stared at Sirius for a long moment. Perhaps the Magus' sharp tone and intimidating gaze would have worked on others, but it simply washed over him. He had dealt with Declan on a daily basis, after all. Bryen smiled knowingly, pleased that he had gotten such a rise from his companion.

"Yes, please."

"So kind of you," huffed Sirius. "Now if you can be patient for just a few minutes, you will understand. When the Magii first appeared in Caledonia thousands of years ago, even though they worked to protect and help the people of the land, there was still a great deal of fear regarding the power wielded by those individuals who could harness the Talent. In part, because they were different. They were able to do things that most everyone else couldn't. But Solomyn, one of the first Magii, also started noticing something else. Some of the people who could make use of the Talent struggled to do so. And when I say struggle, I don't mean that they couldn't touch the Talent. Rather, despite their best efforts, what they tried to do with the Talent didn't work out as expected. For example, someone who could apply the Talent may attempt to use it to help construct a home, yet rather than simplifying that process, such as raising the roof, their good-hearted efforts often led to heartache and harm. They would lose control over the Talent when they were trying to put the roof in place, leading to the collapse of the entire structure. Or someone who could control the Talent would try to do something dangerous, such as a wall of fire for a controlled burn to clear a field, and it would fail with terrifying results, usually with deadly consequences for the person applying the Talent and everyone around them."

"So this Solomyn formed the Order of the Magii?"

Sirius nodded in appreciation. "Indeed he did. The first responsibility, the primary responsibility for those who are members of the Order of the Magii, is to train those who have the ability to wield the Talent. To protect them from themselves and to protect others."

"So by teaching me I can protect Aislinn and not harm anyone else ... unless there's a need to."

"That is your primary responsibility, is it not?" answered Sirius. "But there's a bit more to it as well."

"Dark Magic. The Curse."

Sirius nodded once again. "You've been learning quite a bit as a result of the many hours that you've been spending in Duke Winborne's library, haven't you?"

"It seemed like a good use of my time."

"Apparently it has been. Yes, concern over the use of Dark Magic has a hand in the Order's role in training people capable of using the Talent. Most of the individuals with this unique skill are seeking to apply it for the betterment of others. To help people. To heal people. To protect people. To make the world a better place if possible. But not everyone. As you've probably already surmised, there are some people who are simply out for themselves, and some of these people have the ability to use the Talent. So the Order of the Magii also tries to ensure that the individuals it trains not only have the capacity to employ the Talent safely and effectively, but also that they employ it for the right reasons."

"But that doesn't always work, does it?"

Sirius shook his head sadly. "Unfortunately not. There's only so much that we can do, as a person's natural inclinations always seem to come out in the end. Solomyn established a code that we still follow today, one that sets out the basic rules and expectations that all skilled in the Talent are expected to follow. We'll discuss that more later as we continue with your lessons, but it really all comes down to some very simple strictures. A Magus will use the Talent for good. A Magus will not use the Talent for his or her own personal gain or power. And a Magus will be the first line of defense against the practitioners of Dark Magic."

"Those more interested in helping themselves rather than helping others."

"Just so, lad. Just so. Dark Magic functions in a fashion similar to that of the Talent, but it's been corrupted by the purpose it is used for. You saw it firsthand when you fought the Elder Ghoule. The Ghoules are bent on domination, destruction, on enslaving or eliminating those they view as beneath them. The magic they employ reflects that, because any time an individual exercises power, the reason for its use, the true reason, is manifested in its application, and that very same power will corrupt them."

"So when someone skilled in the Talent applies it for unscrupulous reasons, over time that very same power contaminates them. At some point, they are no longer applying the Talent. Rather, they are applying Dark Magic, and the Dark Magic is using them as well."

Sirius nodded with a smile. "You have been ensuring that your time in the library is well spent. You are correct. A person using Dark Magic is using that terrible power just as much as it is using him, if not more so. Think of it as a parasitic relationship."

"Yet even with the code or rules you mentioned that were put in place by Solomyn, Dark Magic remains a problem."

"It does, lad. It's unavoidable. It's a consequence of human nature. There are some people who are never satisfied with what they have. They always want more."

"More fighting. More blood. More death."

"Yes, what happens in the Pit serves as a good analogy."

"And this requirement that those skilled in the Talent

defend against Dark Magic. I'm assuming this is why the Ghoules have put a price on the head of every Magii?"

Sirius paused, squinting at his pupil. "You have been doing a lot of reading on Ghoules and our history with these beasts. Where did you learn this?"

"A treatise on Arick Winborne's defense of the Kingdom during the Ghoule invasion."

"You're right. Every Magus has a price on his or her head. During the First Ghoule War, the Order of the Magii played an important role in helping Arick, in helping the Kingdom, hold back the waves of Ghoules that came streaming down from the Shattered Peaks."

Bryen looked at Sirius strangely. For a moment, he thought that the Magus was speaking as if he had actually been there. "Many members of the Order were killed, including our most powerful, the Ten Magii who gave their lives to create the Weir. But it was worth the cost. It helped to save Caledonia." Sirius stopped for a moment, as if memories of a harder, deadlier time played through his mind. "Yet we continue to pay the price. The Ghoule Over-lord set a bounty on the head of every Magus, charging his Ghoules with claiming that bounty whenever possible. That evil creature understood that the Ghoules lost that war and were forced behind the Weir by the Magii. It's because of the Order that Caledonia has remained safe from the Ghoules since their first invasion. But rest assured that this is not over for the Ghoules. The Ghoules want Caledonia for themselves, and that means our extermination. Assuming that one day the Weir weakens to the point that the Ghoule Overlord can send his Legions through the Shattered Peaks in greater numbers, the fewer Magii there are to oppose them, the better the chances of their success."

"Which is why there are so few Magii who are known.

You, of course. I don't know of any others but the Duchess of Murcia, and she only revealed her power when helping to heal me."

"Correct, lad. Most of the Magii have concealed themselves and seek to continue to do so. Noorsin, as Duchess of Murcia, is in a position to protect herself as others can't. The only other Magus who is known throughout Caledonia is Rafia Riverstone, but no one has seen her for years. She could be anywhere."

Bryen noted a brief spark of pique in Sirius' last comment.

"And what of Tetric?"

Sirius looked at Bryen as if seeing him for the first time.

"What of Tetric?" he asked warily.

"The few times I've spoken with him or been near him I could sense the power within him."

"Can you sense how much power that I can control?" asked Sirius with some excitement. If so, that was a skill that few in the Order could lay claim to.

"I can. When I look at you, I see a brightness within you. A strong white light. Same as when I look at Aislinn, though a bit more muted. I assume the difference results from your differing strength in the Talent."

"It does," answered Sirius softly, his mind already working on the implications of what the young Protector had just revealed. No one of the Order had demonstrated an aptitude such as this for centuries. When Sirius next engaged Bryen in his training, he would have to explore this finding further. "What did you see when you looked at Tetric?"

"There was a speck of bright, white light, but I could barely see it. It was smothered by a swirling dark that pulsed a pitch black."

Sirius nodded sadly, as if Bryen's explanation had finally confirmed something that he already knew or at least suspected. "Tetric is not one of us."

"He's not part of the Order?"

"No," admitted Sirius, and clearly that acknowledgement hurt him. "He once was, but he changed and was expelled. He chose not to honor what it means to be a part of the Order of the Magii, and we have no use for ones such as him."

Sirius lost himself for a moment, thinking about the time that he had spent with Tetric when he was younger and just learning to use the Talent. Sirius had tried to both teach him and mentor him, because even then Tetric had displayed flashes of not only brilliance, but also a darkness that had worried Sirius, and those worries had only increased with time. Tetric had always wanted more, never satisfied with what he had, never satisfied with what he could do. More power than anyone else. More control. Just more. Sirius had feared that this weakness in Tetric's personality would take him down a dark path that, once tread upon, he had no choice but to continue to follow. Unfortunately, he had been right. There was no way for Tetric to turn back now. He was too far gone if Bryen's reading of him was correct. And it was Sirius who had allowed him to take that path in the first place.

Bryen sensed the change that had come over Sirius, so he allowed a few minutes to pass before he asked his next question.

"Why do they call it the First Ghoule War? It's the only war Caledonia has had with the Ghoules."

Sirius stared at the Protector somewhat perplexed, never having thought about it before.

"Good point," he said finally. "Let's just say that after the conclusion of the First Ghoule War, there's been an expectation that a second would follow, and we may be seeing its beginning right now if stories about the increasing number of Ghoules making their way through the Weir are true."

"You're still not telling me everything," said Bryen.

In a moment of surprising clarity, Sirius replied, "You're right. I'm not. I've told you what I think you need to know. For now."

Before Bryen could pursue Sirius' admission any further, the Protector shot to his feet, sword in his hand.

"What is it?" asked Sirius.

Bryen stared between two boulders out into the darkness, not bothering to look at Sirius. "That same feeling as before, only stronger. I'm going to take a look."

"I'll come with you," said Sirius.

Bryen glanced down at the sleeping Aislinn, who had bundled herself in her cloak and a few blankets.

"Better that you stay here. Keep an eye on Aislinn. I'll be back soon. With the collar, I can't go very far anyway."

Sirius nodded, reluctantly agreeing with the Protector's reasoning.

Bryen then slipped between two huge stones, not wanting to follow the path that they had used to bring their horses among the rocks. For several minutes he stood in the gorge, allowing the silence to wash over him, not moving a muscle, simply getting a feel for the gloom that was still brightly lit by the shining moon. He then turned toward the west and the knoll that rose before him, its wooded slope in sharp contrast to the sand dune that soared behind him. Whatever had worried him, it was gone. But it had only just left. He continued to walk to the west, senses alert for any sign of movement, his eyes tracking the ground. He was beginning to feel that familiar, uncomfortable tug in his gut, the warning that he was close to exceeding the distance that he could safely go from Aislinn, when he stopped and then crouched down.

The terrain was more rock than dirt, but even still he identified a few faint marks in the loose soil beneath his feet. He ran his fingers through the loam, edging the vague indentations that remained from whatever had been there just a few minutes before. Bryen remained where he was for almost a quarter hour, still as stone, confirming in his own mind that he, Sirius, and Aislinn were alone again, before he walked slowly and quietly back to the campsite.

"What was it?" asked the Magus when Bryen returned to his place by the fire.

"I can't say with any certainty."

"If you had to guess?"

Bryen looked at Sirius from across the fire, the flames giving the Magus an altogether different appearance. The façade of the distracted, pedantic instructor was gone, replaced by a man who exercised a hidden power that most couldn't even comprehend, his eyes sparking with fire and just a touch of menace. Bryen believed that he now gazed upon the real Sirius, a man confident in his abilities and comfortable with his purpose.

"I don't like to guess," replied Bryen, "and we can confirm it at first light when we leave, but based on the few scratchings I found in the dirt ... Ghoule."

39

THE AEYRIE

On the morning of the sixth day upon leaving Battersea, the cracked, dry land of the Waste gave way to a lush forest. The trees rose majestically into the sky, some topping out at several hundred feet in height, their bases more than a hundred feet around. Yet despite their size, the sun still broke through the gaps in the foliage and lit up the forest floor, revealing an ecosystem of moss, small ferns, and a rich, dark soil. Heart trees, Sirius had called them. In addition to plunging hundreds of feet into the earth, their roots, many thicker than a man was tall, spread across the forest floor in a haphazard fashion. As Sirius, Aislinn, and Bryen moved deeper into the wood, their path shifted in response to the pattern of the roots. In some places, the roots rose above the path Sirius had selected to form a massive arch, but in others the trio had no choice but to go around the strange and intriguing structures the curled and twisted wood had created over time until they found their way back to the trail.

Bryen struggled to maintain his vigilance, the peaceful quiet that engulfed them upon riding between the trees threatening to dull his senses. They had picked up their pace after Bryen showed Sirius and Aislinn the marks in the dirt and rock that he had identified just beyond their camp-site two mornings before. The scratches could have been nothing, but as Sirius had gazed down upon the faint cuts, he had run through his mind all the possible animals that lived in the Waste that could have left such tracks. Not a single one had matched. So the Magus had decided that on the final leg of their journey speed was just as if not more important than caution.

Several times each day Sirius had searched around them with the Talent, even teaching Aislinn how to do it from the saddle, but they had found nothing out of the ordinary. Still, that didn't satisfy the Magus. When they had bedded down for the night, he had insisted that one of them stand guard while the others slept, but nothing untoward had occurred. The crinkles of concern around Sirius' eyes reflected the sense of worry that emanated from him since Bryen's discov-ery, and it had only worsened as they had ridden deeper among the heart trees.

"You can feel it, can't you?" asked Sirius, as he leaned back along the rump of his horse. Surprisingly, a broad grin had replaced his days-old frown, as if he had just confirmed something that he had suspected but was not yet willing to share. "This forest was tended to by the Order of the Magii. The Order's use of the Talent was strong here and infused the very landscape, thus allowing this grove of heart trees to grow within the Waste. The remnants of their efforts are what's tickling at the edge of your consciousness. It's remarkable, really, what can be accomplished when man works with his environment rather than seeks to destroy it."

They rode on in silence for several hours, enjoying the serenity and the calm that drifted among the colossal trees.

Yet though Sirius and Aislinn seemed to have allowed their worries and vigilance to drop as they continued to the north, Bryen found it difficult to do so, his eyes continuing to scan their surroundings, catching on any flits of movement, whether from an animal or just the touch of the wind playing across a branch or bush. True, there had been no other signs of being tracked the last few days, even with the application of the Talent. But something still didn't feel right to him. Just because there were no obvious indications that they were being hunted didn't mean that they weren't being hunted.

As midday approached, they nudged their horses to a slightly faster pace upon seeing a break in the forest. When they emerged from between the heart trees they were struck by a blinding light. Aislinn and Bryen could only stare at what stood before them, hands covering their brows because of the dazzling gleam. In the middle of the forest, the Magii had carved out a perfect circle. A gleaming tower made of an almost translucent, white stone stood in the middle of the clearing, rising higher than the tallest heart tree. The noonday sun glanced off the stone, discharging a white light that was so bright that they couldn't bear to look at it for more than a second at a time.

"I give you the Aeyrie," said Sirius proudly. "Ancient home of the Order of the Magii."

Bryen and Aislinn rode to the base of the tower, hobbled their horses, then walked the long circuit around the shining spire. Looking up, they saw that the tower narrowed as it ascended into the sky until it reached a sharp point at the very top. They had to look again because instead of soaring straight up, the tip appeared to curl toward the west. Whether it was a trick of the light or how the tower actually had been constructed, they didn't know.

"You see it, don't you?" asked Sirius, having left his horse with the others and come to stand next to Aislinn and Bryen. "The Magii who built this tower sought to capture the essence that makes up the Talent. They curled the top of the spire to signify how the natural magic of the world bends to the will of the Magii. At least that's what the histories say."

"That seems a bit arrogant to me," said Aislinn. "Bending the power of nature suggests an uncalled for conceit when you're really just borrowing the power that nature offers you."

"Well said," replied Sirius. "I have always thought so myself. Perhaps instead we should view it as a lesson. The Talent is a gift from nature as you suggest. We should treat it as such. If we don't, we may be forced to pay a price that we and the world can't afford."

"We can't seem to escape your lessons," Bryen mumbled under his breath with a slight smile, but the sharp look Sirius gave him suggested that the tall Magus had heard him, as had been the Protector's intention. If what little fun life offered him involved tweaking Sirius' nose once in a while, he would take every opportunity to do so. Bryen stepped up to the stone of the spire and ran his hand across it. He was surprised by what he discovered. "There are no mortar or chisel marks. The spire appears to be a single piece of stone."

"Yes, it does," answered Sirius as they all strode around the base. "A clever use of the Talent. The spire was built much like any other tower, then the Magii used the Talent to craft it as you see it now. To give it the appearance of a stream of white light reaching up into the sky. It's supposed to resemble the Talent itself."

"The scorch marks?" Bryen asked, pointing to several places on the spire's stone marred by streaks of black.

"Reminders from the First Ghoule War," replied Sirius. "The Elder Ghoules placed the Aeyrie under siege. They wanted to destroy the tower and thereby eliminate the Order of the Magii at the same time. But their Dark Magic failed against the Talent, which frustrated the Ghoule Overlord and benefited the soldiers of the Kingdom. The members of the Order did all that they could to keep the attention of the Elder Ghoules and their Legions here, as each day the Ghoules sought to break through the spire's defenses was another day given to Aislinn's forebear, Arick Winborne, to prepare the Caledonian army to fight."

"There's no door," exclaimed Aislinn as they completed their circuit.

"There is," corrected Sirius. "But only a Magus can find it."

Sirius walked twenty paces to his left, then stopped. Bryen judged that the spot he had chosen aligned perfectly with the morning sun that rose in the east. The Magus placed his hand on the spire. After just a few seconds had passed, a soft glow appeared in the pellucid tower, white strands of energy peeling backwards from the stone to reveal an open doorway. Peering in, Aislinn glimpsed a winding staircase affixed to the inside wall of the spire that curled up to the very top of the Aeyrie.

"Are you ready, child?" asked Sirius. He gestured with his hand toward the stairway that rose up within the tower.

"Now?" she replied, her nervousness seeping into her voice.

Yes, this was something that she had trained for, something that she had dreamed about and wanted desperately.

But now that the time was upon her, she was a bit frightened of what could happen if she failed.

"There's no time like the present," he replied with a big smile.

Aislinn looked to Bryen for just a second. He must have sensed her trepidation, because she was heartened by the short, sharp nod that he gave her. She felt as if she were taking some of his strength and making it her own.

Turning back to the Magus, Aislinn nodded. She stepped through the open doorway. As soon as she did, globes spaced evenly along the wall that tracked the staircase began to glow, guiding her steps.

"Go ahead, child," said Sirius. "I will meet you at the top."

Once Aislinn had begun to climb the steps, the Magus shifted his focus to Bryen. His face had turned grim.

"I know," said Bryen. "Whatever it is, it seems to be hovering at the edge of the forest, almost as if it's reluctant to enter."

"How do you know where it is?" asked Sirius.

"I watched when you were teaching Lady Winborne how to search with the Talent," said the Protector. "After she had done it a few times, I tried it myself."

"And you timed it to match when she was doing it so that neither of us could tell that you were practicing the skill at the same time."

Bryen shrugged, as if what he had done was of little consequence.

"Remarkable," said Sirius. "But not surprising." He appeared to be thinking for a few seconds before his eyes turned as sharp as an eagle's. "Once Aislinn passes the Test and joins the Order, you and I will be spending more time together. Much more time. Your ability in the Talent is quite impressive."

"I can't wait," Bryen replied, but whether he was being truthful or sarcastic Sirius couldn't tell. The Magus returned his attention to more concerning matters. The darkness that had tracked them to the north.

"Let's hope that reluctance keeps whatever it is at the edge of the forest," said Sirius. "What worries me is that I should be able to sense whatever it is that's been trailing us, especially here, but I can't."

Bryen nodded, having heard much the same from the Magus during the last few days. "How long will you be?"

"If all goes well, Aislinn will have passed the Test and become a novice Magus by early evening." Sirius took one last look at the forest. It appeared exactly as it should. He hoped that it would remain so. "Remember, you won't be able to enter the Aeyrie, and once Aislinn begins her Test we will not be able to come out until she completes it. You'll be on your own. Keep your eyes open."

"I always do, Sirius. I always do."

~

"Allow me," said Sirius.

Spry for his age, though what that age could be no one knew, the Magus had quickly caught up to Aislinn and then passed her on the steps, leading her almost to the top of the spire in a climb that lasted several minutes. Stopping in front of the same almost translucent stone as was on the outside of the spire, he placed his hand against the barrier. Much as had occurred when they first entered the tower, strings of white light pulled away from his touch, revealing an open doorway that led into the Hall of the Magii.

When she followed Sirius through, Aislinn could barely contain herself. The stone on this level was as clear as glass, allowing the midday sun to illuminate the large chamber. Near the wall farthest away from the door stood a large block made of the same stone. It was, in fact, the only distinct feature of the large, circular chamber.

"It's because of the Talent," said Sirius, guessing at why she appeared so surprised. "The builders learned how they could use it to adjust the composition of the stone. They were able to maintain the strength of the stone, but change it at the same time to make it more porous and allow the light to shine through."

"But why?" she asked. "Why not just build a window?"

"Because they could," replied Sirius. "The builders were focused on the new. On innovation. On what had never been done before. If they could do something differently, even if it was more difficult, they would. Come."

Sirius guided her to the stone pedestal, motioning for her to step up onto it. With a small jump she did.

"This is the Speaker's Stone," explained Sirius. "For the most part, there is no hierarchy in the Order of the Magii, no set leadership but for what is agreed upon, other than the Master Magus, who functions as a facilitator. Decisions are made based on consensus. When the Magii gather here, the person on the stone has the right to speak. Once that person does so, all the other members of the Order may offer their thoughts by stepping onto the stone. The first Magus may not speak again on the same topic until all the other Magii wishing to do so have, in fact, done so."

"That suggests some very long meetings," said Aislinn, trying to hide her growing nervousness in humor.

"Yes, you're right about that," chuckled Sirius, remembering some discussions that dragged on for days. "But there is a purpose to this approach. It ensures that all have a say, and that we acknowledge, even when each of us has a different ability in the Talent, whether in terms of our overall strength or what we can do with the Talent, that within the Order we are all equal. We all have the same voice, and it is our responsibility to exercise it."

Aislinn nodded her understanding.

"And later this evening you will likely be in a position to participate in the next meeting of the Magii," said Sirius. "Are you ready? If so, we can begin."

Remembering her conversation with Bryen from the night before, Aislinn smiled as she thought about her quiet, stoic Protector. Then she used the skills that Bryen had taught her while in the training circle to center herself, to push out all distraction and focus solely on the here and now, on what she needed to do. Taking a deep breath, she nodded.

"Good," said Sirius. "I will be here the entire time."

"But Sirius," began Aislinn. "You never told how to pass the ..."

Ignoring her, Sirius placed his hand lightly on her forehead. In a flash of bright white light the world disappeared, and Aislinn fell into a deep, never-ending, still black mist.

AFTER CARING FOR THE HORSES, Bryen walked around the Aeyrie one more time. He marveled at the construction and how the sunlight played off the stone, running his hand across its edges in search of a seam but finding none. At the same time, he allowed his thoughts to drift, but just for a few minutes.

He thought of Aislinn's comment from several nights

past. He knew that she hoped he had missed what she said, that in fact she regretted saying it: "I still like you." He hadn't missed it. But he had little experience with women and didn't know how to respond. And, of course, the collar, always there, connecting them in ways that neither had imagined, complicated his perspective and his feelings. Still not knowing what to make of her words, he turned his attention back to his surroundings.

This place. The spire. The surrounding forest. It all seemed familiar to him. As if he had been here before. But how was that possible? Then it came to him. One of the dreams that he had experienced while traveling from Tintagel to Battersea. He had been right here with his father. They had traveled through the woods and what he saw now looked exactly as it had appeared in his dream. Why would his father take him here? And were any of the chambers that he remembered walking through in his dream actually in the tower that stood before him? If so, and he had actually been here, did that mean that his father was a Magus? His skill in the Talent certainly suggested as much.

He pushed those and the many other questions that popped into his head to the side. He could think about all that later, and perhaps even ask Sirius about it assuming that he could get a straightforward response from the Magus. For now, he needed to focus on his current responsibilities. Whatever had been tracking them in the Waste still remained at the edge of the forest, not yet having entered. Rather than wait for something to happen, he decided to get a better lay of the land. Declan had told him before each training session to not only know your opponent, but also to know your environment.

When he was younger, at first the advice seemed spot

on, particularly the part about knowing your opponent. Usually Declan would sit down with him before entering the Pit and give Bryen whatever information he could about the man or beast he was assigned to fight with the hope that he would survive the combat. But after a time the other piece of advice, knowing his environment, niggled at him, until one morning he decided to question the Master of the Gladiators.

"Why do I need to know my environment?" asked Bryen. "I'm always fighting in the Pit. It's always white sand."

Declan had stopped his constant stream of instructions, surprised that Bryen had spoken. He had been training for just a few months, having already survived several bouts, but when he was not on the white sand, Bryen tended to stay quiet and keep to himself. Which was how Declan preferred it. He was not used to someone questioning him, though Declan realized the value of the boy's curiosity and wanted to encourage it. So instead of launching into a cascade of curses, each one worse than the one previously spoken, which had been his first instinct, he had adopted an even tone.

"Yes, it's always white sand. So long as you're fighting in the Pit, it will be white sand. But that's only a small part of your fighting environment. The Colosseum is open. The sun shines down. On a hot day it heats the sand to the point where your bare skin will burn if touched by those feathery crystals. If you know that, you can use the sand against your opponent. Consider the angle of the sun. Is the light shining down onto the Pit in a way that will blind your opponent if you can direct them to the appropriate place on the sand? Is it raining? If it is, your movements may be slower as the sand clumps and increases your chances of slipping. It will have the same effect on your opponent, and you can use that to your advantage. What of the crowd? Is the Colosseum full? Are they rooting for you or your opponent? That can determine whether you can use the crowd's support to build your own confidence at the expense of that of your opponent. In hard-fought matches, confidence can be the key to your survival."

Declan had continued for several minutes more, and Bryen had taken it all in, standing there quietly. Then he nodded.

From that day forward Bryen's daily training with Declan had changed. The instruction continued, but it gradually evolved more into a conversation that both Bryen and Declan came to appreciate. For just a second, Bryen wondered how Declan was doing. He hadn't seen the Master of the Gladiators for almost half a year. In his time living at the Colosseum, Declan had become the one constant in his life. His trainer. His physician. His friend. His mentor. Perhaps he would have a chance to see Declan again one day, though he doubted it. His life wasn't his own. It hadn't been his own for a very long time. He had no control over most aspects of his life, something that he still struggled to accept. But there was one thing that he could control.

Walking into the forest he began to circle the clearing, taking in everything he could about the grove. The noises the birds made, how the sunlight played through the branches, where the roots of the massive trees stuck out from the rich soil, how the spaces varied between the massive trunks. He extended his circle as far out into the forest as he could before he began to feel the familiar tug in his gut caused by his connection to his charge through the collar that he hated with a vengeance. He walked just a little farther away from the tower, but realized that he had reached his limit as the pull in his gut had transitioned into a sharp, almost crippling pain. If he went any further, he'd collapse to the soft earth, unable to move because of the agony that would surge through his body.

After more than an hour of familiarizing himself with his surroundings, Bryen stopped abruptly. He turned toward the west. Whatever had bothered him for the last few days finally had entered the forest, and it was moving quickly. Bryen ran among the trees, dodging several roots, until he had reached the flank of where he thought whatever this presence that had been hunting them would appear.

As the minutes passed, he stayed hidden behind a tree, peering out from his cover and scanning for any movement. He didn't have long to wait. Looking to his front he caught a few flashes of motion, but nothing substantial. At first, he thought that it could be no more than a trick of the wind. But then he used the skill that he had picked up while watching Sirius train Aislinn. Bryen reached for the Talent. Doing so heightened his senses, bringing him closer to the natural world surrounding him. His vision, his hearing, his smell, his overall presence, became painfully more acute, more aware.

Now when he caught another flash of movement, he was able to fix his gaze upon it. What he saw sent a bolt of fear through him even though he had been expecting it. Ghoules. At least ten. They moved so fast, so fluidly, and they blended into the forest so well with their green skin and brown leather armor. They were approaching the Aeyrie in a skirmish line. Sirius and Aislinn were in the spire, safely ensconced. The Ghoules would not be able to enter. But he couldn't allow the Magus and his charge to walk out into a trap. It took him only a few seconds to develop a strategy. A poor one, and likely to lead to his death, but it was the best that he could do under the circumstances. As Declan had reminded him to the point of annoyance: "Everyone dies. Not everyone dies with honor."

In Bryen's opinion, truer words had never been spoken. Pulling the dagger from his belt, he glided noiselessly along the base of the tree he had hidden behind, his gaze fixed on a Ghoule no more than thirty feet away who stood silently among the trees, the beast's eyes fixed on the clearing just ahead.

40

MAGUS

Aislinn drifted for what seemed like hours through the black mist. Over time her initial fear shifted to a relaxing comfort as the fog filled her with a warmth that infused her entire body. Then in an instant the mist disappeared. She looked around in surprise. She stood on top of a circular, flat, smooth rock that was similar in appearance to the material that was used to construct the Aeyrie. She could actually look through the stone and see that it was balanced on the tip of a towering stone peak. Beneath the summit there was nothing but clouds. She feared that if she moved too far to a side the rock would tilt in that direction and simply slide down the mountainside. Then she looked up, unable to find the sun. Just above her clouds blocked her view, leaving the space that she occupied in a greyish cast. Neither light nor dark. For a moment it unnerved her. Her shock was complete when she heard the voice.

"Hello, Aislinn."

Aislinn spun around, barely breathing. The woman standing before her was just as tall as she was. She wore an impish grin, her dark, curly hair trailing down her back to below her waist, and her eyes sparkled despite the lack of light.

"Mother?"

Sulia Winborne had died when Aislinn was a young girl, succumbing to a fever that ravaged much of the Southern Marches. The experience had changed Aislinn's relationship with her father. Before her death, her father had been fun loving, always ready with a joke or to take her on an adventure. But when her mother had passed, her father had changed. He had grown quiet, introspective. Sadness had settled into his heart. He was still there for her, always, but his focus had shifted. She hadn't understood what her father was doing then, but as she grew older, she realized that most of his decisions were geared toward protecting her. Thus his encouragement of her learning the martial arts, politics, diplomacy. Any skill that he thought might be of use to her in the future, he sought to instruct her in it. And if he couldn't, he found someone who could. She knew why her father did it. But she had missed something along the way. She missed who he had been. She missed having fun with her father.

Upon seeing her, Aislinn's first urge was to run to her mother and embrace her. But instinct kept her rooted to the stone. Whatever stood before her looked like her mother. But it wasn't her mother. Her mother was dead.

"You are right to suspect, child," said Sulia. "I am your mother. I am what you remember of me. An image the Talent has taken from you so that we can have this conversation."

"You're a spirit?"

Sulia laughed, the deep, rich sound bringing back more remembrances for Aislinn of when she was a child. "Not quite, my darling. I am a memory. Your memory, to be exact, of me."

"How is this even possible?"

"Almost anything is possible with the Talent, child. Your training with Sirius has only just begun. There is so much more that you can learn, so much more that you can do. But first, you must pass the Test."

"What is the Test?" asked Aislinn. In all the time that she had trained with Sirius, he had never told her what the Test required, and he had avoided her digging for answers as they rode to the Aeyrie.

"It's not really a test," replied Sulia. "It's more like a question."

"What question?"

"The question is yours to answer," said Sulia.

"I don't understand," said Aislinn.

"You will, child. Are you ready for the question?"

Not knowing what to say or do, but wanting to proceed as quickly as possible, she simply nodded.

"Good. As you know, the Talent is the natural magic of the world. You have touched just a tiny portion of the power that it contains. Now, for the question."

"What happens if I don't answer the question correctly?"

Sulia smiled. "You know the possible results, child. You either pass the Test or you die. There are no other choices. Are you ready for the question?"

Aislinn stood on the rock, forcing herself to look into her mother's eyes. She fought to control the fear that was trying to break free within her. Finally, she took a deep breath, then nodded once again.

In a flash the world around her disappeared, replaced by the swirling grey mist. Images from her life played out in front of her as if she stood to the side watching. First, she was walking through a garden in the Broken Citadel, her mother holding her hand as she reached down to pick a rose. Aislinn pulled back her hand with a cry because a thorn had pricked her skin, a drop of red blood welling from the wound. Next, she was in the stable yard, learning to ride a pony for the first time. Her father walked beside her so that she wouldn't fall, and she could think of no other place she'd rather be at that very moment. Then she stood in the training circle as a teenager, her father standing before her, showing her how she should defend herself the next time he tried a similar strike with his sword.

Another memory appeared. And another. With each image she felt a spark from the Talent, as if it were taking in each memory for itself. More and more images appeared, speeding up, faster and faster until Aislinn couldn't keep up, the swirl of memories seeming to become a part of the grey mist that encircled her. She didn't understand what was going on, but she guessed that the Talent was trying to get to know her, to understand who she was, to get a sense of her character. And then just as suddenly as the kaleidoscope of memories started, it stopped.

The grey mist settled around her like a fog, blocking out any sound, preventing Aislinn from detecting any movement. Time moved slowly. She had no idea what she was supposed to do, so she remained frozen in place, fearing that if she wandered into the mist, she'd fall from the rock she stood upon. As the minutes continued to pass, she detected a rising warmth in her chest, much as she did when she took hold of the Talent. The feeling began to spread, the warmth of the natural magic of the world suffusing her body, her fingertips tingling as the Talent increased its hold on her. More and more of the Talent filled her, reaching a level that she had never achieved while training with Sirius and then going well beyond that.

With every breath she took, more and more of the energy of the natural world sought a place in her body until the warmth became uncomfortable. Slowly, with every new pulse of the Talent that forced its way within her, the warmth began to burn, and it wasn't long before she felt like she was on fire. She tried to stop the flow, to prevent any more of the natural energy from becoming a part of her, but she couldn't. And then she couldn't even think, the pain becoming too much as the burning sensation scoured her very insides.

BRYEN CREPT silently across the forest floor, dagger held out, sword sheathed in the scabbard across his back so that the long steel wouldn't impede his movement. Although he had extended his senses all around him, and he expected a Ghoule to lunge at him at any moment, his eyes were locked on the Ghoule who stood before him, back turned, the creature's gaze on the bright sun that streamed into the clearing just ahead.

Judging that he had gotten as far as he could before the Ghoule detected him, with a lightning quick first step Bryen sped forward, jumping on to the massive root that blocked his way, then using that as a steppingstone to leap through the air. Before the Ghoule could turn at the slight disturbance in the air behind him, Bryen was on the creature, slamming his knees into his adversary's back while placing his hand on the back of the beast's head so that when the Ghoule crashed to the ground, Bryen could push the creature's face into the soft earth as he slashed his dagger across the Ghoule's throat. The Ghoule struggled to free himself, but despite the beast's obvious strength, Bryen held firm, and the creature's resistance slowly ebbed as his black blood seeped onto the forest floor.

Waiting a few seconds more just to be certain that the Ghoule was dead, Bryen stood without making a sound. All remained quiet within the forest. None of the other Ghoules had seen or heard what had happened. If they had, he'd likely be dead already. Bryen grinned, glad that his gambit had worked. One down, however many more to go, he wasn't sure. Still holding on to the Talent, Bryen caught the flicker of movement about thirty feet to his front.

Wiping his dagger clean on the Ghoule's leather armor, Bryen stepped forward silently, his eyes fixed on his next target.

AISLINN OPENED HER EYES, a silent scream stuck in her throat. Her mind could focus on nothing but the heat that had consumed her, that had burned her from the inside out, cleansing every cell in her body, and that thankfully had dissipated. In its place she felt a comfortable, soothing cold. She looked down at her skin, expecting to see nothing but blackened and charred flesh. She breathed a sigh of relief as she ran her hands across her arms. She was all right. It had all been in her mind.

"You passed the Test, child," Sulia said, pride clear in her voice. "I knew that you would."

"That was the Test?"

"Yes, child. The Talent is now one with you. The natural magic of the world has learned who you are and now under-stands your strengths and weaknesses. That is the most important part of the Test. To become a Magus, you must not only be able to touch the Talent, for some a very large quantity actually, and in your case a truly remarkable amount, but you must also be able to control it. The question the Talent needed to answer was whether you had the strength, both physically and mentally, to control the power offered to you."

"You talk as if the Talent is alive. That it has a mind of its own."

"It is alive, child. Some have argued that it is life itself. But it is so much more than that. As you continue your studies, you will begin to understand. You will discover the true meaning of the Talent."

"So that means I am now a Magus?"

"Yes, child. The Talent has tested your strength. It has tested your ability. You may now become a Magus."

A broad grin broke out on Aislinn's face, but then she tamped down the excitement that had begun to build within her as she considered what the spirit of her mother had just said.

"What do you mean by may? I thought that once you passed the Test you were a Magus."

"Choice is involved, Aislinn. Choice is always involved when it comes to power and how that power is exercised. You can become a Magus. Or you can become something more."

"What do you mean by something more?" There was a tone in her mother's voice that gave Aislinn cause for concern.

Sulia stepped closer to her, the image of her mother almost overwhelming Aislinn, as she could see nothing but her face radiating a bright white light within the grey mist that surrounded them.

"Remember what Sirius explained to you, child. The power contained within the Talent is neutral. It is neither good nor bad. How you apply the Talent determines its value. It determines who you are and who you will become."

"But what is there beyond a Magus?" Aislinn had never known that such a thing was even possible.

"So much more, child. So much more. Think about what you want, my daughter. For yourself. For your Duchy. With the Talent, the only thing holding you back from what you want to achieve, what you want to gain, what you need, is you. The Talent offers many pathways. You need only select the right one and you could be more than you ever imagined possible."

Her mother's tone had become more strident, her normally gentle eyes turning stormy. The grey mist surrounding them began to swirl once more, but this time wildly, faster and faster, until Aislinn stood in the center of a gale, the darkness it created blocking out the light that her mother had first created around them. Sulia stepped even closer to Aislinn and then reached out, her hands closing around her daughter's wrists. It wasn't the gentle touch that Aislinn had expected. Rather, her mother's fingernails dug into her flesh. She tried to pull back as she saw drops of blood well up on her skin, but Aislinn was transfixed, unable to escape her mother's hypnotic eyes.

"The power that you will wield as the Duchess of the Southern Marches is great. You will be the master of eastern Caledonia with no one to answer to but a Crown far to the west. But that power doesn't compare to what you can achieve with the Talent. Think, Aislinn! Think about what you can do with the Talent! What you can do for yourself and for your Duchy. I can feel your potential. I can feel the power surging within you that is begging for release. Few in

Caledonia will be stronger than you in the Talent. Few will be able to challenge you. And if you make the right decision, no one will be your equal. With your control of the Talent, with the power you wield, you have nothing to fear from Marden. He can't control you. He can't do anything to you. He's nothing compared to you. He will be able to do nothing but bow down to you."

Sulia's angry expression, the strength of her painful grip on her arms, and the fieriness of her words frightened Aislinn. Her mother never would have said such things. Aislinn sought to step back from the spirit standing in front of her, to pull away from her mother's clawlike grasp, but she found that she was fixed in place. She could do nothing but stare into her mother's black, spinning eyes.

"So why stop at the Southern Marches?" continued Sulia, her voice strident and passionate. "Why not take all of Caledonia? Go to Tintagel. You don't need to marry that sniveling whelp who plays at King. You can use your power to take Caledonia from him. You would be the first Queen of Caledonia. You can mold the Kingdom in your own image. There is no one who can stop you! No one!"

As her mother's diatribe washed over her, Aislinn's fear slowly turned to thoughtful consideration. She found that her resolve was weakening, that what her mother was suggesting made sense. When her father had told her about Marden's proposal, she had feared what that had meant for her. Would she be forced to marry Marden? To become his queen? More likely she would simply become another one of his playthings. But her mother was correct. With the Talent, she could do whatever she wanted. Whatever she needed to do. In fact, she could do anything at all. Visions of what she could become danced through her head, her smile growing wider with each passing thought. She had nothing to fear and so much to gain. She could be so much more than anyone expected. So much more than ...

Then an image of Sirius broke through the reel of images passing through her mind. The old man with the long, grey beard looked down upon her with disappointed, disapproving eyes. All Aislinn's visions of power and grandeur slipped away from her. Now she understood what it meant to wield the Talent. What the consequences of it could be. But she had been looking at it the wrong way. She was not making use of the Talent, rather she was simply borrowing it. Her ability to employ the Talent was a gift and it needed to be treated as such. A Magus developed a harmonious relationship with the Talent. The goal was to direct the natural energy of the world, not control it. It was exactly as Sirius had explained. She could see that now. There was little difference between the Talent and the Curse. Both could be applied to achieve the same goal. But the distinction could be seen within the purposes for which the Talent was applied.

Put simply, it came down to the ethos, or the character, of the individual applying the Talent. Those wielding the natural magic of the world are filled by its energy and are made stronger and whole by it. Those who attempt to use the Talent for their own purposes, for their own gain, become twisted, and the Talent itself is corrupted, becoming instead Dark Magic. Then, over time, there is little difference between the one using Dark Magic and the Dark Magic itself, for that individual is being used by the Dark Magic just as much as the individual is using the Dark Magic. A dangerous cycle from which there is no escape. For the goal is no longer the good of the larger world, but the good of the individual.

Now she knew what she needed to become. With that

realization, Aislinn's mind cleared. The swirling mist disappeared, and for the first time Aislinn could see far beyond the translucent rock upon which she stood, which now glowed a bright white, to the mountain peaks that rose around her.

"Congratulations, my daughter," said Sulia, the anger and acid of the past few minutes replaced by a calm voice and a quick smile. "You are a Magus."

With that, the spirit disappeared.

41

FIGHT OF HIS LIFE

Hearing a guttural growl behind him, Bryen whipped around, pulling the sword from the scabbard on his back in the same motion. Just in time, he caught the slash from the large Ghoule who towered above him before the beast could cut him down. Holding the black blade in place with his own became more of a challenge as the Ghoule exerted his strength, the creature's arm and shoulder muscles bulging.

Slowly, ever so slowly, the Ghoule forced his blade closer to Bryen's face, and the Protector realized quickly that he was in a losing battle. The Ghoule knew it, the beast smiling to reveal his sharp teeth as he continued to push down, applying more pressure, his sharp sword inching closer.

Needing to improve his chances of survival, Bryen rolled to the side, dragging his blade along that of the Ghoule's as he did so, a shower of sparks sliding off their swords. He then pulled free from its sheath the dagger that he had buried hilt deep into the chest of the Ghoule he had just killed. As he rolled on the forest floor, he sliced the smaller blade across the back of the leg of the Ghoule who stood above him, but he missed his mark, cutting through the meat of the creature's calf instead of his hamstring.

Rather than slowing down the beast, the wound only served to incense the Ghoule, as the creature let loose in his guttural language a string of what Bryen could only assume were curses. Rising to his full height, Bryen shook his head in resignation. The Ghoule opposing him was larger than any he had ever come across, at least twice as wide at the shoulders as he was and blocking out the sun that glinted down through the trees. Sensing more movement coming toward him, Bryen realized that he had little time. Several other Ghoules approached, and once they arrived his already poor chances of living through this skirmish would disappear entirely.

Having few other options, Bryen charged forward, his sword and dagger a blur of steel as he attacked the massive Ghoule. At first, the Ghoule appeared confident, knowing that he only had to delay before his compatriots joined the fight. Therefore, the Ghoule decided to absorb the smaller human's assault, blocking Bryen's blade with a speed that matched that of the tall Protector and ignoring the sharp spikes of pain that sparked through him because of the several slashes that crisscrossed his arms as Bryen's dagger sliced across his flesh.

The problem occurred when the Ghoule stepped backward in response to the human's continuing, ferocious attack. The creature stumbled against the large tree root that protruded from the ground behind him. Bryen had positioned the Ghoule exactly as he wanted, using the details of the forest to his advantage and giving Declan silent thanks for ingraining within him the desire to survey his surroundings just a few hours earlier. As the massive Ghoule's injured leg gave way against the root, unable to support the creature's weight, Bryen leaped forward, severing the beast's other leg at the knee with his sword and then slamming his dagger backward in an upward thrust that punctured the Ghoule's leather armor and dug deeply into the creature's gut.

As the Ghoule collapsed to the soft earth, Bryen ran up the large root and jumped to a thick, low branch that extended out from the base of the tree. His agility saved his life, as the sharp blade of another Ghoule slashed down and cut deeply into the root right behind him, missing him by only a whisker. Bryen began to run along the branch toward its end, careful to keep his feet to the center of the wooden path so that he wouldn't slip off. He sensed rather than saw the Ghoule following below him, the creature unable to reach him but biding his time and sticking with him, none-theless.

Then the branch beneath his feet swayed violently, Bryen almost losing his balance. He caught himself just in time, regaining his footing before he fell to the ground and gave the Ghoule tracking him along the forest floor an easy kill. But then the branch began to shake. Confident once more in his purchase, Bryen turned and confirmed his worst fears. Another Ghoule dashed toward him along the branch, sword at the ready, a savage grin revealing the sharp, sawtooth teeth that filled his mouth. Bryen shook his head in annoyance, but his mind had already moved on to what he needed to do next if he was to have any chance of surviving this encounter. His initial plan had worked well. He had eliminated five Ghoules before the others realized that they were under attack. But his circumstances had changed. He had lost the advantage of surprise.

Another of Declan's many sayings came to mind, one that he believed was exceedingly appropriate for the situation he now found himself in. "You are gladiators," Declan liked to remind them when they were on the training ground. "You stand. You fight. You die. That's who you are. That's what you do. Do it well."

Bryen nodded to himself. Stand. Fight. Die. He would do so, and he would do it well. As his resolve grew, so did his anger. At having been forced into the Pit to fight as a gladiator. At being forced to serve as a Protector, a slave's collar circling his neck. At having no choice or freedom for much of his life. At realizing that today he would likely die in a forest that felt familiar and distant at the same time. He growled in acceptance. Such was his fate. He would die today as he would have in the Pit. He would die in a way that would make Declan proud.

Screaming in rage, Bryen raced toward the Ghoule charging toward him along the branch, his two blades at the ready. His action startled the Ghoule, who slowed down, never expecting his prey to attack him. With each step that he took, Bryen allowed his anger to build, to drive him forward, to fill him with purpose. He began to feel a comforting warmth in his chest that spread throughout his body, much as was the case when he had fought in the Pit. He realized that he had unconsciously sought the Talent, and he had found it. Good. He would use it to even the odds. Reaching more deeply for the Talent, he pulled on the natural energy within him, grasping so much that for a moment he thought that he might explode. Then, not even thinking about what he was doing, he allowed the Talent to trickle into his blades. The steel of his dagger and sword began to glow softly, then brighter and brighter as he infused the blades with the power of the world around him.

The Ghoule who had jumped up onto the branch tried to stop his advance, the light from Bryen's blades blinding him and forcing the creature to pivot his gaze away from the human. But it was too little too late. Bryen was too fast and too close. As the Ghoule brought one arm up to protect his eyes while also turning his head, Bryen slashed across the creature's thigh with his brightly shining sword. Bryen tried to contain his astonishment when he realized how effortlessly he had cut off the Ghoule's leg, slicing through the natural armor that guarded the beast's thigh from a normal sword strike but offered no resistance to the power of the Talent. Not allowing that new discovery to slow him down, Bryen lunged forward with his Talent-infused dagger, driving the blade deeply into the Ghoule's chest and finding the beast's heart.

As the body of the dead Ghoule fell off the branch and struck the ground with a loud thump, Bryen stared below him. Two Ghoules now stood there and looked up at him, short swords at the ready. Bryen smiled tightly, his once flagging confidence now soaring. For the first time Bryen detected something in the eyes of the Ghoules that he had never seen before. Fear. These creatures were used to being the hunters. They were used to being predators. But no more. Now they had become the prey.

Launching himself from the branch, Bryen flipped through the air, landing right between the two Ghoules, who were forced to turn away for a moment from the brightly shining steel in order to protect their eyes. But a moment was all that Bryen needed. He stabbed his dagger into the groin of the Ghoule on his left. Hearing the creature screech in agony and sensing the injured beast slump to the ground, Bryen turned his attention to his remaining foe.

The Ghoule tried to exploit Bryen's initial focus on his partner, swinging his short sword in an even stroke that was designed to separate Bryen's head from his body. Having little time to respond, Bryen raised his sword, his steel sticking straight up to catch the Ghoule's strike, the two blades meeting for an instant and forming the shape of a cross. Bryen turned away when the Ghoule's sword struck his own. He heard a clang that sounded like a blacksmith's hammer striking smelted steel followed by a small explosion of white sparks that threatened his own vision for a brief moment.

When he turned his gaze back to the Ghoule who opposed him, Bryen grinned even more broadly. He wished that he had learned this trick with the Talent earlier. It would have proven helpful. When the Ghoule's blade had struck Bryen's shining sword, it had shattered. Pieces of steel littered the forest floor, the Ghoule trying to understand how only a tiny sliver of steel remained attached to the hilt of his weapon. The creature had never experienced anything like it. Not giving the beast any more time to ponder his failure, Bryen struck immediately, driving his sword into the Ghoule's gut. The creature collapsed at Bryen's feet, his eyes glazing over before his knees hit the turf. As he slid his sword free, Bryen heard the sizzle of the blade as he withdrew it from the creature's flesh, the smell of burnt meat wafting up from the wound, its scorched edges plain in the sunlight.

Bryen shook his head in wonder. Just minutes before, he had expected to die. In fact, he was fully prepared to die. Yet instead he now stood victorious. He had defeated three Ghoules with little effort. He had never done so well in the Pit. But before he could relish the fact that he was still alive, Bryen dove to the side, sensing movement to his left. A bolt of black energy aimed for him instead struck the Ghoule that he had just killed. In seconds, the Ghoule's body disappeared, the flesh consumed by a black flame that left in its place an ash that floated in the slight breeze before settling onto the dark earth of the forest floor.

Bryen peeked out from behind the massive root that he had dropped behind for cover, hearing the guttural commands that he remembered so clearly from the skirmish on the north road. An Elder Ghoule. Seeing that the creature was about to send his Dark Magic toward him once more, Bryen ducked back behind the root and crawled away from where he had been hiding, keeping the root between him and his attacker. It was a good thing that he did, as another bolt of inky energy slammed into the root where he had just been, burning through it in a flash.

Bryen glanced to his right, hearing more of the incomprehensible language that he now associated with the Ghoules. Another Elder Ghoule had just entered the battleground. The two Elder Ghoules were communicating with one another, likely developing a strategy for cornering him and then eliminating him. It seemed that his victory was to be short-lived.

A single Elder Ghoule was difficult enough to fight. But two at one time? Even with the Talent he expected that it would be too much for him. Bryen crawled farther along the root, staying out of sight, then he rolled up and over it. Landing on the soft ground, he sprinted between the trees as he tried to put as much distance between himself and his new pursuers as he could.

42

ANOTHER TEST

Aislinn's eyes popped open, and it took her a moment to recall where she was. The translucent stone that she saw all around her confirmed it. The Aeyrie. The shadows of the late afternoon had begun to fill the chamber, so Sirius had lit candles as the sun began to drift down in the west. She had been on that circular stone atop the mountain peak for a good part of the day. She was tired, both mentally and physically, but she felt exultant as she realized that she remained on the stone pedestal in the Hall of the Magii, Sirius standing right in front of her. He smiled broadly, his eyes dancing with delight.

"Congratulations, child! You did it." Aislinn smiled, then stepped off the stone unsteadily. Sirius placed a surprisingly strong hand on her arm to steady her. "This will pass. It is normal. Your body is still adjusting to its new relationship with the Talent. Just give it a little time."

Aislinn nodded, taking several deep breaths. "I feel different, but in a good way."

"You look different," confirmed Sirius. "Though only the eyes of another Magus could see the changes within you."

"How so?"

"Magii can sense one another when in close proximity, particularly when holding the Talent. Moreover, if I look closely now, I can see a spark of white behind your eyes. Every Magus has that spark. It's a mark of your passing the Test and gaining admittance into the Order."

"You didn't tell me what I would face during the Test," chided Aislinn. "What I would have to overcome."

"I'm sorry, child," said Sirius. "I am not permitted to. It would only serve to defeat the purpose of the Test. Who was your guide?"

"My mother," she replied, her heart aching at the memories that her experience with the spirit guide had dredged up within her.

"Yes, that makes sense," said Sirius, nodding his head sagely. "The guide is always someone close to you. Someone you trust. Someone who can beguile you. Thankfully, you weren't tempted."

"What if I had been?" asked Aislinn. "What if I had decided that I wanted what the spirit guide offered me?"

"Then you would have returned here new in your power, just as you have done. But the spark in the back of your eyes would have been black rather than white."

"That's it?"

"No, there's more to it than that," said Sirius.

"What aren't you telling me, Sirius?" she asked, knowing after spending so much time with the Magus when he was reluctant to share or chose to reveal only so much of what he knew.

"If you had returned from the Test with a spark of black behind your eyes rather than white, then I would have killed you."

The harshness of his words took Aislinn by surprise. "But how could you ..."

"The Order of the Magii serves the Talent," said Sirius, his words hard as stone, as he meant them to be. Aislinn needed to understand this, because now she was bound by the strictures of the Order. "We serve others, not ourselves. Therefore, the Order also is responsible for protecting the world from those who have chosen to put their wants and desires first. Over time, those wants and desires consume them, the Talent within them becoming corrupt, shriveling up in the face of the Dark Magic that fills the resulting void. These Magii become the dark sorcerers who have turned away from the Talent, using their debased power for their own ends."

"Have you ever had to do this? Kill a student?"

Sirius nodded, his face as unyielding as granite. "Yes. Several other Magii have had to do so as well. It is not something that we want to do. It is something that we must do. The new Magus may be stronger than their instructor, but not right after they pass the Test. So when they are still coming into their power, when they are at their weakest ..."

Sirius let his words lapse, Aislinn immediately understanding that when such a situation occurred only one Magus could leave this chamber alive.

"How do you feel?" he asked, seeking to shift the conversation. "Your color is better. When you stepped off the pedestal, I thought that you might pass out."

"Tired, but good," she replied. "I feel more alive, more awake. Before the Test, I had to really concentrate to connect to the Talent. It was almost like I had to reach through a shimmering screen that flexed against my efforts. But now, it's just at the edge of my fingertips, always there, just waiting for me. I can reach it in an instant with barely a thought. And the filter of how I used to look at what was around me is gone. Everything here seems to be brighter, clearer, sharper. It's like I'm seeing the world for the first time."

Sirius chuckled. "That's what several of my other students have said. It is a gift and something that will prove useful to you as you grow more comfortable in the Talent. Are you feeling better?"

"Yes, thank you." Relishing the warmth of the Talent as it coursed through her body, she filled herself with it, just to get a sense of how much she could take in now. What she discovered about herself amazed her.

"You still have a great deal of work to do, Aislinn," said Sirius, knowing what she was doing. "In terms of how much of the Talent you can pull in at any one time, you are one of the strongest Magii in Caledonia. In fact, I can think of only a handful of Magii stronger than you, including myself. But if you are to use that much power well and wisely, there is still more training you will need. Having great power matters little if you don't know how to exercise it effectively."

"I understand," replied Aislinn. "That same point was made abundantly clear during the Test." She looked at the Magus with a grin.

Sirius nodded. "As a next step we should decide whether you will continue as my apprentice. As you know, for political reasons, your father thought that it might be a good ..."

Noting the expression that came over Aislinn's face, Sirius' words trailed off. Aislinn clutched at her chest, feeling a sharp pain followed by a burning sensation that took her breath away. For a moment, she was confused, wondering if this was part of the process for assimilating the Talent. But then she realized the truth. It was Bryen. She could feel him more distinctly now, even at this great distance from the collar. Whether this enhanced skill resulted from her new ability in the Talent, she didn't know, and she didn't care. The only thing that she understood for certain was that she needed to help him.

"Something's wrong," said Aislinn. "Bryen's hurt. He's in danger."

Aislinn pushed past Sirius and dashed through the doorway.

"Wait, child. It's not safe!"

Aislinn paid no heed to the Magus, increasing her pace as she ran down the steps, taking them two or three at a time. Bryen was hurt badly. His life was in danger. She needed to get to him before it was too late.

BRYEN DODGED among the heart trees, sticking close to their massive trunks and avoiding the open space between them in order to make the task of the two Elder Ghoules who were hunting him that much more difficult. He felt a surge of cold against his back as another burst of Dark Magic struck behind him, just missing him and leaving a slash of burnt bark in its wake. Rounding the tree, he allowed his legs to slip out from beneath him so that he fell backwards to the ground as another rush of black energy streaked through the space that he had just occupied and slammed into the tree to his right. The Elder Ghoules had trapped him, and that could only mean one thing. There were now more than two creatures stalking him.

This was getting ridiculous, and he was beginning to lose patience. After killing the last two Ghoules that he faced, he had felt a quick surge of pride, much like he did when he walked off the white sand of the Pit, as he was simply glad to still be alive. That feeling had disappeared quickly now that he was running for his life once again. As he pushed himself up off the ground, Declan's primary saying passed through his mind, one that had left an indelible impression on the Protector: "Everyone dies. Not everyone dies with honor." If there were truer words than those, Bryen didn't know what they could be.

He was done with this game. No more running. If he was going to die, he was going to die fighting. Steeling himself for what he had just planned, he ignored the Elder Ghoule who waited for him to appear once more from behind the tree. Instead, sword and dagger still in hand, he turned to face the Elder Ghoule who had emerged before him and now stood no more than twenty feet to his front, a swirling black cloud of Dark Magic spinning around the top of the creature's black staff.

The Elder Ghoule offered an evil grin, revealing his sharp teeth. "We remember you, boy," hissed the creature. "You were a hindrance by the sea, as you are now, but no more. You will not escape us again. You die. Here. Now."

Bryen forced down his surprise at hearing another Ghoule roughly speak the Caledonian language, for he didn't have time to think about it. Pointing his staff directly at him, the Elder Ghoule shot a shard of Dark Magic as long as a spear toward him.

Functioning solely on instinct, Bryen used the Talent that still raged within him. Benefiting from the constant practice that Sirius had required of him, he crafted a shield of white energy that instantly took shape to his front. Bryen raised his forearm, the spear of black energy striking the edge of the shield. A thunderous crack echoed throughout the forest.

The power of the Dark Magic slammed Bryen back

against the heart tree. The shield had deflected much of the energy, but unfortunately not all of it. A sharp sliver of corrupt sorcery had sliced deep into his chest on the left side, the tainted energy burning into his flesh. Bryen screamed in agony, but he did his best to ignore the sizzling wound even as he felt his flesh crisp and smolder, the Dark Magic burrowing toward his heart. He raised his shield once more. This time he caught the strike dead center on the white energy that spun in front of him, another thunderous clap sounding throughout the forest. Looking up from behind his shield, he saw the look of anger on the face of the Elder Ghoule. The creature had expected him to be easy meat. The Elder Ghoule should have known better.

Ignoring the searing pain in his chest, Bryen stood up and braced himself against the tree behind him. The Elder Ghoule pointed his staff at him a third time, screaming in his harsh language as the spear-like bolt of Dark Magic shot toward him. Bryen's wound continued to burn, and he could feel the putrid energy beginning to spread out from his chest to other parts of his body. He was beginning to weaken, the Dark Magic boring its way into him, filling his insides with a blisteringly cold fire. But he refused to yield. If he was going to die, it was going to be on his terms, and his terms only. More of Declan's words passed through his mind as he battled against the torment that pulsed through his body: "Stand. Fight. Die." Raising his shield one more time, he deflected the Elder Ghoule's third attack, but just barely.

Hearing an unintelligible scream of agony, Bryen glanced quickly to his left. The second Elder Ghoule, who had almost killed him when he rounded the tree, had sought to make use of his comrade's attack, sneaking around the trunk of the tree to strike him in the flank. Unfortunately, the creature's timing proved to be poor. Bryen's deflection with his shield directed the Dark Magic the other Elder Ghoule had sent toward him into the chest of this one. The creature's scream ended in seconds as the Curse consumed the beast, leaving only a cloud of black ash as a reminder of what had once stood there.

Turning back to his primary adversary, Bryen smiled, enjoying the shock on the other Elder Ghoule's face. Stand. Fight. Die. He had done the first two. Now it was time for the third. Gathering what little strength remained within him, and holding his shield of white energy to his front, Bryen pushed off the tree and charged toward the Elder Ghoule in a painful, stumbling run, a roar of anger escaping his throat.

AISLINN RUSHED OUT of the Aeyrie into the early evening, the shadows beginning to dominate as the sun offered a final radiant burst of strength over the tops of the heart trees, the last light of the day shining off the western side of the spire. She ducked instinctively as a sphere of Dark Magic slammed into the white stone of the Aeyrie just a few feet above her head.

Crouching in the long grass, she took in everything going on around her in an instant. Bryen had fallen to one knee in the middle of the glade. He held a rounded shield of white energy in front of him, doing his best to defend against a steady stream of attacks by three Elder Ghoules, each sending bolts or shards of Dark Magic slashing toward him with the hope that they would overwhelm him. But their opponent had proven tougher and more resilient than the beasts had expected. So far, Bryen had not only maintained his defense, deflecting the attacks, but he had gotten in a few strikes of his own, Aislinn identifying a dead Elder Ghoule crumpled at the edge of the trees with his staff thrust through his chest, the knob rising toward the sky.

For just a moment, her thoughts turned toward the shock that she felt upon seeing her Protector make use of the Talent. Even with the collar, she had no idea that he could harness the natural power of the world. She pushed that thought aside. He was badly injured. She could feel his pain and suffering. She needed to help him. He faced three Elder Ghoules to his front, but she also noticed blurring movement on the northwestern side of the glade. It had to be Ghoules. Perhaps as many as five were attempting to sneak around Bryen and take him from behind while the Elder Ghoules kept him in place.

A sharp, white-hot anger imbued her. The Talent came to her in an instant, cascading within her, beckoning to her, wanting to be released in response to the Dark Magic that hurtled through the glade. She had fought one Elder Ghoule just weeks before and survived. Then, she had not yet known the full extent of her strength. Now she did. Now she would show these evil creatures what she could do. She quickly fashioned several balls of condensed, blazing energy, juggling them from hand to hand. She was about to release them when she heard a shout from behind her.

"No! Eliminate the Ghoules! Leave the Elders to me!"

Aislinn turned to watch Sirius stride into the long grass. What she saw amazed her. This was not the normally distracted teacher she had come to know during her training. This was a Magus demonstrating the full might of his power. He crackled with the Talent as he passed by her and stalked toward the three Elder Ghoules, his body shimmering from what appeared to be a cloak of white energy, strands of the Talent jumping to and fro across his billowing robes.

Confident in Sirius' abilities, Aislinn turned her attention to the Ghoules, several of whom had left the cover of the trees and were now sprinting toward Bryen. Aislinn flung the small, sizzling spheres toward her targets. Several balls struck the two Ghoules who had outdistanced their peers and were closest to Bryen, blasting through their backs and exiting through their chests. The creatures remained standing for just a second longer, not yet realizing that they had died, before collapsing to the ground. A third Ghoule slid to a stop in the long grass, shocked by what he had just seen. His delay in moving proved to be his downfall, as three more spheres of white energy ripped into him. But that delay proved useful to the remaining Ghoule.

Knowing the danger that the girl with the Talent presented, the surviving Ghoule glided from the trees, moving impossibly fast directly toward Aislinn. For just a moment, she was mesmerized by the Ghoule's mask of hate. The beast roared in fury, short sword raised to cleave her head from her neck. Realizing that the creature was too close to do what she had done to his comrades, she relied on her instincts.

Just before the Ghoule swung his blade down at an angle, aiming for her collarbone, she rolled to the side. Not having her sword in hand, she added her own twist to the maneuver. She crafted a sword from the Talent that blazed with a clean white light. She swung the weapon backhanded through the space that she had just vacated. The fiery energy of the sword cleanly sliced through the Ghoule's blade and his midsection, the beast falling to the ground with his body almost cut in half.

Amazed that the fight had lasted only a few seconds,

Aislinn took just a moment to center herself once more as her adrenaline swept through her. She was pleased that she was still alive and shocked that she had eliminated the Ghoules so quickly and viciously. But that wasn't important right now. She looked back toward Bryen, ready to assist her Protector against the three Elder Ghoules. She quickly realized that her help wouldn't be needed in that respect.

As Sirius walked through the tall grass, he left a smoldering path behind him, the energy surging around his robes setting the stalks ablaze. Approaching the three Elder Ghoules, the Talent filling him to the point of bursting, the Magus felt better than he had in years, more like himself, more like when he was younger. He had pretended for so long to be someone else that he had almost forgotten who he was. But no more. There was no longer a need to pretend. Now he could be who he was meant to be. He could exercise the power that he controlled to its fullest extent.

With a flick of his wrist a wall of white energy settled in front of Bryen, blocking the Elder Ghoules' attacks and allowing the Protector to release his shield. The strain of maintaining his defense was evident as Bryen's legs gave out beneath him and he collapsed into the grass. Before the three Elder Ghoules realized that they faced a new danger, Sirius released a bolt of blazing white energy that struck the Elder Ghoule on his left directly in the chest. The blast went straight through the Ghoule's body, and the creature fell backwards into the grass, dead before he hit the dirt.

The remaining Elder Ghoules quickly shifted their focus toward this new threat and attempted to defend themselves, shards of black energy streaming toward Sirius once they realized they could not penetrate the shield protecting their initial target. For several seconds, Sirius disappeared within a cloud of inky black as the Dark Magic tried to devour him.

Then with a thundering boom the Curse disappeared, consumed by the blazing white energy that spun faster and faster around the Magus.

With Sirius occupying the Elder Ghoules, Aislinn ran to Bryen, propping his head on her knees. His shirt was torn and charred in the front, and a shiver of fear shot through her when she saw the massive burn that covered the left side of his chest, tendrils of black quickly spreading out to his body's extremities. She wanted to do something for him, anything to stop the advance of the Dark Magic, but she didn't know what. Even with her newfound strength in the Talent, she felt helpless. All that she could do was wait for Sirius.

As she turned her gaze back to her instructor, he appeared to be more vengeful demon than man, his normally unkempt long hair sticking straight up, sparks shooting from the tips, threads of the Talent springing across his robes. But what really scared her were his eyes. Their normally dark color had been replaced by a white fire. She watched as Sirius brought his hands to the sky and then made a quick motion toward the remaining Elder Ghoules. Two bolts of white lightning shot down, obliterating the beasts and leaving two large circles of ash in the grass, small fires burning at the edges of the charred space.

Satisfied with his efforts, Sirius took a quick look around the glade to ensure that no more Ghoules would be rushing out from the forest and then trotted over to Aislinn, crouching down next to Bryen and putting his hand just above his burned chest.

"Can you help him?" Aislinn asked, tears forming in her eyes as she realized that Bryen's breathing was growing fainter.

Kneeling over Bryen a few seconds more, Sirius removed his hand, closed his eyes, and bowed his head.

"I'm sorry, child. I wish I could, but I do not have Noorsin's skill in healing. I cannot help him."

"Please, Sirius, you must try," Aislinn said, her tears now streaming down her cheeks. "You must at least do something. He doesn't deserve this."

"He doesn't deserve much of what he's gotten in his life," muttered Sirius, his frustration at not being able to do anything to assist the boy evident. "At least he will have not died in vain. He will have died protecting you, fulfilling his primary responsibility."

"He's required to do that, Sirius," Aislinn replied, wiping her eyes with a dirt-streaked hand. "Because of you and my father. He has no choice."

"If he were a free man, child, if placed in this same situation, I have no doubt that he would meet the same fate just as bravely as he has done now."

Aislinn stroked a strand of Bryen's curly, white hair from his eyes, taking in the full weight of Sirius' words. "Please, Sirius. His death is on our shoulders."

Sirius snarled in anger, irritated by the lack of options as several scrolled through his mind and just as quickly he discarded them. Except for one. One that could save the boy or could kill him, but at this point, as he watched the Dark Magic continue to advance from his chest, the last concern really wasn't relevant. He began lifting Bryen up, demonstrating a surprising strength for an old man.

"Help me bring him into the Aeyrie. There is an artifact in there that might help him when we put him through the Test."

"But how could he ..."

"You saw what the boy could do against the Elder

Ghoules," Sirius said raggedly, not wanting to deal with a series of questions as he started to walk toward the entrance to the spire carrying Bryen. "Besides, the boy has the skill to become a Magus. I've been training him privately. I don't think that he is ready for this now, he could have used more time to learn about the Talent, but it doesn't matter now. If he fails the Test, he dies, and if he doesn't take the Test, he dies."

"But how can the Test help him?"

"If he passes the Test, his body will be filled with the natural energy of the world, more than he's ever controlled before. If we do this right, he can heal himself during the Test with that reservoir of power. That's the only way. And perhaps it will work. Noorsin suspects that's how Bryen healed so quickly when he was first wounded by the Elder Ghoule on the coastal road. He should have died then, but somehow, he tapped into the Talent to heal himself. Perhaps he can do it again with a little extra help. Now no more questions. Help me. He has little time."

43

THE SEVENTH STONE

After what seemed like hours but was only minutes, Sirius finally trotted into the chamber at the top of the Aeyrie, Bryen slumped across his shoulder. The Magus had hustled up the winding staircase as fast as he could, feeling Bryen's body growing colder with every step that he took and knowing that every second counted. Aislinn followed right behind, her fears for her Protector increasing the higher they went in the tower. She could sense everything that was going on within Bryen's body through the collar. The Dark Magic was spreading faster than she thought possible, and although he continued to fight it, his strength was waning. He was dying.

"Sirius, we need to move faster," she said as the old Magus gently shifted Bryen off his shoulder and placed his back against the small stone pedestal that she had stood on during her Test. "I can feel the Dark Magic poisoning him. It's almost to his heart."

"I am doing all that I can, child," mumbled Sirius, having suspected as much himself. "Now hold him against the pedestal. He can't stand on it as you did, but he must be touching it through the entirety of the Test. It is the only way."

Aislinn dropped down to her knees, then grasped Bryen tightly by his shoulders, pushing her Protector's back against the stone and holding him there.

"Keep him in place," ordered Sirius. "Do not let him move, no matter what."

Aislinn nodded, then watched in fascination as Sirius placed his palm against Bryen's forehead. A flash of white blinded her, and then she was struggling, using all her strength to keep her Protector against the pedestal, his eyes popping open for just a second and his body flopping about as if he had been struck by lightning. Just as fast as his frenetic movement had started, it subsided to a few random spasms, and then he sagged back against the stone.

"Is that it?" she asked, keeping her hands on Bryen's shoulders and making sure that his back stayed in contact with the stone.

"For now, yes," replied Sirius. "He has begun the Test. All we can do is wait."

"How long will it take?" asked Aislinn.

"It is different for each person, child. For you, it was most of the afternoon. For your Protector, who can say? It could be an hour. It could be a day."

Nodding, Aislinn shifted her position so that she could be more comfortable, sitting next to Bryen, her shoulder touching his so that her Protector remained in contact with the stone. Sirius sat a few feet across from them, his gaze never leaving the boy. Every few minutes, Aislinn glanced down and studied the wound on Bryen's chest, ignoring the many scars that marred his arms, chest, and abdomen, her curiosity piqued about what he had endured in the Pit, but she knew that it was not pertinent in that moment. The scorched flesh remained as it was, enough layers torn away to reveal the muscle beneath. The veins of black persisted, but since Bryen had been sent into the Test by Sirius, it didn't appear as if those threads of darkness had continued to spread, which gave her some hope that perhaps Sirius was correct. Perhaps if Bryen passed the Test he would be able to heal himself as he had done after the fight on the north road.

Aislinn's hope was quashed less than an hour later when Bryen's eyes shot open again and his body shivered as if another bolt of lightning had shot through him.

"Sirius!" she screamed, as she draped herself over Bryen's body to keep him from unintentionally moving away from the pedestal.

The Magus was there in an instant, helping her to push her Protector back against the stone. Bryen's body continued to shake for more than a minute before he settled into an uncontrollable shivering, a white energy blasting out from the Protector's wound. But after just a few seconds, the bright light transformed into a muted glow that slowly turned a sickly yellow. After less than a minute, the light could barely be seen any more, and then it simply winked out, Bryen becoming still.

"He's losing," whispered Sirius.

"What?" asked Aislinn. "No. No, he can't. He must fight it. He must."

The old Magus nodded toward Bryen's wound, and she saw that the veins of black were once again beginning to spread higher up his chest to his neck and also down to his abdomen. Then the veins began to pulse a deep black as they formed what resembled a haphazard spider's web across the Protector's chest.

"The Dark Magic and the Talent are contesting with one

another. But Bryen is too weak. He is too far gone. The Dark Magic is taking him."

Aislinn looked up at Sirius with pleading eyes. "There must be something else that we can do. Anything. Please, Sirius! He doesn't deserve to die this way."

Cursing in frustration because he knew that Aislinn was correct, his mind rapidly ran through a dozen possible options for trying to help the boy, but just as fast as an idea popped into his mind, he knew that it had no chance of working. Except perhaps for one. The one he had been thinking about since he first brought Bryen into the Aeyrie. It was a long shot, but it might be the only chance the boy had of surviving this. It also had a good chance of killing him, but what was the harm? He was dying already.

"Keep him here," said Sirius. "I'll be back as soon as I can."

The Magus jumped up from where he was kneeling and sprinted out of the room and across the hallway. Another doorway beckoned, and he dashed through into the chamber beyond. It appeared to be just a large, circular room. Like every other chamber in the Aeyrie, there were no windows. But Sirius knew that this space was so much more than that. He took a few steps further in, then stopped, sensing what he had expected to be in his way. He put his hand out in front of him, but couldn't extend his elbow. His movement was blocked by an invisible barrier. Although it appeared that there was a large room right in front of his eyes, he could go no further.

Knowing that the magical barricade extended for the length of the room, having been put in place by the Order when the Aeyrie had first been built, he placed his hand against the invisible barrier and closed his eyes. After several seconds of probing with the Talent, he opened his eyes once more. With just a little pressure, his fingers disappeared into the imperceptible wall. He smiled. Then he pushed his arm farther into the invisible barrier, the image in front of him shifting, becoming more fluid.

Satisfied that everything was working as it should, he pushed his entire body into the unseen barrier. When he stepped across, there was nothing on the other side except for an empty room.

He hadn't done this for a while, so he stopped for a moment. He could sense the power in the chamber, something old and exceedingly strong. But it was muted and could only be detected by those who knew to look for it. He wandered about the room with a purpose. In what he judged to be the center of the chamber, taking into account the space segmented by the invisible barrier, he found what he was searching for.

He could feel the ancient energy pulsing just beneath his feet. Basing his next action solely on memory, he reached down and touched one of the tiles in the floor, then moved back quickly to avoid the thin, stone pedestal that shot up. The stone was the same as that of the spire, very pale, almost translucent, but what unavoidably caught his eye was the object that sat on top of it and was held in place by three barely visible gold threads.

The diamond was the size of his fist. He stared at it for just a second, dazzled by the play of the light across the gem, looking for imperfections, but finding none. He sensed the power that the diamond contained, both good and evil balanced on a razor's edge. That power could be nudged to either side. It would take barely the touch of a feather. He hoped that he was right. He hoped that this ancient artifact would be the difference and give the boy a fighting chance. Carefully removing the diamond from the pedestal, he pushed his way back through the barrier and sprinted across the tower, sliding to a stop right in front of Aislinn's Protector.

Sirius had been gone for only a few minutes, but Bryen's condition had worsened drastically. His entire chest was now a mass of pulsing black. How the boy could endure the agony he likely felt, Sirius couldn't comprehend. Not really knowing what to do, he did the only thing that came to mind, placing the diamond against the Protector's wound, which had begun to ooze a thick, black pus.

"What is that?" asked Aislinn, entranced by the beauty of the diamond. She had to force herself to look away, the effort required to pull her gaze free from the stone almost too much for her.

"The Seventh Stone," replied Sirius.

"The Seventh Stone?" Aislinn had to think for a moment, the name bringing to mind some of the lore that she had learned when she had first begun to study with Sirius. "You mean from the time of the Ten Magii?"

"Yes," replied Sirius, though his attention remained on Bryen. "The Seventh Stone of the Seven Stones. The most powerful of them all."

He believed that the Seventh Stone could help the boy, but he wasn't sure how to activate it for the purpose that he desired to put it to use. Although he held it against the Protector's wound, nothing had changed.

"What are you going to do with it?"

"I'm going to try to stimulate the healing process within Bryen. I can try to heal him with this."

"Could it harm him?"

"The Seventh Stone is neither good nor bad. It's an artifact that was used as a gateway or a circuit that allows for the user to manipulate both Dark Magic and the Talent, allowing the two distinct powers to coexist, though I can't say it's an easy relationship. An Elder Ghoule employing the Seventh Stone could make use of the Talent as well and finally exercise the power to destroy the Weir. A Magus could use it to harness the Dark Magic needed to rebuild the Weir. It is simply a tool. How it is used depends on the intentions or goals of the individual employing it."

"Will it save him?"

"It could. But it could also hasten his death."

"Do we have a choice?"

"No, we don't. This is our last and best hope."

"Then we need to do this. Do you know how to make it work?"

"Enough questions, child," said Sirius, a tinge of irritation rising in his voice as he continued to consider what he had to do next. "Let me concentrate."

Realizing that time was of the essence, he did the only thing that came to mind, sending a small stream of the Talent into the Seventh Stone. The huge diamond flashed in response, but then just as quickly it returned to its normal coloring.

"Were you expecting it to do that?" asked Aislinn, her concern for her Protector becoming more and more urgent as the seconds passed. His breathing had become shallower to the point where she could barely tell if his chest was rising and falling.

"I don't know what to expect, child. I've never done this before."

He was about to send another stream of the Talent into the Seventh Stone, this one much stronger than the first, when a blinding flash of white light shot from the diamond, illuminating the entire chamber with its brilliance. Both Sirius and Aislinn had to turn away from the blast of energy,

and when they were finally able to look back at the
wounded Protector, the Seventh Stone pulsed brightly but
slowly, seeming to match the pace of Bryen's almost nonex-
istent breaths.

"Did you do that?" asked Aislinn.

"No, I didn't" answered Sirius, who couldn't take his eyes
away from the pulsating diamond. "It's doing it on its own."
But then he corrected himself, allowing a small smile to
escape. "Actually, I think Bryen is doing it. He's connected to
the Seventh Stone somehow. Look."

Aislinn stared down at the wound in her Protector's
chest. The pace of the diamond's pulses had begun to
increase, staying in sync with Bryen's breaths. Though still
shallow, he was breathing more regularly now. As the
seconds passed, the pace continued to increase. Then a
bright white light blasted from the Seventh Stone into his
chest. Bryen shot up from where he was slumped against
the pedestal for just a second before collapsing back against
the stone, Sirius catching him before he could hurt himself
and making sure that he was as settled as he could be. That
flash of energy grew brighter and brighter as it began to
spread throughout Bryen's body. The black pus that had
been seeping from Bryen's wound slowly dried up and then
flaked off his body.

Aislinn watched in amazement and hope as a small ball
of misty black began to spin just above the pulsing Seventh
Stone, the inky sphere growing as the Seventh Stone began
to extract the Dark Magic that had infected Bryen. Slowly at
first, then faster and faster, the tendrils of black that had
crisscrossed his body began to shrink and then shriveled up
and disappeared entirely as the poison was pulled out by
the magic contained within the diamond.

When it appeared that the last of the Dark Magic had

been removed, the wound in Bryen's chest began to heal itself, the muscles that had been shredded rebuilding themselves, followed by his skin, which knitted itself back together. When the wound was no more than a faint mark on her Protector's chest, and the sphere of Dark Magic, now a swirling mass of black that threatened to blot out the last rays of light that shone through the translucent stone of the Aeyrie, spun so fast that her eyes couldn't track it, a flash of white light erupted within the chamber followed by a deafening boom.

When they could both see again, Aislinn and Sirius looked down at Bryen. He lay against the pedestal, but his wound was gone. Now only a faint scar remained. His color had returned, and he was breathing easily while in a deep sleep. The Dark Magic had been drawn from his body. He had been healed. But the Seventh Stone was gone.

"Sirius, you did it!" exclaimed Aislinn, as she hugged Bryen to her. He had survived!

"I did nothing but bring the Seventh Stone here," he replied, sighing from both exhaustion and relief. He was glad that the boy had lived, because when he had first seen the wound, he didn't think that he would. "Your Protector healed himself. It's one of his skills."

"Is he a Magus now?"

"He is," replied Sirius. "I can feel it. He passed the Test, and he healed himself at the same time, harnessing the power of the Seventh Stone to do it. A truly remarkable accomplishment for one so inexperienced in the Talent."

Aislinn glanced back down at Bryen, and then up at Sirius with a questioning expression. "Then if he used the Seventh Stone to heal himself, where is it?"

"It's in him," replied Sirius. "It's a part of him now."

"It's what?" Aislinn failed to contain her shock.

"At the very end of the healing process, before that last flash of the Talent, the Seventh Stone dissolved into a white mist that flowed into Bryen. They are now one and the same, the Seventh Stone and your Protector."

"That was a diamond," protested Aislinn. "There is no harder stone than that in the world. How could it dissolve?"

"I don't know, child. But I mean to find out."

Though he wasn't a skilled healer, Sirius reached out for the Talent and used it to scan Bryen. The boy was in a deep sleep, his body exhausted by the internal battle that he had just fought. When he awoke, would he be the same as he was before he received the wound that had almost killed him? Or would he be different? The Dark Magic was gone. Or rather the Dark Magic that the Elder Ghoule had struck the boy with had been destroyed. The boy's ability to heal himself, strengthened by the power contained within the Seventh Stone, had seen to that. But Sirius sensed that Dark Magic still existed within him. It was in the boy now, just as the Talent was. Both forms of energy, one used for good, the other for evil, had melded together when the Seventh Stone fused with him.

The Seventh Stone had saved Bryen. Of that, Sirius had no doubt. But what would happen to the Protector now? How would the Dark Magic that now rested within the boy affect him? Would he be able to control it as he did the Talent? Or would the Dark Magic gradually consume him and leave him nothing but a hollow shell? A warlock who could do nothing but obey the Dark Magic that coursed within him?

And what would result from the unexpected and frightening development of the Seventh Stone now being a part of Bryen? What did it mean for the Weir? That barrier had been deteriorating during the last few centuries, thereby allowing small groups of Ghoules to be forced through the magical shield with the application of the Elder Ghoules' Dark Magic. The Seventh Stone was essential to maintaining the integrity of that obstruction and reconstructing it, if need be, but if the Seventh Stone was now a part of the boy, did that mean that the Order had lost the ability to strengthen the Weir? Would the magical barricade continue to degrade over time until it reached a point where the Ghoule Legions could once again march through the Winter Pass and invade Caledonia?

There were so many questions and so few answers. The uncertainty and his own fears left Sirius with but one course to take. He would need to visit the one place that he had been avoiding for the last decade. He would need to meet with the one person who unnerved him. Hopefully she could help him determine whether the Protector should be allowed to live, because Sirius really didn't want to kill the former gladiator unless absolutely necessary.

BONUS MATERIAL

If you really enjoyed this story, I need you to do me a HUGE favor – please follow me on BookBub. And if you have a few minutes, consider writing a review.

Keep reading for the first two chapters of Book Two of *The Tales of Caledonia, The Protector's Quest*.

THE PROTECTOR'S QUEST

BOOK 2 OF THE TALES OF CALEDONIA

By Peter Wacht

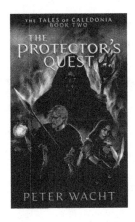

This book is a work of fiction. Names, characters, places, and incidents are the product of the author's imagination or are used fictitiously. Any resemblance to actual events, locales, or persons, living or dead, is coincidental.

Cover design by Ebooklaunch.com

Kestrel
Media Group, LLC

Published in the United States by Kestrel Media Group LLC.

ISBN: 978-1-950236-20-6
    eBook ISBN: 978-1-950236-21-3

Library of Congress Control Number: 2021918526

SETTING THE STAGE

The Protector's Quest, Book 2 of *The Tales of Caledonia*, is set more than one thousand years before the events that occur in *The Sylvan Chronicles* and takes place in a separate land of *The Realms of the Talent and the Curse*. Caledonia, though a monarchy, functions more like a loose confederation of Duchies, much to the displeasure of the Crown.

It is during this time that some of the more adventurous and grasping members of the Caledonian nobility accept King Corinthus Beleron's territorial grants and begin to colonize the Territories far to the west on the other side of the Burnt Ocean. These Territories will eventually become the Kingdoms.

In Caledonia, as in the other realms, the ability to use the Talent sets apart the person gifted with this unique skill. But being able to use the Talent is only part of the dynamic. For if a Magus chooses to follow a darker path, the Talent becomes the Curse.

CHAPTER 1. FIRST BLOOD

"I take it, Duke Winborne, that your lovely daughter has not yet returned from her sojourn?" asked Tetric, his tone suggesting that he already knew the answer. The small man, his hypnotic black eyes glaring balefully at the Duke of the Southern Marches, exuded a malice that pervaded the library situated in the base of the turret, putting both of its other inhabitants on edge.

The Duke and Noorsin Stelekel, Duchess of Murcia, had been deep in conversation, sitting on one of the couches at the far end of the room. Kevan was a large man, both tall and broad-shouldered, but the more petite Noorsin didn't mind sharing the couch with him. Their close proximity simply served as a reminder that there could be more to their relationship beyond the obvious political and economic alliances between their two Duchies. If Kevan was willing to take the chance. She thought that he had been about to, and she would have welcomed his advances, but for the rude interruption of the King's Advisor.

Kevan stood slowly, giving himself time to gain control over the vexation that flashed across his face because of the intrusion. As he did so, the back of his neck prickled, a sense of imminent danger, a feeling normally reserved for the battlefield, coursing through him. Tetric had walked right into the library without being announced. The Battersea Guards stationed at the door never would have allowed that to happen unless they were under duress ... or worse. Heeding his instincts, Kevan took a step forward and faced off against Tetric, placing himself between the Advisor and Noorsin. His right hand rested on the hilt of his sword, having grasped with his left hand the scabbard from where it lay against the couch.

"She has not," he replied coldly, his voice strong and unyielding. "She continues her instruction with Sirius, so you will have to wait a bit longer for her return."

"I think not," said Tetric, his voice barely above a whisper, his bald pate caught in a colorful halo as he stepped beneath the skylight made of colored glass. "I have waited long enough, but I can wait no longer." As was his habit Tetric pulled down on his beard with his left hand, twisting it, before smoothing the oiled hair with his right hand into the sharp point that he favored. "I must admit that it was a clever play on your part, Duke Winborne, to send your daughter away with the Magus, but your success will only be temporary. There are cards on the table that must be played. If the first play doesn't work, then we must move on to the second before the game changes."

"And your meaning?" asked Noorsin, rising from her place on the couch and standing next to Kevan. She was a beautiful woman with long, chestnut hair running halfway down her back, the curls framing her face. But she was not unaccustomed to confrontation, and she sensed the threat in Tetric's words, her eyes flashing dangerously.

"Today I must return to Tintagel," Tetric responded,

ignoring the Duchess and focusing his full attention on Kevan. "While you delayed, the world turned, and I must catch up." Tetric took a step closer to the Duke, unfazed by the difference in size and height or the steel that Kevan could draw from his scabbard in the blink of an eye. "And since the Duke's lovely daughter isn't here to begin the journey to her betrothed, I will allow Duke Winborne to join me instead on my journey west. His daughter can then follow along at her pleasure, though I would suggest that she not wait too long. The groom and I have only so much patience, and it's wearing thin. Paper thin. Her father's life will depend on the speed with which she reaches the capital."

"You will allow," chuckled Kevan. "You believe that you can threaten me in my Citadel? In my Duchy? You have gone too far, Tetric."

"Enjoy your laughter, Kevan," hissed Tetric, purposely withdrawing the Duke's honorific, and it was not lost on either Kevan or Noorsin. "For it will be the last bit of humor that you will enjoy for a very long time. I tried to be respectful, acknowledging your position and authority in the Southern Marches. But now I see that rather than offering the carrot I should have used the stick. That I have not gone far enough in forcing you down the path that you have no choice but to take. That stops now."

With a motion of the Advisor's hand, Killen Sourban entered the chamber with a handful of soldiers arrayed behind him, weapons drawn.

"No need for that, Duke Winborne," said the Captain of the Royal Guard as he nodded toward the scabbarded sword in Kevan's hand, his ice cold blue eyes revealing his disdain for the Duke of the Southern Marches. "If I see an inch of steel, we'll deal with you as we do any who are foolish enough to disobey the commands of our good King Beleron. We are supposed to protect you on the way to Tintagel. But we can't protect you from yourself, so I suggest that you think carefully about what you plan to do next. If you feel the need to be put in your place, we'd be happy to oblige. It would be quite enjoyable, in fact."

Kevan stared at Killen with a flinty gaze, and then a smile devoid of emotion revealed the fighter hidden beneath the lord. He slowly pulled his blade free and flung the scabbard onto the couch behind him, making clear his contempt for the Captain and his men.

Killen's frigid smile twisted into a sneer, clearly welcoming what was to come. "So the Duke has a backbone after all," he said. "I hadn't expected that." The Captain of the Royal Guard looked at Tetric, catching his eyes. "With your permission, my Lord?"

For just a moment, Tetric hesitated, wanting to be done with this contest as quickly as possible. He needed to be a day down the road before the Captain of the Battersea Guard attempted any pursuit, and the Duke's resistance now would only delay him. But then he nodded, deciding that an example needed to be made of Kevan Winborne in order to ensure an uneventful journey. The lesson the Duke was about to learn would serve him well on the road to Tintagel.

"Be quick about it. But don't harm him too badly. Although watching the Duke die certainly would be entertaining, he still has a role to play. We need him healthy and whole if we're to use him to get the girl."

"As you command, my Lord." Killen pulled his blade free from its scabbard as he stalked across the library. "I'll just have a little bit of fun with the arrogant arse before we truss him up like a pig and take the good Duke with us."

The soldiers of the Royal Guard spread out behind their

Captain so that the Duke of the Southern Marches had no chance to make a run for the door, as they expected that he would seek to escape rather than take on so many assailants at once. Clearly, they didn't know the Duke.

Kevan's dispassionate smile turned barbaric. He felt as if he had been released from the bonds that had weighed on him ever since Tetric had arrived in Battersea. Finally, the time to fight with words, whispers, and insinuations had come to an end. It was time for steel. He stepped forward confidently to meet the Captain of the Royal Guard, knowing that if he were to have any chance against the five fighters arrayed against him, he needed to move fast. He also needed to even the odds if he could.

Raising his sword above his head, he pretended to swing down toward Killen's shoulder, who raised his blade to block what the Captain viewed as the most obvious attack the Duke could have made, but at the last moment Kevan twisted smoothly to his left, slashing downward and across the chest of the soldier standing farthest away from the door. The man's sword clattered against the stone floor as he collapsed to his knees in shock, his hands going to his gut, the deep slice first welling up with a bright red blood, his internal organs then threatening to spill out. The soldier fell forward as his life seeped out onto the tile.

Realizing the danger presented by the Duke, the soldier next to the one who had fallen got his blade up just in time, parrying the backhanded slash that Kevan had aimed for his neck. But the soldier was so focused on Kevan's primary attack that he failed to see the Duke pull his dagger free from the sheath on his belt. It wasn't until the soldier felt the foot-long steel slide into his throat that he grasped his mistake, and by then it was too late. When Kevan pulled the dagger free, the soldier sagged to the floor, choking on his own blood, the light leaving his eyes with his last breath.

Kevan stepped back then, bloody dagger and sword in hand, pleased with what he had accomplished in less than a minute, to stand protectively in front of Noorsin once again. His attack and elimination of the two soldiers happened so fast that it left Killen and the remaining members of the Royal Guard stunned and rooted in place.

"I believe you said trussed like a pig," said Kevan, his eyes murderous. His quiet, confident words sounded out of place in the strange silence that had descended in the library. "Would you care to try again?"

The two soldiers standing to Killen's left prepared themselves to charge forward, but the Captain of the Royal Guard raised his hand to stop them. His frosty eyes blazed with fury, but Kevan identified other qualities there as well. Anticipation. Eagerness.

"He's mine," Killen said in a deathly whisper. "I've been looking forward to this challenge for quite some time."

The Captain of the Royal Guard took a few steps forward, his blade singing as he whipped it through the air several times.

"Careful, Kevan," whispered Noorsin. "He means to kill you. I can see it in his eyes."

The Duke nodded, expecting no less. "Good. Because I plan to kill him as well."

Kevan raised his blade, catching Killen's steel before it could slice into his neck. He then twisted his wrist to force his opponent's following lunge past his right hip, and then again to push the thrust that came right after the first past his left hip. Killen was fast, in fact faster than any man Kevan had fought in quite some time. But that discovery only served to increase the adrenaline flowing through his veins.

As the Duke of the Southern Marches, he dealt with a barrage of problems daily, the administration of his Duchy taking up most of his day and often leaving him exhausted and drained by the end of it. There were never any simple solutions to the challenges that he faced, and often when he applied one potential cure to what ailed the Southern Marches it simply led to a host of other unexpected issues that needed to be addressed, which meant the investment of more time, energy, and resources. A never-ending cycle that could be both satisfying and frustrating at the same time.

But what he did now, his blade a blur of steel as he absorbed Killen's deadly assault, offered him an often difficult to attain clarity. A duel was crystal clear. There was never any doubt or confusion. Kill or be killed. It was as simple as that. And he appreciated that simplicity more than he was willing to admit. Because he much preferred the black and white of combat to the grey of everyday life.

A smile broke out on Kevan's face as he teased Killen around the room, always keeping Noorsin behind him, the other soldiers of the Royal Guard having backed off. The Duke was in his element, leading the Captain this way and that, dictating the tempo of the combat.

After a few minutes of chasing after Kevan and failing to draw blood, Killen's aggravation burst to the surface as he spewed a string of curses and taunts. The Duke was a better fighter than he expected, and he hoped to gain an edge by weakening his focus as Killen had done so many times before with lesser fighters. But Killen was disappointed quickly, the Duke not taking the bait.

Instead Kevan realized that it was time to change his strategy, and he did so in an instant. Forming a cross above his head with his dagger and sword to catch Killen's steel as it slashed down toward him, he then spun on his right heel and whipped back around. His overconfident adversary blocked his sword with his own, but missed Kevan's dagger as it sliced across his forearm, a splash of blood staining the carpet.

Killen stumbled back more in anger than pain, shocked that Kevan had drawn first blood. But the Captain had no time to ponder what had just occurred as the Duke of the Southern Marches refused to allow the Captain to disengage. Kevan maintained his assault, his dagger and sword slashing, cutting, and slicing through the air at a speed that would have impressed his daughter's Protector. And with every strike, a streak of red appeared somewhere on the Captain of the Royal Guard, first at his hip, then across his other forearm, then his thigh, followed by his shoulder.

The wounds weren't deep or debilitating, each slice into his flesh setting off within the Captain a slow burn, physically and mentally. Killen realized with a hint of uneasiness that every wound was a message. Duke Winborne was playing with him. His opponent could have struck him down any time that he wanted to in the last few minutes, yet he had chosen not to in order to make a point. The Duke wanted to put Killen in his place, and he had. Killen could see it in his adversary's confident posture and the gleam of his eyes, and that realization released a burning fury within him. He would not be toyed with! The Duke should have killed him when he had the chance, and Killen would make him pay for his arrogance.

Killen was about to lunge forward, sword aimed at Kevan's chest, when he felt his feet being swept out from beneath him. He landed hard on his back, his breath knocked from his lungs, and his hand losing its grip on his sword as he tried to cushion his fall on the hard stone. When he attempted to raise his head, Killen felt the tip of Kevan's sword pressed into his throat, drawing a small trickle of blood. He knew without a doubt that the Duke of the Southern Marches was about to kill him, and for the first time in a very long time he felt a cold lump of fear settle in his belly. Killen's haughtiness had cost him his life.

"It appears that you'll be playing the role of the pig on this day," said the Duke of the Southern Marches, his voice calm and commanding. But before Kevan could finish the duel as he so desperately wanted to, the King's Advisor stepped toward him, a mist of black energy drifting outward from his hands.

"Enough of this foolishness!" Tetric shouted shrilly, the mist continuing to stream from his hands to become a dense black cloud. "My patience is at an end."

It was in that very moment that the disparate pieces regarding the King's Advisor fit into place for Noorsin. She knew that Tetric had been expelled from the Order of the Magii, and she and Sirius had surmised that he had turned down a darker path, but they had not been able to confirm what they suspected. Now as she watched the black energy spin faster and faster around Tetric's palms, she knew beyond a doubt that he had accepted the insidious gift of Dark Magic, giving up his soul for the deadly, addictive power. Perhaps even more concerning, she had not sensed his depraved, pernicious abilities the entire time that he had been in Battersea. How was that possible? How had he kept it hidden from her and Sirius?

Noorsin didn't have the time to think on her questions any longer. The swirling mist in Tetric's hands instantly coalesced into a black claw that reached for the Duke of the

Southern Marches, seeking to ensnare him before he could drive his blade into Killen's throat.

"No!" shouted the Duchess of Murcia.

Lunging forward, she pulled the shocked Kevan behind her while also reaching for the Talent, a barrier of white energy springing up between her and Tetric in the nick of time. The black claw slammed against the shield, causing a blinding flash and a thunderous boom as the Dark Magic and the Talent met, Noorsin's defense holding.

"I knew you were a Magus, my dear Noorsin," laughed Tetric, his psychotic tone sending a spasm of fright down the Duchess of Murcia's spine. "I just never knew how weak! Watch and learn, woman. You will pay for your insolence, for trying to impede someone with a power that no one can resist."

Incensed at being obstructed from achieving his goal, Tetric redoubled his efforts, pulling in more of the Dark Magic that he controlled, pushing more and more of his corrupted power against the pulsing barrier of shimmering white that Noorsin had formed. But she refused to yield, as she too called on more and more of the natural magic of the world, filling her shield with the Talent. Each time Tetric's clawed hand struck her barrier, the meeting of the two powers caused a blinding flash followed by an ear-splitting roar that shook the very foundations of the tower.

At the start of the fight, Noorsin's barricade maintained its shape. But as the minutes passed, and the strength of Tetric's assault increased, her defense began to waver. Tetric's black claw slammed into her shield at a constant rhythm, the shimmering power flaring and flexing backward wherever struck, tiny wisps of darkness beginning to spread across the shining barricade.

Noorsin desperately wanted to fight back. To strike at

their aggressor. But she could sense Tetric's power now, and he was stronger than she ever expected that he could be, all because of the Dark Magic that raced through him. It was all that she could do to keep the tendrils of black energy that now probed her defense from burrowing their way through the magical barricade. Because of his overwhelming strength, each time Tetric's claw hit her shield, more and more threads of darkness wriggled like worms across her barrier, searching for a way through. Although she had no intention of surrendering, her analytical mind had already come to a painful yet inevitable conclusion. It was only a matter of time before Tetric destroyed her shield. Still, she refused to give up, even as the tendrils of black continued to spread across her shield, which was becoming more and more compressed, tightening around her and Kevan.

Her mind worked furiously in search of a solution. There had to be something that she could do to stop Tetric. But she discarded every idea that popped into her head. She already had reached the limits of the power that she could employ. There was little else that she could try that would have any real effect against her adversary.

"Noorsin, can you hold?" asked Kevan, poised to attack, his dagger returned to its sheath but his sword still gripped tightly in his hand. "Allow me to pass, and I'll take care of this snake once and for all."

Noorsin reached for his free hand, tears streaming down her face as she grasped his fingers warmly. "I'm sorry, Kevan. I tried. But Tetric is too …"

A deafening explosion tore through the turret, much like the whoosh of a gust of fresh air feeding a blazing fire. The blast destroyed Noorsin's shield, throwing her and Kevan back against the far wall.

Kevan struggled to his feet, his sword somehow still in

his hand. But his vision was blurry, and his ears rang with the sound of a thousand bells. He looked down at the floor and glimpsed Noorsin curled up against the stone wall, blood trickling from her nose and a deep cut on the back of her head, her hair matted in blood. He didn't think that she was breathing as he couldn't detect her chest rising and falling. With that discovery a white-hot rage surged through him as he turned his gaze away from the fallen Duchess and toward the King's Advisor, who, seemingly unconcerned, had stepped closer to him. Kevan tried to swing his sword in a curling arc designed to take off Tetric's head, but all he succeeded in doing was to throw himself off balance. He fell to his knees as his concussed brain failed to function.

"You have no need of that," said Tetric, who now stood over him, an evil grin revealing his grey teeth. "Steel can't help you now."

Despite his best efforts to fight the compulsion that he could feel closing around his mind, Kevan acceded to Tetric's command and released his sword. Tendrils of black smoke circled around him, crushing his arms to his side and solidifying until he was held by wispy cords that were stronger than steel. Frozen in place, unable to move, Tetric's Dark Magic too powerful for him to resist, Kevan turned his hate-filled eyes on the King's Advisor.

"You will pay for this, Tetric," said Kevan in a garbled speech, the room spinning in front of his unfocused eyes. "I will avenge Noorsin. That, I swear."

"Promises, promises," replied Tetric. He nudged Noorsin with his foot, finding her unresponsive. He saw the gore in her hair from where her head had struck the wall as well as the bloody trickle running down her chin. "So much for your lover. A pity, really. Such a beautiful woman, I may have taken her myself if I had the time and the inclination. But I doubt that she will survive the night. We will leave her here, a fitting resting place for one so weak in the Talent."

"You scoundrel!" mumbled Kevan, still not hearing the words he was trying to say, the explosion having damaged his eardrums. "I'll make you pay for what you've done."

"Enough!" shouted Tetric, a tendril of black mist wrapping itself around Kevan's mouth, silencing him. "You fail to understand that you are no longer in charge. I am. And that's the way it will remain for the foreseeable future."

Tetric then reached into his robes and pulled out a collar of blackened steel.

"Does this look familiar, Kevan?" Tetric knelt down with a spark of glee in his eyes as he held it up for the Duke to see, flipping the metal torque across his fingers. "I got the idea when I saw the boy. I hadn't heard of a Protector being made for decades, yet you took it upon yourself to do so. Looking back, it was clearly a good decision. The boy protected your daughter from my assassins, and his actions forced me to come to this backwater Duchy in order to accomplish my mission. A waste of my time and my ability. Or so I thought at first, because coming here gave me the idea for this collar. When I saw what you did to the boy, a thought struck me. Why couldn't I do the same thing? Why couldn't I craft my own collar? So I did, and you get to be the first to try it out."

Tetric reached up and placed the blackened steel around Kevan's neck, then snapped it shut. Kevan immediately began to feel even more lethargic than from the effects of the concussion that he had suffered, as if he could barely think, barely move, as if all his thoughts and his energy were being drained away into a bottomless pool of black. No matter how hard he tried to resist the inky tendrils that seeped into his mind, he could do nothing to stop the darkening haze from settling over his brain.

"Wonderful!" exclaimed Tetric. "You're already beginning to feel the effects of my creation. That should make our journey to Tintagel quite delightful. Now, off to see the King."

CHAPTER 2. MORE TO ADMIT

"There is much that you've been keeping from me, Sirius. More than you should have."

"Not just from you, Aislinn. It is a hazard that comes with the responsibilities and burdens that I bear."

"As the Master of the Order of the Magii."

"Yes, in large part," replied Sirius, feeling that he could no longer hide that fact from her. As always, his wispy long white hair stood on end, and though he now appeared to be no more than the mild-mannered teacher she had grown up with, she remembered how he had looked when he strode mercilessly from the Aeyrie toward the Elder Ghoules, strands of the Talent leaping across his robes and setting the long grass ablaze, his eyes burning with a frightening fiery intensity.

"Then why were you really in Battersea and the Southern Marches? I'm certain that you didn't come here just to teach me or to advise my father."

"I admit that I called Battersea home for multiple reasons," replied Sirius. "But I was there to instruct you in the use of the Talent, and I was there to advise your father. You know, he was the one who called for me."

"You're evading," challenged Aislinn, her voice becoming harder, assuming the tone she would have used if she faced an emissary from another Duchy who was attempting to dissemble in front of the Stump. "For what other reasons were you in Battersea?"

"For this," Sirius replied, knowing that there was no point in trying to avoid her question as he gestured toward the young man lying down on the bed who was breathing slowly in a deep sleep beneath several blankets.

After the Seventh Stone had fused with the Protector, Sirius had carried Bryen down several flights of stairs to a floor where the quarters for Magii visiting the Aeyrie were located. Each of the dozen rooms were similar. Small but functional with bed, desk, washstand, mirror, and shelves lining the inner walls that were filled with books and scrolls. As the contents of the library at the Aeyrie had expanded over the centuries, more space was needed. The guest rooms were the most obvious solution. The outer wall always remained free of obstructions so that the sunlight could shine through the stone and warm the space even on the coldest winter day.

"For Bryen? A former gladiator?"

"No, although his arrival in the Southern Marches was certainly a surprising but valuable and fortuitous development," replied Sirius. "No, I came to Battersea in part to protect the Aeyrie. Or rather to protect what the Aeyrie protects."

"The Seventh Stone." Aislinn was finally beginning to understand. She flicked a lock of her auburn hair out of her eyes and curled it around her ear as her mind followed this new path.

"Yes, child. The Seventh Stone. When the Order of the Magii first constructed the Aeyrie, it was done with several goals in mind. It was to be a place of instruction for those learning the Talent and for those who have already mastered the Talent to continue their studies and construct new knowledge regarding its application."

"But it was also to be a fortress," suggested Aislinn. "To protect that knowledge from those who might wish to steal it or the artifacts tied to it."

Sirius couldn't help but smile. His student's ability to pull truth from a web of disparate threads was truly impressive. "Indeed. That's why the Aeyrie was attacked in the First Ghoule War. The Ghoule Overlord believed that if he could destroy the Aeyrie and the Magii within it, he would have little to fear from the forces your forebear, Arick Winborne, was gathering to defend against his Legions. The Overlord could then conquer Caledonia at his leisure."

"But he didn't succeed."

"He did not. The Elder Ghoules failed to take the Aeyrie, though it was a closer thing than the histories suggest. But the Overlord came for another reason as well. If he conquered the Aeyrie and destroyed the Magii he could also take ..."

"The Seven Stones."

"Yes, child. The Ghoule Overlord knew of the power that could be harnessed through the Seven Stones. He feared them and how they could be used to hinder his plans, so he wanted them for himself. The Order suspected as much, so during the First Ghoule War they were hidden within the Aeyrie."

"If the Ghoule Overlord gained the Seven Stones, then the Order of the Magii could not have stood with Caledonia against him. As you said, the Seven Stones are neither good nor bad, but they serve as conduits for the power exercised through them. The Ghoule Overlord could have destroyed every Magus in the Kingdom in one fell swoop."

"Indeed," sighed Sirius. "Correct again. But the Ghoule Overlord and his Elders didn't achieve their goal, and we were able to buy the time that Caledonia needed to defend against the Ghoule Legions streaming down from the Shattered Peaks. Nevertheless, I would argue as well that if we did not have the Seven Stones in our possession here in the Aeyrie when the Ghoule Overlord attacked, that foul creature would have achieved his objective."

Aislinn chuckled softly, her laugh lighting up her beautiful face. "You speak as if you were actually here. The First Ghoule War occurred ten centuries ago."

"Why do you find that so strange, child. I've explained to you many times that a person using the Talent will be changed by that power in some very unique ways. Longer life is but one gift that a Magus receives from the Talent, though perhaps in certain situations that can be a curse as well." Sirius leaned back in his chair, contemplating that somewhat depressing conclusion for a moment. Then he shook his head as if to clear it of a bad memory before turning his attention back to Aislinn. "Regardless, it was because the Magii here in the tower could employ the Seven Stones during that attack that the Aeyrie still stands. The Ghoule Overlord, realizing that he could not achieve his objective here, turned his Legions to the west, but by then it was too late, and Arick Winborne was ready for him. We know how the rest of the story plays out. There is no need to go through it all again."

"We do, but that's only part of the story, isn't it?" Aislinn's raised eyebrows formed a question, as if she expected more of an explanation from Sirius. The Magus smiled again because of the Lady of the Southern Marches' instincts and tenacity for getting to the truth.

"Right again. That is only part of the story. For the Seven Stones played an essential role at the conclusion of the First Ghoule War. Arick defeated the Ghoule Legions at the now aptly named Bay of the Dead and succeeded in pushing them back into the Shattered Peaks to the northern boundary of those mountains, almost to the Lost Land itself from which the Ghoules first emerged. But Caledonia was still at risk. We expected the Ghoule Overlord to counterattack at any moment, and we knew that we weren't strong enough to prevent the additional Legions coming from the north from spreading across all of Caledonia if the Ghoules succeeded in reaching the Breakwater Plateau again."

"The Weir," said Aislinn, having guessed at the direction the story would turn next.

"The Weir," confirmed Sirius. "The ten strongest members of the Order of the Magii used the Seven Stones to construct the Weir, the magical barrier that since the First Ghoule War has prevented these beasts from invading Caledonia once again. Those men and women gave their lives to do it, using the Seven Stones to harness both the Talent and the Curse, but in the end, making use of the Dark Magic contained within the Stones proved too much for even them. We owe them a great debt. Without the Ten Magii, the Ghoules would have overrun the Kingdom long ago. Caledonia would have belonged to the Ghoule Overlord."

"But I thought that the Seven Stones were still in the Shattered Peaks."

"Six of the Seven Stones are where they should be," replied Sirius. "Each Stone is different -- emerald, ruby, black opal, white pearl, sapphire, jade -- but all serve the same purpose. They remain at the Sanctuary, the lonely stone spire in the Trench where the Ten Magii used the Seven Stones to construct the Weir."

"Then why was the Seventh Stone kept here in the Aeyrie rather than the Sanctuary with the other Stones?"

"For its own protection," explained Sirius. "The Seventh Stone serves as the catalyst for all of the other Stones. The Ghoules cannot breach the Sanctuary. At least not yet. The magic of the Weir is still too strong for them to destroy the barrier with their Dark Magic. But there is no place to keep the Seventh Stone at the Sanctuary. The power of the Seventh Stone alone is so great that it could disrupt the purpose of the other Stones if it remains there too long."

"You mean that the Seventh Stone could weaken the Weir simply by being in close proximity to the other Stones?"

"Yes, I mean exactly that. Remember, the Stones are neither good nor bad. They are receptacles for the Talent and the Curse. How those Stones are used is what makes all the difference. That's why the Order has kept the Seventh Stone here. If the Ghoules were ever able to gain the Seventh Stone, they would have the ability to enter the Sanctuary and destroy the Weir. We have protected the Seventh Stone since the Weir was built, assuming as well that we would need it again at some point in the future."

"Then how did you know that the Seventh Stone would help Bryen?"

"I didn't," Sirius replied honestly. "I hate to admit it, but it was just a guess. A throw in the dark. You need to understand that when the Ten Magii created the Weir, they did it by merging the Talent with Dark Magic and then infusing that merged power into the Seven Stones. What they did worked, but what they didn't realize when they did that was that the Seven Stones took more than just their power. The

Stones also took their spirits, so in a sense you could say that the Seven Stones still contain not only the power of the Ten Magii, but also their essences." The Magus leaned his chair back against the wall, placing his head against the stone as he tried to stretch out his aching back, a painful reminder of the fight with the Elder Ghoules and his carrying the wounded Protector to the top of the Aeyrie. "Because your Protector was using the Talent to fight the Dark Magic that threatened to consume him, because both powers were fighting within him, I hoped that the Seventh Stone might be able to assist him, to serve as a catalyst and give him the additional strength that he needed to defeat the Dark Magic. And it did."

"But you didn't expect the Seventh Stone to dissolve and become a part of him?"

Bryen shifting his position beneath his blankets drew Aislinn's eyes, her concern obvious. But it dissipated when her Protector returned to his healing slumber.

"No. I didn't even know that that was a possibility. I was just trying to help Bryen and no other options came to mind. What happened was the most remarkable thing, though completely unexpected. It was almost as if the Seventh Stone knew him or recognized him and wanted to be one with him."

"How could that even be possible?"

Sirius took a moment before responding, as several possibilities ran through his mind. But as was his wont, for now he chose to keep that information to himself. "I don't know, child."

"But it worked."

"Apparently, yes. But ..."

"But what?"

"The Seventh Stone is a part of him now. It merged with

Bryen somehow. That's the best way that I can describe it. So ..."

"So what?"

"So I didn't know how the use of the Seventh Stone was going to affect him, but I didn't expect that to happen. The Seventh Stone is a receptacle. Its utility in constructing the Weir resulted from the fact that it could hold both Dark Magic and the Talent. That's how the Ten Magii were able to work with the Curse without it corrupting them for a time. Without it destroying them the instant they began their work on the Weir. But the Seventh Stone is gone now. Essentially, Bryen is now the Seventh Stone. Which means ..."

Aislinn finally understood why Sirius seemed so concerned, and it wasn't all because of a concern for her Protector's well being. "The Dark Magic from the Seventh Stone is in Bryen now. It's a part of him. Just like the Talent."

"Yes."

"What does that mean for him? Will it hurt him? Change him?"

"That's just it. I don't know. But we have to assume that it can and will, because the Curse is aptly named. Those using Dark Magic are soon also being used by the Dark Magic. The Curse is not like the Talent. It takes more than it gives."

"How can we find out for sure?" asked Aislinn, her concern for her Protector clearly seen in her eyes. For just a moment, Sirius wondered if there might be another emotion there as well, something stronger, more powerful, more intimate.

"There is little that we can do but watch him," responded Sirius. "We need to see if the Dark Magic that's now a part of him manifests in some way. Keep in mind that he is a strong young man, and by that, I mean both physically and mentally. He could not have survived in the Pit for so long otherwise. Plus, his acuity for and skill in the Talent is extraordinary, though not entirely unexpected knowing his bloodline. So perhaps we have nothing to worry about. Perhaps his strength in the Talent will contain the Dark Magic, keep it under control."

"Are you willing to risk Bryen's life on that assumption?"

Sirius looked at Aislinn. He was certain now. There was more to her relationship with the boy than simply his role as her Protector, whether she was willing to admit it to herself or not.

"No," he responded quietly, trying to ignore the feeling of shame that threatened to overwhelm him. He did care about the boy, but he was just a piece in a larger puzzle. Rebuilding the Weir and keeping the Ghoule Legions from Caledonia had to come first. "I'm not. I will reach out to another Magus who might have some knowledge that could be helpful. But keep in mind that there are no guarantees. We don't know as much about the Seventh Stone as we would like, and we don't know how its fusion with your Protector will affect him."

Aislinn nodded, shaking her head as an unexpected sadness washed over her. "He's had a hard life."

Sirius was about to reply, but he needed to take a moment as a surge of unanticipated emotion washed through him. *Harder than you could ever imagine, child,* he wanted to say, having more knowledge about Bryen's upbringing and how the young man found himself in the Pit than anyone else, but not yet ready to divulge that information.

"Yes, but he is still alive. That's the most important thing. The trick will be making sure that he stays that way."

LOOKING FOR MORE ...

I hope you enjoyed the first two chapters. To keep reading
The Protector's Quest, Book Two of *The Tales of Caledonia*,
order your copy today on Amazon.

Made in United States
North Haven, CT
12 August 2024

55958021R00290